IN BETTER TIMES

SEVEN STORIES

Fiction By Ken Hinrichs

BOOKSIDE Press

Copyright © 2024 by Ken Hinrichs

ISBN: 978-1-77883-274-1 (Paperback)

All rights reserved. No part of this publication may be reproduced, distributed, or transmitted in any form or by any means, including photocopying, recording, or other electronic or mechanical methods, without the prior written permission of the publisher, except in the case brief quotations embodied in critical reviews and other noncommercial uses permitted by copyright law.

The views expressed in this book are solely those of the author and do not necessarily reflect the views of the publisher, and the publisher hereby disclaims any responsibility for them. Some names and identifying details in this book have been changed to protect the privacy of individuals.

BOOKSIDE Press

BookSide Press
877-741-8091
www.booksidepress.com
orders@booksidepress.com

Contents

Part One: The Lawyer 1
Part Two: The Lagniappe 35
Part Three: The Deed 42
Part Four: The Media Star 54
Part Five: The Lady 88
Part Six: The Ticket 319
Part Seven: Ticnup 365

In Better Times
Fiction by Ken Hinrichs

"Neither can the wave that has passed by be recalled, nor the hour which has passed."
Ovid – The Metamorphoses

"Maybe we just keep comin' back over and over again until we get it right."
David Jackson to Art Carney – St. Helens

"Time starts now."
Steve McQueen to Jacqueline Bisset – Bullitt

"Pluritas non est ponenda sine necessitate."
Attributed to William of Ockam, The Principle of Occam's razor

"Nach vorne Willkommen. Sie können anfangen, Kapitel Eins jetzt zu schreiben."
Field Marshall Erwin Rommel to his newly arrived biographer prior to the Second Battle for Tobruk
and
A Christmas Tail
A Very Short Story
"Please sir, I want some more."
Charles Dickens – *Oliver Twist*
and finally
An Ode to the Longevity of the Siphonaptera
Adam had 'em.

In Better Times

THE LAWYER

I

May 18, 2016 – Cottonwood Pass, near Turner Peak, Colorado

Charles Pierre LeBlanc IV – *Pierre* to his associates, not *C.P.,* that was his father – not, *the Baron, that* was his grandfather . . . *just Pierre* – turned off I-270 southwest of downtown Denver onto Highway 285. He was fascinated each time he caught sight of railroad crossing gates at the entrances to the Colorado Interstates. At first, he believed they'd been installed to control traffic in the event of major traffic accidents. Then the reality hit him that the gates were used to shut the highways down when blizzards struck. He shivered at the thought. This was definitely not Louisiana. It was going to be an out-of-body experience for him anyway because back home roads rarely varied in their flatness. Today, he'd be driving mountains for the first time ever. He was pumped.

Another checkmark on my bucket list!

When his associates had heard that Pierre was planning a two or three-day business trip in the Rockies, they'd razzed him about taking advantage of a business trip to get in some sightseeing in one of the most beautiful areas of the country. Worse than that, they got on him about his dismal driving record . . . and that was earned on the

In Better Times

straight non-icy roads of Louisiana, not on Colorado's high mountain switchbacks. It was true he'd never driven higher than a sand dune and that had been in a dune buggy.

Isn't most of Louisiana under sea level anyway?

He'd laughed off their derision as jealousy and horseplay.

Yeah, maybe I've never seen a live mountain, but I've played road-race video games set in the Alps, and I've watched mountain driving videos taken by friends who ski the Rockies. And that was in the winter, wasn't it? And it was *in Colorado, right? So, what's so tough about driving uphill?*

"I'll be driving in the middle of May for crying out loud!" he'd told his associates. "Maybe, just maybe, I'll need a long sleeve shirt when I get there. But even if the temp drops to 60, I plan on going casual! Hey. Anyway, this isn't really a heavy business trip! I'm just running an errand for my father. That's all. Just to see some old hippie and his wife, partner, or whatever. He's got some money comin' from an estate."

Their warnings about driving conditions had been a waste of words. The roads were fine, and the scenery was gorgeous! Frankly, this was unlike anything he'd seen or experienced in his life and the beauty gave him almost a crammed buoyancy in the *too-small* driver's seat.

Everything wasn't all hunky-dory though. He *was* running seriously late. He still had more than 150 miles to go just to get to the hotel, a cabin of some kind at a place called Taylor Park Trading Post. It was the only lodging he could find within hours of his final destination which was situated along the route . . . a town bizarrely called *Ticnup*!

He'd gotten an *okay* start that morning from Louis Armstrong International in New Orleans and the flight to Dallas had been uneventful. The next leg though had been delayed over and over because of "mechanical problems." By the time they'd landed at Denver International, it was four p.m. instead of noon. *Still, I should be okay,* he considered.

The Google girl told him it would be a four-hour drive and that sunset was due at about eight, so more scenic thrills weren't far down the road. When he checked his course yesterday, he'd noticed that he had at least one mountain pass to cross. It was higher than 12,000 feet. Ticnup . . . *sounds Alaskan* he thought . . . was supposedly situated on the edge of yet another big peak he'd climb. He couldn't be certain about that though, because using his Garmin GPS, he was unable to find any town called "Ticnup" . . . in *any state.* Fortunately, the Baron had had one of the interns write down directions for him.

Pierre was upset over the airport delays because he preferred to drive as much in daylight as he could so he could check *mountain scenery* off his short list of the things he'd never before experienced. And who knew? Louisianans weren't known for leaving their bayou homes much, he might never again get the chance.

A ringtone pulled his attention away from an incredible view of a snowcapped peak not far off in the distance.

"In 1814 we took a little trip, Along with Colonel Jackson, Down the Mighty Missisip . . ."

Johnny Horton was singing from his shorts. Pierre

tried to wrestle the phone from his pocket while steering around a sharp curve. Answering the phone took second place. It took longer than usual. The call, though, had to be from *The Lady Jolie*, his fiancée.

"We took a little bacon, And we took a little beans, And we fought the bloody British, In the Town of New Orleans."

"Hey, Babe! How y 'all doin', Sweetheart?"

"Where have you been, Pierre?" came the clipped West Midlands British accent of his fiancée. "I have been worried to death over you. The last time I heard from you was nine hours ago after you *supposedly* landed in Dallas. Bollocks! You said then that there were mechanical problems with your flight to Denver and it had been delayed. Then, nothing! I have heard *nothing!* Have you collided? Are you alright?"

"Long story, babe. First off, it wasn't a mechanical problem. That's what they told us though. After we finally got on the plane almost four hours late, I found out what really happened."

Word by word she responded, "But . . . why . . . did . . . you . . . not . . . call . . . me?" She was obviously unhappy.

"Sorry. They kept tellin' us it would only be a few minutes and to stay close to the gate. Then I forgot to call until we were in the air."

"Well, why did you not call me when you landed. . . if you ever did?"

"Oh, yeah. Of course, we landed! I'm on the road now heading for my hotel . . . . or cabin . . . . or whatever it is. That's a long story too.

Jolie was about to comment but heard the tone in Pierre's voice and held off.

"Let me fill you in on the delay. It turned out that on the leg *into* Dallas, the plane we were scheduled *out* on to Denver hit some turbulence coming in. A bunch of the passengers got sick. They had to bring in a Hazmat team at DFW to clean up the mess. You should have seen them. They were dressed like it was anthrax they were cleaning up. The ground crew replaced three or four rows of seats and a couple of pieces of carpeting, and all that took a while. So, it really wasn't a mechanical problem at all. They just had to call it that because . . . well, if they hadn't, no one would have gotten on board. Didn't smell too bad though. They probably sprayed something to cover it . . . ."

"Yee gads! Disgusting!" Jolie interrupted. "I am not at all certain I would have gone aboard even then."

"Well, they never did tell us about anyone getting sick on the previous flight. I learned about it from one of the flight attendants after we took off."

"So why did you not ca . . ."

The connection went dead. Pierre checked the signal. No bars. "Aach! Hey, I'll have to call y'all back when we get a signal," he yelled into the useless phone.

Pierre found an indention in the dash that fit the phone well, placed it there, and left it face up. He was proud that he'd plugged his route into his new GPS App. He'd need it before long. He'd always known where he was going in the Big Easy as well as in the rest of Louisiana, so he'd never had a use for a GPS until now. It was a cool program.

In Better Times

Even better than Pong! A sharp curve with a big drop-off on his side came up. His attention refocused on the drive.

Anyway, life was good, and he was making great time. The two-lane winding road he'd been on gradually had him climbing up and into the foothills. Coming into Denver on the plane, his ears had announced the change in elevation as they'd descended. Now, as his small car struggled up progressively steeper hills, his ears again warned him to swallow and reset his internal barometer.

No wonder I lost cell coverage. Mountains are blocking every microwatt that could get through. Wonder why they don't have cell towers on top of these ten-thousand-foot-tall chunks of dirt and trees?

Pierre curled around another mountain featuring a nice drop-off on the passenger side. Out of his sightline, his phone signal reappeared, and immediately another call came through.

Two bars. Good enough.

"I loaded sixteen tons and what did I get? Another day older and deeper in debt . . ."

This time it was Tennessee Ernie Ford introducing a call from his office. He pushed the *Speaker Phone* function.

"Yeah, this is Pierre . . ."

"Hey, guy. How's it goin'? Where are y'all?"

"Hey, Jerry. I'm in my rental, heading to Ticnup. What a stupid name for a town!"

"So, you got a car? Good for you! We had bets going here at the office that you'd be thumbing your way, probably smoking something you got from some old hippy and getting a Rocky Mountain High!"

Pierre ignored the smoking weed comment.

Just like Jake to throw that in. My dad's probably passing his desk! I'm pretty sure I'm on Speaker Phone in the office!

"Well, you were right. I should have reserved a vehicle ahead of time. That and some flight delays really cost me. But I'm clicking along at a healthy 52 miles per hour in a fancy 1980 International Scout. I'd give you the mileage, but the odometer froze before I got in her at 278,496.3 miles. Who knows how long ago that was!"

"You're kidding me! Bright orange, right? All those old Scouts were bright orange. We told you to reserve an SUV for the trip ahead of time . . . somethin' with four-wheel drive. Sounds like you got an SUV ancestor."

"Yeah. Bad decision on my part. And it's not bright orange . . . but it might have been 36 years ago. It's a three-speed stick on the column and, if it has a working suspension, it hasn't shown up for duty yet. Fifty miles down and about a hundred fifty to go and my rear end already feels as if the next bump in the road will take out my own undercarriage!"

They both laughed, Jerry a bit cynically.

"So, why'd you choose a Scout, for heaven's sake? Or are you just a fan of old mini station wagons that were crap when they were new?"

"Well, when I got to DIA, I went to *all* the rental counters. All of 'em! Started with AVIS and went down the alphabet. Didn't expect that there would be such a demand for rentals. Every story I ever heard was that you skiers took shuttles from the airport when you went back into the mountains, not cars . . . and not *rentals!* Anyway, the summer migration to the Rockies is apparently underway and no rental company at the whole airport had *any* vehicles that weren't already spoken for."

"So, what did you do, buy this one from some airport employee?"

"No. Unh, unh. Very last rental counter. *Z-GUT Rentals.* Stands for *Zach's Good Used Transportation.* I think it was Zach himself at the counter. And even he told me he had nothin' available. I almost got on my knees to plead with him. Finally, after I offered big money to rent his personal vehicle, he remembered that a scrap company was coming in tonight to take away an old *International Scout* that hadn't been rented in almost a year. I could have *it* if I was really desperate."

"Wow. Pretty sad. Pretty funny too. Hope you got a discount! Everyone in the office is listening on speakerphone, by the way."

Pierre could hear pure Louisiana joviality, whistles, and catcalls behind Jerry.

"Just remember, we all tried to get you to reserve an SUV ahead of time. You are *definitely gonna* catch it when you get back. You better watch your weather too! Frank says he was at a wedding in Aspen once on the fourth of July and they had to move inside because of a mini blizzard. He says that if you're not prepared for changes in the weather in Colorado, you're liable to be in deep Doo-Doo. As the TV weathermen in Denver say, 'Overnight, we're expecting six inches of Doo-Doo!'"

Pierre heard a tone sound over the call telling him someone else was trying to get through – Jolie probably. Meantime, he could hear laughing in the background and then a bunch of his office mates chorused, "Told you so. Told you so!" Jerry leaned in toward the speakerphone to be heard over them and said, "Hey. Do us a favor: Get someone to take your picture next to the Scout with a snow-capped mountain in the . . ."

The signal dropped, and Pierre was glad to be alone again. He turned on the ancient rental's radio, hoping it worked, because a bunch of the car's other features didn't. He'd made certain that at least the headlights and taillights functioned but Zach had had to teach him how to work the manual choke! Fortunately, the weather was cool so he didn't mind the fact that there was no A/C. The windows, in the old car rolled up and down on cranks – most of 'em did anyway. And the old radio was a Philco that only received AM with no satellite or FM . . . but at least it worked!

He swept the band which was full of hissing and buzzing until a male voice came through strong and clear saying, "You're tuned to KOA, the News Voice of the Rockies . . . Hey, Denver: We've got a surprise for you tonight! We're all gonna get a couple of inches from a late spring storm. But, for you folks above 8,000 feet, you are gonna get slammed! Welcome to mid-Spring in Colorful Colorado! Maybe a foot or more, and if you're higher than that, you could even see *more* of the white stuff. And . . . you know what that means . . . chains, folks! Yep. Dig 'em out, drivers! One more time. Oh, and get the cows and brass monkeys into the barn! But don't worry. It's May. This system should pass quickly, and we'll get a thaw going when the sun comes out in the morning. And, for you folks on the northern slopes, hang on! It's gonna be windy! . . . "

Pierre turned the radio off but not because he didn't want to hear the bad news. One colleague who'd spent time in Fort Collins had told him that it wasn't unusual to find 18 Wheelers on their sides along I-25 north of Denver having been nailed by the ferocious North Plains Winds. He'd even pulled up a photo on his computer a guy had taken of a coal train lying on its side, just off the interstate between Cheyenne and Fort Collins.

"In 1814 we took a little trip . . ."

It was Johnny Horton singing again and that meant two things: a) he had a signal, and b), the Lady Jolie was calling.

"Hi, babe. I'm in the mountains and I may lose you again. Where were we when we got cut off?"

"I was asking why you did *not* call me from the Denver Airport?" Her voice leaked with tension and irritation.

"Oh, yeah. Well, I was just tellin' my office about my experience at the rental . . ."

"Your office? Is that why I was sent to your voice mail? Well, what did Blah, Blah, Blah want?"

"Jolie, my dear. It's not Blah, Blah, Blah, it's LeBlanc LeBlanc LeBlanc . . ."

". . . and *Blois*. I know. But when you put your last names together, it sounds like you're saying, 'Blah, Blah, Blah . . .'"

"and Blois," finished Pierre. "Yeah, I know. But if my dad or Grandfather ever heard you say. 'Blah, Blah, Blah,' you'd get excommunicated from the family even before we got married! They're not fond of hearing that from anyone, especially from other attorneys in the city, and really-especially from a future daughter-in-law."

"Well, speaking about our pending nuptials, are you about ready to set the date, my darling?" She sang the last two words.

"Yeah, gettin' close, babe. Both *the Baron* and C.P. have got me on this assignment here in Colorado. It's a big one. They've been workin' it for more than 15 years and it's worth over $60 million to the firm . . . and to the guy we're looking for, of course. If I can pull this assignment off, it should elevate me from my lowly back-office job . . . and the least senior of our eleven associates . . . to one of *Superior Confidence* from the Partners. An', I think I'm pretty sure I can pull this off. Then we can set *The Date!*"

There was a longer pause than necessary.

"Jolie? Jolie? Oh, crap! Signal's gone again." Pierre pounded a fist on the dashboard nearly shaking his phone loose from its resting place. As it was, a coating of dust a sixteenth of an inch-thick rose in the air and settled everywhere, including on the phone.

This last short conversation with Jolie had pulled his attention from the surroundings and now that the call had ended, he realized the skies had darkened enough that he needed headlights. Strange blobs of brown stuff now lined State Highway 360. He'd left 285 behind back in Buena Vista and had been switch-backing up a major mountain ever since. Of course, he realized, the blobs were old drifts of extremely dirty snow left over from the last storm. He'd never seen snow in person, much less driven in it . . . much less driven in it in the dark . . . much less driven in it in the dark while climbing a mountain! In Louisiana, the biggest hill was the occasional Mount Trashmore one would pass at parish landfills. He'd always wondered how they'd look with a snowcap. Now he knew. Mountains were bigger.

Thanks to the steepness of the climb, Pierre's confidence in his reckoning skills and the logic of his GPS steering him this way was beginning to wane. However, instincts honed over a lifetime of traveling across Louisiana's swamps kept him moving forward. Doubts were pushing at the edges though. Surely, he was heading generally for Ticnup, right? Behind was Denver, and ahead was Ticnup. Where else was there to go? At the back of his mind though was the fact he'd not been able to find Ticnup, Colorado even using Google. He'd tried MapQuest as well with the same luck. No Ticnup! Still, he had the Baron's instructions . . .

A sign finally came into view. There had been none for a while and, come to think of it, he hadn't seen any indications of population for a while either . . . . no homes, no stores, no shelters of any kind. The Scout's engine was beginning to labor also. The mountain was taking its toll on the miniature Pre-SUV. A small thermometer symbol next to the word, "Engine," was glowing bright orange.

"Crap!" he said. And then, "Crap and Double Crap!" A sign on the side of the road that had come into focus read, *'Cottonwood Pass, Altitude, 12,226 feet.'* Pierre's highway designation changed at the pass as well. More doubts were creeping into his mind. Baron's notes said the road composition would change to packed gravel. Instead, it appeared to be relatively new asphalt. He was now traveling State Highway 209 . . . it was going downhill . . . fast . . . and now snow was falling! Big flakes. He'd left DIA with the temperature at 58, a big drop from the morning's 79 degrees and 100 percent humidity of New Orleans. He guessed that outside the temperature was now in the 40s.

Since he was near the top presumably of Cottonwood Mountain, he checked his phone again and, voilà, found a signal. Three bars!

Yee-hah! Must be a cell tower here on the peak somewhere!

Punching up the weather channel app, he was stunned to see that the outside temperature had dropped to 33 degrees.

Yeah. I've been cranking that heater up over the past hour. I guess I can believe it!

Getting a solid estimate of the distance from the Pass to where he intended to spend the night was tough. Another sign at the Pass informed him that State Highway 209 was normally closed from October to the end of April, and he could see why. Yesterday, Google, because of the possibility of poor road surfaces, possible snowpack, and impossibly steep inclines . . . *or declines, I guess you could say*

... tried to route him from Buena Vista south to Salida, then west to Gunnison, and then back in toward the Taylor Park Reservoir where the trading post was located ... hours longer than he had available to him. 209 was a switchback road down the mountain, and he guessed the *'as the crow flies'* distance to Taylor Reservoir was about 15 miles. The switchbacks would make this trip at least two or three times that distance but this was the route he'd chosen and he rarely changed his mind about something once he'd decided. Jolie said he was *just plain stubborn.*

Stubborn? Me, stubborn? Bollucks! My hunches have always led me true.

Within a mile though, Pierre's confidence began to crash and burn. Snow was falling at an astounding rate. Already several inches were on the ground, and there was old snow beneath that! The windshield wipers on the Scout were working, but brittle. He couldn't find a windshield washer. *May not have been standard equipment back then,* he thought. The defroster was having trouble keeping up and a bad gasket behind his head on the backseat window allowed in an enormous amount of frigid air which threatened both his equilibrium and comfort.

The moon was mostly full but because of heavy snowclouds, it rarely made an appearance. At one point while rounding a curve, conditions were momentarily perfect for him to look down into a moonlit valley far below where, for a second or so, he thought he saw the lights of a small town. They were quickly erased by more blowing snow and, while the view had been beautiful, he realized that he was looking almost straight down . . . . hundreds of feet.

This is what it must be like in Tibet or the Andes, he thought, *or maybe even Shreveport!*

II

Just after nine p.m., Highway 209 began to level. Pierre breathed a sigh of relief. As it slowly flattened, he began to un-claw his fingers from the steering wheel. It had been a tough drive – hairpin turns every quarter mile, big drop-offs, and surfaces that seemed greased by the snow. The Scout's wipers couldn't keep up. They were brittle enough from old age that he joked to himself that they might scratch right through the windshield. While there had been mounds of dirty snow at Cottonwood Pass, the trip down brought fresh flakes that were accumulating up to seven or eight inches by the time he reached the bottom of the mountain. Pierre estimated that because of the switchbacks, he still had eleven or twelve miles to go.

* * * *

Through fog and an iced-up windshield – and with continually accumulating snow – Pierre saw a puzzling array of soft lights before him in the distance. Closing in, thankfully, the tallest of them advertised *The Taylor Park Trading Post . . . his cabin for the night!* They were red neon letters, and some had either burned out or were blocked by snow. The *Post* itself was a two-story building housing a welcoming center, a restaurant, and an indoor pool. Nearby were a dozen large mounds of snow with smoke rising up from chimneys. Cabin Seven, *my cabin, must be one of them,* he thought. The most baffling part of the view though was the parking area.

Thirty or forty plumes of exhaust wafted up through the still-falling snow. The exhaust apparently rose from vehicles of all descriptions that were crowded into a parking lot that looked smaller than it should have, but then because of the deep snow it was impossible to discern where the parking area ended and grasslands might begin. Some vehicles were fully covered by a foot or more. Others, because their engines were running, were partly clear of the white stuff. There were people inside them, probably toasty warm.

Pierre was relieved to note that the *Engine Overheat* warning light on his Scout had shut off. Coasting down the mountain, plus the even colder temperatures outside were no doubt helping bring the old car's engine back to normal operating status.

"You may be old, beat up, and worn, but you've got stamina," he said aloud, patting the dashboard in affection.

Finally, the brave little car sloshed and danced around a bit but did a respectable job of pushing enough snow aside for Pierre to open a parking space.

He had been dreading this moment. At least he'd been smart enough though to throw his carry-on into the backseat at the airport instead of stowing it in the far-back of the vehicle. That meant he wouldn't have to trudge through the snow to open the hatch. Even that wouldn't be a major concern though. The real problem was . . . he wasn't dressed for any of this.

It's May for crying out loud!

Pierre fished around in his carry-on and found his Wingtip Oxfords. Slipping off his flip-flops in the crowded space of the front seat, he wrestled his chilled bare feet into his best pair of dress shoes. By pushing the driver's door outward, he created a small area free from heavy snow, clear enough, at any rate, to allow him to at least emerge from the car. Now with shoes on his feet, he began to pull his carry-on behind him, wading a hundred feet or so through knee-deep snow toward the entrance of the lodge. *Hope they got the walk to my cabin shoveled,* he thought. The wheeled carry-on acted like a reverse snow shovel and dragged at him, so he hoisted it up and over the white stuff, pulling it like a sled.

As he pushed through the Trading Post's front doors, he was greeted by a gasp, and then a scattering round of applause . . . even some cheering. At least a hundred people were crowded into the lobby and restaurant. Every chair and couch was filled to capacity! The crowd's focus was on the front door to see which poor soul would next emerge from the Yukon wilderness outside and make his or her way into the safety of the lodge.

"Close the doors! Close the doors!" The chant from the spectators was like a cheer at a football game at LSU's Death Valley!

People were stretched out on the floor everywhere.

But they were all cheering, applauding, and whistling *at him. This is sort of like the reception Norm got when he entered Cheers,* Pierre thought. Of course, the fact that he was wearing cargo shorts, a maroon tee shirt that offered directions on how to properly eat crawfish, a Saints cap, and black dress oxfords containing sockless feet, had something to do with the reception he was getting. He waved at them with the flip flops in his free hand and smiled, acknowledging them in his best Elvis impersonation, saying, "Thanks! Thanks, y'all! Thank ya' vera much!" The crowd laughed and then went back to its business, which wasn't much, apparently.

In normal times, the Trading Post would have been considered rustic and western . . . probably even, *quaint.* Huge wooden beams hovered over the lobby with the highest part of the ceiling perhaps twenty feet off the floor. A restaurant sat off to the right and a gift shop to the left. There were people everywhere. No chair was left unsat upon, or in many cases, unslept upon. Twenty or fifty kids were running circles, yelling, and dodging in and out of groups of adults, some of whom were playing cards. The noise, even when people weren't cheering and applauding, was deafening. And then there was the smell. Probably because everyone in the lodge had walked through the same kind of snow Pierre had, a sour, heated, wet sock aroma seemed to permeate everything and everyone in the large room.

Pierre was frozen and wet, and his expensive black oxfords were soaked and disintegrating. Against one wall near the entrance, he saw a sign saying, "Registration." He edged his way up to the desk where several people were already waiting for assistance from two harried-looking young women. Finally, it was his turn. He found himself facing the younger of the two.

"LeBlanc," he said, pronouncing it La *Blaw*, "Pierre LeBlanc. I have a reservation for Cabin Seven tonight. Sorry, I'm a bit late. The snow, you know."

Her name tag read, *Hello! Welcome to Taylor Trading Post. I'm Shelly. How can I help you enjoy Colorado?* She stood before him behind a counter that was in complete disarray, and she appeared to be on her last legs herself. Shelly wore a wrinkled bellman-style top. Her hair was messed beyond repair. Her makeup had run, and her face showed perhaps the after-stains of tears. With stiff pursed lips lacking even a hint of lipstick, she sorted through a file of reservations and pulled one from the stack.

"Yes, Mr. La Blanc" – she'd mispronounced the name as Blank – "but, I'm afraid I have bad news." She looked as if she was prepared to duck if Pierre took a swing at her. "We held your cabin until seven, but when you didn't show," she held her hands up showing the huge throng of humanity in the lobby, "we gave it to two families totaling nine people. They're camped out there now sleeping on the one double bed and a pull-out. I am so sorry."

Pierre was set back on what remained of his dress shoe heels. Melted snow squirted out. "Well," he stuttered, "what *can* you do for me then?" I have a meeting in Ticnup in the morning at nine and I need a place to stay, catch a shower, and get something to eat."

"Again, I am so sorry. We have no food. Our restaurant ran out two hours ago. We've got people sleeping on the tables in the restaurant area in the lodge. There's no room even in our lobby. The storm, you know. It was totally unexpected, and all these people pulled in here because we're the only place to stay between Gunnison, Crested Butte, and Buena Vista! Many folks are camping in our parking lot in their travel trailers, their RV's, or even in their cars."

"Well, what am I gonna do?" Pierre asked.

"Well, you're certainly welcome to stretch out in our lobby," she replied. "We'll refund your deposit, of course. It *is* supposed to warm up tomorrow, and while it's such a heavy snow – we've had 14 inches so far in the last six hours – it should begin to melt off quickly in the morning . . .

"Wait a minute!" she said interrupting herself, her eyes brightening a bit. "Did you say you were heading to Tin Cup?"

"No. Close though. *Ticnup*."

"That's gotta be Tin Cup." It's only about fourteen miles up the mountain and the road's a good one. My uncle lives there and there's a B&B in Tin Cup called the *Birdcage*. Let me give them a call."

Shelly had brightened considerably. She pulled out a small, laminated reference page with highlights of the area listed – mostly views, trails, fishing, swimming, camping spots, and so forth – and picked up the phone, punched in a couple of buttons, and in a moment was speaking to someone presumably at the *Birdcage B&B*. "Hey, Annie. Shelly at the Post. We're getting' slammed here. Fourteen inches so far and it's still comin' down. We're packed, people trippin' over themselves in our lobby. We've got one woman in the restaurant goin' into labor. How's it up there?"

She listened to the phone for a minute or so as "Annie" gave her the weather report in Tin Cup, *not Ticnup!* Finally, she said, "Oh, yeah. That's what I was callin' about. We got a nice guy here . . . believe it or not, he's wearing a tee-shirt, shorts, and dress shoes. . . and he's got a meeting in Tin Cup, of all things, tomorrow. He needs a place to stay. Are you full?" A pause. "Hold on. Mr. Blank? Great news! Annie's got a *really* nice room with a bath at the *Birdcage,* right where you're heading. You can be there in under an hour. Are you interested?"

III

The trek back to the car from the Trading Post was even more difficult and colder than the one going *into* the lodge. Pierre was exhausted, hungry, wet, and cold . . . and he needed an Abita, *bad*. In place of the beer, he'd bought a bottle of water, Hostess Cupcakes, and a crushed praline at the gift shop.

At the covered entrance to the lobby, he checked his phone.

It had frozen up.

Literally? he wondered. *Or is it just it's usual, 'Hey. I'll think I'll just quit working!'*

Even before it went down for the count, Pierre's phone hadn't shown a single bar of coverage since Cottonwood Pass. Worse, there was not only zero cell coverage at the Taylor Trading Post, but its Wi-Fi was also out of commission. From folks near the registration desk, he'd heard two different mileage estimates to Tin Cup – *Tin Cup! Not Ticnup, Tin Cup! Damn paralegals!* – One was 13 miles; the other 27 . . . both up one more mountain to climb. *Isn't that a song?*

Just as he was set to step out from under the canopy, Shelly rushed out from the lobby and stopped him, presenting him with an emergency road kit. She told him that it was pretty common in the *Colorado Wayback* to carry one in your car.

He recalled a story from one of his skiing friends that such a pack unusually consisted of a blanket, a can of canned meat, a bottle or two of water, a couple of candles, and a pack of matches. What all these items were for seemed a bit obvious, but Shelly insisted on explaining each one to him anyway.

"Compliments of the Taylor Trading Post," she concluded! "I'll back-off the charge for your cabin, too. Thank you for considering the Taylor Trading Post, Mr. Blank," she said with a renewed and cheery smile. Pierre realized that his was probably one of the few problems she'd been able to resolve all evening long. She deserved to be pleased with herself. He smiled.

"Thanks," he said sincerely, as he looked out at the

snow-covered and frozen parking lot. Vapors rising from the exhausts of forty snow-covered lumps of cars looked like bonfires in an Indian village. "Thanks," he said again. "I'll return this stuff when I come back through here tomorrow or the next day."

"Don't worry about it," Shelly said. "It's part of our Rockies Good Neighbor Philosophy. Keep it. Or pass it forward. Never know when you're gonna need it! Good luck on your trip to Tin Cup. Just take a right out of the Post, then a left onto 742, and then another left onto 55. Take it east for about ten miles, then a right onto 765. Keep goin' past Abbeyville and you'll run right down Tin Cup's Main Street. Maybe 25 miles."

"I thought it was only 14."

"That's if you're a crow and you're flying!" Shelly laughed. "All our roads around here twist and turn a bit going up and down the mountains. You'll be okay. But watch the roads carefully. Not too many signs out here, and now most of 'em are covered in snow. Be careful. Say, 'hi' to Annie at the *Birdcage* for me."

Shelly had certainly perked up from when he'd first met her, but Pierre thought he also detected sort of an *"if you're ever heard from again"* inflection in the way she gave her directions.

He spent a few minutes cleaning snow from his windshield, the side windows, and the hood of the Scout. He should have spent more, but his feet were beginning to feel like dry ice. He wanted to check them and see if steam was coming out of the holes in his shoes, but he needed to get moving. Climbing into the Scout, he cranked the engine over. It didn't catch. He tried twice more before recalling Zach's cautions about the manual choke. In no time, the engine was revving, and the heater was putting out reams of cold air. *Well, okay, wisps of cold air.*

"Holy cats! I hope I survive," Pierre told the dashboard. "The Baron ought to make me a full partner for this," He checked his phone again. Still no signal, but at least the GPS seemed to be functioning. "How can that be?" he asked himself. "Doesn't that thing work off the same phone signal?"

Turning right out of the entrance to the Trading Post, it was a short-haul to get to 742 where he took a left, and then another left onto Highway 55. All he had to do now was stay on 55 until he got to 765 and turn right. Right?

Immediately he realized the problem. In the valley where the Trading Post was located, snow had built up to 14 inches or more, and much more than that in the drifts. The roads were barely discernible in the darkness and there were no streetlamps. Over and through numerous quiet moments of abject fear, he drove, not telling if he was even on the road, sometimes, except by the *feel*. Fortunately, there was a full moon. Unfortunately, snow clouds covered it most of the time. There were almost no buildings or trees in sight but every so often it appeared that an unmarked road forked off to the right or left. His GPS was now showing roads and distances to Durango. *Where the heck is Durango?* he wondered. The last time he'd heard of Durango, Marshall Dillon was there after transporting a prisoner from Dodge City!

His ears popped. Because of the limit of his headlight beams, the only indication he had that he was climbing another mountain was the discomfort of his ears popping. At one point he was blocked – if, in fact, he was even on the highway – by a large mound of snow that vaguely resembled a pick-up. He hoped there was no one in it and cautiously sashayed passed it just as the moon made another appearance.

"Oh, my God!" he exclaimed as he hit the brakes. To his left was a drop-off, and in a break in the whirling blizzard, he could make out the tops of snow-covered pine trees at least a hundred feet below. The Scout sloshed to a stop, and Pierre sat still for a few moments breathing heavily, flexing his aching fingers. He hadn't realized until now that he'd been hanging on to the steering wheel with a death grip and vowed to slow down from his speed of nine or ten miles an hour, exerting a bit more caution. "This sure ain't the bayou!" he said to the dash. It still refused to answer. He'd begun to think they were better friends than that.

Forty-five minutes after leaving the Trading Post, he turned right onto Highway 765 and recalled from a map Shelly had shown him that he was almost halfway to Tin Cup. Maybe another hour. It was already close to ten p.m.

What will I do if they've given up on me and shut the Birdcage *down for the night?*

The higher he climbed though, the less snow he encountered. But even that was relative. There was a good six or eight inches of fresh stuff on the road.

In reality, Pierre was proud of himself. For one who'd never driven in snow or on mountains, he seemed to be doing alright. He suspected it was because the wind had picked up and was now blowing the freshest snow off the road. There were still very few trees to be seen through the darkness. That made the wind seem even fiercer.

He'd only met one vehicle coming the other way and they'd jockeyed to get past each other, narrowly missing. The driver had waved to him, and he'd belatedly returned the greeting.

"In 1814 we took a little trip, Along with Colonel Jackson, Down the Mighty Missisip . . ."

Back at the Trading Post, he'd shoved the phone back in his pocket. The ringtone was coming again from his shorts and he was unprepared to release his death grip on the wheel to find the phone, pull it out, and answer it.

"We took a little bacon, And, we took a little beans, And we fought the bloody British, In the Town of New Orleans."

His fingers were stiff and didn't react well to hunting for the phone.

"We fired our guns and the British kept a-comin', There wasn't nigh as many as there was a while ago, We fired once more and they begin to runnin', Down the Mississippi to the Gulf . . ."

"Hey, Jolie. How are you, my love?"

"Well, son, I suspect a bit Bloody Hell better than you are. I have been watching the Weather Channel and they are having a *delightful* time talking about a late spring blizzard over the Rockies. I am hoping you are finally at the Trading Post enjoying a cocktail. How come you have not called me . . . again?" There was still that element of irritation in her voice.

Doesn't she ever use a contraction? he asked himself.

"Yeah. Sorry. Not a lot of cell coverage up here. And worse, I'm still on the road. You wouldn't have believed the chaos at the Trading Post. They gave away my cabin to two families because I was running so late. And in the lobby there must have been a hundred other travelers hunkering down for the night, completely filling the place!"

"Oh, my dear man. So, what are you doing?"

He filled her in on the *Birdcage*, on Tin Cup versus Ticnup, on the snow, on the car . . . and he could tell she was as exhausted from hearing about it as he was from living it. He knew his moments of cell signal were precious, so he said, "I can't imagine that we aren't going to get cut off again, Jolie. I think I'm okay. I've still got at least a half-hour to go, I think. But now I have emergency stuff in case I have to spend the night in the car. You know, blankets, candles, and . . . hey, I was told I've got a can of meat! Yum! I forgot to get something to eat at the Post and hadn't thought about it until now. Anyway, I should be okay, although this may be the adventure of my life."

He was about to tell her where he'd hidden his will but paused first to hear her response. There was none. Reluctantly he placed the phone back into the indentation on the dashboard and pressed on the accelerator, churning on, and depressed at the way the call had ended. In truth, he was a whole lot less confident about the next hour than he'd let on. And he hadn't even said, "Goodbye," or "I love you, babe!"

Highway 765 had been a dirt and gravel road from the beginning but the more he climbed in altitude, the messier it became. The two lanes often narrowed to one and it seemed he was traveling along one of those roads that hug a mountain in commercials, with steep sides on the left and a precipitous drop-off on the right. If he met another pickup, given the snowpack, there might not be enough room for them to pass each other. On the other hand, traffic coming the other way would certainly indicate that there was indeed civilization ahead. He'd not seen a sign of life in a while. Yeah, he'd passed a small cemetery . . . *probably travelers that hadn't made it to Tin Cup in a blizzard* . . . but no homes, and worse, no signs indicating that he was still on 765. Wasn't he supposed to pass Abbeyville? He loved Abbeyville, Louisiana. Nice casino and great Cajun food! But Abbeyville, Colorado? Where was that? Maybe it washed away in an avalanche!

"Another vehicle coming the other way!" He shouted to Scout.

The two vehicles each gave way, but their rearview mirrors kissed each other goodnight.

He tried Scout's radio but even KOA's 50,000 watts weren't making it through the ether. All he could get was an occasional understandable word or two. The more he climbed in elevation, the more the temperature dropped. He was now crunching through icy snowdrifts that completely transversed the road. Rounding a curve, the skies cleared enough so he could see where he was: on top of another precipice – a wall of snow or stone on the right and a big drop-off on the left. He felt his left front wheel drop down and instinctively jerked the Scout's steering wheel hard to the right. That's when he felt the left rear wheel wallow into a deep pothole. He hoped it was only a pothole.

The little Scout settled in nicely and no amount of jerking her old transmission would help. The vehicle had tilted about 20 degrees off vertical and was angled so that it completely blocked the road. *Ain't no one goin' nowhere on this road tonight,* he thought. He considered getting out and hiking but didn't know where he was or how far it was to either Abbeyville or Tin Cup. Worse, he was unsure of what was outside the driver's door and worried about getting out, slipping, and sliding down some hundred-foot, 45-degree slope, and off a mountain. *If that happened, my body would never be found!* He couldn't get out of the car on the right side of the vehicle either, because of a wall of snow.

"Come on, Scout!"

He imagined for a moment he was sitting on the front porch with Jem and Dill and Boo Radley talkin' about those great old summer days. That brought his attention back to the car. "You can make it girl!" He ground the gears a bit and tried to jack-shift the old car back onto solid ground. The old girl just settled in deeper.

"Well, that's it I'm afraid. We're here for the duration .

". . or until somebody rescues us," he said to the dashboard. It occurred to him to regret that he hadn't told Jolie exactly where he was because she might have been able to summon help. That required a cell signal and he still had none.

Assessing his situation, he checked the fuel gauge. "Ah! Hooray. We've still got more than half a tank. That should keep us warm through the night." His conversation now was entirely with Scout. The girl still wasn't returning his attempts at communication. He realized he still needed to conserve fuel because dawn wouldn't make an appearance for another six or eight hours.

To preserve gas, he shut the engine down, vowing to run it and the heater only five minutes every half hour. The wind whistled through the bad gasket in the rear window behind him and he could feel the chill on his neck. Wrestling his carry-on from the back seat, he pulled out pajamas, socks, and a suit coat.

Yeah, I brought a suit. He answered the rebuke from his head.

The Baron would never have approved of him representing LeBlanc LeBlanc LeBlanc and Blois in anything but a suit. Now, that decision might save his life. He wrestled on the trousers and suit jacket and tried to make himself comfortable.

It was then that he remembered Shelly's, Emergency Kit. It was packed in a cloth Taylor Trading Post shopping bag in the back seat. Hungrily he popped the top off a can of Spam and with a plastic fork and knife, devoured the contents within five minutes. "Not bad," he had to admit.

"Wonder what it would taste like with grits?" Next came and went a bottle of water. The car cooled quickly after he turned the engine off, so he lit one of the candles and waxed it onto the dashboard.

I find it hard to believe that a single candle could keep a person alive in the cold. Sounds like an old wives' tale.

On the few occasions the full moon showed itself, he looked around. The road curved slightly to the right just ahead, so he couldn't see much that way, mostly because of a wall of snow blocking his vision. To the left was a drop-off. Nothing but blackness was visible below. It seemed to have stopped snowing but the blowing wind coming down the mountain was still sending a steady stream of large flakes across the Scout's hood and windshield.

"Good night, Scout. Dill. Jem."

No reply.

He had nothing to do but close his eyes and think . . . of carbon monoxide!

Quickly Pierre rolled down each window an inch or so. *Hope I'm not too late.* He'd heard of people in Louisiana who'd tried to survive cold nights using space heaters and barbecue grills to warm their homes, only to wake up dead in the morning thanks to carbon monoxide poisoning. *Could a candle emit enough CO to kill me?* He was cold regardless, especially for someone from Louisiana, and he rolled the windows back up until only a quarter from closed. Freezing cold air poured through the slit.

What's the point of heating my car with a candle if all the heat is lost out a window crack?

Wrapping himself in the blanket as best as he was able, Pierre squirmed into a moderately comfortable position and closed his eyes . . . and . . . *he was certain he smelled carbon monoxide! I thought you weren't supposed to be able to smell it?* He argued with himself. Pierre was exhausted, wet, cold, miserable, hungry, and desperate for someone to talk to.

Gotta change my attitude, he thought, interrupting his melancholy in mid-stride. *It has been a fun day! I saw some incredible scenery, I can check off Colorado on my list of visited states, I've seen snow for the first time, and I've driven both in it and over mountains . . . and I'm still alive!*

That brought a note of reality mixed with confidence to his situation. Exhaustion was taking over. He tried to open his eyes but realized he was in that state where one could doze off and yet be both awake and asleep at the same time. He chose not to awaken and then smiled. *Things could be worse!*

His mind seemed to be functioning just fine. With nothing better to do, he reviewed the trip so far: the flight delay, the hunt for a decent rental car, the incredible changes in the weather, the slide down the mountain after Cottonwood Pass, the undependability of his outside communications, his failure to find shelter at the Trading Post, and now this: Stuck in the middle of a dirt road on a mountain in Colorado in a snowstorm! He heard his colleagues back in the office singing, "Told you so! Told you so!" Even in this somnolent state, he gritted his teeth and mumbled to himself, *I gotta think positive!*

The scenery had been magnificent: Incredible snowcapped mountains! He'd been through his first tunnel and his second! Wouldn't it be great to be flying on a tiny ultra-light aircraft, floating above the mountains in the fresh air of summer accompanied by a squadron of pelicans, looking down at incredible scenery below? He'd land in a lush green pasture full of mountain flowers of every color next to a boutique hotel perched on the side of a steep cliff, a swift-running stream full of jumping alligators beside it. He'd sit by the huge swimming pool looking out on snowcaps, even in August. A soft sea breeze would blow the fronds of the palm trees . . . and a large sign on the hotel roof would read, "Welcome to Tin Cup Colorado."

Ah, everything is perfect, even the . . . carbon monoxide?
This time Pierre didn't wake up.

The Lagniappe

I

New Orleans – 2 a.m. – Fat Tuesday 1991

"One hundred-fourteen. Yep!" the boy proudly said to himself as he skipped out the fire door into an alley. It was dark with only a half-moon scuttling in and out of clouds, but usually hidden this night. He knew from his daylight excursions in the neighborhood that what he'd find in this particular alley was mostly trash, often of the vilest sort. After a few minutes of searching, he smiled. He'd been able to locate the item he was looking for lying mostly in a puddle of foul greasy water. Wringing it out, he pulled the worn shirt once again over his bruised chest. He was happy to get it back and began a carefree whistle as he headed for home.

* * * *

An hour earlier

The rooms and other spaces in the abandoned hotel all seemed to reek of misery and debauchery, even the fire stairs. It was dark and without electricity, the stairs emerged in the deep night thanks only to obscured moonlight peeking through the small dirty windows of each landing. They provided just enough light for a trespasser to move around without tripping over something.

In Better Times

The twelve-year-old boy followed his father up the evacuation stairs of a building that had once enjoyed a more celebrated past. *The Lagniappe,* a faux Jackson Square edifice built in the early fifties, crowded the north edge of the French Quarter. Since the hotel's days of greatness and popularity, its landings, as well as most of the stairs, had been graced by the noted decorator, *Debris*.

Even where refuse was absent, the Lagniappe's stairs and walls had grown greasy and gritty over disuse. The boy wished he'd brought a flashlight so he could see where he was stepping . . . and on what he was stepping. He could discern almost nothing around him when the clouds blotted out the moon. The building's low-wattage bare-naked emergency bulbs, located on each landing, were either missing or shattered. On one or two floors even the fixtures were missing, stolen by scavengers he believed. In their place, dust-grimed wires hanging from the sockets were all that remained. The *Exit* signs were equally dark and grimed over.

And on this night, the moon seemed to prefer hiding its half-face through the mud-colored clouds that hurried past New Orleans, seemingly wishing to avoid the sourness below. When he *could* make out objects on the stairs in his path, the boy found himself often stepping and sliding on things most unpleasant. More than once on the trek up, a rat scurried through his legs.

"Com'on, kid! I gotta 'pointment *right now* up on the roof and I ain't gonna miss it because of you."

The boy was dressed in shorts, flip-flops, and a torn

and bloody basketball jersey featuring a small, faded number seven on its front and a much larger seven on the backside. The shirt had once been a brilliant green and gold, the colors of the Jazz, the city's former NBA franchise, but it was now a pale-yellow monochrome. It was dirty and torn with dried blood staining it in a few places. Parts of the shirt were hidden by the boy's long tousled and matted hair. A small stream of blood dribbled from the boy's nose and down his chin.

The boy . . . Paul . . . sniffled a whimper every so often as he recalled the beating his mother had taken just before *this* man, *supposedly* his father . . . the man who climbed the stairs in front of him . . . pulled him from their Ninth Ward slum-home, requiring him to accompany the old man on his adventure. There had been no desire on the part of the boy to go anywhere with his ole man but he had no choice.

What he preferred rather was to be home administering to his mother's injuries He hoped she'd not been hurt too badly from the beating he'd been forced to watch. Sniffing back another sob, the boy paused to wipe his nose with his wrist and then, after a call to 'catch up' by his ole man, he again began following him up the stairs of this creepy, decrepit building . . . . floor after floor. The boy wondered why the city would allow the abandoned and decrepit building given its condition. He shuddered when he thought about what probably went on even in the landings.

By the time they climbed past the fifth floor, the old

man had begun stumbling on every tenth stair. He was out of breath from three decades of too many cigarettes and twenty-five years of too much alcohol. Following him, the old man radiated back a mix of body odor and booze, and who knew what else. The combined effluence seemed to be leaking from his pores.

Without considering the possible consequences, the boy let out a big sigh.

"Cheer up, kid. You're gonna get an education tonight," came the response, coupled with a loose rattily cough. The boy subconsciously ducked in response.

On the other side of the dirty windows, the clouds seemed to descend even further over the French Quarter, threatening a deluge.

Paul knew from the moment they'd entered the old hotel that he'd better show some enthusiasm for whatever it was his father wanted him to see. No sense in aggravating the old man further. When they finally opened a barrier door to the roof, the boy announced with forced cheerfulness, "114 steps, Pop! Fourteen steps between each floor, plus two extra ones in the lobby. Altogether we climbed a hundred and fourteen! How 'bout that?"

"Huh?"

His hopes of impressing the old man with his counting skills had apparently missed the mark. He'd try anything to convince the old man to like him at least a little because it might mean fewer beatings and humiliations. "Seven stories. Sixteen steps on the first floor and each floor after had 14 more. Plus, there were another 14 to get to the roof! 114 altogether. How 'bout that, huh, Pop?"

For his counting skills, the ole man slapped him across the face, this time bloodying an ear. "Your mom never hears anything about this, kid. Right?"

A soft downcast, "Yes," was the response.

"Yes, what?"

"Yes, sir."

"And take that damn shirt off! The Pistol's gone. That jerk cost me a lot of money anyway! I'm glad he left for Tabasco Lake, Salt Lake, or wherever the hell it is. That shirt's ruined anyway."

The boy felt the old man's rough hands pulling his most-favorite-shirt-of-all-time above his head and out of reach. He reached out in protest but was too late, he watched as the worn and faded jersey sailed over the edge of the roof and disappeared into seven stories of darkness below.

A woman was waiting for them in a corner on the roof. She was cloaked in darkness. To this point she hadn't acknowledged their arrival, quietly smoking, her left hand cupping her right elbow. From the shadows, he heard her inhale deeply, then exhale. He thought enough smoke came from her lungs to warm a ten-by-ten-foot room. As she took a puff, the glow from the cigarette highlighted the dark circles under her eyes.

Paul looked away from her as his father left his side.

Mardi Gras 1991 was now officially *history*. Below them . . . seven stories below . . . garbage trucks were rolling through the streets of the French Quarter. They were the only sounds of Mardi Gras that remained.

And then Paul heard, unmistakably, the sounds of heavy breathing.

Thirty minutes later, perhaps ten minutes after his woman had left them, the boy fled his way down those same dark stairs at three times the speed it had taken him to climb. Reaching the darkness of the alley, he edged past the crumpled body of his old man. It lay face down on the filthy broken pavement, blood still oozing from the crushed skull.

He gave the body no pause. He was on another mission. Searching, searching until he spotted his old shirt lying in a huge puddle of fowl-smelling liquid fifty feet away. He gave the stench of it no mind but waded in anyway, finally slipping his prized possession, a soggy old Pete Maravich shirt, back on over his scarred shoulders. As the moon poked its face out of the clouds, Paul began the long walk back to his home to the Ninth Ward.

The few sober individuals who were still on the streets at that hour, some poking through the remains of Mardi Gras, marveled that at that early hour, a young boy was out and walking alone. He was whistling a happy tune as he hurried down the streets and alleys, seemingly on a mission.

THE DEED

I

New Orleans – 2005

On a day when rain threatened, two men sat opposite each other at a 17th Century Partner's Desk in a plush office on the northwest side of the French Quarter. One appeared older than the other but that may have been because he wore a heavy scraggily beard and was dressed in bib overalls, a blue flannel shirt, no socks, deck shoes that should have been discarded months ago, and a New Orleans Baby Cakes baseball hat. The other man, the one with his back to the wall, was dressed much smarter: a blue pinstriped Saville Row suit, crisp white button-down shirt, a $200 tie, with a slicked-down haircut straight out of a Hollywood salon.

Mr. Bib Overalls rocked contentedly in his office chair while Mr. Pinstripe paid no attention as he dictated letters from his command seat behind the desk. The desk was genuine, not a recreation by an artist active in the fake antique industry that did surprisingly good business in the Crescent City. The desk was the genuine antique article though. Its nicks and scratches could tell incredible stories had they been able to speak.

A portrait-style photograph of the building in which they met covered a large space behind the desk's owner.

It was a night shot. Theatrically the building was bathed in white lights. The structure had been declared to be an architecturally positive edifice critical to French Quarter history, even though it only dated to the 1820s. From the photograph though one could easily imagine the building as a four-hundred-year-old castle on the Rhine.

The office spoke of wealth almost unimaginable to customers of the business. Bookshelves lined one side wall as well as the back wall. The other sidewall featured a large window, but it was hidden behind a beautiful leather tapestry, blotting any view of the intersection of Governor Nicholls and Bourbon Streets. On either side of the office door on the back wall stood tall display cases. Inside each was a collection of trinkets collected from the life of the younger man. Dominant in both cases was a partially deflated basketball, each one had a Pete Maravich autograph written on it in black magic marker, plus *#23 LSU* on one, and *#7 The Jazz* on the other.

A visitor might have expected to find the shelves full of old books and first editions but the dozen or so volumes that were on display had been written by authors with a more modern connection to New Orleans: Anne Rice, Tennessee Williams, James Lee Burke, and some with more tenuous claims to the city, novels by Grisham and Isles, and several autographed Cookbooks by local famous chefs.

Framed and autographed photographs were on display on other shelves. Generally, these featured the younger man standing next to or shaking hands with celebrities, politicians, or sports figures. There were also a few with the man's family. One of the largest of these showed him holding a monstrously large Grouper with the help of a beautiful young woman wearing a tiny bikini, presumably his wife. She was smiling while helping him lift the big fish. One might swear that a sparkle of sunlight glinted off her teeth. Next to them holding a smaller Flounder was the older man. The boat they were aboard appeared in a few other photographs as well. It was named, *The Good Times*, a 42-foot fishing boat. Oddly, in the photo of the Grouper, neither man was smiling.

One large outdoor photograph showed Saville Row smiling with his arm around the strikingly beautiful young woman from the fishing photo. Another appeared to be a family portrait aboard *The Good Times*. In it were the desk's owner, the same woman/wife, a young boy, and a perfect golden retriever. Of course, the sky was blue, and the water was perfectly calm.

Bib rocked on. If he'd really concentrated, he might have heard Henri Mancini's *Moon River* playing in the deep background. The soothing music wasn't registering on *his* brain though, or for that matter, the brain of the younger guy.

"So, why the meeting?" It was the younger man breaking the silence as he finally closed a large corporate checkbook and pushed it into a desk drawer, locking the drawer. For him, that act seemed to signify the closure of his bit of business. He glanced at his watch. It was now time to move on to the next. When Bib failed to respond, Saville Row made more of a show of checking his Rolex again. The question he'd originally asked had been inflected with a bit of irritation as he'd not expected an interruption to his day by the older guy.

Bib, however, was content to rock in his chair and made a small show of examining the office. A leather inlay was on the small table that sat alongside *his* office chair. Both pieces of furniture were centered on a smallish rectangular Persian rug, no doubt an expensive *pièce d'accompagnement*. A vase of fresh lilies posed on the table broadcasting an entrancingly sweet smell. It was mostly lost on the two men however as the building's heavy-duty ventilation system kicked in noisily, sucking the emitted fragrance up and through a vent in the ceiling.

Competing with the lilies and the powerful ventilation system was an even stronger aroma. It issued from a nine-inch long Cuban Partagas Serie P No. 2 hand-rolled cigar and rested in a large ashtray in front of the younger man. The pleasant aroma successfully defeated the industrial environmental vacuum cleaner. Over time it and its many sister Partagas had imbedded their aromas into the carpets and draperies of the office. Even the Partaga was a loser though to one more scent. What fragrances not lost to the ventilation system were beaten down and subdued by an artificially induced perfume of carnations and roses that issued from a small odor emitting device mounted in a corner of the ceiling.

For the younger man, the extended silence became too much to bear.

"I repeat, John, why are we here?"

But the older man remained silent, continuing to rock, apparently in contemplation of the announcement he was about to deliver. Just as Saville Row again reached the end of his patience, Bib cleared his throat and answered. "Paul, I've spent the past month making some unpleasant decisions." He paused in his opening soliloquy to bat away cigar smoke, "I am here today to put my decisions into action." Bib . . . *John* . . . wrinkled his nose, leaned forward in his chair, and now seemed ready to get down to business.

As one might have guessed from the beginning of the conversation, the two men were partners. Several years earlier, the one with the money, the older man wearing the beard, overalls, and baseball hat, had staked the other in an opportunity. Since then, he'd become somewhat of a recluse and now was almost invisible in the New Orleans Social Set. The younger man, conversely, was well known in town, even recently serving as King of the Krewe of Bacchus, an honor normally unavailable to non-celebrities. He'd worked hard to make that happen. Public visibility was a plus in *his* line of work and, unlike the older man, he worked it every way possible.

Of the two, the younger man was *the* public persona who was linked to the success of this joint endeavor. He alone possessed the medical and scientific knowledge critical to its operation. But, he was also the partner with the least *business* acumen for his instinct was to spend, not generate profit.

It was early in the afternoon. This was a unique

business, sometimes operating until late at night and sometimes closing as early as noon. All business to be transacted on this day had either been already concluded or was being intentionally left unfinished. The employees had departed. Only the two partners remained in the building.

What *really* was left behind though was the conclusion to a conversation that had begun months before, had experienced few good moments, and sustained many that were dark and unhappy.

"Sorry, bro," said the bearded one a bit too casually. He'd always been the more flippant of the two. "I am aware of course that we've had many good moments, but nevertheless I've decided to sell off the business. I'm leaving town. It has been my money that got us here but I've become exhausted from the drama that you bring into my life. And, the truth is, I've had it up to here with your mistakes and deceptions. They've cost us dearly. Oh, and one more thing: I am tired of covering for you. I need to move on to a place where I'll have no worries over money, conflict, . . . or even prison. I want clean air, fish to catch, and a chance to begin my life over."

A pregnant silence ensued as the two men each contemplated the bearded man's revelation. Each of them simultaneously exhaled.

The ventilation system cycle took that moment to shut down and the office became deathly noticeably quieter. That allowed another sense to take over. The air seemed to become noticeably wet with the fragrance of flowers, both genuine and artificial.

Neither man noticed.

The silence, however, allowed, just for the moment, *The Girl from Ipanema* to be heard as she played through suppressed ceiling speakers. The volume was dialed low though. At this tense moment, the *Girl* broke into neither man's consciousness.

The older man finally broke the quiet.

"So, this is the end. I'm leaving tonight. My attorney will close the books in the morning and then put the business up for sale. I can tell you, my friend, I won't look back."

He paused again as the younger man continued to sit silently, hands steepled, staring through him to infinity.

In the absence of a response, the older man again picked up the conversation. "I don't need to tell you how much you've let me down. All the faith and love I once had for you has been exhausted many times over. Please, clear your personal effects out today, and . . ."

He was interrupted from his short monolog by the younger man as he, with perfectly manicured nails, reached down and opened a lower desk drawer. From it, a Glock 9 emerged and Mr. Saville Row aimed the polished weapon at the chest of the older man.

Time seemed to slow as each man stared at the other silently.

The younger man finally spoke, his voice hoarse with nervousness. "Sorry you feel that way, but you know I cannot allow you to shut us down. I've invested too much time, money, and risk in our endeavor. You *are* correct though; we *have had* many good times. That is why I fail to understand why you feel you must take this action, especially now. You've certainly known all along that I would never allow anyone to close us up . . . you, especially. This attempt to wreck us ends today, and to be truthful, I never imagined that *our* own relationship would *also* end this way. I thought we were way too close."

The bearded man opened his mouth to reply but before he could object or even blink, he felt the pin prick sting of a bullet. He was deaf to the concussive thunder though because . . . he was gone – instantly – lurching back in the chair, falling sideways and onto the table. His collapse began a chain of chaos, toppling the table and taking with it his body, the vase, and the flowers.

Everything crashed to the floor as one. Water from the vase puddled on the rug, mixing instantly with blood that now seeped freely from the older man's chest. He lay face down in the debris, his eyes lifeless and frozen in disbelief.

Saville Row casually rose from his chair, pocketed the Glock, and stepped around the desk, righting the older man's chair. He struggled to lift his former partner into it because of the chair's wheels. After the body was propped into place, it threatened to slump back to the floor. The younger man was finally forced to shove the rolling chair back and into one of the tall sports cabinets before successfully shifting the dead man's weight and making certain the body would remain in place.

Blood from the chest wound had already begun soaking into the small carpet and had also migrated into the dead man's beard. Because of the younger man's difficulty in positioning the body in place on the chair, the blood also managed to soil his expensive suit. He swore at the discovery and then interrupted his efforts with a sudden worry over the noise of the shot, the falling chair, and the sound of the body hitting the floor.

Ironically, he uttered a quick and silent prayer . . . and he hadn't done that since he was a small child. His prayer was that he was the only one left alive in the building. The moment passed and he rolled up the small rug, collected the fragments of the vase and flowers, placed as much as he could in the waste basket, and then placed it and rug in his former partner's lap. He stood up and turned to the doorway.

Quietly opening the office door, he whispered down the hallway, "Anybody here?" There was no response and he exhaled in what seemed to him like his first breath since pulling the trigger. Now his heart was beating fast and he began to sweat. He finally wheeled the chair and its cargo through the office doorway, out, into, and down the dark hallway. A few seconds later the small procession passed through another doorway, this one first required the entering of a code before it opened by itself into the hallway.

As the two men, only one of whom still breathed, entered a dark sterile room, fluorescent lights began to flicker to life, humming loudly enough to drown out the soothing melodies that continued to play throughout the building. Frank Sinatra was now singing *The September of*

My Years. The younger man pushed his cargo into the far corner of a large antiseptic-smelling room as the entrance door began to swing shut behind them.

Two stainless steel tables stood starkly alone in the center of the room, each positioned above dual floor drains and were bathed in spotlights.

On the same wall as the doorway but down from it, index cards had been wedged in slots on the faces of meat-locker-style waist-high doors. These cards listed the name of each locker's current occupant along with the date he or she had been admitted into a room the employees had nicknamed *The Pale Horse Hotel*. Only the middle locker held no card. Saville Row unloaded the waste basket and its contents, and unlatched the middle cooler door, extracting a long empty drawer. As he did so, a puff of humidified air escaped, dispersing noiselessly. Then came the task the younger man dreaded. Fortunately, he was in excellent condition. Still, he needed to wrestle the dead man's flaccid body up and onto a thick cardboard tray that lined the drawer.

Succeeding, he covered the body with a plastic sheet. Saville Row then checked his watch, showing surprise at the current time. In contradiction to the heavy somber atmosphere of the room, in a light cheery almost sing-song tone, he informed the corpse: "Ooh! So sorry, my friend. I gotta go. Must change before the big event tonight! See you later big guy. I want you to know, it's been *great* working with you!"

The killer closed the locker drawer containing the

body of his former partner. Latching it shut, he walked back toward the door he'd entered just two minutes earlier. Holding it open, he turned theatrically to face the center of the room and spread his arms wide as if to take in everything in the room. "Now," he announced to only the five souls reposing in the lockers, "It's *all* mine!"

With a smile, Saville Row pushed the empty office chair into the hallway and followed it out. The door to the sterile room swung closed and secured itself. Thirty seconds later, the lights in it automatically shut down as Johnny Mathis ended a beautifully soft version of *I'll Be Seeing You*. Darkness quickly settled as Terry Jacks took over the microphone and began singing *Seasons in the Sun*.

There was no applause.

THE MEDIA STAR

1

**7 A.M., SATURDAY MORNING, APRIL 16TH
BELOW THE WESTERN I-610 – I-10
INTERCHANGE IN NEW ORLEANS**

With his foot extended, Albert Breaux probed the body, pushing a leg that protruded from a work blanket.

"Sir?" tentatively asked the best-known Feature Reporter for the *New Orleans Times*-Picayune. "Mister?"

Breaux continued to nudge the body. Nearly a minute went by with no sign of life.

"Sir?" Breaux asked again, now shoving the body hard with his foot. These were Breaux's fourth and fifth attempts to get a reaction from the guy and there was still no indication he was even alive.

Is he breathing?

Breaux was uncomfortable. His bowed head barely cleared the underside deck of the I-610 overpass. He could actually feel traffic vibrations in his aching neck. An old injury from his days as a competitive swimmer aggravated the problem. He'd been exploring similar areas under several bridges along both I-610 and I-10 without luck for the last half hour looking for this man. He looked around himself and sighed. It was amazing how many trash dumps had popped up under the city's bridges, and within many of them, homeless people – mostly men – were camped out.

Most of the spots were vacant at this hour of the morning but Breaux was looking for late risers.

Early morning rush hour traffic roared overhead. The wide moist underside of the viaduct seemed to vibrate. Two sections of concrete met just above Breaux's head and the thump-thumps of passing vehicles were jarring. Five minutes earlier, he'd found this guy. Just one more sleeper among the thousands of homeless camped out in the city. If this bum didn't cooperate, it might take another hour to find someone else. It probably was getting too late in the day to identify another target anyway . . . someone who'd agree to the strange concept he was prepared to offer.

If he's dead, should I walk away, or risk police involvement by reporting an unexplained death?

From his time as a cub reporter for *The Advocate* in Baton Rouge, Breaux knew that reporting the discovery of a body would likely require several hours to explain to the police how and what he'd found, what he suspected, and why he was there in the first place. On the other hand, a dead body under an Interstate Highway bridge might get him a byline in the Local News section of the *Times-Picayune!* And, if it was a murder, the story would probably get moved up to Section One. He decided to wait it out and try to awaken the guy one more time.

The smell rising from the man was intense. It seemed to waft upward from him in waves. But, based on his experience, it wasn't the smell of death. Breaux had tagged along at enough body recoveries to know *that* smell well. This though was the rancid odor of unwashed human flesh, flushed with a bouquet of cheap wine and urine . . . with a hint of . . . well, he didn't want to dwell on it anymore.

Movement? The heavily bearded form that was snugged up tight against the incline of the deck of the bridge moved its arm and snorted. It coughed a loose raggedy cough. Brown flemmy eyes flickered open, looked up at him, and then closed again. Then they reopened. "What the hell do you want? Get away, dammit!" He spoke! The man's voice was scratchy and imaginatively slurred. "Go 'way! If you ain't a cop or you don't wanna contribute to my foundation, get the hell away from me. Lemme' be dammit!" The eyes flapped shut again.

So much for the front page.

"Sir, I'm a reporter for the *Times-Picayune* and I'd like to interview you for a feature we're doing on New Orleans Homeless People. Do you have a few minutes we could talk?"

"Lemme' alone or I'll call my lawyer!"

"Please, sir. This will only take a minute."

"I said, get the hell out of here. I don't wanna see you when I open my eyes again, or you're gonna wish you'd never come here! I've got friends, you know."

"I don't think you'd attack me," responded Breaux. "Com'on out and let's talk, Huh?"

"I might not attack you, but I sure as heck *can* piss on you! For the last time, get outta my life!"

Breaux hadn't seen any other vagrants for the last half hour, so he knew the two of them were alone. "But sir, if you agree to my proposal, you *could* earn $200 cash for just talking to me . . . and of course, by doing something rather innocuous over the next few days."

The brown eyes opened and stayed open. It was a look of hatred mixed with fear mixed with Ripple, but this time a raised eyebrow and a softer but still scratchy voice issued from the chapped lips, "Tell me more, my friend."

Breaux needed to get himself out from under the bridge deck and into a standing position. He often felt a bit claustrophobic, and this was becoming one of those moments. His neck, once broken in a swimming accident, already was aching badly. Even more pressing, he badly needed to get upwind of the man.

"How much did you say?"

"$200 for three days work . . . and there's really no *work* involved." Breaux regretted using the 'work' word when he didn't need to. A few seconds passed. He gagged slightly, swallowed, turned his head, and took a deep breath of only slightly tainted air. Please, sir. Could we step outside," Breaux said, gesturing a few feet to the left where they'd be in the fresh air and sunshine and where he wouldn't need to stoop.

"Alright," the man replied. "I might agree to do what you want *if* you tell me what's involved . . . and you make it a thousand dollars. I got a degree, you know."

While he spoke, the man rolled over and began struggling to his feet. He then began brushing all sorts of environmental debris off his coat. Finally, he stood up and stretched amid the old newspapers and other trash that probably served to keep him warm on cold nights. If it hadn't been for the smell, in Breaux's eyes, this vagrant could have been Rip Van Winkle fresh from his twenty-year sleep. Albeit this Rip was wearing torn . . . *really* worn out . . . jeans with holes in all the wrong places. He was coiffed by bushy, grey, oily, matted hair and a scraggy beard. The beard came complete with bits of food crumbs and other unmentionable bits of debris matted into it. There were stains on his clothing whose origin Breaux didn't even want to consider.

Breaux could see deep-set brown eyes which were surrounded by long greyish hair and sun-wrinkled, cracked, and dirty skin. The man looked to be on death's door. *He may kick off at any moment and I'll get my story yet!* Breaux considered.

Whether his appearance came as a result of poor lifestyle choices, bad nutrition, a fatal disease, or some other factor, wasn't obvious. *Probably all combined.* In short, the man was disgusting and neither he nor his jeans looked as if they'd last the day.

"You keep calling me, sir. I don't like it," said the man, "I'm proud of my name and it ain't Sir! It's Paul . . . Wait a minute, I ain't giving you my name . . . not at least until you decide to write me a check. No, make that cash! I don't trust banks! I put twenty bucks in one once and a year later tried to get it out. It was gone! Robbers! You say you work for a newspaper? How 'bout me getting' robbed for a story? Crooks!"

The vagrant noticed that Breaux was looking over his filthy jeans, "Yeah. Gotta get me some new Wranglers. I know. Been wearin' these for most of two months." He said this with a gesture indicating a bit of thrifty pride. "Haven't taken 'em off once! First thing on my shopping list though. Wouldn't want to stake me to some new ones, would ya'?"

"Actually, I might! Tell you what," said Breaux. "we're trying to interview at least ten *People of the Street*. If you won't give me your name, that's okay. I can live with that. How 'bout I call you Seven? We're giving all our subjects numbers for names anyway."

"Seven. Why Seven?"

"We have six of you down for the project *so far*. Loyola wants ten altogether.

"Seven? Hmmm. Yeah! That would work! It's my favorite number, my friend. My favorite color's blue, too. And my favorite food's steak and mashed potatoes with gravy. Oh, and I like nice quiet walks on the beach at sunset. You need anything else for your interview? I'm ready for my check. No, no. Make that cash . . . right now!"

Breaux found himself chuckling. "No, sir. . . uhh, I mean, *Seven*. It's not quite that simple."

For just a moment, Breaux thought there was a small possibility that he might someday be able to like the guy, given time. Maybe 200 years . . . but before that happened he'd have to brush his teeth and take a Clorox bath. Given the strength of the man's body odor, even bleach might not be effective. Behind the beard, what little of the man's face that showed was speckled with ground-in dirt, some of it perhaps permanently imbedded in the crevices and wrinkles. Pock marks, probably caused by continued exposure to the wind and sun, added to his patina. A few of the markings on his neck and arms could even be mistaken for tattoos. Actually, some probably were.

During the conversation, Breaux closely studied what appeared to be a tattoo on Seven's right arm. He wasn't certain if it was of a naked lady, the word *Mom*, or an American Flag. He was about to ask the man about it but then thought better of it. Seven wore a pink wife-beater tee shirt with the Energizer Rabbit on it. "Hey, man," he said, his curiosity getting the better of him, "I like the shirt. Where'd you get it? I don't think I've ever seen one like it."

"Got it at the Zulu Parade. It's the best of all the Mardi Gras parades, you know. An incredible great lookin' woman dressed in not much was wearing it when she tossed it to the guy behind me. He'd tossed her a bunch a' beads. I dove for it and got it first. She was throwin' those beads from the bed of a '54 Chevy Pickup decorated with pink four-foot rabbit ears. After I came up with the shirt, she thunked me in the head with a pack of 16 Double A Batteries. I guess I was supposed to duck but I got distracted when she took off her shirt! Sold the batteries for five bucks! Kept the shirt because I thought she liked me. Don't know her, do you?"

"No. 'Fraid not." Breaux caught himself smiling.

Seven wore no shoes even though it was April. But this was New Orleans after all, and one could almost comfortably go without shoes or sandals most of the year . . . usually.

"If it's not a thousand, how much money is this interview worth?" Seven asked.

Breaux knew then he had a keeper, and of all things, maybe he *was* beginning to like the guy.

"I'm authorized to go to $250. All you have to do is allow me to interview you on tape. That'll take an hour at the most. And then you wear this device until Tuesday night . . . three days from now." Breaux held up a small black boxy-looking piece of plastic with about a twenty-inch strap on it.

"What the hell is that, a bomb? I ain't no terrorist!"

"No, it's like a small telephone that will send your running commentary directly to me. I'll be in a closed room at Loyola, listening to you. You see, like I said, my paper is working with Loyola on a homelessness project and we want to follow you and other homeless folks that we get to sign up for a few days . . . . all to see what life on the street is like. You just interact with others, and especially any homeless folks, as usual. Describe what you're doing out loud . . . you know, how you feel, and things like that. We'll be able to hear you through a GPS feature and then . . .

"What the crap is a *gyp's* feature. I don't want nothing or nobody knowing where I go. Understand?"

"Yeah, sure Mr. Seven." Breaux saw he was making progress and fudged a little to sell the deal, "GPS stands for Global Positioning Satellite. With it, we'll be able to hear everything you say . . . *when* you want us to hear it. We won't tell anyone where you are. And everything we record will be kept confidential. We won't release any of it unless you approve. Okay? You control the on-off switch on the microphone, so we won't hear anything unless you want us to!"

Breaux knew that the on-off switch had been disabled so the mike would be on 24/7 whenever it was activated by Seven's voice, so if the vagrant wasn't talking, the unit wouldn't be recording. Seven didn't need to know that though.

"What's my *commentary* for? And will that thing..." he asked pointing at the black box, "... give me cancer? I don't want no cancer. My mom died from it an' she went to hell! No, I mean she went straight through hell."

Breaux knew then he had Seven in the bag. The homeless man likewise was sure that he could negotiate more than $250 if he applied a little leverage. The reporter just needed a bit more convincing. This could be his big day! He might even go from this to interviews on Oprah.

"Loyola has asked us to help them with a study titled, *Life Ain't Easy in the Big Easy*. The project will start right after we conclude a short interview . . . over breakfast at the IHOP."

"*IHOP?* Alright! Why didn't you say so? You're on, Dude! Let's go. There's an IHOP a block away."

"I know. I've already scouted it out and got us a booth. Let's get started!"

They began walking toward the IHOP with Seven leading. He now seemed to be operating with a burst of enthusiasm for the project.

"Tell you why I agreed."

"Okay. I'll bite. Why'd you agree?"

"*Seven!* I like the name. Seven is Pistol Pete's old number when he played for the Jazz. He was my idol when I was ten or eleven. I wanted to play for the Jazz so much I planned to drop out of school."

Breaux interrupted. "Seven? This is a bit late to tell you, but I've been recording our conversation . . . and forgot. It's a legal thing. I have to get your permission to do so. I was gonna erase all this early stuff, but I like what you just said about Pete Maravich. It'll help sell the story. So, I gotta get your permission to record what you've said, and what you're about to say."

Seven nodded *yes*.

"No. Unh, unh.' Said Breaux. "Won't work. You have to say it out loud so the machine will record my question and *your* verbal affirmative."

"My what?"

"You have to agree to allow me to record you for the story. The paper requires it and I think, so does the government."

"Damn bureaucrats! *Yes!* I agree to allow you to record me. I'll be a star!"

"Alright. Let's get this thing started."

"You wanna go in and order breakfast first?"

"You're absolutely right. Let's do that."

Breaux led them into the IHOP and found the booth he'd reserved for them in the back. He wanted to wait until they'd ordered breakfast before beginning with the questions. Seven ordered pancakes, sausage, orange juice, coffee, toast, and three eggs over medium. As he spoke, Seven's breath nearly gagged Breaux. And Breaux continued to be incredibly put off by the man's body odor. At the moment, he wasn't sure he'd be up for food for a couple weeks. When they sat, instead of breakfast, Breaux decided just to settle for black coffee.

A few customers within smelling range were beginning to look their way with hard stares. Breaux figured he'd give Seven enough time to talk, and he'd have more later, so he waved at the silverware as a way of prompting Seven to begin eating his breakfast.

"So, even at ten or eleven, you planned to drop out of school?"

"Of course! At the latest, I was gonna do it maybe after some high school, just like my parents and their parents. Maybe even earlier. Gotta maintain family tradition, right?"

Without realizing it, Breaux wrung his hands. He was thinking, *Pulitzer*!

Despite the attention they were attracting, Breaux and Seven spent a few minutes talking about the food and the service at IHOP.

Breaux wasn't too worried because he'd already alerted the IHOP manager beforehand to get his approval to do what he wanted, and to make certain they knew with whom he'd be talking. Most importantly, the restaurant needed to know that the *Times-Picayune* was involved. That was always the clincher for things like this . . . free publicity for the IHOP! Management had readily agreed, believing the story would make the news for all the right reasons. But after ten minutes, the manager realized he'd vastly underestimated the fragrance factor. Customers as far as twenty feet away from the two men began leaving or asking their waitresses to be moved to other tables.

To speed things up, Seven and Breaux spoke little over breakfast, the better to get that over with. Over the next 45 minutes though, Seven consumed enough food for them both, plus the waitress, and the cashier. The manager, who'd only made one visit to that point, began showing his second thoughts, frowning and pinching up his nose.

Breaux guessed that away from the restaurant, Seven was less likely to be comfortable talking. One way to get him going was to ask him about a subject in which he was interested. "First off, Mr. Seven, tell me about Maravich."

After ordering a fourth cup of coffee, the words poured out of Seven. "I loved Pistol Pete both for what he did at LSU and then what he did for the Jazz. I was too young to remember seein' him play in the NBA, but when I was a kid and a member of a Boys Club, we went to an exhibition where he was one of the guest stars. That was after he retired from the *Utah* Jazz an' the Hawks, a' course!" Seven made a disgusted face to indicate his opinion of both teams. "The exhibition game happened not long before Pete died. He was a *great* man! I decided then and there that I wanted to be an NBA Star too. You know, earn a billion dollars, buy the Jazz, and bring 'em back to New Orleans where they belong."

"Pardon me, Mr. Seven. But you're at best five feet

eight. I doubt that any player in NBA history stood only five feet eight inches tall."

Seven demonstrated a knowledge of basketball for which Breaux was unprepared.

"Was too! There've been a bunch. Spud Webb was only 5'7" and played mostly for Atlanta. He was an All-Star and was terrific! Muggsy Bogues, who played for the Charlotte Hornets? He was only 5'3" an' he was pretty good too! He was the shortest NBA player ever."

"Didn't know that. Still, you'd have certainly been a long shot at 5'8" unless you were a spectacular player . . . and then you'd still have had to play in college before the NBA. Did you?"

"No. Never got the chance. But I had a great jump shot. And, there've been a bunch of NBA players who never went to college and they still became great players. Look at Daryl Dawkins . . . and of course, there was the first and, except for Pistol Pete, the greatest player ever, Moses Malone! Besides, I used to be 5'11"!"

"Com'on Mr. Seven. You're nowhere near 5'11"."

"Hey, just call me Seven. Cut the 'Mr." crap. We're friends now, right?"

Breaux was about to say, *No. Actually, you're an employee and I'm your boss, idiot!* But he thought better of it.

"I *was* 5'11" once! Now I'm not 'cause I'm permanently stooped, thanks to an accident . . . and no thanks to a buncha' dumb doctors at Charity Hospital.

"By the way, '*Mr.*' was my dad. I'm *Seven* from now on, Breaux. I think I'm gonna legally change my name.

I like it!"

"Seven . . ."

"I know. I know. Back to my story! I *was* 5'11" until a couple years back. That's when a damn streetcar nearly killed me . . . *Old Number 024.* She ran me down on Magazine Street. I spit at her now every time I see 'er comin' down the line. Anyway, the docs at Charity cabled, screwed, and glued my spine back together and here I am today, handsome, permanently stooped, and rich as ever . . . 'cause I didn't have to pay for none of that hospital stuff."

"The city paid for everything then, right? If you sued 'em for a bunch of money, why are you living under a bridge?"

"The city should have paid but it didn't!" Seven growled. "The bill and all the hospital stuff ended up being free. I coulda' won a bunch though. Trouble is, six months after it happened, the judge ruled I wasn't *accidentally* hit by the streetcar, or even that I tripped on the rails. He said I was drunk and asleep on the tracks!"

"Were you?"

"No, dammit. Yeah. Well, maybe I *had* done that once or twice before, but not that time! I was robbed. Robbed I tell you!"

"Well, okay. Enough on that. I can check out our archives for the story. Tell me a bit about yourself and then I'll hook up the transmitter."

Seven ordered another cup of coffee and a stack of pancakes and settled in. "Do you want to hear more about why I should be six-foot-two?"

Twenty minutes later Breaux began to wonder how Seven could possibly swallow that much coffee and still not need to use the restroom, but he didn't ask because he was certain that if Seven made a trip to the john, they'd get kicked out of the IHOP for sure.

He waited for Seven to continue, then realized the man was waiting for him to answer his question.

"I thought it was 5'11". Enough on that. Tell me about your childhood."

"Not much to tell. First thing I remember was living in the Ninth Ward. I had twin a brother but he left for the West years ago. My dad disappeared when I was 10 or 11, an' my mom died of cancer not long after that. My brother an' me quit school when she died.

Life punched me pretty hard, Mr. Breaux. I know it wasn't all their fault, but my mom and dad . . . teachers, school officials, cops . . . and even my brother caused all this. I am an *innocent victim of fate.* Now I *squat* in a house off Canal . . . sometimes. But the best pickings are up here in the North End. You're not gonna print that are you? It's where I camp sometimes. Things may go missin' from some of the nice homes around here and I'd just as soon keep quiet about where I live, if you don't mind."

"Anything you tell me *not* to print, I have to honor, Seven. The Journalist's Credo, you know. So, you have two *luxury* homes, huh? A house in the city, and a place up here near Pontchartrain . . . under a viaduct?"

"I'm getting' the feeling you're makin' fun of me an' I'm thinking I may not want to do this . . ."

Breaux interrupted and apologized, urging Seven to continue.

"Sometimes I camp out in abandoned buildings, sometimes in public restrooms that are open all night, an' sometimes up under the bridge where you found me this morning. I actually got an ID card with an address: 472 Vacant Lot, Canal Street, New Orleans, Louisiana! Was sleepin' it off there one night when I got rousted by the cops. A social worker forced me to go to the license bureau to get an official ID card. So, now I got one."

Seven's head had been bent down into his plate all the while he told the story. Suddenly he stood up and shouted maniacally, "Sic Semper Tyrannus!"

The staff and customers in the restaurant looked up in fright and it was less than twenty seconds before the manager escorted them to the checkout stand.

Breaux paid for Seven's breakfasts. *Or was it seven breakfasts? Did three breakfasts times Seven make 21?* The bill for the homeless man alone was over $35 plus tip and Breaux had to leave a big one given the man's bad odor and worse behavior. He shoved the receipt in his pocket figuring to put it on the project's expense sheet. They left the IHOP as staff descended on their table with buckets, sponges, disinfectant, and deodorant spray. The two men walked out the door and began heading back toward the overpass.

Away from the restaurant, Breaux asked Seven why he'd shouted *Sic Semper Tyrannus* inside. "Do you know what that means?"

"Naw. Sometimes it just overcomes me an' I yell it out. It's somethin' my dad used to say whenever he got really mad at us."

"No, I mean, do you know where the phrase came from?"

"Hell, I told you. My dad used to say that. I don't know what it means, or where it came from before that. Do you?"

"Actually, yes," said Breaux a bit condescendingly and immediately regretted the tone, "The original derivation isn't absolutely known. Many folks believe that Brutus called it out just before he killed Julius Caesar. But it was definitely shouted by John Wilkes Booth just after he shot Lincoln."

"Lincoln who?" asked Seven.

"You know who Spud Webb is, but you don't know who Abraham Lincoln is?"

"Oh! Him! Yeah. My mom taught me that he sacrificed his son to God. Wonder why he would have said, 'Sic Semper Tyrannus?' Did they speak Hungarian in the bible? What's it mean anyway?"

"Thus, always to tyrants."

"Huh?"

"Never mind Mr. Seven. Let's get you wired up and wrap this process up. Boy, have I got a story to write!"

Once under the bridge, Seven warned him, "Okay, Mr. Breaux. I don't want my buddies seeing you, so don't ever come back here again. Just with that box on me, they'll think I hit it rich and they're likely to rob me tonight.

They might even kill me for it. It's a tough life out here, and it's been tough for me and my family for a long time."

"Okay. But I'll eventually need to get the box back and talk to you some about your family and other things." Breaux gave the phone device to the homeless man, who was now named *Seven,* and clipped a small microphone to his dirty collar.

"Now put the unit itself inside your shirt. Just make sure you keep the microphone plugged into it at all times. The cord is the antenna. It's voice-activated to save battery, so anytime you want to make an observation, just speak in your normal voice. Everything you say will be recorded and sent back to Loyola. We'll let it run for three days. I'll meet you in front of the IHOP Tuesday night about 10 p.m. for the final payoff. Okay? Maybe a different manager will be on duty, and he'll let us in and I'll buy you dinner. The batteries should last that long unless you talk too much."

"I want my money upfront."

"Sorry, Seven. A'int gonna happen. Here's $100 now and I'll have another $400 for you Tuesday night. See you then. Remember, you are *live* on Candid Microphone as of right now!"

"Huh?"

The truth was, Seven was beyond being thrilled at having a hundred dollars in his hands.

"Hot pajamas!" he said as he walked away from Breaux and headed for a nearby liquor store. He knew they wouldn't be open for another half hour though . . .

. still, he'd be first in line.

* * * *

When Breaux returned to the small audio lab at Loyola, he closed the door to one of several smaller listening rooms and began playing back "Seven's" recording. The first thing he heard was, "Testing! Testing! Testing! Can you hear me, Breaux? Hope so!" followed by a click, and then, "Gimme' that bottle of hooch over there. (mumble) Yeah, I got money! (mumble) Shit, yes! Here!" Then he heard another click which apparently signified the shutting down of the microphone and another period of silence. Since the machine shut down between utterances, Breaux had no idea how long the intervening silences were. Run consecutively, this made for difficult listening. A single pause could be seconds or even hours, but when played back it sounded like only a half-second pause. Breaux had no idea how long Seven had stopped talking each time he heard a click.

Next, he heard, "Hey, Breaux. I'm in an alley if you can hear me." Click. "For the last couple of weeks, I been thinkin' of updating my wardrobe. I'm here in a dumpster behind a strip mall clothing shop and I've found two boxes of brand-new jeans the store is dumpin'. Maybe they're flawed. In my broad experience of shopping only the finest retailers, these are probably outta style too."

Breaux could hear boxes being ripped apart. Click.

"Alright. Tried several of them on. Most of 'em are too small, but I found at least two pairs that might work. Left my ole Wranglers upside down on a garbage can. Was gonna give 'em to someone worse off'n me, then I realized, hell, ain't no one worse off'n me. Left 'em on the can." Click. "I'm going over to a dry cleaner's window to see what I look like, wearin' 'em in the window's reflection. Doin' that only 'cause I noticed you lookin' at 'em this morning, I'll continue my play-by-play in a minute, Breaux." Click.

"Wish you could see me now, Breaux. Had to throw one pair away. Too small! But these ones fit real good. Maybe they're a bit short on me and I'm not sure I like the spangles, but the price tag says $149! I'm turnin' around now so I can see my butt in the window. (A pause, but not long enough for the machine to shut down.) Definitely do NOT like the spangles on each cheek. They outline big four-inch stars. People 'round here will take me for a Cowboys fan . . . an' I die for the Saints. I'll probably get murdered by the *Who Dats* just because you didn't like my ole Wranglers and they won't like my Cowboy jeans." Click.

"Now I need a haircut. Maybe even a shave. The way people was lookin' at me in the IHOP, I probably need a shower too. Ain't had one in a while. Now that I think about it, ain't had one since I put those ole Wranglers on and that's been a couple months. If I get all that done, I might go on a job hunt. The Del Champs Grocery back near the bridge had a sign sayin' they're lookin' for a night manager." Click.

"Boy, I sure do love this rabbit shirt!" Click.

Albert Breaux put down the headset. He'd check it again later to make sure it was still recording properly but he wasn't sure he could take much more of this . . . or find much usable for his story.

II

It was Tuesday evening at about 9 p.m. and with nothing better to do, Albert Breaux was at Loyola again catching up on Seven's recordings. They were due to meet at the IHOP in another hour. The only thing of any interest he'd heard so far was a segment from earlier that afternoon and it promised to be worth a spot in his story all by itself.

"Hey, Breaux. Three o'clock on Tuesday. Hot day for April, ain't it? Got something here. I'm in another dumpster trying desperately to keep my new blues clean, but I found somethin'. I was hungry and saw what looked like a completely good banana, but it turned out only to be a peel. You see, the peel was wrapped around somethin' that made it look like a good banana. When I picked it up, the *banana* under the peel turned out to be the barrel of a pearl-handled thirty-eight-caliber *pistola!*" Click.

"Next to it was a black trash bag wrapped around something big and squishy. The bag looked interesting but since I'd already found somethin' worth a bunch on the streets, I stayed away from checkin' the bag out. Maybe I should have. Anyway, now I got a gun! Five cylinders got bullets in 'em. The last one's only got a shell. Things have been kinda' tough for me lately so I'm lookin' for anything I can turn into cash. Worse, I'm crazy if I believe you're gonna give me $400 tonight." Hell, I probably won't even get dinner outta' you!" Click.

"Hey, Breaux, I know what I'm gonna do with my banana special." Click.

"It's comin' up on nine-thirty and I gotta do some plannin' so I'm signin' off for a while."

Albert checked his watch. It was 9:28. The recording he was listening to *wasn't* really a live recording. It was a playback of something that had happened before . . . . perhaps even an hour ago. He had a bad feeling in his stomach though. Worse, what he was hearing could be a live broadcast, but from where? Seven hadn't said.

Suddenly Seven was back on the air again.

"Been checking the gun over and the serial numbers are filed off or have been treated with acid or something. You know most throwaway guns got a history. Makes me wonder what was in that trash bag in the dumpster where I found the gun. I got my fingerprints on the bag and on the gun too, so that ain't good. Now I'll have to dump it when I'm done with it or toss it in the Mississippi later. Or, maybe I can clean my prints off it an' sell it to some joker for $50 as is. Might do that!" Click.

"Where are you, Seven?" Breaux asked aloud. Like magic even though Seven couldn't hear Breaux's question, he came back on and told him . . . or at least partly did.

"Just so you know, I'm outside a convenience store behind some trees. At the moment there are two customers in the bodega. Each of 'em came in their own car a couple minutes ago. When they leave, if no other customers show,

I'm going in. I scouted this store about a month ago in case a chance ever came along to rob it. It has. They got only one security camera and it covers the front doors, so I know it'll get me comin' in and goin'. First thing I'm gonna do though is shoot that sucker straight to hell." Click. "The clerk's a little tiny Asian woman; she's the manager. Couldn't lift a candy bar if it was half-eaten." Click.

With the recorder running only when sound activated it, Breaux had no clue whether the clicks were only seconds long, or hours. Either way, real-time was catching up to record time quickly.

"They're gone. Between 'em, the man and woman bought a six-pack of beer and a bottle of cheap wine and left . . . might'a been a couple driving two different cars and meeting back at her place. I dunno'. Anyway, I'm goin' in. I'll give you the play-by-play Breaux, but I'll be speakin' low 'cause I don't want her to know. Okay?" Click.

Albert Breaux leaned forward on the desk. His mouth was dry. This was unexpected and, of course, not at all what the subjects of the study should be doing. On the other hand, he couldn't imagine anything better than this. His notepad was ready, and a pen was in his hand. He, himself, would be in the clear for he had no idea at all where Seven was. He could do nothing to prevent a robbery from happening.

"Hold up, Lady! Hold up!" Three shots sounded. "I just fired three shots at the camera! Holy crap, I think I missed. The clerk's backing away from the register." Click.

The sound of another shot started the recording

again. "I shot one into the ceiling over her . . . just to let her know who's boss!"

Breaux could hear heavy breathing, and, in the far background, a tiny female voice shouting in a high-pitched tone, "You bad man! You in deep shit. You go 'way now. You get no money! You no make *more* trouble. Go you . . . *now*!"

To Breaux, his guy in the Pink Rabbit Tee Shirt and fashion statement jeans with spangled stars on each cheek sounded unafraid. Seven yelled, "I know you're hiding it, Mee Maw! Gimme' the money, right now!" Seven's confidence and voice had risen in pitch.

In his mind's eye, Breaux could picture the scene. The stooped and limping homeless man, victim of a personal collision with a streetcar, was now apparently waving a 38 pistol in the air inside a small bodega.

He debated calling 9-1-1 but still didn't know where the store was located, so he couldn't do that. He'd just have to let it play out. Maybe Seven would say where he was. Breaux imagined that the homeless man, now armed, believed he was 6' 2" and in command.

"All of it! Right now, lady!" Another shot sounded and the Pink Rabbit Robber suddenly could be heard screaming and falling into a stack of what sounded like canned goods. Everything was falling to the floor.

Oh, my God. Did she shoot him? Breaux wondered

"Owww, oww! Breaux! I shot myself in the ankle. Oh, crap!"

In the background, an alarm began sounding loud

enough that the recorder kept transmitting. Evidently, the clerk had triggered the alarm. Breaux wished he had this all on camera. Why hadn't he thought of that? Then he realized the store's cameras probably had audio capability. If they did, they just picked up *his* name when Seven shouted it. Seven continued to moan and seemed unable to come to his senses and get the heck out of the store. This whole thing was taking much too long. What was going on?

"Hey Lady, what are you doing with the bat? Come on, for crying out loud. Can't you see I'm bleeding, here? That last shot ricocheted off something and hit me in the ankle, Lady! Take pity, for cryin' out loud! Breaux, help me! Please! . . . No, don't! . . . Please, don't!"

Breaux heard a noise like, "Cloumph" and the audio stopped.

III

Albert Breaux was frozen in place. He didn't know what to do. He couldn't call the police because he didn't know where the robbery attempt had taken place.

Suddenly, the audio came back on. "Breaux, are you there?"

"Don't use my name for crying out loud!" Breaux yelled. Of course, he remembered that Seven couldn't hear him because this was a one-way broadcast. Breaux could hear Seven but couldn't speak to him; Seven could speak to Breaux, but couldn't hear him.

"I winged myself in the ankle. I don't think it's broken but it's bleeding like a son of a gun . . . and it hurts like crap! I managed to roll out the door and crawled into some bushes next to the parking lot just as two cop cars showed up . . . lights flashin' and all. They're inside now and I'm hot-footing my way as best I can through the woods next to the store. Damn, I think I'm leavin' a blood trail though." Click.

Breaux took the moment to place a call into the paper. There was always someone there listening to the police radio. They would know where the robbery was taking place.

But what could, or what would he do when he learned the address? Should he try to rescue the man named Seven? Should he stay out of it? If the police found Seven, they'd realize he'd been broadcasting his attempt to someone . . . maybe even the man named Breaux whose name the robber had called out during the attempt. Eventually, the police would trace the signal back to him! This was nuts!

"Hey, Breaux. My head hurts. That little B-I-itch hit me with a baseball bat. I think she broke my nose, my back, or neck . . . or something. I'm seeing stars. Wait a minute. I'm almost finished crawling through a path through some woods outside the store. Hey, now I'm up at a street, but I'm still hidden in the bushes. There's a car coming down the street. Oh my God, it's stopping right in front of me. A guy's getting out. Is he a cop? Did he see me?

"Oh, thank God. It's not me he's after, he goin' around the car. There's a woman in the car too. Now he's opening her door."

Breaux was entranced by the personal play-by-play of the robbery and the aftermath. For a second, he thought about selling the recording to CNN or Larry King. Faintly in the background, he could hear a woman's voice saying, "Thank you, Robert."

Seven was whispering now. "She's getting out and they're walking up the porch stairs across the street. Hey, the dude left the car running. It's right in front of me! The door I need to go through to get outta' here has literally opened! Now, the guy's gonna kiss her goodnight. This is too good to pass. My luck is changing, Breaux! I'm goin' after the car!" Click.

Breaux then realized that the police might mistake "Bro," for Breaux! Maybe all was okay. He was still hanging on to the phone trying to reach his office back at the *Picayune*. No one had answered. He gave up so he could better concentrate on the live audio coming from Seven's microphone.

"Hey, Breaux. Does the signal transmit even when I'm in a car? Can you hear me?

"When the guy heard his car door slam, he stopped in mid-kiss and started chasing me down the street. I left him in the dust. Ha, ha!" Click. Seven's laugh had taken on a strange maniacal quality.

"What am I up to by now? Attempted robbery? Discharging a firearm in a public place? Vehicle theft . . . and, who knows what kind of history this gun has? I could be up for murder. Probably will be. That bag in the dumpster probably had a body in it an' It was squishy when I touched it.

"Well, anyway, I know where I'm going. Remember I told you I've got a shelter up on the fourth. . .

"Crap, it's started raining *real* hard . . . and now there's lightning. Where did this come from? That's all I need. Haven't driven a car in three years, and now I'm in a rainstorm in a stolen car and running from a bad robbery! Crap!" Click.

There was a sound of a lightning boom.

Breaux thought that if the mike had picked it up, it had to be nearby . . . and loud.

"Wow, that one was close! Lightning just took out a tree behind me. Where's the switch for the wipers?" Click.

Breaux was about to wet his pants. He couldn't imagine how Seven's own plumbing was holding up. For a moment, the sight of Seven chugging five cups of coffee at the IHOP without taking a pee break – all within 45 minutes – flashed in his mind.

"Hey, Breaux. Remember I told you I've got shelters all over the area? I'm gonna need help here. You'll come for me, right? I'm heading for the golf course. But first, to get there safely, I gotta dump this car." Click.

"What golf course, Seven?" asked Breaux knowing there would be no answer.

The wait for the next transmission took two minutes. Breaux was hanging on to his desk for dear life.

"Okay, Breaux. I'm outta the car and goin' through some woods just on this side of the golf course and . . ."

Seven kept talking while Breaux shouted to the tape recorder, "What golf course, you idiot! There are dozens. Where are you?"

". . . damn this ankle," continued Seven. "I'm leavin' a trail of blood from my head *and* from my ankle, and they both hurt like hell. You gotta pick me up, Breaux. I'll be at the fourth green." Another intense crash of lightning and thunder exploded close to the microphone. Click.

"Oh, crap. They followed me! Gotta get through these trees and sticker bushes. And now, of all things, it's beginning to pour again. If I find out you led 'em to me, Breaux, I'm quitting your homelessness study!" Click.

Breaux deduced that Seven had left the car and was running, or limping, more probably, down a path through some woods, heading somewhere toward a golf course . . . but which golf course? There must be twenty in the city. There were four courses in City Park alone. He could be anywhere!

"Okay, Breaux. I made it to the course, but it's pouring rain. I can see my shelter only a couple hundred feet ahead. Actually, they're only outdoor bathrooms but that's okay. The cops'll never think of looking there. But there must be fifteen of 'em pouring out of the woods and comin' after me. Cripes! Now they're letting dogs loose! Jeez, Breaux, I may have to sign . . ."

There was a loud burst of static and then . . . Click.

IV

Breaux tried the newsroom again. This time he got through and was quickly plugged into the police audio of the chase. He was now remotely following a breaking story about a failed bodega robbery on the north side, a car theft near there, then a foot chase through the woods in a downpour, generally all in the same area, and finally news of an intense lightning strike right in the middle of the chase. Preliminarily, no police officers had been injured but damage to the course was significant as several large old trees had come down. Worse, the *unsub* who was in the middle of it all managed to escape. The storm had passed over and a search for the suspect was underway. BOLOs were being issued.

* * * *

The next morning every newscast in the city covered the attempted robbery at a New Orleans convenience store, a car theft that left two lovers on the doorstep, and then a foot chase through a forest. As one cop called it, " . . . A supernatural bolt of yellow lightning ended the chase." Another cop's best guess/theory was that the unsub who'd been involved in all three events had been vaporized by the lightning strike. Either way, the suspect had gotten away.

Television had some videos that WWL Radio – the 50,000-watt radio news giant of New Orleans – couldn't duplicate. One station had video copies of not one, not two, not three, but four versions of the attempted robbery taken by the bodega's security system.

From four angles, the tapes showed a running video of an attempted robbery at a convenience store on the north end. Even if Seven *had* managed to shoot out one of the cameras, three others had recently been installed and all of them recorded the chaos in amazingly clear quality.

As shown, the attempt made for incredibly humorous footage which was shown on all the morning news shows. Most of the nation's evening newscasts that Wednesday featured at least one of the videos, and the audio was crystal clear. Breaux noticed that his name had been bleeped out. *Thank goodness . . . I think!* That had to mean that the police believed it to be *Bro*, or they were, perhaps, looking for him even then. How many Breauxs were there in the phone book anyway? "Ahhh," he said aloud, "This is New Orleans! There's lots of 'em."

The next night the videos made *Entertainment Tonight*, and, because of tape delay, the late evening shows had them a day later:

The Tonight Show Starring Jay Leno

"Kevin. Man, if you haven't seen this yet, hold on. It's a video of a robbery-gone-bad at a convenience store in New Orleans two nights ago. Here, look to the bottom right of the screen and you can see the robber coming into the store. There's no one else in there except the clerk who's a small, frail grandma; she's standing behind the register in the upper left.

"There's the robber coming through the doors. The robber, some bum in too-tight jeans, immediately tries to shoot out the camera, missing badly. What was it? He shoots at it from five feet away three times and he can't hit it? (audience laughter) Now he's shouting commands at the woman who then yells back at him, (he pauses for the woman's voice shouting), 'You bad man! You in deep [bleep]. You go 'way now. You get no money! You no make more trouble. Go you . . . *now*!' (more laughter and then applause)

"Then for some reason, the robber decides to fire another shot into the ceiling. (small pause for the shot), and (pause) then another! He goes down as the last shot ricochets and hits him in the foot, taking down a display case full of donuts and soup cans! Listen to him howl! (moaning, then intense audience laughter) Now the clerk hits the alarm button. You can see the flashing beacon and hear the alarm. Now she hits him with a bat! (laughter) The robber, apparently unable to stand, crawls out the doors. Now you can hear sirens as police pull up and run into the building. (pause again for lengthy audience laughing and applause).

"Now, Ladies and Gentlemen, please help me welcome this overnight national hero to the Tonight Show stage, the 90-pound, baseball bat totin', 4'9" grandma, slash, clean-up hitter, Lisa Sun Ling! (more applause)

The Late Show with David Letterman

Letterman: "You know, I think at some time or another we all have wanted to join a really exclusive community and one that pays slightly better than minimum wage too . . . and that's: *Holding up Your Local Convenience Store.*

(laughter) So here's tonight's Top Ten List. It's called *Best One-Liner for Shooting Yourself in the Foot While Robbing A Bodega* . . . (laughter) Heh, heh. Here. Here we go!

Number 10: *Take that, 7-Eleven!*

Number 9: *Judge, Can I get a copy of the video when the police are through with it?*

Number 8: *Ma'am, you got a roof leak stain on ceiling tile number twelve!*

Number 7: *Does this qualify me for the Army's Sharpshooter Badge?*

Number 6: *Hey Lady, will this make the Top Ten on Letterman's Stupid Human Tricks?*

Number 5: *I shot myself in the foot while trying to rob a bodega . . . and I'm gonna sue!*

Number 4: *Damn! Here I'd passed all the* other *tests to join the Secret Service!*

Number 3: *Are ya' feeling lucky, Armstrong Ceiling Tile?*

Number 2: *Clean up on Aisle Three!*

And the *Best One-Liner for Holding up Your Local Convenience Store.* is: "*Will this make the Top Three on America's Funniest Videos?* (laughter). Not a chance son. Not a chance." (intense laughter and wrap-up music)

But it did. The best of the four videos had been given by the bodega parent company to the clerk, Lisa Sun Ling. She submitted it to AFV and six months later took home the $10,000 Top Prize.

THE LADY

I

April 18th, 2005 New Orleans

Paul Pope's nearly hidden driveway lay down a treelined lane just off of a similarly exclusive street named *Swan* in New Orleans' north end. His home was a driver and a wedge down from his entrance gate and was one of the city's newest and most expensive homes. In it, to the background of soft jazz coming from numerous ceiling speakers, Paul patrolled his 20 by 20-foot living room checking for dust. He was a bit of a neat freak and wanted everything in order and in its proper place should a member of the city's Social Register stop by for a visit or call on him seeking advice on a matter of importance.

The home's plantation shutters were open to incredible views on three sides. To the north, the view was of Lake Pontchartrain's sparkling sunlit waters extending to the horizon. Today the view was enhanced by seagulls circling three racing sailboats, but it was also spoiled slightly on the left by the infinitely long bridge fading to mist as it stretched across the huge brackish body of water.

Including North America's family of five Great Lakes. Pontchartrain ranked as the eleventh largest. Of the six *longest* bridges in the *world*, three were in Louisiana with the two longest stretching out from New Orleans. Lake

Pontchartrain's bridge, the world's longest, began three miles west of Paul's home and only marginally stained his view of the lake. It departed land in Metairie and returned to it in Mandeville, 24 miles to the north. As was often the case, puffy white clouds floated over the lake's dark blue waters. Because one typically cannot see the far shore from Paul's home, it was easy to suppose that one was gazing at an ocean view from Paul's to-die-for living room.

The second set of corner-to-corner windows faced east and showcased a port side view of Number Four, the signature hole of the Bayou Oaks Golf Course. From its tee, a golfer's attention was drawn to four highlights off in the distance: the 4th Green itself which was set on a slight dogleg-right, majestic Lake Pontchartrain in the far background, corridors of 50-foot-tall Live Oaks on each side of the fairway, all with magnificent swooping branches extending out 150 feet, and finally, Paul Pope's architecturally significant home which was sited on a man-made incline just to the left of the 3rd Green. A photograph of this same view was often used to market the course to the PGA.

The Bayou Oaks course, the city's oldest, opened in 1902 as part of City Park. It made great scenic use of the thousands of huge native Live Oak trees that dotted the park. It was beneath these beautiful trees in the early 1800s that many of the young country's *duels d'honneur* took place. It was said then that on any given Sunday afternoon, hundreds of witnesses would gather to watch three or four duels.

II

At the moment, two golfers were on the 3rd Green, putting in a modern-day duel. From the looks of their efforts, their putts would not make for *grand honneur*.

The home's third set of monster windows faced south and framed a long brick driveway set against yet another backdrop of oaks. Paul's property bordered the northwest edge of City Park while the course itself wound its way around the north end of the huge facility. Everywhere one turned, giant oaks spread their canopies over large carpets of lush green grass, the course, and of course, Paul's property.

City Park was so large that it played host to four different 18-hole courses as well as a football stadium that was once home to the original Sugar Bowl. For a brief period of time, the park also served as home to the fledgling NFL Saints. It is where Tom Dempsey, a player with only half a kicking foot, set a mark for NFL Kickers in 1970 with a 63-yard field goal as time expired, giving the hapless Saints only their second win in a long losing season. Today many football fans believe the kick occurred in the Superdome where there were no winds to affect it but the kick actually took place out of doors, clearing the City Park crossbar by several yards. City Park was also famous for its art museum, soccer stadium, a music venue, and was also once the site of a racetrack where a young George Armstrong Custer was photographed standing proudly near the betting windows, smiling, and holding up a winning slip.

Even though Paul's property only bordered the park, he'd made certain to landscape it to have it appear that his home was actually a *part* of City Park . . . or perhaps the other way around.

Just beyond the home's south windows sat Paul's brand new, bright red 2005 Ferrari F430 Spyder, License Plate, *Louisiana 7*. It had been three weeks since Paul had taken possession of the automobile, but its MSRP sticker remained affixed to the passenger side window. On it, one was almost compelled to note that while the vehicle's suggested price came in at just under $200,000, not included on the sticker were all the factory bells and whistles one could order. Paul Pope's new Spyder had cost significantly more. Still, with a high-end Ferrari, there weren't too many features one can add to make the price that much higher, right?

Paul Pope himself was standing in the living room. He was of medium height, toned, tanned, and handsome. Looking out the south-facing window, his gaze washed over the Ferrari. He smiled to himself, possibly more because of his own good fortune than because of the car. He currently reigned as the King of Bacchus, had an incredibly attractive wife, owned a well-respected and *very* successful business, lived in a majestic home overlooking the lake, and retreated when necessary to one of two well-appointed fishing and hunting lodges – *Camps*, as the native Louisianans call them – one located in the Atchafalaya Basin and the other near Monroe in the northern end of the state where duck hunting was king. And of course, he paid cash for the only brand new 2005 Spyder F430 in New Orleans, much less in Louisiana . . . and likely even in all the adjoining states.

Below him, the golfers were moving on, hurrying perhaps because of the coming dinner hour. As their cart sped toward the fourth Green, Paul again checked his watch. "Hey, Babe!" he called behind him. "Time's runnin' out. We need to leave soon." He picked his cell phone up from an end table and punched in seven numbers. After a pause, he said, "Jerome. Where are you? We need to be movin' on in a few minutes." He listened for a few seconds and then disconnected without saying goodbye.

With those two little reminders behind him, Paul resumed his inspection of the living room, straightening out a few pillows and leveling an expensive modern art painting that, along with its brothers and sisters, dotted the long fourth wall. All were vibrant with color. In fact, they provided the only real color in the room, as everything else was black and white . . . even the clothing worn by the owner. The furnishings in the room were tasteful, new, very expensive, very modern, very toney, and *very* obvious.

Looking over the room for a final review, Paul smiled again, appreciating the fact that nearly everything in the room was white with black or chrome trim. He paused for a moment to lean down and scratch the head of a perfect, although golden, retriever resting comfortably on the floor. "Good boy, Trip," he said. The dog raised its head to accept the head-scratch and praise, and then rested it again on its manicured paws.

Noting *Space Ghost*, a cartoon showing on a state-of-the-art 50-inch Panasonic plasma television that had set him back $8,000 the previous Christmas, Paul checked to see if his son was paying the show any attention. He wasn't, so Paul used the remote to mute the sound. The boy sat cross-legged on the floor below the screen playing with more Legos than a single human being could possibly count in a week. Hearing the cartoon's audio drop out, the boy looked up and moaned, "Dad! I can't hear *Space Ghost!*" Then, after a brief pause, "Hey, Dad, look what I built. Check it out." He proudly pointed to a foot-high facsimile of a fort, surrounded by Lego debris. The television's sound remained muted.

"Looks great Ace!" said Paul after a minute, bringing the program's audio up, genuine interest in his son's Lego Fort lacking, and moved on. In fact, Paul's interest *was* elsewhere. He stepped to an end table and withdrew a glossy magazine from beneath several others and rotated the stack, placing the magazine he'd withdrawn on the top. Now only one magazine was visible, and it would remain so for observation by anyone entering the room.

The cover featured face shots of three young adults below a headline reading, "2005's Three Under Thirty." The magazine was the current issue of *New Orleans Entrepreneur*, an annual chamber publication. The face in the middle belonged to Paul who was pictured wearing a somewhat somber expression and an equally somber, but expensive, black suit.

Nodding approval, Paul again smiled to himself. He stepped back from the table and returned to reorient the stack slightly for an even better cursory examination by any passersby. The other two *Under 30s* were also attractive people: a woman wearing a radiant smile and dressed in a flashy business suit, and a man wearing a week-old luminescent green, yellow, and purple tee shirt. He wore a week's growth of beard and held a Mardi Gras mask in one hand with a full champagne flute in the other. If one looked closely, the man's eyes were severely dilated, and his smile appeared to have been designed by *Booze*. Empty bottles of Abita were scattered about the room behind him.

Still moving about the living room, Paul sidestepped an auburn-haired teenage girl perched on the edge of one of the room's three white leather couches. She was chewing gum and humming to Mario's *"Let Me Love You"* as it leaked noticeably from her headphones. The girl swayed to her music and because the headphone cans were clamped tightly to her head, heard none of the jazz coming from ceiling speakers. Paul suspected that the teen had deliberately set her music loud enough to drown out Kenny G. He predicted to himself that she would have lost most of her hearing by the time she reached her twenties. As he listened to the mix of Mario, the sax, and the trumpet music, he concluded that *"Let Me Love You"* competed reasonably well with Kenny G's *"At Last."*

Paul stepped to a wall mirror and looked himself over. He liked what he saw. For this evening's event, he was dressed in Black-Tie. In the mirror, he examined everything about his appearance. Fussing with his hair, he finally said something over his shoulder to the girl, "Hey Layla. How ya' doin', girl?" Layla, the gum chewer on the couch, was oblivious. *She's ignoring me,* thought Paul . . . *or probably she's already deaf.* He called out again, louder this time, and the girl pulled one of the cans off her right ear. As the music poured out, she replied, "Hey, Mr. Pope. How ya' doin'?" Without waiting for an answer, the girl popped the can back over her ear, smacked her gum loudly, and began again to sway to Mario.

An audible chirp sounded from an unseen ceiling speaker. Paul checked his watch. Reaching again for the television remote, he switched the channel. From security cameras mounted perhaps four feet off the ground and to the side of his private gate, he viewed two live side-by-side images. One was a slightly blurry black-and-white image taken from behind a dark-colored limousine, The second image showed a close-up from a camera mounted on a post aimed directly at a driver's window. Paul recognized the driver and pushed another button on the remote. The gate began to swing open, and the limo moved through it. As it began to close, Paul shut the TV down to the dismay of the boy. "Hey, Dad . . ." cried the boy, and before *Ace* could finish his complaint, Paul clicked the remote again and the cartoon resumed.

"Sherrie," Paul yelled, just loudly enough to be heard in adjacent rooms, "Jerome's coming up the drive. We need to go, babe!" There was no response, so Paul yelled again, even louder this time. "Hon! We need to be out of here in one minute. Jerome's coming up to the portico."

This time a pleasant feminine voice responded from another room, "Okay, hon. Gimme' two!"

Paul checked his watch. He was certain that Sherrie's *two minutes* were code for *ten, minimum*. He walked through the front door as a stretched black limousine pulled in, parking next to the Ferrari. Exiting the portico and walking to the front of the arriving vehicle, Paul was acknowledged by the limo driver, Jerome, with a two-fingered salute. The man was dressed in a full chauffeur's dark blue uniform complete with the hat. The driver lowered his window and spoke as Paul came up to his side of the vehicle.

"Nice!" said Jerome, nodding to the red Ferrari.

Paul ignored the compliment. "Hey, Jerome. Twelve minutes. If I've done the math right, Sherrie will step out of the bedroom in exactly twelve minutes. Can we make it to the event on time if we don't leave 'till then? By the way, you look great in the uniform. You might oughta' take a second job!"

"Thanks, sir. No problem with the time, sir. We'll get to the Dome early enough for a couple cocktails."

While they waited, Paul pulled at the collar of his tuxedo, "Damn it's hot! Can you believe it's this warm in April?" He checked to the west where dark clouds were building. There were no golfers in sight, possibly because of forecasts for thundershowers.

Jerome was still admiring the red Ferrari parked next to him prompting Paul to fish in his pocket and retrieve a set of keys. "While we wait for her, you wanna put the Spyder in the garage?"

"Absolutely, sir. Your wish is my command!" Jerome brightened and eagerly jumped from the limo taking the keys from Paul. "You sure you don't want to take her to tonight's event?" Jerome said as he lovingly patted the Ferrari's front fender. Paul grimaced. Noticing it, Jerome used the cuff of his jacket to polish the spot he'd just touched.

"Love to. Not enough room in it for three though. And even if there was, I'm bettin' Sherrie would have a fit 'cause it would mess up her hair. Another time, my friend."

"Yes sir. You got it." Jerome stepped to the other side of the Italian sports car.

Paul walked back to the portico and said, without turning his head, "Eleven minutes. The countdown is underway. See you in a bit. Have fun."

"Oh, yeah!" said Jerome, actually licking his lips as he wedged his six-foot-two frame into the Spyder and cranked it up with a huge roar. Paul turned at the front door and the two exchanged smiles . . . one as driver, and one, more importantly, as owner.

Three seconds short of 12 minutes, Sherrie emerged from the back bedroom into the living room. A strikingly beautiful brunette, she was wearing a tiny black dress that only a Size Zero, twenty-six-year-old woman could wear . . . a woman who knew she possessed a killer body, had a face for the ages, and a voice that dripped with sex. The dress was a special order from New York purchased just for this occasion. Six of them might buy another Spyder.

Seeing her through the south-facing windows, Jerome again absentmindedly licked his lips.

As Sherrie glided into the living room, the boy stood from his Legos to welcome his mom. The dog also rose to attention, tail wagging hard. Back inside now, the husband's eyebrows lifted and then hooded. "Whew!" was all he said, but the word was uttered in praise and with an obvious tint of lust. Sherrie was the center of attention at this moment and would be again later in the evening at the event.

"How do I look," she asked, already knowing what the answer would be.

"Nice!" Paul said appreciatively and whistled softly. Sherrie kissed him on the cheek in thanks. He accepted, then tried to return the favor with a bit more enthusiasm.

Sherrie backed off saying, "No. No. No! The makeup! The hair! Later, big boy. Later!"

Then, for the first time, she looked *him* over.

"Whoa! Paul, *you* look fine! *More than fine*! Are you sure you want to go to this thing? We *could* just stay home, have a couple glasses of wine, and . . . uh . . ." Her offer was punctuated with a seductive smile, and her question, while left unfinished, was no doubt one of double entendre.

It was accepted by Paul with a return squint and leer. But, instead of responding similarly, he made a point of clearing his throat and nodding back toward Layla on the couch, mouthing to Sherrie, *I'm ready if you are.*

"Oh, Paul. She can't hear a thing with those

headphones on!"

On the couch, and looking in another direction, Layla's eyes rolled and she smacked her gum loudly.

Sherrie glided over to the girl and lifted one of the headphone cans. Heavy metal leaked from it this time. To compensate, she spoke more loudly than necessary and the girl grimaced in return.

"We're leaving now Layla. You have all our contact information, right girl? We should be back by 9:30, ten at the latest . . . and Jerome will give you a ride home." She leaned down and kissed her son on the top of his head. "PJ, Mommy and Daddy love you. You be good for Miss Layla."

Finally, she turned to Paul, "Well! What's the holdup? Set the security, dear. Let's go. We'll be late!" With that, she was halfway to the door before Paul could react.

Paul reached down to nuzzle the dog's head. "You'll take good care of Shanna and Ace, won't you boy?' He looked toward his son and said, "Goodnight, Ace."

"Paul, please don't call him *Ace*. It sounds like you named him after a crap game!"

"Poker, Sherrie. That's my game and Ace is my Number One Son, right, boy? I'll call him what I want."

PJ/Ace looked up, questioning the response from his spot on the floor in the middle of the Legos.

His Mom and Dad moved out the front doors passing a security panel positioned on the foyer wall. For a few seconds, a bit of tension floated in the air between them over the boy's nickname. The door closed behind them.

The security remained unset.

III

THE EVENT

The limo was only a year old, but over those twelve months, a deep fragrance of carnations had imbedded itself into the upholstery. The smell was strong enough to overwhelm some riders, but it went unnoticed by Paul and Sherrie. As the limo passed through the changing New Orleans cityscape, Paul and Sherrie observed the passing scenery but didn't really absorb it. Their minds were elsewhere, and neither was moving down the same track.

Part of the trip took them onto I-610 and then onto I-10 leading south to the New Orleans Central Business District . . . or the *CBD* as most local Orleanians called it. Traffic gradually slowed to a standstill.

"The Hornets are home against the Timberwolves tonight," Paul said, more to Jerome than to Sherrie, and more to end the silence than anything. "One would think that a last-place team looking for only its 19th win would be lucky to attract a dozen fans, much less a capacity crowd. The *Jazz* sure never enjoyed this kind of support. I guess that's why they left for Salt Lake City. It would seem, with their win-loss record, the return of the NBA to the Big Easy is still in its grace period. Given the Hornets' 60-loss season (and maybe a few more before it's over), if you combine that with the Saints' wretched historic win-loss totals, the old New Orleans Jazz looks pretty damn good."

Jerome was aware of Paul's strong desire to witness the NBA's return to New Orleans. Because of their relationship as employer and employee, he'd taken to paying close attention to how both the Utah Jazz and the New Orleans Hornets were doing. Nevertheless, he had no intention of irritating his boss.

"Boy, I'll say!" Jerome responded with political correctness.

Paul sighed. "You know, the good folks in Salt Lake can thank us for not naming our former team the *Pirates*, or the *VooDoo*, or maybe even the *Flaming Rum Punches,* because the ownership in Mormon Town would never have taken them in, or maybe they'd have decided to rename 'em, *Joe's Wives!*"

Jerome loyally chuckled at his boss's off-color attempt at humor.

"Still, the name *Jazz* just doesn't really seem to fit for Utah does it?"

"I think I like the Utah Flaming Rum Punches better. Good one, sir," Jerome correctly responded.

"Yeah, I'm impressed that they may get a full house tonight. But, it's the second to last home game of the season, and a lot of the fans, I guess, want to be able to say saw the team win a game. It doesn't happen often. They've missed that experience too many times this season. Last place by far in the division! And, who knows? This team could disappear in the middle of the night too, and maybe show up in Cincinnati or some place."

Traffic hadn't budged at all during the exchange.

Jerome changed the subject.

"Because of the big crowd expected . . . plus all the folks going to your event at the Dome, I think I'm gonna take Canal downtown rather than I-10, sir. Shouldn't put us more than two minutes behind schedule. We'll still get there in plenty of time."

The limo slowed even more and made a hard right, cutting across several solid white lines and into an interstate exit that had begun several hundred feet back. Horns honked in irritation at the move. It didn't help that the stalled drivers were envious of the *big folks* in the limousine.

"Excellent move, Jerome. And don't call me *sir*. We work together every day for crying out loud."

"I know, *Paul*," said Jerome, emphasizing the name. "But when you put me in this crazy uniform, I become someone else!"

"Well, I appreciate your willingness to be our chauffeur tonight. This beats what you drive most days."

As darkness settled in, the limousine picked up a bit of speed, but traffic still delayed their arrival. This alternate Canal Street route took Paul and Sherrie through several of New Orleans's unique and ancient above-ground cemeteries. Neither of them seemed to find the big plots of much interest. Closer to downtown, stately old homes replaced the cemeteries but they too held little importance in a battle for the attentions of the limo's three occupants. As they closed in on the CBD, event traffic stopped the limo completely. Canal Street became the same bumper-to-bumper-stop-and-go mess that I-10 had been. They still had two miles to go.

Half a mile from the Dome, Sherrie awoke from her daydream, looked out the windshield, and watched as search lights swept across the dark clouds over their heads probably drawing attention to the events at the Superdome and the NBA game at the Arena.

Still blocks from their destination, she panicked and said, "Jerome, it looks like it's gonna rain. I don't want to get my hair wet. Is there any way we can get there sooner? If not, can we pull into the parking garage?"

"Afraid not, ma'am. This is as good as it's gonna get. We're stuck in it 'till we get there. I don't think it'll rain for a while though. Either way, I'll do my best."

"I'm sure you will. Thank you, Jerome."

Paul's Blackberry rang. He glanced at the caller's name on the face and took advantage of the delay, answering, "Hey, man. We're on our way to the *Three Under Thirty* event. Anything going on?" He listened for a few seconds and responded, "Okay. Okay." Holding the unit away from his head, he turned to Sherrie: "Hon, we've had a late delivery. I may have to have Jerome drop me off at the office after tonight's event and then have him take you home. OK? If so, I'll grab one of the company cars and be home as soon as I can . . . but it'll still probably be close to midnight before I make it there."

Sherrie, with undisguised scorn, replied to an empty space in the limo, "24/7. Always was. Always will be. 24/7!

In Better Times

Humph. What about John? Will he be there tonight? Maybe I can hang out with him."

Paul squinted, shook his head, and mouthed *No,* but didn't say anything aloud because he was still listening to the conversation on the phone. A minute later he smiled and said into the receiver, "Okay. See you later," and hung up. A slight rain began to fall.

Full darkness descended upon the city as the limo finally crept into the CBD. By now traffic had grown much denser and even more congested. A bit on edge because of the delay, and now the falling rain, Paul and Sherrie sat on the edges of their seats looking forward as the New Orleans Superdome, bathed in lights, grew larger. Searchlights flashed back and forth sweeping across the now-dark sky. The rain took a break, and at the Dome's VIP entrance, a slightly soggy New Orleans-style jazz band was playing *When the Saints Go Marching In.* A mammoth ticker-tape style electric sign proclaimed: "Three Under Thirty – 7 pm Tonight!"

The limo pulled up to a red carpet. Many couples passed by it dressed to *their* "nines" but most weren't in formal attire. Many stooped and tried to see through the shaded windows of the limo to try to determine whether or not its occupants were recognizable celebrities, for this was the only VIP entrance to the Dome. The rain finally slackened to nothing as Jerome opened the Limo's rear door.

As Paul and Sherrie stepped out and began to make their way down the carpet and into the VIP entrance, a few people recognized them, calling out "Hey, Paul!

Congratulations!". Once inside the Superdome, the stylish couple pushed their way down a crowded hallway leading to the football playing surface which had been left in place for this event.

The Superdome had been the site of numerous prize fights, Super Bowls, Sugar Bowls, NCAA Championships, and hundreds of other events from celebrity funerals to tractor pulls. As well, it had been the home stadium for most of the 207 Saints home games played up to that day, excepting a few as the expansion Saints played in the stadium in the City Park while the Superdome was under construction.

In the Dome's hallways, the night's attendees passed wall posters commemorating many of those same events as they made their way to their tables. Nearly everyone had a drink in his or her hands. Many were two-fisted drinkers.

Coming out onto the main floor of the Dome, several attendees including Archie Manning, Fats Domino, and the Mayor, stopped Paul to shake his hand and offer congratulations. Many greeted Sherrie with compliments, faux leers, and *air-kisses.*

Paul and Sherrie searched the floor as they moved through the crowd, shaking more hands, hugging, and air-kissing, and eventually steering themselves to a circular head table. A hundred more tables filled the football-playing surface behind them.

The head table was located where the goalposts were normally planted for football. They framed the field-level entrance where, prior to each game, the Saints emerged

In Better Times

to ear-shattering cheers from a crowd that was the envy of the league . . . but oddly, for a team that had yet to compete in its first playoff game in 32 seasons.

The head table was reserved for the Master of Ceremonies, his escort, and the *Three Under Thirty* honorees and their guests. Before taking their seats, Paul and Sherrie looked back across the floor and noted that the tables perfectly aligned with each other and with the yard lines. The lighting in the Dome was subdued, almost too dark in fact to see things properly. As their eyes adjusted, white tablecloths stood out and easily showed off a hundred vases containing dozens of red and white roses.

Other than Mardi Gras, this was New Orleans High Society's biggest affair of the year. A little *self-congratulation* dinner where tickets ran $200 a seat or $1,500 for a corporate table of eight. Those present and those still arriving were among the city's most elite citizens. They were being thanked for serving as leaders of the major American City they wanted New Orleans to become.

"Once, with a Chamber Committee, I was given a VIP tour of the Dome," Paul remarked to Sherrie. They were both looking high into the dark roof of the Dome. "I was able to view this same scene from as high up in the Dome as one can go." They looked up to see a catwalk where a worker was adjusting one of the spotlights far above them.

"Were you afraid? That guy looks like a bug, crawling across a ceiling," said Sherrie."

"Nah! That's where I was though," said Paul pointing to a walkway just behind the worker. "But you're right in one respect, the people down on the floor looked like tuxedoed bees buzzing around a honeycomb." He paused to imagine what the worker above was thinking as the man checked lighting and security from his *way-high* vantage. *Eight hundred people, all dressed in their finest, moving from table to table,* Paul thought. *Even the noise of the crowd probably sounds like bees from up there.*

Around three sides of the seating area were eight large screens showing an endless loop of slides featuring the three honorees in different situations in their daily lives including some with them counseling with city leaders. Occasionally interspersed in the shots were slides thanking the sponsors. Some displayed company names and logos congratulating one or more of the honorees.

Attendees who bothered to pay attention to the slide show viewed family shots of the three, shots of them in their daily work lives, shots of them in front of their office buildings, and of course, the obligatory shots of the *Three Under Thirty* awardees doing volunteer work to make New Orleans a beautiful, cultured and socially responsible community. Occasionally attendees might catch themselves pictured with the honorees because nearly every person in attendance personally knew at least one of the three.

It was no surprise of course that each of the home companies of the honorees was a major sponsor of the event and had purchased and filled many of the tables. Their employees were there to celebrate their bosses, to enjoy a fine *company-paid-for* but probably rewarmed dinner at no charge, and to drink their way through a long evening.

In Better Times

The awardees needed to be sponsors of this event because it was likely that many of those in attendance would take the hint, become sponsors, and hope to be so honored in the future or have one of their employees so honored. That guaranteed that next year's event would be paid for by three *other* companies as another set of three hard chargers was honored.

"At least there won't be a silent auction!" a few veterans of the evening dinner circuit said, laughing.

Two much-larger screens were positioned to the front and each side of a small stage set about 15 feet behind the head table. The left screen showed a static message that read: *Welcome to the Louisiana Superdome*, while the right screen displayed a message reading: *2005 Three Under Thirty*.

The tinkling of glasses and the general hum of conversation were clearly louder by far than classical music played by a string quartet appearing courtesy of the city's symphony. Very few attendees though, even those near enough to hear the quartet, could profess to identify either the names of the composers or the compositions performed. Nevertheless, virtually everyone present swore, under oath if asked, that he or she was a supporter, financial donor, and a regular attendee of every performance of the New Orleans Symphony.

At precisely 7:50 p.m., an amplified baritone voice that could well have belonged to God . . . and in fact was amplified from speakers aiming down from the dark interior sky of the Superdome . . . announced, "Welcome to *Three Under Thirty*. Please thank our pre-event entertainment,

The Fourth Concerto." There was a pause for a smattering of applause. The voice now continued in a more casual, less perfunctory, and more Louisiana-friendly, tone: "Folks, I know the Superdome soaks up applause but, com'on, let's show these men and women who've donated their time to entertain us, just how much we appreciate them!"

The applause was much stronger this time and the four performers stood and bowed their thanks. Under their breaths, they asked each other, "Donated? We *are* getting paid for this gig, aren't we? Why is *Mr. MC* saying we're *donating* our time? We're at least going to get a free dinner, right?"

Mr. MC continued again as the applause died down. In his best announcer's voice, he said, "Our program will begin following dinner. Please take your seats."

The Master of Ceremonies, he'd been nearly invisible up to this point, was standing to the side of the Saints' entry tunnel, microphone in hand. He was about to turn away when he was confronted by the members of the string quartet. *Mr. MC* professionally made certain the mike was turned off and in a non-announcer voice said in anticipation of their question, "Just kidding folks! You'll get paid . . . and you got thanked much more appreciatively this way. Your dinner is waiting at one of the corner tables in the back of the room."

He abandoned them to find their own table, which both he and they knew would be at the extreme rear of the audience. He then headed toward the small stage and locked the wireless microphone in place on the stand of a small lectern sitting in its center.

Finished, he stepped down, making his way to the head table where he said to those already seated, "Folks, I'm Tommy Tijon," as if they didn't already know. "Tell me, with whom do I have the pleasure of dining tonight." Tijon made the rounds at the table shaking every hand save one, memorizing names, and took the last open seat with his back to the mini-stage. Turning to his right he said, "And you, young lady, are my wife of the evening, I suppose. Right?" He chuckled at his own joke and then introduced his spouse to the others.

At precisely 7:57 p.m., the lights in the Dome faded to dark, came back up, dropped again, and then went to full bright. Tijon, owner of the same electrified voice as before, echoed throughout the Dome over the crowd-noise saying, "Please return to your seats. *New Orleans 2005 Three Under Thirty* begins in one minute." Three minutes later, an intense spotlight sparked to life with a honk and a hum, and all the screens went blank.

The two large screens at the front replaced their "welcome" slides with a live shot of Tijon standing behind the lectern. He asked the crowd to stand and remain standing following the invocation and then introduced the Arch-Bishop of the Diocese of New Orleans who generically provided an after-the-fact stirring prayer, mentioning the honorees by name, listing several of the good works of the Chamber, and prayed thanks for the city officials in their midst.

In true chamber form, a student from Loyola performed

the national anthem acapella. Motioning for the audience to remain standing, Tijon then introduced a boy of nine to sing the state song, "You are my Sunshine." They were all thanked profusely by Tijon who finally motioned to the restless crowd to be seated so dinner service could begin. All screens resumed their slide shows.

During the dinner, every male present seemed to make at least one trip to the portable bars that formed a "U" around the crowd. Not a few women made the same trips. The bars had opened ninety minutes before the dinner, so the crowd was now well past caring about how boring the event promised to be. As dinner began to wind down, movers and shakers refilled their drinks and moved from table to table shaking hands, glad-handing their superiors, deprecating their inferiors, slapping backs, and laughing. With the event finally ready to begin, most attendees were well-lubricated, talking, relaxing, and waiting. Many were seen surreptitiously checking their watches.

To an audible rush of surprise and with no warning, at exactly eight-twenty the Dome went dark. A few seconds passed, and the honk of the spotlight was again heard. It blanketed the empty stage in brilliant incandescence. A pause of another few seconds occurred as Tijon's scripted opening drama began. He waited for the first rustle of anxiety from the crowd and then stepped up and onto the stage and into the light, moving behind the deliberately short lectern. There were a few *oohs* and *aahs*. A few whistles were heard. This was New Orleans of course, not Paris where whistling would be considered gauche after all.

In Better Times

Gradually the rest of the lights in the Dome came up to 30% of their previous level. The room became adequately silent. Unnoticed by most, when the lights had been extinguished the nine screens had also gone dark with them. Now only the two large screens at the front were still lit, showing their previous messages.

"Good evening. Welcome to *Three Under Thirty*, the 2005 version of the Annual Presentation of our Chamber's most prestigious community awards." Tijon paused.

Mr. MC was a very tall man. Of course, almost everyone in the place knew Tommy Tijon already, or at least knew who he was, and many of the less sophisticated attendees who might not have been sure of his identity learned of him over dinner. Quite a few had passed by him at the head table doing double-takes, asking their escort, "Is that . . . uh . . . uh . . . what's his name?" The question was asked with no small amount of pointing. Tijon was incredibly handsome and well-toned. His tuxedo fit perfectly, and he stood before his admirers with well-coifed silver hair. Even though it was April, Tommy's tan said *August. The* lowered height of the lectern added another two inches to his 6' 3" frame.

The two larger screens at the front blinked and then projected a full-length image of the man behind the lectern who offered a small wave and a warm, confidence-producing, professional smile. As the camera zoomed in on his face, Tommy's eyes seemed to bore in on every member of the audience. He stared directly into the camera, visibly accepting the applause as well as the envy that many in the audience broadcast to him. *I should run for president,* he thought . . . *or, even better, for Governor of Louisiana!* Finally, he closed his eyes, nodded his head, and held his hands palms-out to quiet everyone. The applause continued anyway . . . and he expected as much.

Because the large screens *had* been dark but now showed an image, every set of eyes in the Dome moved to them and watched a close zoom to the MC's face. It ended and Tommy *quick-smiled,* raising his cheeks slightly without opening his mouth, accepting the cheers and whistles. Finally, he'd drunk the admiring stares from the women empty . . . along with a fair percentage of the men. He quick-smiled again and cleared his throat to speak. Instantly the crowd noise abated.

It was time to start the show. The deep resonant voice majestically echoed again throughout the Dome, "I am Tommy Tijon, Lead Anchor for Channel 12 News," he said unnecessarily. Tijon paused again to acknowledge the brief applause he'd expected. Once again there were a few whistles. Everyone recognized Tijon of course, but he wanted to make certain everyone knew his name. Following this brief applause, it became deathly quiet in the Dome.

Another pause occurred, perhaps a bit longer than necessary. Then Tijon raised his right fist in the air and shouted, "Laissez les bon temp rouler!"

A huge and prolonged period of thunderous applause began. Many in the crowd got to their feet, cheering, and whistling at the well-known Louisiana slogan, *"Let the Good Times Roll!"* A chant began: "Laissez les . . . bon temp rouler! Laissez les . . . bon temp rouler!" It was echoed back at Tijon by the crowd for thirty seconds before his hands rose up, palms forward to shush everyone. The moment verged on the religious. Then again, the communion wine hadn't hurt. The crowd now settled down.

This early part of the show of course was scripted and at more than one table one person said to another, "Tommy sure knows how to milk this, doesn't he?"

It didn't take much to get a Louisiana audience ready for the main event. Yes, Tommy did know how to *milk it*.

Lights came on spotlighting the head table. A camera woman, dressed in all black for better invisibility, and who'd previously provided the close zoom on Tijon, reappeared . . . almost, and pan-shot the head table from the position where Tijon had sat just a few minutes earlier.

There was still a buzz from the chanting as the two large screens up front switched from Tijon to a panoramic shot of the head table. The three honorees, along with their spouses, smiled and waved in recognition. A softer and more dignified round of applause followed. Now that the hurrahs were over, the crowd was beginning to show its growing anxiety.

Tijon first introduced his young wife whose face was shown in close-up on the two big front screens. Subdued applause followed. Following her script, the camera woman concluded the close-up of the woman and began slowly panning the head table clockwise, keeping time as Tijon introduced each of the honorees and their escorts. The shot ended on Paul Pope as he gazed dutifully at Tijon in the unfocussed background. Paul professionally ignored the camera. The camerawoman then circled behind him and followed his sightline to show Tijon on the stage in the distance. She then began zooming the focus from Paul's side profile to the full-length shot of Tijon bathing in the unfocused spotlight. It continued to zoom until it became an extreme close-up of the Master of Ceremony's face. A drop of perspiration sparkled on his handsome upper lip.

"Tonight, we honor three young residents of our fair city who have, through hard work, inspiration, and a passion for this town inspired us to love and care for *Naw'lins* and its residents..." Once again Tijon anticipated applause and wasn't disappointed, "... and frankly," he continued over it, "they've inspired all of *us* to love and emulate *their* appetite for success. This evening, if you know anything about them at all, you'll learn how they emerged, in each case from very humble beginnings, to succeed as leaders in our town. *Each* of their stories is unique and by the end of our program I think you'll agree," Tijon again paused with drama, "we are *all* better off for *their* presence in our lives and in our town!"

There was no *ask* for applause, but Tijon was not to be disappointed. The response by the big audience was respectable. The tuxedos and cocktail dresses, the dinner, the drama, and especially the alcohol had all done their duty. The crowd was poised to explode with love and admiration. The three honorees were equally stoked by their moment in the spotlight.

"Our first honoree is a native of the city." Tijon paused

In Better Times

and organized his papers to allow the audience to settle in.

The lights dimmed again but stayed at a hushed level. The *theatre* had been well managed and the latest silence in the big room now became overwhelming.

Tijon looked up from the short lectern holding high a yellowed copy of *The Times-Picayune*. In his best lead anchor voice, he said, "I'd like you to recall the front page of my competitor, dated October 17th, 1978 – 27 years ago." The camera lady dutifully zoomed in on the paper. "Two noteworthy events occurred in the world on that day. Both made the front page . . . *above* the crease:"

There were a few laughs from those who recognized the newspaper phrase.

"One . . . *Pope John Paul Ascends to the Throne of Rome*, and . . ."

Tijon paused for effect one last time . . . .

"Two . . . *Local Couple Honors New Pope by Naming Twins after Him*. In smaller type below the main headline is a sub-headline reading, *Identical Twins, John and Paul, are born to Martha and John Pope at Charity Hospital.*"

The crowd laughed and then began to applaud. A few stand, and soon all 800 attendees stood and applauded until Paul Pope turned in his chair, into the spotlight and, a camera now on him, and acknowledged the honor. The two large front screens flipped from his face to an eighties-style, slightly fuzzy photograph of a humbly dressed young couple awkwardly holding twin babies standing in front of a typical but run-down New Orleans Shotgun home.

Tijon continued Pope's introduction but for Paul,

the wonderful baritone voice had faded to insignificance. He stared unblinkingly into the darkness above Tijon's head and recalled the day a few weeks ago when a feature reporter for the *Picayune had* interviewed him seeking personal background.

Oblivious to Paul's mesmerization, The dulcet tones of Tommy Tijon's voice continued to pour from speakers high in the dome, "Life was tough for the Popes."

IV

THE INTERVIEW
MARCH 16, 2005

"So, Mr. Pope," said Albert Breaux, feature writer for the *New Orleans Times-Picayune*, "the Chamber is looking for *bullets* to use in your introduction by Mr. Tijon at the *Three Under Thirty* event. My Assignment Editor wants me to write feature stories on you and the other two honorees. The features will likely appear in the paper the week preceding the event, partly to promote it of course. If you're not aware, our publisher is chairman of the chamber this year and he wants a big crowd. Makes him look good, you know. Part of today's interview will also be used for mini-biographies on the winners that will be a part of the program for that evening."

"I'm all in" said Paul, only slightly nervous and hoping this interview wouldn't be too *in-depth*."

In Better Times

"Okay. Let's get started. . .

"First, you seem very familiar. Have we ever met before? Maybe on a story?"

"Don't think so, and I've got a pretty good memory," replied Paul.

"Well, perhaps then in another life . . ."

"Yeah. Perhaps."

"Maybe I've seen you on TV. You just look familiar. Okay, then. We'll need some casual photos of you, of course. One of our photographers will be contacting you in the next few days to make that happen. Here's her card in case she calls your secretary. Most Gate Keepers try to shield their bosses from us, you know. So, I'd suggest you let her know that she'll be calling. You'll need to give Sarah several hours of your time. Be thinking about where you might want to be when the photographs are taken because, given your business sign out front, I'm not really certain that is where you want to be photographed."

"Sure. I understand. Smiling's probably something we shouldn't do in front of the sign."

Ignoring the reply, Breaux added, "We'll also want to get several shots of you with your family, preferably at home. Is that a possibility?" Breaux didn't wait for an answer and grimaced, "I understand you own horses and a small farm near a fishing camp in the basin, right? That might present some nice photo ops as well. Our readers love horse photos.

"Nice office, by the way."

"Yeah," replied Paul, sensing the reporter's slightly

resentful tone. "We can make that happen." He grabbed a miniature plastic casket from his desk containing business cards, took two out, wrote the name *Roberta* on the back of one, and handed both to Breaux. "Here're *my* cards. I've written my secretary's name on one; her phone number is on the front. She keeps my schedule. Have your photographer call her and we'll knock this thing out in no time."

"Cute, hmm?" Breaux said, pointing to the unique card holder."

"Yeah, well . . . What can I say?" was the reply.

"Alright," Breaux said, pulling a small old-style tape recorder from an inside jacket pocket. From another, he produced several cassettes, placed one in the machine, placed both the recorder and the spare cassettes on the desk between them, and pushed the *Record* and *Play* buttons simultaneously.

Showing that he could multitask, at the same time and with the other hand he pulled a small notepad from yet another jacket pocket and a pen from his shirt pocket. "I want to honor your time . . . and this session is scheduled for only an hour, so why don't we start by you telling me the story of your life. Can you do that in an hour?" Breaux chuckled because he'd never interviewed a subject of a feature article yet who couldn't talk about himself or herself for several days. Without pausing, Breaux turned to the recorder's internal microphone. "Paul Pope, March 16th, 2005, *Three Under Thirty*.

"Now . . . let's begin. Mr. Pope, do I have your

permission to record this conversation?"

Paul nodded.

"Please Mr. Pope, for the recorder . . .?

"Yes, I consent," he said, "and could you please call me, *Paul*?"

"Okay, Mr. Pope. Let's hear your story."

Paul had been preparing for this interview for several days and had made a few notes that he especially wanted to include. He opened a leather binder on his desk and, visible to Breaux in an almost elegiac penmanship, produced his notes.

"In elementary school," he began, "my pop, John Randall Pope, and my mom, Martha Eloise Landry, tested pretty well but never planned on even attending high school. And so, they never gave *us* any encouragement to study or to excel either. You know, none of my grandparents went to high school. In fact, you *could say* my father's father was even *anti-education.* My parents were destined to become high school dropouts right from the start . . ."

Frankly, Paul thought, *in all three cases, the trigger was teen pregnancy. Dropping out and unwed pregnancy was sort of family tradition for the Popes . . . and for the Landrys too, come to think of it!*

". . . and, John and I followed that tradition. Neither of our parents nurtured any hopes for us to have a life filled with successes, achievements, and joy.

"For the most part, our parents were two peas in a pod, too. I think by sixteen they'd already seen every bad thing life could offer. If there was a real difference between them, it was that my mom stayed extremely close to the Catholic Church while my father held an iron-strong belief that the world had crapped on him." Paul paused and smiled. Breaux ignored the attempt at humor and said nothing.

"That latter conclusion probably took root in grade school, and it blossomed when Pop's Natchitoches High School science teacher flunked him. My ole man was hopeless in nearly all subjects including general science. But *physical* science, especially astronomy and the study of the moon, the sun, the planets, the stars – (*in fact*, the whole solar system) he loved it! Astronomy was one of two subjects for which he showed good aptitude in and a fair amount of enthusiasm for."

Even more so than for nights on Main Street with the guys and a trunk full of ice-cold Dixies, Paul thought to himself.

"But even that ended. When Pop got an *F* in Science, he gave up any attempt to climb out and away from what he'd believed was his destiny as an astronomer or an inventor, and I guess he committed to a life of *poverty and alcoholism*. At least, that was my mom's opinion. Her view was that Pop was book-smart but life-dumb. I learned that from her after Pop just disappeared from our lives one night when John and I were eleven or twelve."

"Tell me about your brother John," interrupted Breaux.

"I will. I will. Give me a moment. Let me finish with my mom first."

Breaux seemed to realize that he'd lost control of the interview but nevertheless allowed Paul to drive on.

"Mom, who'd been born and raised across the river

In Better Times

in Algiers, and who'd been sent to her aunt's home in Natchitoches by *her* mother to escape our horrid school system (Well, I guess some things never change, do they?). She dropped out of Natchitoches High School for the man she loved, John Randall Pope.

And, the father of her child-to-be. Make that children-to-be.

"With twins on the way as almost their only wedding presents, Mom didn't have to try very hard to convince Pop to move us to her parents' shotgun house in the Ninth Ward, and perhaps more importantly, where she could give birth in a real hospital. Back then, *Nack-a dish* didn't even have a medical facility with a birthing option. You had to go to Alex . . . at least an hour away for that sort of thing. As you can imagine, twins require a lot of help. I think they also made the move to the Ninth Ward at the time because she could count on getting a little help there from her mother. Pop's mom had died giving birth to him so there was no Mee Maw Pope to get help from.

"It was here, then, in the Big Easy that my father, hoping to support his growing family . . . and without a high school diploma or even a GED . . . found work at a number of entry-level jobs. By the three-month mark of each though, especially the last one at the Falstaff brewery, he succumbed to the temptations of golden liquid libations to wrap up his days of manual labor, 100% humidity, and 90-degree temperatures. My mom had watched *her* father plow this same field, so she accepted Pop's choices with little comment . . . and probably committed herself to a future like *her* own mom . . . in other words, carrying on as best she was able with little or no help from a husband. Life was tough for us Popes."

Paul paused and asked, "Hey, Mr. Breaux . . . Albert . . . Is this the kinda' stuff you're lookin' for?"

Breaux frumped up the corners of his mouth and replied, "Yeah. Exactly. I'll take out some of the gritty stuff to make you look better, but I need the background for context. Don't forget your promise to tell me about your brother. If we have to, maybe we can meet again here at your office?

"And, hey, uhh, I'm a big basketball fan," said Breaux. "At some point, whether it's relevant to your story or not, you gotta tell me about this display, here . . ."

"Display?"

"Yeah! The Maravich jersey and the two autographed basketballs. Never seen a Maravich one from LSU before! It'll make a good background and, it's a photo waiting to be taken!"

After a swig of water, Paul took a deep breath and said, "Yeah, okay. I will. Now, where were we?"

V

POST TIME

"Despite challenges," continued Paul, as Breaux scribbled notes that to Paul's eyes appeared completely illegible, "... you know, generational poverty, alcoholism, absence of culture, and on and on ... my parents managed to hold things together fairly well for nearly a decade. Us boys, if you haven't guessed already, were named after that Pope who was crowned on our birthday, John Paul II."

"Yeah, yeah, responded Breaux, "that's probably gonna be the headline."

"Well, neither our mom nor our Dad really knew how to parent us because *their* parents had done a lousy job of raising *them*. How could they know how to bring us up anyway?

Our education wasn't school, it was real life. In fact, you really could call it *Life in the Ninth Ward*. How's that for an original title? It was there that we *lived* what was actually happening. We were forced to accept everything, right or wrong, good or bad. *You* might see it as the *only* thing to do and then move on, but to us, it was the way things were *supposed* to be. We grew up quickly. Even at six or seven, we were carrying on conversations with our parents, our teachers, and ... everybody ... as if we were their friends or neighbors ... not their children.

"My father refused to acknowledge that he wasn't as educated as other folks, or at least he didn't act like it. He just thought he'd been unlucky, or maybe even jinxed. From experience he didn't trust schools to provide a worthwhile education anyway, so he took it on himself to educate *us* ... so that we would, like he had ... excel at life. Right!

"From his minimal schooling my father – he preferred us to call him Pop – didn't read much. I don't think he liked books in fact. Bizarrely though, he was deeply impacted by his high school English teacher's reading of Ray Bradbury's short story, *A Sound of Thunder*. Maybe it was because he enjoyed looking at the stars and planets.

"I'm pretty sure a high school philosophy course would have captured his attention too 'cause he often talked a good line about philosophy. But remember, his short go at a formal education was at a rural Louisiana high school, and the only philosophy available there came from street corner conversations or, if he was lucky, a one-day study of famous Greek figures. Still, Pop worked to instill into both of us favorite sayings of his that he learned from *his* father, including – and chief among them – *Keep Doing It Until You Do It Right!*

"We heard that one every day of our lives! I'll never forget it. Matter of fact, I've got it hanging over my desk, see?" Paul pointed behind him to a wooden plaque hanging on the wall with the same phrase burned into it. "That plaque belonged to my father . . . made it himself in Wood Shop. Another thing he was fond of saying to us – I think to show us how intelligent he was – was, '*Boys, never forget what William Shakespeare said, Make use of time, let not advantage slip!*'

Wow, I can't believe I can still remember that one! Another one that he first began using, came about around the time he was hangin' out with an old crazy guy who claimed to be a real scientist who lived near us. *'Got that? Got that?'* He'd ask us that every time he forced us to memorize one of his favorite quotes. *Got that, Breaux?*

"And he'd trip over the last few words of any Shakespeare he ever tried to quote, mostly due, I think, to having downed a few too many ice-cold Dixies before he tried to teach us something. Havin' a beer under his belt . . . or two probably . . . turned him into a teacher!"

To Breaux, Paul Pope seemed to drift back in time for a moment, recalling the power of his father. Breaux thought it was a good moment and he added it to his notes about the man.

"We once asked him what the quote about *not letting* advantage *slip* really meant, but if I recall correctly his explanation was a bit cloudy. All he said was, 'It's not so much about letting advantage slip as it is about managing time.'"

"Do you have a name?" asked Breaux.

"Huh?"

"The scientist. There might be a local connection here I can talk to for background."

"Oh. Yeah. He was, uh . . . Let's see, uh. His name was, uh . . . Doc, uh . . . Doc . . . *Doctor Anderson*! David, I think. David Anderson. My father always called him, Doc. Anyway, *Doc* . . ."

Breaux interrupted again. "With what facility or university was he affiliated?"

"Oh, hell, I don't know. I'm lucky to even remember his name. He wasn't around that long and then one day he just . . . vanished."

"Okay. Continue, please."

"Yeah, he just disappeared. Well, Doc and my father

were working on some experiments in Doc's garage. Pop called it a *Time Control Machine*, or something. I think they were mostly drinking beer. Anyway, about that time, Pop was lecturing us a lot about time loops."

"Time loops?"

"Yeah, like when you're doing something, and all of a sudden you go back in time to some event in your life and start all over again. Sorta' like getting a second chance to get it right."

"That happened?" asked Breaux There was a look of pure incredulity and cynicism in his eyes.

After a few seconds of non-response, Breaux spoke up, "Mr. Pope. To be honest, that sounds like a whole 'nother conversation. What I'm looking for here is mostly about you, and to a lesser degree, about your brother and your mom and dad. I'm probably not looking for some guy who was just a beer-drinkin' buddy of your dad's. What I'm looking for really is what happened to make you what you are today. Okay?"

"Yeah. Right. Okay.

"The other subject that caught Pop's attention, *philosophy*, wasn't a required course at Natchitoches High School, and his school counselor who was more knowledgeable about Pop's background perhaps than his potential, enrolled him in wood shop when he was a freshman . . . and, truth be told, Pop learned some pretty good skills there. Maybe the counselor knew better than he did what his talents were.

"He didn't pay much attention to math in grade school,

In Better Times

but even as a freshman in high school, the counselor was pushing careers at him. For my dad, high school math was light years above him. School wasn't something he'd been encouraged by his parents to enjoy anyway, so he lived down to some pretty low expectations."

The recorder made a stuttering clicking sound and Albert Breaux held up his hand to put Paul on *pause* while he replaced the old cassette with a fresh one. He pushed the *Record* and *Play* buttons again and said, "Paul Pope, Tape Number Two. Go ahead, Mr. Pope. It's recording again. Remember, we want more information about you than about your dad."

"Okay. Okay. I'll wrap this part up but it all relates to who I am today. My father once tried to land a spot on the NHS Wrestling Team, but he met with disappointment pretty quickly there too because strength and coordination were totally foreign to him. He considered football briefly but, as with wrestling, Pop left the team early, settling I guess, for his highest-scoring after-school activity: a round of pool and a beer with the guys at *On the Q* in downtown Natchitoches."

"On the Q?"

"Yeah. It was a pool hall. Still, is. I think though he always felt a responsibility when we were kids to help us improve. Always! *At least, while he was around.*

"And, truth be told, John and I actually helped *him* understand elementary school science and philosophy. We'd throw a question to him about science and, if he didn't know the answer, which was most of the time, he was bright enough to want to know the answer."

"Mr. Pope. Please, let's move on from your father. Tell me more about your mom."

"I'm not finished with my father yet but, okay..."

I'll make sure I get a chance to come back to the son of bitch later, Paul thought.

"... Their marriage was a rocky one and my mom often stole away with us boys to visit *her* mother. She'd lean on Mee Maw Landry for sympathy and advice. Mee Maw's responses were almost always taken straight from the Book of Psalms but my mom took 'em all to heart. The Mass and its mysteries offered her a better life anyway than the one my father was giving her, especially because it predicted *eternal* happiness.

"Pop fought back, arguing that everything she learned in the scriptures was wrong. He attacked *her* religion with *his* science. As the years passed, Mom began to get really confrontational when Pop pushed science."

"Your mother, please, Mr. Pope. Your mother."

"Yeah, sure. Sorry 'bout that.

"There was no good time for twins to arrive in the home of a couple already barely surviving in the Ninth Ward – as desperate a place then as it is today. Even when we were six or seven, the burden of caring for two babies, mostly alone, strained the few threads that bound her to him. Mom's religious beliefs spoke harshly about divorce or spousal abandonment and so she made certain the two of them stayed together... even if it meant an occasional black eye or two... and on more than one occasion, a trip to the Charity Hospital Emergency Room.

"Often though, my mom called on Mee Maw for help and *she* was the one who watched over us. Mom took on cleaning jobs in the low-end hotels and motels at the edge of the Ninth Ward. She once thought she'd made it big when the Lagniappe hired her. That lasted about a week if I recall correctly.

"I know you want me to talk about my mom, but are you wondering why my father stuck around?"

Paul picked up before Breaux had a chance to respond.

"He wasn't ever gonna leave. As far as Pop was concerned, their marriage could, should, and would always hold intact. As much as he pitied and abused her, Mom was really the only good thing that had *ever* happened to him in his whole life and he wasn't about to let her get away . . . even if she might have wanted to."

Breaux interrupted Paul again and said, "We're closing in on an hour already, Mr. Pope, and we've still got a lot of ground to cover. What say we give it another 15 minutes and then either decide we're done or schedule another session?"

"Okay, but I think we're getting' there, Albert. I'll move on to the toughest part." He paused for a few seconds and then began again.

"John and I were tested early on in school, and we showed reasonably good IQs. Frankly, that was because we'd inherited them. But just like our parents' early lives, John's and my windows to the world were at ground level, mud-spattered, and never really open to fresh air. For us, life was *the present* and that meant scrabbling with our buddies to see who was king of the trash pile . . . not who stood at the top of the Honor Roll. In scrapes, fights, and other encounters . . . even in high school . . . we learned to be independent and to not even pretend there might be education for us after age 16. Why break tradition, right?

"But all that was to end even sooner than anyone expected. One day when we were about ten or twelve, Pop died in a fall from a French Quarter hotel. My mom's death came not long after, although hers was because of lung cancer, probably triggered by second-hand smoke from my father's smoking.

As identical twins, we had many similar interests, and sharing DNA, we stayed close even after being orphaned. Our grandparents had passed on by then too. Worried that we'd get separated by the foster home cops, we never told our school about Pop's suicide or our mom dying of *the Lung*. After a while, when school counselor questions about our home life got a little too personal, we just quit going and hid when the truancy cops knocked on the door.

"A couple of times they came close, but we'd already decided we'd be better off on our own than in foster homes. But because they kept comin' after us, we finally decided to find some other place to live. It didn't take long 'cause there's lots of abandoned homes in this town, especially in the Ninth Ward. For a long time, we *exercised Squatter's Rights,* I guess you could say, over a tumbled-down shack of a home, not in the Ninth, but up on Rue Waterloo, about half a block off Canal in the Mid-City area. But the truant cops were everywhere.

"To keep from being picked up, we became nocturnal. It was the kind of neighborhood anyway where neighbors would choose not to report two young kids living alone in a run-down home with no electricity or running water for fear of drawing attention to their own sad state of affairs.

"I think I gradually ascended to the role of the Alpha Male and, most times, John didn't take kindly to it. Leadership by one identical twin over another is just one of *many* areas in which we seemed to find a reason to disagree . . . and argue . . . and shout . . . and fight.

"By 15, our squabbling became pretty constant and we hit a tipping point. At first, we just became more distant from one another. Then we fought – *really fought*. One day I nagged John about his smoking habit. You see, I blamed Mom's passing on Pop's bad habits and smoking was his worst, even worse than being drunk ninety percent of the time.

Our split came not long after. I'm afraid I caused it. One warm night during Mardi Gras – *I'm ashamed to admit this here but* – I mugged a drunk on Bourbon Street and John got arrested for it. Twins, you know. The guy looked at a lineup and said, literally pointing, "That's him! That's the little bastard that hit me!"

Paul noticed Breaux scribbling fiercely.

"Hey, you can't use that stuff about the mugging, okay? That was a long time ago . . . and it won't help your *Three Under Thirty* stuff either, or your relationship with your boss. Remember, I know him pretty well."

Breaux looked up; eyebrows raised. "Really?"

"Really. So, I got away with the mugging and John spent a month in Juvie for it. When he was released, the Child and Family cops tried to put him in a foster home but he ran away the first night.

"One morning about two a.m., I came back to our Mid-City shack and found him there pouting and standing in a boxing pose. That night we fought over my failure to pay for *my* crime and a bunch of other stuff. I thought I might lose him for good then. We had a knock down drag out . . . and John lost.

"Sulking after getting beaten like he usually did, John took his black eye and his cratered self-esteem and moved in with a friend, a tough kid named Cleon. Cleon and I had run together for a while but we'd fallen out. He was two years older than us and living in a similar housing situation, but he was still back in the Ninth Ward. Cleon had a girlfriend named Cyndy, and, while she was from the Quarter – her parents owned a business of some kind – she wanted out of Naw'lins and kept pushing Cleon to take her out west.

"John later told me that a month after our final fight, Cleon stole a black 84' Firebird with painted flames trailing from both front-wheel wells – *it had Mississippi plates, if I recollect* – and picked up Cyndy and him and they split to Lafayette for jobs, drugs, booze, and fun at the Cajun and Roughneck bars over there. Whether John was involved in the theft of the car, he never said, but he sure went along for the ride. During their three-hour drive, he later told me, he listened to Cleon's travel stories. John began to realize, for perhaps the first time ever, that there was an entire world out there waiting to be explored.

"Cyndy loved Cher, you know, Cher - *the singer* . . . and wanted her life. Said she was a Hippie wanna-be just like Cher. I think John liked Cyndy for himself and he told her he was curious about the 70s too. 'I thought that whole hippie thing was dead', he told me.

"'Pretty much, yeah', she'd replied, 'but accordin' to my cousin, there's still a bunch of hard-core communes up in the mountains.'

"I've got an older cousin who got dealt a low lottery number back when we had the draft and one day he just flat out disappeared. No one claimed to know where he'd gone . . . but no one seemed too worried about him either. I never even met him then, but he showed up at our place about a year after John left, wearing a headband and a full-length tie-dyed robe. Weird, huh? I talked to him a little. He said he'd been hiding out, avoidin' the draft in one of them communes up in the mountains, and that was even after the hippie movement started falling apart because of the war ending.

"Back to Cyndy and John for a second . . . While they were on the road, Cyndy told John, 'there are still hundreds of communes makin' a go of it in Oregon, New Mexico, back in the hills in California, and especially in Colorado.'

"Just past Baton Rouge, as they crossed the 22-mile bridge over the Atchafalaya Basin, John decided that he'd been missing a lot in his life. After listening to Cyndy, he decided he was gonna set out to see as much of the world as he could, and stayin' for a while in a commune looked like a good way to start. That night in Lafayette, the three of them partied hard. But the next morning when they woke up, Cleon and the Firebird were gone . . . Cleon had flat out disappeared.

"While waiting around for him to come back, John and Cyndy talked again about the hippie life and, when Cleon still didn't show up, they started hitch-hiking up I-49. They were halfway up 49 – I'd guess probably near Alex and heading for Denver when Cleon got pulled over back near Baton Rouge by the State Cops driving that stolen Firebird. He'd been on his way back to the Easy.

"I heard about it later and that's when I learned John was in on it. Anyway, Cleon got busted for car theft and ended up back in New Orleans anyway thanks to the State Cops. Because he was 18 and older than Cyndy and John, he got sent away to the men's prison just south of Baton Rouge. Haven't heard anything of him since.

"Anyway, at the time, I was still back in our shotgun in New Orleans and was the loneliest I'd ever been. I'd never been without my parents or my brother in my entire life. I really missed John. I was so used to running around with my . . . *doppelgänger* . . . *I think that's what they call them* . . . on a twenty-four-hour basis that I didn't know what to do. Time dragged. Of course, that also meant I had more of it to get into trouble.

"I'm not proud to say that my less-than-legal activities moved more from Petty, to *Grand* theft. It gives me no great pleasure to say that I also discovered I had a natural talent for con games. You can't write about that neither. By the way, Mr. Breaux, can I interest you in a nice fishing camp in Breaux Bridge at a real good price?"

"Nice try Mr. Pope, but no thank you. What happened to Paul out west?"

"Okay. You're going to hear about a pretty wild life, but I think John's arrival in Colorado and his first couple of months there were fairly laid back and gave him some time to mature . . . or maybe it was the drugs. I don't know. He and Cyndy joined a commune in the mountains north of Crested Butte and he let his hair grow. He told me he recalled growing a nice prophet's beard – don't know if I mentioned it or not, but John came back from the mountains with memory problems – probably from bad drugs.

"But, back to the story. When they got to Colorado, both of them found others of like mind, and *friendship-with-benefits* became sort of a way of life. Can you imagine that?

"It wasn't all love and warmth though. Colorado winters were hard. Used to our mild winters here, John and Cyndy just weren't ready for temperatures in the single digits, winds gustin' to 50 miles per hour in blizzards, and overnight snowfalls measured in feet instead of the number of snowflakes.

"About two years after they left, a friend of mine who'd tried the hippie life for a while ran across John in a different commune somewhere near Montrose or

Durango. He said John was wearing Huarache Sandals and a multicolored tie-dye shirt under a not-very-clean white floor-length robe. The story I heard from my friend was that underneath that robe, there was . . . nothing! Whew!

"John'd taken to calling himself, Jesus – pronouncing it like the Spanish do, *Hay'-sue* – and seemed to always walk slowly . . . always in clockwise circles . . . around the commune with his hands folded in front of him chanting the Hare Krishna. Must have been on some really strong stuff! He needed a haircut and by then had a long scraggly black and grey beard going. Didn't smell too good either, I was told by my friend.

"After John came back to me a few years later, he said that growing up in our sub-tropical climate here with no AC was pretty tough but that weeks of blizzards with zero degrees-and-below temperatures on a mountain top were far worse. You can see, can't you, the end of his adventure wasn't far off.

"After three-and-a-half years . . . now wearing bib overalls, a flannel shirt, and a cowboy hat, Brother John figured it was time to end his western vacation and leave the commune life behind. It didn't hurt at the time that he had no job, had lost both Cyndy and 40 pounds, and was crashing in a small, abandoned church in a ghost town somewhere up on top of a mountain in the Rockies.

"As that third winter raked the Colorado mountains, even into April, John's Cajun blood and a craving for jambalaya pushed him to head home. Carrying a small suitcase holding his few possessions, he hopped a freight in Gunnison and aimed for the Big Easy.

"Over his three years there, he'd weathered, matured and, I think, maybe even grown up a little. When his freight train began to pass the Montrose stockyards though, John had second thoughts and almost jumped the train. Despite his Cajun blood, the communal existence, coupled with the beauty of the Rockies – *in the summer that is* – still held his spirit hard. In the end, though, he never got off that southbound freight. It was the end of April and still winter in Colorado. As his train picked up speed, he told me he finally realized it was time to head back to 100 percent humidity and the only real family he'd ever known . . . me."

"That's gonna have to do it, for now, Mr. Pope. I've got a deadline to meet," Breaux said as he shut the recorder down. "How 'bout tomorrow at three, here in your office? We'll finish this then. Will that work for you?"

"Oh, yeah! You wanted me to tell you about John so, I've got more. . . much more."

VI

THE REUNION
MORNING, APRIL 10ᵀᴴ – NEW ORLEANS
DOWNTOWN FREIGHT YARDS

Finally, back in the *Easy*, a fully bearded John Pope gingerly climbed down from an empty freight car. His arm was in a sling. A badly stained bandage was wrapped around his head and part of his face. Another large bandage showed around his upper chest, appearing whenever his shirt flapped open. John hurt all over. Life had been tough again for the Popes . . . at least for him.

This time it had happened just as his freight pulled into the Fort Worth rail yards on the trip back from Montrose and Gunnison. John had been robbed, stabbed, and beaten by two fellow *transients* who were after his suitcase. Expecting no one to open the boxcar for weeks, they'd slid the door closed and left John locked in to die.

But every railroad car has a purpose and on the same morning John's arrived in Cowtown, it was routed two hours later to a siding owned by a lawn mower manufacturer in South Fort Worth. It was empty save for a severely injured John Pope. The boxcar was opened upon arrival and John was found unconscious, bleeding, and barely breathing. He was rushed to John Peter Smith Hospital, X-rayed, operated on, dosed up, bandaged, and admitted, two heartbeats short of *Condition Critical.*

John had no money or identification and because he didn't appear to be mentally acute, the well-known charity hospital kept him overnight for observation. Two days later, still heavily bandaged, John was fragilely mobile and breathing shallowly. Most importantly, he was intensely desirous of moving on. At his own insistence – actually ranting to be released, which they did after he signed proper papers. Had the hospital had sufficient beds, John would never have been released, but he wanted out. He promised never to sue and signed another paper to that effect, this one in the presence of a notary. He was released and, truth be told, the hospital wanted him gone. A team of sanitation employees quickly descended on his room. Nevertheless, it was still held patient-less for three days to help get rid of the lingering odor.

John had been fed real food for several days, so he ended up leaving the hospital in better shape than when he'd first arrived . . . healthier, in fact, even than when he'd boarded the freight back in Gunnison. As a testament to his durability, John's still emaciated frame was now five pounds heavier than when he'd been admitted.

Having never before been to Fort Worth, John had no clue where John Peter Smith Hospital was in the city. However, from his hospital room, he'd been kept awake by sounds of train couplings, air horns, and other rail yard noises. He knew transportation was nearby and available. That was instinctual though for he'd lost his memory. John didn't know who he was. Worse, his life had been saved in a city he'd never been to before. No one there knew him.

He had no recollection of any past life and the only thing motivating him was a driving desire to get to New Orleans. Perhaps there he might recover his memory and identity.

Within an hour of his release from Peter Smith, the man with no name crawled into an empty container car that he suspected might be heading east based on some freshly applied instructions affixed to the side of the car. His only cogent thought at the moment though was that he needed to get to the Crescent City as quickly as possible. The weather was cool in Cowtown but a vision of palm trees and warmer temperatures in New Orleans drove him forward.

Still, the man once known as John Pope wondered to himself, *Am I heading in the right direction?* Fortunately for him, at a stop well past New Orleans – Mobile, actually – he was befriended by a fellow homeless railroad enthusiast. The stranger recognized John's confusion, for many of his friends who traveled the rails shared similar symptoms. He steered him to another empty freight car in the Mobile rail yard, this one heading west and *back* to New Orleans.

Arriving in the Big Easy before dawn, John managed to avoid yard cops and began walking in the general direction of the Superdome. Since his beating, John's memories occasionally surprised him but they were at best inconsistent. He certainly wasn't thinking with clarity, but he recognized the skyline of New Orleans as a place he was certain he needed to be. Arriving at the Superdome, John couldn't decide what to do next. After wandering around the French Quarter for several hours, on a whim he began hiking out of the CBD, randomly choosing a direction. His internal GPS hadn't suffered a concussion and it helped him make the correct choice.

By early afternoon he turned down a street called Rue Waterloo and stopped in front of a ramshackle shotgun home that looked vaguely familiar. John didn't know it at the time, but it was the same old house he'd shared with Paul three-plus years earlier. While the dilapidated structure looked familiar, John still didn't recognize it as his old home. Because nothing had been done to improve the shotgun's squalor over the past three or four years, the building was in worse shape than it had ever been.

Sleeping on a porch swing supported by three rusty chains was a man about his age. "Hey, mister," John called out, "can you tell me where I am? I think I'm lost."

It had been a late and alcoholic night for Paul Pope. Waking with an intense hangover at the sound of a man calling him out, Paul did a bleary-eyed double-take, nearly falling from the precarious swing. He stared back at a man who now was stooping over him. The man's arm was in a sling, he had a full scraggly, and mostly grey beard, and he sported a healing black eye. The stooping stranger appeared to have been injured in a serious accident that had also left a long scar across his forehead. He wore a crumpled cowboy hat along with dirty, wrinkled, and bloody bib overalls. Despite all this, there was something familiar about him. Paul paused as images flashed through his aching head like a mechanized police lineup.

Buzzers finally went off in his hungover brain and he asked, "John? Is that you? Holy jambalaya! Good to see you, man! You look like shit!"

Within an hour, Paul and his long-lost twin were singing, "We're back in the saddle again!" To anyone watching the reunion, it was obvious that Paul had missed his prodigal brother who had now returned, seeking forgiveness. Paul couldn't wait to catch up.

VII

For John, a return to somewhat familiar territory provided the healing environment he needed. Within a few days, even his memory began improving. Nevertheless, anything before the previous month remained a murky mystery. As best he could recall, he filled Paul in on the mugging he'd taken in Fort Worth and told him how he'd traveled there from a place called Gunnison, which could only mean Colorado. His head was filled with massive memory gaps though. But, like a fog lifting on a cool damp morning, the past was slowly becoming a bit clearer day by day.

At one point, John lit up a cigarette he found on a sidewalk and lit it. Paul instantly castigated him for still having the habit. "Gonna kill you some day, John," said Paul, "just like it did Mom."

Because Brother Paul's life was filled with booze, John began riding the same bottle. One morning a few days after their reunion, the boys' hangovers were interrupted by neighbors assembling on the street in front of their shotgun. One man waved an American flag and was discussing a bombing in Oklahoma City that had taken off the front half of the Murrah Center, a federal office building housing a myriad of government agencies including a Day Care Center. Many people died in the explosion including children. Worse, many adults and kids were still among the missing. The death toll might end up in the hundreds before all was said and done. Television newspersons quickly claimed that it was one of the worst terrorist acts in the history of the country.

It was too overwhelming for Paul though. He became bored by the news because of the return of his twin brother. He'd become unrelentingly anxious to explore John's faulty memory to learn everything he could about John's exciting adventures in the communes of Colorado and the women he'd met along the way.

In the days that followed, the news coming out of Oklahoma continued to retard John's mental rehab. The two young men stood in the middle of the street for the daily meeting of twenty or so outraged neighbors. Finally, Paul herded John back toward the old Shotgun. Leaving the neighbors on the street, Paul said, "Okay John, so, tell me 'bout them hippie women again . . ."

Over the next few weeks, the brothers fell into an old routine following in the steps of their father in his fondness for alcohol and disdain for employment. They both owned minor criminal records before John had taken his Colorado sabbatical. Now that they'd reunited, the two returned to petty thievery and rabble-rousing with a gusto. Within a month, NOLA PD knocked on their battered front door and, while not arresting them, warned the twins that the paths they were headed down would ultimately lead to Angola, the big death-sentence prison north of Baton Rouge famously known as *Home of the Green Mile*.

With his brother's return, Paul quickly reverted to his role as the Alpha Male. He led John on food and drink runs in the French Quarter . . . begging for handouts on street corners, rummaging for food scraps in trash containers in front of Bourbon Street bars in the small hours of the morning, committing small acts of burglary, and pickpocketing tourists in the Quarter, or when the Carnival season was on, the especially lucrative Mardi Gras parade routes.

It was February 20th, not quite a year after John's return to Rue Waterloo. It was Fat Tuesday or Mardi Gras Day. The boys were working *Rex*, the parade that features the *King of Carnival*. Within an hour they'd *fingered* the pockets of so many inebriated parade watchers that they were forced to hunt for a black plastic trash bag in which to carry their haul. They finally stole one from an empty city trash basket and headed back to the shotgun with their haul.

"Next time," they promised each other, "we'll *each* pack a pillowcase for that purpose." In addition to the wallets and purses they'd claimed, they'd also thrown and caught enough beads to float a float on the Mississippi.

"Hey John, in your commune, where'd you find the beads to get girls to lift their tops?" asked Paul.

"Didn't need 'em," replied John with a little look of satisfaction.

It was a repressed memory that had suddenly popped into his head. John smiled at the unexpected flashback.

In terms of popularity, *Rex* was sometimes considered the *Santa Claus Parade* for Mardi Gras, because its star, Bacchus, the King of Carnival, made his appearance on the very last float in the parade. That day, John and Paul stationed themselves near the parade's end where crowds would be the largest, and where, because of congestion, the floats usually slowed to a crawl. While beads flew, and booze flowed, the brothers made off with the King's mask when it was set aside for a libation break by its celebrity owner. When the twins arrived home and poured out their booty, they found enough cash and credit cards to live on for months. John put on the Bacchus mask and danced around their living room throwing beads and announcing, "I am the Monarch of Mardi Gras!"

The huge haul of Mardi Gras cash and pawnable booty eventually ran out. Still, even when it became tough to come by, the twins still managed to find enough cash for beer and liquor.

Inconsistent memory lapses though continued to plague John even a year after his return from Colorado. He found that the *blackouts,* which typically came and went and lasted six or seven hours, were frequently lasting longer. Paul wondered if the amnesia that still affected John was occasionally causing him to hallucinate. At other times he wondered whether John was perhaps suffering from Early Onset Dementia.

"You need to watch your drinking an' smokin', Bro! Somethin's goin' on wit' your brain!"

Like his father before him, Paul imagined himself to be the smartest person in any group of at least two. One rainy day, given his brother's unpredictable memory, Paul lectured him on Pope Family History.

"I know you probably forgot this, Johnny . . . or never heard it before . . . but life has been tough for us Popes."

John groaned. Amnesia or not, he'd heard these same stories *too* many times already. At times he wondered if *Paul* was the one suffering from senility because he never seemed to recall that he'd given the same *family history lecture* many times before. Nevertheless, as the more laid back of the two, he allowed Paul to steer these conversations.

"Mom didn't work and Pop either couldn't keep . . . or more likely, didn't want . . . a job. But he *was* a proud one, wasn't he, John? Remember how he told us over and over that he was the smartest person in our family . . . that Mom had a low IQ, but *he* had a big one. Because we'd inherited *his* smarts, us boys would probably do okay in life. He said we might not be as intelligent as he was, but we were smarter than Mom. One thing I never could figure out though was how that could be if he and mom were the same age . . . and yet, Mom was two grades ahead of Pop when they dropped outta' high school? That probably had a lot to do with the booze though. The ole man sure loved his hooch!"

They both laughed at the recollection, John wondering privately if this was true or not.

More seriously, Paul moved on, "You'd think though, that as a dropout Pop might take it easy on us, but he'd ask us questions all the time! If I think about it, it was about then that Pop began to spend a lot of time with that old neighbor, *Doc . . . ahem . . . Doctor* Anderson." Paul made a *La De Dah* face at the title, *Doctor* as if no college would ever think of awarding the man that title.

"Who was he again?" asked John because he liked this part of the story.

"He was that scientist guy who lived a block over. Pop'd come back from a session with the Doc, and he'd be really hopped up. He'd quiz us on science and philosophy. Pop always said those were his two favorite subjects. Some of his questions though were ones he couldn't figure out the answers to, and he'd ask us over and over, like 'Is time travel possible?' . . ."

John: "Where does space end?"

Paul: "Is perpetual motion possible?"

John: "When did time begin?"

Paul: "Will man ever be able to travel at the speed of light?"

John: "Is there such a thing as fate?"

Paul: "Live! Die! Repeat!"

John: "Can you make something outta' nothing?"

Paul: "Hey man! Your memory ain't so bad after all! We heard those things over and over when we was kids and they never seemed to end. God, did we ever get sick of 'em!"

John thought that likewise, Paul's history lessons would *never* end. He was beyond bored by the same lectures he'd received several times just in the past month. He'd even considered getting away again. Colorado popped into his mind. *I love Colorado!* Still, he nodded in acquiescence to help Paul believe he was paying full attention.

The next day Paul lectured, "There was a time before

Doc Anderson left when Pop really started pushing Mom's buttons whenever he got the chance. He'd tease her by asking *us* questions like, 'Can you make something from nothing?'

"Mom had heard his not-so-subtle criticism of the biblical creation one too many times before and she knew where this conversation was going. 'Of course, you can, silly!' she cut in. 'Boys, God says in John, Chapter One: *Through him all things were made; without him* nothing *was made that* has *been made today.*'"

That resurrected an old memory for John. "Remember this one, Paul? 'Persistence. Persistence. Persistence!' Pop'd say that to us at least once a day. And also, 'You just keep doin' it 'til you get it right! Persistence!'"

For hours on end, Paul worked to help John recall *The Philosophy of John Randall Pope*.

"Remember when Pop and Doc had a falling out and he lectured us on how it was impossible to travel back and forth in time. Mom actually sided with the Doc that time. She told him that God lived forever and so He was able to move in and out of time.

"Pop threw a fit. 'It just ain't possible, Martha,' he said. 'Think about it. Let's say you go back in time exactly a year . . . *to the second*. You press a button or something, and you're gone. You've dropped back exactly a year. But guess what! There ain't no '*here*' to go to! You see, that's because exactly a year ago, the earth was half a million miles behind where it is in its orbit today. It's why we have one extra day every four years in a Leap Year. So, if you just pressed a button and went back exactly a year, you'd just reappear out in the middle of space lookin' at ole Mother Earth a few thousand miles away! And that doesn't even count the fact that our whole solar system, including the earth's orbit, is always movin' at hundreds of miles per hour headin' someplace else in the cosmos. Time travel just ain't a realistic option for just that reason, boys. Period! End of sentence.'"

John laughed to be polite, but the quasi-lecture was becoming old news to him.

Paul continued with little pause: "Mom'd open her mouth to respond, but he'd cut her off and say, 'And, don't forget about the Butterfly Effect too, Marty! A scientist named Bradbury wrote about it in a treatise called, *A Sound of Thunder*. It's a scholarly book, I'll tell *you!*'

"That's the only time I ever recall Pop admitting to having read an entire book all by himself.

Paul kept going, "Remember when we were about eleven? He lectured us all day several times. Some days it would be about parallel universes, but mostly it was about goin' back in time. 'The whole point of this,' he'd say, 'is that if you *could* go back and did so – say a million years – you'd undoubtedly mess up somethin' . . . say kill a butterfly . . . even accidentally. That bug wouldn't spin no cocoons anymore and the loss of that one butterfly would kill off all its next generations. Eventually, the loss of that one bug millions of years ago would have an impact leading to chaos in our time. Heck, you probably wouldn't even be here today if some joker'd gone back in time and killed a butterfly a million years ago! *A butterfly!*

"'*That* butterfly,' he'd say. 'Boys . . . that's the *real* butterfly in the room!'*

"Mom rolled her eyes at his explanations and then frowned every time. She shook her finger at him. 'Don't you dare teach our boys that nonsense!' She'd pause for a moment and then cut to the chase – no pun intended – warning him, 'If you do, I'll hack it off!'"

They both laughed at a memory that appeared fresh in John's amnesiac mind. Still, John thought to himself, *I don't know if I can take much more of this . . . but it is working! My memory is coming back . . . I think.*

"Pop knew when he'd better back it down an' replied, 'Calm down Marty,'" said Paul, speaking as his father, " 'I didn't mean nothing. It was just science for cryin' out loud.' And then he went out back where he stashed his booze, swearing at Mom for her ignorance, and for his poor choice in selecting a wife unequal to himself in IQ. I think that was the time he got skunk drunk, he did. It was also the night that they had that big fight. It woke me up, it was so loud. I got up and saw Mom trying to stop her nose from bleeding, an' she had a black eye too! I got so mad at the old man. He was out back looking for his hooch. I grabbed a butcher knife off the counter an' went after him. I wanted to kill 'im, I did."

"What happened?" John was being polite, for he'd heard parts of this story more than a few times.

Paul paused for a few seconds, trying to catch his breath. His eyes were watering. He was in distress over something that had happened on that night long ago. When he was breathing better, he started talking again where he'd left off, "An' I would have, too, but he took it away from me!"

Paul paused again and it took a full minute this time before he regained his composure. When he finally continued, he seemed to have won an argument with himself. "The next day," he said, "they found Pop's body in an alley at the bottom of the old Lagniappe Hotel . . . left us all behind and kicked off on us!" He swallowed and then looked up at John with a satisfied frown on his face.

"After Pop committed suicide, Mom moved us to Algiers so's we'd be close to Mee Maw. That's when she took her first full-time job ever. It got tougher for us then . . . an' especially for her. She'd put us up with Mee Maw so she could work, and so we all could get by. Some weeks she'd work at three different Seven-Elevens . . . all of 'em in the Ninth Ward, too – toughest neighborhood in Naw'lins it is. She got robbed a couple times too. It's a wonder she never got shot."

VIII

Near the second anniversary of his return from Colorado, John concluded that he could pretty much . . . *generally* . . . get along with his brother . . . *almost* . . . every day. At least for a while. The arguments they had just weren't serious enough to cause another three-year rift. Paul remained the more antagonistic of the two, but

John compensated for it by trying hard to be easygoing. And so, in some ways, their personalities meshed.

As Paul sometimes said, "We're like two jigsaw puzzle pieces."

John called it, "My Ying for your Yang."

When he would say that, Paul would look at him as if he were crazy.

While he hid it from Paul, John believed his time in the commune had helped him become more enlightened, wiser, and the more mature twin. He certainly felt older. *That helps me get along with my crazy brother,* thought John whenever he ruminated over their clash of personalities. With his memory improving bit by bit, John recalled that when they were younger, he believed he could read Paul's mind and could predict what he might do next. That seemed to still hold, or so he felt. It was something he needed to work on to confirm.

On a whim, one summer day John walked through the doors of the Jackson Square cathedral and into a meeting of Alcoholics Anonymous. He was greeted like a long-lost brother and came back the following week for the free cookies. At least, it was a place where he could smoke without his brother nagging at him. The woman who led the sessions gave him a lucky coin, too.

Things began to return to a routine that was in place almost four years before. Life then varied little from day to day until early May 1997 when John was asked by Paul to *borrow* electricity from a neighbor. Of the two, John had a few innate talents in carpentry, electronics,

In Better Times

and lock picking. To accomplish this task, John ran a 50-foot orange extension cord he'd stolen, from under the neighbor's crawl space back to their own. In the damp, humidity, and filth of their crawl space, John discovered an old mold and mud-covered brandy bottle containing something other than Brandy. Breaking it open, he found almost a hundred dollars in ones and fives along with a meaningless note. John shoved the note and the money into his pocket, ended his electrical project early, and wasted no time looking for his drinking partner/twin brother with the good news. Paul though was nowhere to be found. Suspecting that he might find him at their favorite Back-Quarter retreat, John headed to a bar called the *Time Zone*. With cash in his hands and the smell of bourbon in the air, John's AA pledge of abstinence became an unrealistic pin-dot on the horizon.

It was over a couple drinks an hour later that Trip B entered the boys' lives.

IX

THE PREACHER
APRIL 1999 – THE FRENCH QUARTER

"Give the cowboy a beer an' put it on my tab," slurred John. He was at the *Time Zone, waiting for his brother* and spending money from the brandy bottle he'd found. John was feeling no pain. A hulking cowboy-hat-wearing-man was drinking next to him. John was considering starting a conversation with the man. The only topic that came to man was the Dow Jones average. The cowboy beat him to the punch.

"Howdy, brother," the Reverend Billy Bob Buckmaster drawled, extending his ham-sized hand. It's great to meet y'all." Billy Bob stood about five feet eight and looked like he pushed 270 pounds. He wore a white cowboy hat complimented by a dirty clerical collar under a black tunic. The tunic barely showed under his overalls. Beat-up alligator boots completed the outfit.

"Thank you kindly for the beer, brother. By the way, I'm Trip B."

"Say again?" responded John whose senses, especially his hearing, were dulled by a live band and too much alcohol. "You said, *'dripped beef?'* I like them dripped beef samiches."

Actually, he was already two sheets past caring who this crazy cowboy was.

"Honestly?" replied a slightly more than irritated Billy Bob. "Trip B . . . Trip B, you idiot! *Not dripped beef!* . . . Triple B! . . . Billy Bob Buckmaster! . . . *The Big B from the Big D!* The Reverend Billy Bob Buckmaster, if you must know. You don't hear too good, do you, son?"

"Goo'ness, Mr. Honey Bee," John attempted in a response. "You got as many names as a Decoration a' Innapenance!"

Billy Bob grabbed a bottle of Jack Daniels from the barkeeper's hands and poured John a fresh plastic cup of whiskey.

John picked the cup up in one hand and grabbed the bottle from Billy Bob with the other, holding it high. "Speakin' 'bout the holiday," he said saluting the fat man, "Happy fifth!"

John started to laugh at his own joke but Trip B slapped him on the back, harder perhaps than intended, and most of John's new drink sloshed out of last season's plastic Mardi Gras cup and onto the sticky surface of the *Time Zone's* bar. Since he was holding the bottle of Jack in his other hand, he took a pull from it instead."

Buckmaster couldn't believe that his message wasn't getting through to this new drinking buddy. "Let me say it slowly, my friend, so you can understand it: Bill-lee Bob Buck-mas-*ter!* Got it?"

"Well, howdy-do, Bill Lee! I'm Jawn Pope today."

John was a bit distracted from the conversation with his new friend because he was seriously contemplating licking the counter dry.

As it developed, the Reverend, or so he claimed . . . Billy Bob Buckmaster, *the Big B from Big D* . . . was in town after making a tour of Louisiana's casinos. After the rough start, and over the next twenty minutes, the Texan began to grow on John, or more likely, it was the booze. Billy Bob talked about his visits to various casinos around the state and said, by way of explanation. "We ain't got none in Texas."

"Well, we ain't got none in Texas either," John replied.

Over a few more sips from the bottle of Jack, all paid

for by John with his crawlspace-bottle-money, they shared *Get Rich* schemes. When the subject of lotteries came up, Billy Bob said, "I like you, Mister Jawn! Lay hands on me with your inspiration! Gimme' six numbers to play on the big board back home in Tay-hass. An', gimme' a couple of your family's birthdays too! I'll make it worth your while!"

John had switched from the hard stuff in favor of a foreign brew, but he hadn't touched a full plastic cup of whiskey. Tossing back a shot followed by a chug of Abita, John paused to make certain he understood his new friend's request. After a moment, muddled comprehension set in. He responded, "10 – 16 – 78 and 10 – 16 – 78. Those are my brother's and my birthdays. How's that?"

"Nope. Won't work, son," drawled Trip B. "The numbers cain't be the same. Looks like y'all don't know nothin' 'bout lotteries."

But John's head had hit the bar. His tongue had taken residence in the sticky aftermath of spilled booze.

X

Half an hour later John was rudely awakened by the bartender. As his head cleared somewhat, he noticed that the stool next to him was empty. *The cowboy must have gotten on his horse and headed back to Texas*, John thought, and decided to head home himself. In appreciation to the anonymous crawlspace bottle donor though, John bought another bottle of brandy, drank it while he walked home, and stuffed into it what little cash remained, plus the note

In Better Times

he'd found, into the now empty bottle. Arriving home, he tossed it into the crawl space where he'd found its mother.

John awoke to a beautiful morning. He felt chipper and surprised himself by crawling back under the shotgun to finish the electrical project and, while there, slipping what was left of the anonymous donor's money into the new empty he'd tossed into the crawlway. He told himself that he was doing this because he wanted to turn over a new leaf . . . and there were plenty of them in the crawlspace. Until this moment, John could recall only having a soft spot for his late mom and *maybe* his brother . . . maybe. It was a fuzzy recollection though. He vaguely recalled buying drinks for a preacher called Trip B and remembered that he'd spent money on booze that might have gone for a better, or at least a tastier purpose. Both acts of low-level generosity were completely out of character for him. *Hmmm. Perhaps it was the hangover.*

A few days later, after separating a tourist from his wallet, John again felt pangs of guilt. To atone, he made his way into the crawlway again and replenished the full amount. He then did his best to forget about the cash and the bottle in the crawlway . . . for a while.

To John, this second moment of payback to an unknown benefactor was even more cathartic. Coupled with the memory of his late mother and her verdant religiosity, John found himself in Jackson Square and the pews of St. Louis Cathedral for Mass the following Sunday morning. There, John was healed, *got religion,* and vowed to reform.

His quest for purity didn't last long. During Father Jacque's sermon, John couldn't get his mind off the Reverend Billy Bob Buckmaster and the lottery. *Have I seen The Big B before?* he wondered. *Perhaps it was seeing the priest's collar that reminded me of Trip,* he thought.

A month later, while scrubbing pots at a nonprofit bar called *Bon Temp* on Magazine Street and working off court-ordered *paid* community service – actual employment that John had seldom experienced – his ears perked up as the name Billy Bob Buckmaster was broadcast from a TV mounted over the bar. Tingles went down John's leg as Trip was introduced as the sole $36 million-dollar winner of the Texas Lottery. Billy Bob looked into the camera and intoned, "All my life I've played the birthdays of my kids. Last week I threw a few of my favorite hymn numbers into the mix: 3 – 11 – 16 – 28 – 40 and 44. Winner. Winner. Chicken Dinner! Yee-hah!"

The anchors chuckled over Trip's response and seemed buoyed by his good fortune.

Even John felt good about Trip's good luck, and he'd never felt better for anyone's good fortune . . . except his own, and that hadn't been often . . . or often enough!

John dwelled on Buckmaster's good fortune all that night. The truth was, he'd been set on his heels by the news. Something unnatural had occurred. The next day he dug around until he found a mostly dry copy of *The Times-Picayune* in a trash bin on Bourbon. On the front page of Section B was Trip's picture, big as life. In it, Trip was holding up a wrinkled piece of yellow-lined grade

In Better Times

school paper with the winning numbers printed on it: 3 – 11 – 16 – 28 – 40 – 44. The handwriting on the note was a mirror of his own! And the note looked familiar. *When did I write that? Where have I seen that paper before?*

The following Sunday, the shock of lost opportunity pushed John to again attempt atonement for his sins and failures, chief among them, not getting to know Trip better. As he exited Mass, Father Jacque pulled him aside and said, "Son, I know you're trying to do right, and, with all my heart I believe you're on the right path. Stay on it. Here's a way to help make that happen: One of our parishioners has a job for you . . . *if you want it*. It's not a great job, or even a fun one, and the hours are bad . . . and the pay is too. Worse, the work isn't pretty . . . but John, my son, it's a job!"

"Father," John responded with a bit of newfound personal pride, "I'm working part-time now and keeping myself pretty busy at the *Bon Temp*. It's a non-profit bar. They seem to like me there. It'll probably lead to at least a part-time *paying job* after my community service is over. I've got a twin brother who doesn't have a job. Maybe I can convince him to apply for *your* job."

"Do that," said the priest, who also knew brother Paul's story as well, once having given him last rites after an overdose only to have him recover mid-rite. "It's a miracle!," the former corpse said.

Now, Father Jacque responded to John's effort to pawn off the job reference. "Do that! And bless you, son."

John took the pink phone message slip from the

priest's hand and read it while walking home. It was an entry-level job all right . . . and *all night* . . . a part-time position of some sort at Beiderweil Funeral Home at the corner of Royal and Nichols in the Quarter, not terribly far from the St. Louis Cathedral on Jackson Square. It was also only a block from one of Paul's and his favorite places in the whole wide world . . . Bourbon Street! *That might make it easier to sell Paul on the job,* thought John.

Nevertheless, because the job would take actual hands-on work, possibly even some manual labor, and a commitment to show up for work on time, it took a great deal of urging to get Paul to respond to the opportunity. Still, Paul had seen what having a bit of spending money was doing for John. Thanks to his work at *Bon Temp*, John was now buying drinks instead of mooching them.

"I was really holdin' out for management, but I'll give it a go," responded Paul. John gave him a few interview tips such as looking his possible future boss in the eyes whenever he spoke. He helped him dress for the interview too. Finally, he pushed the priest's note with the Beiderweil address into Paul's hand and wished him luck: "Break a leg!"

"Why? What kind of a job is this?"

With twenty minutes to spare, Paul set out for Royal on the Canal Streetcar and returned three hours later with a huge smile on his face. He'd stopped off on the way back for a beer . . . or two.

"$6.65 an hour, three nights a week, and all I have to do is roast some andouille!" Paul chuckled. "I got the job. I start tomorrow night *and* . . . I get a *uniform!*"

"What do you mean, *roast some andouille?*"

"I am now, officially, the Part-Time Assistant Crematorium Attendant. Anytime I'm on duty and someone croaks and his family wants him toasted, I get to do it! What could be more fun?"

John was repelled by the twenty-word job description Paul showed him, but he wanted to be supportive. Because their neighbor had discovered the extension cord, they'd lost their electricity. John popped warm cans of beer for them both as they rehashed the interview.

"Yeah," Paul said, "It's an old funeral home that's run as a family business." He looked at a business card he'd come back with. *Walter Beiderweil* is the owner. He inherited the business from his father, and his father had inherited it from *his* father, who inherited . . . well, you get the idea. I think the place was built back in the twenties . . . the *eighteen* 20s! Somewhere back then the name must have been the *LaLurie* because there's one of those historic plaques *about the LaLurie Mansion* mounted near the front door. Mr. Beiderweil told me the place was haunted. I believe it, especially given what the guy does for a living."

"Haunted? You've got to be kidding!" responded John, thinking, *Glad I didn't go for that job!*

"No, no. Not really. I don't think so, anyway. The place is okay though . . . maybe a bit moldy on the inside. Sorta' creepy too! I met both him and his wife, Emma. They live above the place on the second floor in an apartment along with their 15-year-old daughter, Cynthia. She's a kick! Got this long hair the color of carrots! Not bad lookin' either. There's a third floor there too but I don't know what they use it for."

After Paul roasted his first *andouille*, he told John about the process and was on a high for a week. John was even happier he'd not gone for the interview and happy that he had pawned it off on Paul. The whole concept of crematorium work repulsed him. "Ooof! I look back on what we've been through, and it wasn't pleasant," he said showing off the family history Paul had taught him, "but I wouldn't want to work . . . *or* grow up in a funeral home! Yuck!"

And so, both twins entered corporate life: John scrubbing pots at *Bon Temp*, and Paul occasionally pushing a cart bearing a person who'd recently made the transition to room temperature . . . and then to an oven and a toasting. He really loved the *whooshing* sound he heard and felt when he flipped the switch and the burners kicked in. For the next few weeks, whenever something or someone irritated him, he'd hold a hand in the air pretending he was flipping a switch, and mimic the sound of ignition – *"Whoosh!"*

Meanwhile, John's life continued to bend erratically on occasion. His memory continued to marginally improve but it still hadn't completely returned. On some days it would show improvement, and on others, he had trouble even remembering his own name.

Within a month of hearing about Trip's windfall, John committed to attend weekly AA meetings at the Cathedral. Not long after, when he considered the changes he'd made, it seemed life had begun to turn for the better. That was

In Better Times

about the same time he'd run into Billy Bob Buckmaster. *Is there a connection?* he wondered. Still, there was no mistaking it, both he and his twin had ascended half a rung on the tall ladder to success. They still had another twenty rungs or so to go before even considering things like paying taxes or being kind to one's neighbor.

Nevertheless, before long, John was *122 days sober,* thanks to his trek up the 12 steps. He began making plans to build a new life for himself and his largely clueless twin brother.

Just after midnight on the evening of Day 123 while walking home from *Bon Temp*, John was staring at a glorious night sky and considering how old the universe was. He should have been watching where he was going. Crossing neutral ground on Canal Street, he was struck by Streetcar Number 024.

John Pope was declared dead at the scene by the conductor who believed he was authorized to do so because he was *an official employee* of the city.

"9-1-1? I jus' run down a jay bird! Lord have mercy on me! He's daid, he is! Come quick!"

After police confirmed the conductor's diagnosis, John's body was taken to the nearest funeral home – Beiderweil's – where, as luck would have it, Paul was on duty, holding forth alone in what he'd begun to refer to as, *The Tacky Palace of Eternal Rest*. The Beiderweils had left for the night to spend some time at their fishing camp near the Atchafalaya basin leaving their daughter behind. Paul was interrupted from flirting with Cynthia by the arrival of the morgue wagon.

"Oh shit John, what have you done now?" Paul asked the corpse after the ambulance crew had departed.

Paul had been without John for a few years while he'd been in Colorado, not long before. He'd seen many of his relatives and street friends die early deaths over the years. The sight of his brother lying on a cold steel preparation table stopped him only for a moment. With no cash to bury or memorialize John, he assessed his position and made a quick decision to cremate John before the Beiderweils' returned.

Paul knew nothing of filling out death certificates and so none was created or processed. Afterward, he collected his brother's ashes and placed them in a faux silver urn he found in a dusty carton on the floor of a seldom-visited closet in the casket display room. As *Ole Walt* had taught him, Paul handprinted and affixed a label to the urn that read: "Pope, John." He then carried the urn back to the same closet and placed it on the uppermost shelf.

In the space of five hours, John Pope had transitioned from *part-time hippie and former hard-life resident of New Orleans* to past tense and now a permanent resident of an urn gathering dust on a shelf in a run-down funeral home on a back street of the French Quarter in New Orleans, Louisiana, the Big Easy.

For all intents and purposes, from that moment on, John Pope ceased to exist.

Left to his own wants and desires, the bad seed in Paul blossomed again and he quickly failed to live up to the positive changes his brother had helped make in his life. He drank more than ever; he burgled more than before; and he pick-pocketed the rest of the time. A few weeks after John's passing, Paul missed work at Beiderweil twice in a row and was fired. The next day, the shotgun home he'd squatted in for several years was sold by the city.

In many respects, things didn't change all that much. His abandoned house may have been sold for its tax value, but the new owner had purchased it as a cheap investment, never intending to set foot on the property. Paul continued to squat there, unnoticed, free of charge.

In December, a tipsy Paul clumsily attempted to pick-pocket a large man leaving the Superdome after the Saints had, as customary, blown a great chance to make the playoffs, losing the last game of the regular season to the Falcons in the final three seconds.

Paul's pick-pocketing target turned the table on him and body-slammed him into a light pole. Paul was sent to his birthplace, Charity Hospital, where he lay in what was called a *Pauper's Bed*, unable to get up even to change channels on an old black and white TV tuned to CNN. For a week, all the news anchors could talk about was the fallout after the Supreme Court decided to award the presidency to Al Gore. Chad made all the difference. Paul wondered when the newsman would interview Chad.

Life in the hospital though was better than on the streets. When it came time to be released, Paul complained of complications and comically limped around the hospital room. The hospital staff, however, was wise to this sort of bad acting by a member of the city's large homeless population and pushed him out the front door anyway . . . and not in a wheelchair. Paul returned to his shotgun home on Rue Waterloo, broke again, and was, for all technicality, still homeless. But, for the first time in a long time, his stomach was full thanks to terrible-tasting but nutritious hospital food.

John had told him what to expect if he ever spent time in the hospital. He missed John.

XI

THE FALLEN HERO
LATE EVENING APRIL 18, 2005

Furtively Paul slithered up Canal Street heading toward New Orleans City Park, taking refuge behind anything large enough to hide him as he checked the route behind him for anyone following. He planned on taking Rampart Street and then Esplanade to get where he was going. It was a long walk, but he had nothing better to do. Dressed shabbily, and when spotted, he was easily mistaken for a homeless person or a drunk. At several points, he paused for a few moments to consider the state of his life. If he thought about it at all, he was in fact a member in good standing of each of those populations. Perhaps he was not technically homeless because he claimed a leaky, unheated, and uncooled roof on Rue Waterloo as his home. It at least mostly covered his sleeping bag.

Paul Pope was, and had been for some time, a homeless person in a city with one of the largest populations of homeless people in America. He was also a bona fide card-carrying perpetual drunk. He might even qualify for honorary status among that specific segment of the Big Easy's population because he was far younger than most.

This week had been even tougher than the one before.

Friday around eleven p.m. Paul had pulled a snub nose 38 caliber pistol from his hoodie's front pocket in an attempt to rob a convenience store on Canal Street. He'd found the gun while rummaging for food in a dumpster behind *Mama's,* a well-known Canal Street Italian restaurant a block from where he now stood. He could have just gone home with the weapon because at that moment he was only three or four blocks from his shotgun, but he didn't. Inspecting his new acquisition, he discovered that the gun's serial number had been filed off, but five of its six chambers were still loaded so, of course, it became a keeper. The other chamber contained a used and empty shell.

The robbery attempt went poorly.

Intelligently, Paul had waited until all the bodega's customers had left the parking lot. He entered the small store and announced his presence by firing two shots at the store's security camera. Both shots missed badly but because he'd stood three feet from the camera and was looking directly into it as he aimed, he assured his identification by police. The camera rolled, capturing crystal-clear images of Paul along with his running audio and a command ten seconds later to, "Put 'em up and shut up!"

If an unbiased observer could find humor in the attempted holdup it would be when a technician froze the recording upon a specific frame. It was the moment Paul's face was perfectly focused. He was squinting and aiming the gun while his tongue was slapped to the side of his right cheek. That moment became the image later shown on television newscasts and it made Paul both identifiable and sadly comedic. Because he knew the police would now be looking for him, certainly at his shotgun, he decided to seek alternate sleeping quarters.

Paul had scouted the convenience store for months because, like his Pop had told him, "It never hurts to be prepared when an opportunity presents itself." His father had pounded that phrase and a dozen others into his head as a kid.

He'd been confident that the camera he'd shot at was the only camera on the premises. Unfortunately for him, two more had been added since his last scouting visit a few weeks before. They were also rolling, assuring the NOPD of multiple great-quality videos of the attempt. Better, because of the humorous squinted face shot, the cops had no problem getting local stations to carry all three recordings on newscasts for several days. Even better, after what transpired, the videos were found to be so hilarious that they were circulated to the national networks. They were played all day on CNN. Paul should have felt better afterward than he did though because, thanks to him, the videos turned a tiny elderly Asian convenience store manager into an overnight national hero and a late-night celebrity.

At the sound of Paul's opening volley, she'd pressed an alarm button under the counter and backed into an open doorway leading to a back room for safety. When Paul yelled at her to return and empty the cash drawer, she refused, yelling in a high-pitched voice, "Drawer open. You get money yourself! Then you go! You no hurt *no* one!"

In the version of the video shown most often, Paul leans over the counter and reaches a bit too far to grab as many bills from the cash drawer as he can. In the background, the woman becomes visible again, stepping back into the cash register area carrying a baseball bat.

Both he and the small woman are in full frame as she swings her bat high and fast. Catching the movement at the last moment. Paul ducks. An audible thump is heard on the audio track. Paul slumps down for the count, his arms falling to the far side of the counter. For a full five seconds, he lies there like a body tied to a horse in an old western. The tiny woman drops the bat and runs out the door. She can barely be heard screaming, "Police! Police! A killer! A killer!"

Paul groggily comes to life a few seconds later. We hear moaning. He slides to the floor knees first, his chin bouncing on the counter's edge. Sirens are heard in the background. Paul makes it back to his knees and barely manages to crawl through the doorway into the darkness as two squad cars of officers arrive.

He's been on the run ever since.

The next day, thanks to the video, police mug shots, and word that their suspect is a lefty, NOPD announces to the press that for all practical purposes, it has solved the attempted robbery. Thanks to a history of petty thievery and other brushes with the law, police center their search for the perpetrator to one Paul J. Pope who was last known to be squatting in a shack on Waterloo. An arrest is imminent.

Knowing in his heart that he was smarter than they, Paul had already chosen an alternate location to spend the night if, for some reason, he was unable to make it home, say perhaps being too incapacitated, drunk, or on the run from the law, as silly a thought as that might be.

A week prior, while visiting a shelter to recover from too much gin, Paul had accidentally discovered his future overnight luxury accommodations in the fairway restrooms of one of the oldest golf courses in the United States. The former New Orleans Golf Club in City Park was designed and built in 1902 beneath thousands of towering Live Oaks. Years later, when the Golf Club relocated to a more fashionable part of the city, the original course was purchased by city officials and renamed Bayou Oaks. The course became crucial to the park's future expansion, but almost as important, with it, New Orleans City Park became known as one of the largest city parks in the entire country. The chamber loved it and promoted that fact for nearly every event imaginable.

Outdoor Bayou Oaks restrooms were located in three

different locations on the course including between the fourth green and the fifth tee. They became Paul's secret hideaway whenever he needed to scout the north side of town for burglary targets. Never locked, the only question about their occupational candidacy was one of cleanliness. There were two other lesser concerns as well: The restrooms and an attached small storage room were neither heated nor air-conditioned, and the doors and windows of all three buildings lacked screens.

That first time Paul had attempted to sleep there he met with zero success. At morning's first light, he checked his body for welts from a thousand mosquito bites. At the time, he desperately required a good night's sleep. It hadn't happened. A homeless friend suggested that getting his system free of alcohol, plus showering, might make him less attractive to Louisiana's State Insect. Paul agreed and planned to get one sometime in the next few months.

Before committing again to a night's residence in a golf course restroom, Paul briefly considered turning himself in to the police as a vagrant, hoping that he wouldn't be recognized. A one-night stay with a good hot meal would certainly be a welcome change of diet. And it would likely be free of mosquitoes. On the other hand, Paul was not one to willingly bend to supervision. And of course, if somehow he was to be connected to the robbery attempt at the bodega, his stay in the hoosegow might last a bit longer than he could handle.

Before he was forced to make that choice though, Paul decided to chance it and creep back to Rue Waterloo in his old neighborhood where he hoped to get into his shabby shotgun home unseen, find something to eat, and get a few hours of unmolested sleep.

The move nearly cost him his freedom as he discovered NOPD officers staking out the shack, front and back.

Finding cops at his home had Paul again mulling alternate housing options. He contemplated choosing a different, and perhaps air-conditioned set of restrooms in the newer version of New Orleans's Golf Club where it had relocated years ago. The newer course lay less than a mile from his now staked-out shotgun. In the end, though, he chose the more distant, but less policed, mosquito-ridden restrooms of the old Bayou Oaks Country Club on the north end of City Park. He'd steal up some mosquito repellent and defeat those suckers this time!

With police hovering around Rue Waterloo, he had no choice in the matter. Leaving the alley behind his home, Paul turned back for the long hike to the Bayou Course . . . and, while he was certain the restrooms there would be safe, they would at best be a sad alternative.

He began the five-mile hike to *Hotel Mosquito*. The course took him the length of Canal Street and through several of the city's landmark above-ground cemeteries. The meandering path had him skirting Greenwood, home now to three Civil War generals, a Congressman, a Governor, and three major league baseball players. It lay adjacent to the famous Hope Mausoleum where 20,000 former Crescent City residents lay interred, including three more Congressmen, and the same Abner Powell who'd invented baseball's Ladies Day. It then took him next to St. Patrick Cemetery Number One and, once through it and onto City Park Avenue, his trek brought him into and through the Masonic Cemetery. All of these aboveground cemeteries offered excellent temporary hiding places should police patrols spot him.

I am so smart to think of that!

With heavy clouds seemingly hovering only twenty feet above him, the night rocked darkness. But he was distracted by other things. As he passed through Masonic, chills suddenly ran down his arms. Buzzers sounded in his brain. Paul became convinced that he felt that he was being pushed around by unnaturally cool drafts of wind. He was certain he heard ghostly shrieks. With his sense of apprehension growing larger, even the rustling leaves began triggering what few anxieties were left sober in his mind.

A nearly full moon occasionally peeked through the clouds and a middle-of-the-night thunderstorm seemed to be building, promising inundation to anyone crazy enough to be out of doors. Paul decided he needed to find shelter sooner than the golf course. He didn't want it though to be in Masonic Cemetery.

Finally, having lost a pound by shivering, Paul arrived at the Bayou Oaks Golf Course unscathed by demons. He was exhausted and hungry. Forgoing a search for a free dinner of someone else's leftovers, Paul chose sleep, and the women's restroom at Bayou Oaks because it featured side-by-side stools. Over them, he placed two boards he'd stolen along the way at a construction site. He was proud of his ingenuity because by laying them across the two stools, a make-shift bed was formed.

"It ain't the Sheraton, but except for the mosquitos, it'll do" he mused. Paul stretched out and was asleep in seconds.

Over the night the weather front passed through into Mississippi. When it was over and the sun peeked over the horizon, New Orlean's temperature and humidity both began to climb. April weather in southern Louisiana is always fickle. Heavy tropical deluges often occur with no warning. The violence accompanying these short storms often does enormous damage. The sudden unexpected lightning strikes alone are said to be more than sufficient to wake the dead who normally sleep peacefully in the city's above-ground cemeteries. "It is true!" said Paul to no one. "Four or five French Quarter tour operators have confirmed the story for me.

Unfortunately, after only an hour's sleep, Paul awoke, uncomfortable on his plank bed and fearful because winds continually whipped through the towering old oaks. One might come crashing down at any moment. The rising humidity and dropping barometer also contributed to his edginess.

Restless, trying again for sleep, Paul couldn't help but believe his life was edging toward failure. With the loss a few years ago of his twin brother, he had no relatives left . . . and no friends. Still unable to fall asleep, he decided to step outside for a walk down the cart path to the fifth hole to take a leak. He preferred not to pee in his bedroom. Paul looked out the door and stared at the swirling clouds,

In Better Times

imagining the stars behind them.

His mind though kept revisiting the night before.

The humiliating moment a 4-foot-10 inch seventy-year-old woman clubbed *him*, a reasonably fit, armed young man, resonated in his head. The moment replayed itself in his mind and made him feel lower than the scum and mold on the ancient cement cart paths. As well, ever since he'd discovered the weapon, he'd moved toward concluding that the best use for it wasn't in robbing convenience stores, it was for ending a failed and futureless life.

As he turned around and walked back toward his golf course motel, the muzzle of the cold steel sent a tingle to his right leg as it slid back and forth, creating a widening hole in his pants pocket. "Shoot me. Shoot me," it seemed to sing. With a storm now bordering on explosion, Paul approached the fifth tee of the Bayou Oaks course and, with the opening rays of sunshine, oddly began feeling better, his fears and apprehensions fading with the darkness.

Ah, Home Sweet Restroom!

As could be predicted, the storm finally blew up. Paul had walked too far. He began to skip across the cart path back to the restrooms trying to beat the sure-fire heavy rain that, through a lifetime of experience, he knew was about to pummel everything between it and the ground. Through a sudden dimness, and now, swirling debris, Paul finally found the restrooms a few hundred feet away. His mind again ran images in fast forward about the mosquitos and the hot, oppressive, and sleepless nights he'd spent there. A boom sounded not far way. He was now regretting he hadn't hurried in his walk. The storm was almost on him. Just as bad, he realized he'd never done what he'd set out to do. He had no choice now but to make use of his restroom/bedroom.

Shoot me. Shoot me.

In the distance behind him and to the west, sirens wailed. His life seemed to be swirling around him. It stopped with a slam and then began to pass before him like an old-style reel-to-reel tape recorder in fast forward: no education . . . not even a GED . . . no family . . . no friends. He could still feel the clubbing he'd received from the baseball bat last night.

Another vision flashed before his eyes. It was of a different beating that hadn't ended well . . . *for his father.* An hour after the old man had slapped around his mother one too many times and left her lying on the floor semiconscious, he'd grabbed Paul by the hand and dragged him downtown. There he met a woman on an old hotel rooftop. Finally, in his mental video-review of a hard life, Paul relived the moment in the funeral home when his twin brother, his only relative, had been reduced to ashes at his own hands.

Shoot me. Shoot me.

With time now in slow motion, Paul considered his future, tainted by numerous criminal listings in NOPD logs. Following last evening's attempted robbery, he was also wanted for discharging a weapon in a public establishment. Worst of all, the gun he'd used probably carried its own criminal history. In New Orleans, throwaways were almost always traced back to capital crimes. No friends. A failed family – all of whom were now dead and gone – and criminal charges ahead of him that could send him to the Green Mile.

Shoot me. Shoot me.

He shook his head and decided to end it all . . . and decided the time to take this action was now.

Heavy rolling thunder sounded and within seconds the skies opened. Torrents of rain began to pummel him. A bolt of strange yellow lightning struck at the far end of the fairway with an electric boom that seemed to echo forever. Paul instinctively ducked toward a large old Live Oak to find shelter and then thought better of it.

What difference does it make how I go? he asked himself, but he knew that being struck by lightning offered no guarantees either.

Shoot me. Shoot me.

It was time. With but a second's thought of the consequences, he struggled to pull the 38 from his pocket where it had snagged in the hole. Finally, placing his finger on the trigger, he pointed the weapon's short muzzle at his right temple and squeezed.

A boom sounded.

Night turned to day.

It was a monstrous bolt of lightning. The explosive sound hadn't come from his pistol after all. A giant yellow lightning bolt occurred at the same moment he tried to pull the trigger. The 38 had misfired. In its place, a 40,000-volt bolt of supercharged lightning struck hard and loud a few feet from him, zigzagging across the ground and into his right hand.

It was midnight, April 18, 2005.

XII

A TRIP BACK
APRIL 19TH, 1995 – BAYOU OAKS
GOLF COURSE, NEW ORLEANS

Sounds of crickets, tree frogs, and night birds usually overwhelm New Orleans nights. Bowing to the violence of a passing storm though, an eerie quiet had replaced the noise and mayhem in this forested part of the city. By three a.m., Mother Nature had expended all her energy. Skies cleared, winds stilled, and the tree frogs nervously regained their croak. The rain clouds were replaced by a silky black sky with a waning moon, the bright pin pricks of stars emerging to compete with it for brilliance.

A naked bearded man lay in a fetal position on the grass next to a cart path. A wisp of smoke rose from his charred right ear and hand. Twenty feet away a large tree stood in shock, many of its leaves withered and torn. Apparently struck by lightning a few hours earlier, finger-thin wisps of smoke rose from its damaged trunk. A large broken bough hung by a wooden thread, its extremities resting on the ground, now blocking a cart path.

Oddly, a cart path streetlight only twenty feet from

the tree continued to operate. Canted twenty or so degrees off-center though, it seemed to be spotlighting the man's body with a bone-white illumination as if the body were a prop on the city's Orpheum Theatre stage. It was cool for mid-April in New Orleans, the temperature barely above fifty degrees, but thankfully New Orleans' famed humidity had taken a break. Had it been its usual 75 percent or more, the damp would have driven perceptions of the temperature down significantly. The fact that there were no breezes also helped chase away the chill.

The body on the ground remained still. There was no sign of breathing. Were there passing golfers, they would have bet each other that the man on the ground had been struck fatally, but it was only three hours past midnight and there would be no golfers on the scene for hours.

Following the massive boom and light show, silence had enveloped the scene. That was half an hour ago. The only sound now was the frogs' chatter and the faint resonance of a lightning strike that in their tiny minds rippled to infinity, similar in every way to the impact of a small stone splashing into a pond. Cricket by cricket, frog by frog, bit by bit, the rhythm of night sounds returned, gradually increasing in intensity to the point where it returned full blast . . . comfortingly overwhelming.

An hour went by, then two. The eastern horizon began brightening.

With a sudden jerk, the man kicked out his legs and sat up. He was stunned and confused. He wrinkled his brow trying to recall what had occurred, gingerly touching his charred ear. Absently sucking on a burned thumb, he was amazed at the numbed crispness of his skin. He tried to make sense of what had happened but failed. He remembered nothing . . . *nothing!* The only thing he knew for certain was that he was naked, hurting, and outdoors.

A bit wobbly, he stood, pounding the right side of his head with the heel of his palm to bring back his right ear's ability to relay sound to his brain. When he thought about it, he also realized he had no idea where he was . . . or, even *who* he was. Finally, he shook his head, committing to the likelihood that at least for now he would only be able to hear from his undamaged left ear . . . and that in time his memory might return. He would not allow himself to even consider that the memory loss might be permanent.

Fortunately, it was dark, and no one was around to be offended by his nakedness.

Behind him, a *For Sale* sign fronted dense foliage. It read:

Million Dollar View!

Large Lot for Sale. Ideal Luxury Home Site.

180-degree view of beautiful Lake Pontchartrain. 142 feet of shoreline.

Lot overlooks Bayou Oaks Fourth Green. $999,900.

Antebellum Realtors. (504) 867- 5309.

"What the hell?" he asked aloud as he tore fronds from nearby bushes to hide his nakedness. There was no one within sight or hearing to respond. "Where am I?" he asked again . . . of no one.

It was dark, but under the partial moon, the man easily

could see several small nondescript buildings a hundred or so feet away. They were the only structures within view. He trotted over while awkwardly covering himself. The small buildings turned out to be outdoor restrooms for golfers and included a small, attached storage shed. He forced the door of the last one open and found filthy work clothes probably belonging to maintenance workers. Dressing hurriedly, he was pleased, at least, to see that the clothes fit . . . mostly.

Nakedness covered; he could now more comfortably look about him. Nothing had changed. He could discern only the restrooms, two fairways, a putting green, and a break in the trees in the far distance. Far beyond them in the even further distance, he could barely make out lighted windows in a few tall buildings. *Population! People!* With no thought as to where he was or what he might encounter, those buildings became his goal.

An hour later, the sun popped over the horizon. He appreciated the feeble warmth offered by the sunrise as he walked unsteadily through above-ground cemeteries in whatever city he was in. Before long he passed a large mausoleum and continued down a street which, from a sign, he identified as Rue Canal.

New Orleans. New Orleans! At least I know where I am now! he thought and sighed in relief. The tall buildings in the distance though remained his goal.

The walk helped settle his mind some. Obvious clues helped him identify missing bits of information that would eventually . . . hopefully . . . help him figure out who he was. Somehow, he knew the makes and years of automobiles. From the age of the vehicles parked along the streets, he deduced that the current year must be somewhere near 1989 or 1990. Obviously, he had some prior knowledge of automobiles . . . but that conclusion offered little else. Gradually, he came to the realization that everything he saw, and yet nothing he saw, was new to him. It was curious. *This area must be a part of my prior life,* he guessed. While he may have thought he knew where he was, he remembered nothing of that past, including his own name. Worse, he seemed to have no clue as to how his whereabouts related to him.

He was guided by a subconscious instinct. While the business district of the city *had* been his goal, about halfway down Canal Street, for an unexplained reason, he chose with confidence to turn left down a narrow side street listed as Rue Waterloo. Within two minutes he stood before a weathered and dilapidated shotgun house and found a young man sleeping on the porch in a broken swing. "Excuse me!" he gently called from the sidewalk, "Can you tell me where I am?" The young man on the porch wore a dirty muscle shirt, torn jeans, and a week's growth of whiskers.

Except for a slight age difference, the two men resembled each other in size and hair color. The younger man stirred, came fully awake, and looked out from his porch to see a bearded maintenance worker addressing him. He paused for a second or two in apparent disbelief and blurted out, "John, is that you? Man, you look like shit!"

"Do you know me? I think I have amnesia," the man in the dirty work clothes called back. "I woke up on a golf course this morning, naked, and my clothes mostly burned to shreds! I must have been clubbed senseless or robbed and left for dead. I don't remember a thing," he repeated. Someone may have even tried to set me on fire!"

Paul Pope, apparently the younger of the two men, didn't respond to the other's plea, but said, "Last time I heard about you, John, was two years ago. You were living in a commune back in the mountains somewhere. Town had a strange name like Beer Mug or somethin'. You say you got amnesia? Well, if you can't remember what happened, you left me alone here in NOLA and hitchhiked west a couple years back! Left me high and dry, you did! I know! I heard all about it from a guy who said he ran into you there. He told me you'd grown a beard, that your hair had turned grey, and you'd let it grow 'till it was down to your pecker. And, he said you were heavy into booze and drugs. And you was shackin' with an older woman with three kids!

"Have you dyed your hair man, 'cause it sure ain't grey? But you do look like you've been smokin' some serious dope, Bro! Where's your woman and her kids?"

The lightning-bruised man from the golf course stared cluelessly as the younger person left the porch and approached him, still rambling. The talker finally ran out of questions, laughed, and slapped the older man on the shoulder. "Forget it! Come on, John. Let's go get us some hooch!"

"Hooch? Liquor? It's still early in the morning!" The man was amazed that he knew what hooch was.

"Yeah, bro. But you know it! This is New Orleans! You can find a bar open 24 hours a day! Get with it, man. Anyway, I got a couple of beers in my cooler. They should still be cold."

Over the next few minutes, foggy memories of his days in several communes emerged from a mental fog like neon signs turning on, flickering to life for a moment, going dark again, and then finally settling into a glowing permanence. As the apparent twins sat on the front porch in the broken swing with open bottles of mostly warm Pearl in their hands, they began telling each other stories from their time apart. Mostly it was Paul doing the talking and often asking *John* about stories from his time in Colorado. But *John's* memory of those times was still jumbled and incomplete. At times he wondered if he wasn't really this *John* person. It wasn't at all a familiar name.

Suddenly, neighbors from all around erupted from their homes and gathered in the street in front of the shotgun. Because he knew a few of the neighbors, the man who had awakened on the porch – *Paul* – reacted first, "What the heck's going on? I've never seen anything like this before, John. Somethin' big must be goin' on.

In a loud alarmed voice, one neighbor woman asked another: "Who would do such a terrible thing? All those babies!"

An old man was in tears. He saw the questioning looks coming from the two men on the porch and said by way of explanation, "The TV pictures are so sad. They're carryin' out bodies of little kids and lottsa' women. Few men, too. Maybe a few is still alive in there."

Another woman said, "I heard one report that they're pretty certain *nobody* made it out . . . and they're guessin' at least a thousand may have died. It's a tragedy, it is. Wonder what caused it?"

Another old man turned to her and said, "One of them TV guys on the scene says it was a bomb! An', CNN says some folks saw a big rental truck racin' down da' street, clippin' parked cars 'n trucks. One woman says she was a block away lookin', sorta', out at that buildin' when a truck done drove past 'er an' ran right tru da front doah, sat dere wedged in place fo' a few seconds, and then she blow! She was lucky. She was behind a pillar of a buildin' down de block. Took down dat whole 20-story building in front o' her, it did. Flat out leveled it!"

Finally, Paul spoke to a neighbor he knew but who was not very fond of him, "What's happened? A building got blown up? Here? In Naw'lins?"

The woman replied, "No, no. Tulsa. Up in Oklahoma. Must be a casino, 'cause it's call' the Harrah Building or somethin'. Leveled! Just blowed up. Must be tousands dead in Tulsa and a lot of 'em's kids. They doan' tink no one lived tru it includin' a bunch a people out on da' street. You wanna come in and watch it on my TV? I knows you ain't got no 'lectricity."

The younger man said," No thanks. We have some catchin' up to do. This is my twin brother, John."

"Nice to meetcha', John. Hope you're a better neighbor than yer damn brother!"

With that, she turned her back and marched back to the crowd out in the street.

* * * *

The boys talked all that day. By evening they'd resolved to forget all about the problems that caused their break-up more than three years earlier. *John* just nodded his head though because he recalled no disputes with the man who claimed to be his twin brother. Other than a sketchy memory and a sore ear and hand, John was now feeling mostly normal.

Paul convinced John to party in the French Quarter that night on some cash he said he found in an alley. They returned to the Shotgun at three a.m., far from sober.

Since he was an amnesiac looking for an identity, *John the Older* gradually adjusted to his new role as Paul's twin. The scenario made sense anyway as the two obviously were of very similar appearance. And how could he have unconsciously chosen *this* house to return to if he hadn't had some hidden or repressed memory of it?

Over the next few days, the two men – the slightly older one seemingly in his mid or late twenties, and the other one, who said he *knew* his age was 16, going on 17 – got to know each other better. The younger man called himself Paul Pope and addressed the older one as John Pope, his identical twin brother. While to *John* this seemed a bit crazy: the fact that fate had led him here and that this person recognized him, stood for something, didn't it? He began to believe Paul's tale as a genuine possibility, but still . . . *something just wasn't* right with this whole scenario.

John accepted Paul's invitation to move into the dilapidated twelve-foot-wide shotgun house, a residence, Paul told him, that was common to many parts of the south but especially to south Louisiana. It was called a *Shotgun* because most were built with a hallway running from the front door along one side of the house, all the way to the back door. Rooms were stacked behind each other for the length of the house. Almost always, Shotgun Homes were built several feet above the ground on small piers of bricks. That way, theoretically, a breeze blowing under the house would help cool it. Also, theoretically, a shotgun-wielding person standing on the front porch could fire a weapon through the open front door and down the hallway, and the buckshot would travel completely down the length of the house, exiting out the open back door without doing any damage. Hence, the name, *Shotgun House.*

John noticed pellets lodged in the front door frame, as well as in both walls lining the hallway. So much for the theory.

His gut told him that he was older than Paul even though they appeared to be twins. The belief would nag at him for the rest of his life.

I'm more set in my ways and thankfully more mature about the realities of the world than my supposed twin, believed John.

The two men found themselves to be generally

compatible, and to aid in the recovery of his memory, Paul convinced John to shave. Then they cut each other's hair in a crude style, similar to one another's, and stood before a mirror, comparing features. It was a convincing demonstration by Paul that, *yes*, they were indeed twins. John still saw an age difference, but he finally told Paul he agreed, that he was, *indeed*, John Pope. He promised to do his best to become the brother that Paul said he'd missed for far too long.

XIII

THE NUMBERS

John's memory still had holes. He seemed to know more about Paul's life than he knew of his own. After several arguments about whether he had, or had not, gone to Colorado, John gave up on his conviction that he'd never done so. He relented, telling Paul that he'd been correct; he *had* gone to the mountains. That explained a lot of things. Maybe Paul *was* right, anyway. Regardless, it was nice to have a family, even if it was just a brother. Behind his back though, he crossed his fingers and hoped that the real John Pope didn't return unannounced to expose him.

Because of John's on-and-off amnesia, Paul tried to fill in the gaps for him. At one point he completed a somewhat biased review of their lives and told John what had occurred since a dispute had set them against each other a few years back, prompting John's departure to Colorado.

"What sort of dispute?" asked John.

"Well," Paul hedged, failing miserably at eye contact, "I got messed up and did something bad and somehow the cops blamed you and locked you up by mistake. I *tried* to get 'em to let you go 'cause I'd done it, but they didn't want to admit *their* error," he lied. "You paid for it with time in juvie when I *should* have. That's when you left for Colorado. I'm sorry, man. I really am!"

John feigned appreciation for Paul's apologies, but he'd also begun to understand and accept the fact that this was the normal life of a Pope. Alcohol and minor criminal activity did then, and would regularly now and in the future, play a big part in *their* debilitating family history. The problem was inherited from Paul's . . . *their*. . . father and it would likely play a major role in their lives going forward. That would explain a lot of the things that Paul had told him.

One day, during such a family history session, Paul explained all there was to know about their parents: "John, the two of us are identical twins. We were born on October 16th, 1978. I think I know why we don't look exactly alike. I think it's because of whatever happened to you while you were in the Copper Kettle, or whatever that town in Colorado was called . . . *Bad Drugs*, probably."

"Tin Cup. Tin Cup was the name of the town," John interrupted and immediately wondered where his correction had come from. Until that moment, despite Paul's claims, he'd had no recollection of living in any town in Colorado, especially one with that unusual name.

"Tin Cup then. Whatever. While you was gone, you probably lived a tougher life than I did . . . maybe even camping out during those cold winters . . . and that, and the drugs, probably made you look a year or two older than me. That probably happens sometimes with identical twins anyway.

"Okay," continued Paul. "Let's get back to the history lesson. Our father was John Randall Pope. He was born on the same day that John the 23rd was named Pope of the Catholic Church. As a joke, or maybe because our parents were good Catholics, Pop was given the name *John* . . . *John* Randall Pope. *Randall* was after *his* father. Time rolled on. Our dad grew up and met mom.

"In 1978, a few months before we were born, an Italian Cardinal became Pope when John the 23rd died. On the day when the white smoke went up in the Vatican, our mom was six months pregnant with us. She wasn't scheduled to deliver for another three months . . . *if she went full term*. Anyway, the new Pope chose as *his* Papal name, John Paul, to honor two previous popes.

"Mom and Pop knew that twin boys were on the way, and Pop was disappointed that we wouldn't be born on the new Pope's big day . . . *like he'd been*. "Damn!" Pop supposedly said. "We could'a named our boys, John and Paul Pope!"

"But . . ." started to interrupt John.

"As luck would have it, Pop got his wish. That new Pope . . . John Paul . . . died just a month or two later and on October 16th, 1978, another Cardinal became Pope and he took the *papal* name, John Paul the Second. That was the same day mom gave birth to us. I don't know if Mom approved of it, but Pop made sure our birth certificates listed us as John and Paul Pope!"

* * * *

Time went by in *John's* education. Paul began Session II of his lectures from the course *Pope Family 101* by telling a whole series of stories about their parents.

"Mom would go to Mass at the Cathedral on Jackson Square every Sunday. Pop wouldn't. He'd swear at her when she took *us* along. One time when we came back from Mass, Pop got real high and mighty about how smart he was and started runnin' us through the coals with science questions. He knew Mom was as much anti-science as he was anti-religion. Mom, of course, jumped into the conversation on the side of religion. Back and forth. Back and forth!

"I think that was the day he kept on asking, '*When did time begin?*' He went on and on about it. Mom finally interrupted his sermon by tellin' us, 'Boys: Genesis, Chapter 1: *In the beginning God created the heavens and the earth. And God said, Let there be light, and there was light. God called the light day, and the darkness he called night. And there was evening and there was morning – the first day.* I'll never forget her words.

"'And so, Randall, you and the boys should know that your ... your ... evolution theory ... probably ... *really* did *happen but it happened* before *that very* first *day was over! And, God made it happen that way! The billions and billions of years you keep talkin' about just happened before we . . . before God, that is . . . started countin' time the same way we humans do'.* She doubled down, '*Evolution happened* before *that first day was over!*'

"Over another meal for us that was barely enough for two chickens to eat, I remember her stopping Pop in mid-sentence while he was talking about the age of the earth. *'Psalm 90,'* she said. *'For a thousand years in your sight are but as yesterday. In other words, a day to us is like a thousand years for God . . . or is it the other way around?'*

"Pop laughed so hard he nearly fell off his chair." Paul paused for a few seconds, swallowing before continuing. "And then . . . the *Ole Man* died when we was 11."

"Yeah," interrupted John spontaneously, "I got him good, I did! I hit him with a big board and pushed him off a building!"

"Hush, John," replied Paul looking over his shoulder to make sure no one was listening. "You didn't do it," he whispered. "I did. How'd you come to figure that out? But, if you want the deed, it's yours to have."

"Don't know. I don't know where that came from," said John with a bewildered look on his face.

"We'll just forget about it . . . like everything else, including your promise to quit smoking!" Paul said with irritation, then continued, "If you don't remember, when we was 12, Grams died, and mom followed not long after. It was *The Lung* the doctors said, but *she never smoked*! I'm sure if it *was* cancer; it came from Pop's smokin' so much . . . an' John . . . you better stop too, right now, you hear?"

John didn't even know that he smoked but he thought it was curious that his brother, who drank heavily, incessantly chewed tobacco, injected toxic drugs into his body, and routinely burgled small businesses and homes which sometimes led to armed showdowns with homeowners . . . that *he* would lecture *him* on the evils of smoking.

A moment occurred a month later that stopped John in his tracks. He and Paul had spent a reckless night in the French Quarter . . . pills, booze, injectable heroin, meth, and worse . . . with three *very* young women. They were all recovering in an empty, hundred-degree, trashed-out room in the old Hotel Lagniappe. A copy of the previous day's *Times-Picayune* lay on the floor in a corner and caught John's attention. His hungover, bloodshot, swollen eyes fixed incomprehensibly on the headline: "30M Americans now on the Internet."

"Paul, look at the paper," said John. "That headline's all wrong! There's more people than that on the internet. I read it in Newsweek eight or nine months back. There are now more than 200 million people on the internet. The *Picayune's* screwed up and . . . hey, it's even got the wrong date! It says it's 1995, *not 2005!* Nobody's proofing or checking facts anymore! If they can't get the date right, no wonder they got wrong numbers about how many people are usin' the internet. You know, those newspapers are gonna have problems when more people start usin' the internet."

Paul laughed at John's reaction. "What the heck are you talkin' about, John?" Then he stopped and attempted to clear his own head. With a slurred voice he asked, "It *is 1995*, shithead! You still trippin'? It's not 2005, idiot! It's 1995! Maybe it's you who's nuts. You need a drink, Bro."

It was yet another moment when John had spoken without really thinking ahead about the current topic, in this case, what year it was. Where did these weird memories and comments come from? For several days, John tried to figure out how he could have lost ten years. Or had he gained ten years? "It was all in how one perceives it," he told Paul when they discussed his memory lapses.

Paul just shook his head saying, "You sure you ain't our father? He'd say crazy crap like that, too."

Because of the amnesia, John had no solid memory about what had happened up until 1995, or even 2005, or any time before. In his heart, though he knew the current year *was* 2005, not *1995*! *What happened between these two dates . . . or did nothing happen because it hadn't occurred yet* he asked himself, and then puzzled over the last possibility.

One morning, John told Paul about concerns over his sanity. His twin responded, "Let's face it, John. You are one sick, dude! You just don't know it! We may need to get you some help. I just hope I don't inherit it." He'd said and accompanied the comment with a laugh that was a bit revealing.

Over the next year, the two men . . . really a teen and a young man . . . bonded to a degree. Their lives though remained mired pretty much at the bottom of New Orleans society.

In May 1997, John attempted to repair faulty plumbing under their home ... actually, illegally hooking their house up to city water. The only water line to the home had been turned off years before. While making connections in the crawlspace beneath the house, John happened on a dirt-encrusted brandy bottle with $100 and a note in it.

Because of Paul's hands-on training, John's first thoughts were to spend the money on booze. He rushed out of the crawlway to tell Paul the good news about finding the money. Unable to locate him, he rushed from the crawlway heading for the *Time Zone*, a bar in the French Quarter where the brothers liked to drink, quickly going through a quarter of his newfound cash. In his final half-hour of sobriety, he bought an Abita for a heavyset man sitting next to him at the bar.

"Get one fer' him too," John slurred to the bartender, elbowing the big man sitting next to him in the ribs.

"Hey, my brother," the Reverend Billy Bob Buckmaster said extending his meaty hand, "Thanks for the beer. I'm Trip B."

"Say again?" quizzed John. His mind was performing one of its *déjà vu* buzz flips at the moment and he was caught off guard. *Trip B? he asked himself.* Still, with a bunch of drinks already under his belt, John was only two notes away from a samba. The moment passed.

"Trip B ... *Triple B*! Billy Bob Buckmaster of Dallas, Texas!" said The Reverend Billy Bob, not willing to let the issue die. "But, because I like you, you can just call me Pastor B, son." The fat man said what he said very loudly and slapped John on the back in an attempt to shake him loose from his alcoholic stupor. Half the dark brown Louisiana beer in John's cup splashed out onto his threadbare shorts.

For a moment John considered leveling Pastor Bobbi Ann or whatever the heck his name was, but a heavy thumping inside the back of his head refrained him.

Turned out *Trip B* was in New Orleans visiting from Dallas while touring every one of Louisiana's casinos. Over a few more beers, the two men shared schemes and, when the subject of lotteries came up, Billy Bob said, "I like you John an' I done hit it big time once't for $5,000! An', I kin do it again, son! But the key is, I gotta get fresh digits – *not my own*! Gimme' some numbers to rock the charts."

"Say what? Ro*ck the Charts?"* asked John, lapsing again into a confused state.

"The Lottery, man. The Lottery!" said Triple B, disappointed at having to repeat himself for this Louisiana backwash of a drunk.

And so, while tossing back a shot following a last gulp of his Abita Amber, John took a moment to make certain he fully understood Trip's request. Another *déjà vu* vision stole the moment and clouded his firewater impeding short-term memory even more.

Unable to stabilize a vertical hold on the image before him, John came up with, "3 – 16 – 40, uh, and uh, 10 – 16 – 78 – 11 – 44 - 48," giving Trip the numbers from a

Psalm he thought his mother had taught him, his alleged brother's birthdate, and a few other numbers just for the heck of it.

Trip had been ready and was jotting the numbers down, growing progressively perplexed.

"Are you sure these are good numbers, son? For one thing, it's three too many! For another, one of 'em's a double, an' worse . . . you don't seem too sure of any of 'em. I need winners, son!"

* * * *

By the time John stumbled back to the Shotgun, he'd gone through all but $40 of the money he'd found in the bottle. In appreciation to its donor though, John bought another bottle of brandy, emptied it in the handiest receptacle, his throat, slipped the last $30 into the empty, and tossed the bottle back into the same crawl space where he'd found its twin. Later that night he pulled a crumpled-up wad of yellow-lined paper from his pocket. He read it, but the notes made no sense. *Bunch a numbers,* he thought, recrumpling it, and pitching the note in the weeds.

For John, these two tiny moments of payback – buying a beer for a stranger and repaying a *found* bottle with cash . . . or, maybe paying a gift forward to an unknown donor . . . was almost life-changing. Sunday morning, with church bells clanging between his again hungover ears, he dreamed he was in the pews of the St. Louis Cathedral with his mom listening to a priest named Thibodaux.

During the sermon, John had trouble concentrating on the Gospel because a vision floated above Father Thibodaux. It was that of the Reverend Billy Bob Buckmaster. Billy Bob's voice echoed in the sanctuary as he sang, *Shoulda' given me the numbers! Shoulda' given me the numbers!* And then, *Winner! Winner! Chicken Dinner! Yee Hah!* It was a dream within a dream . . . a sure omen of something!

After waking, John speed-walked to Jackson Square, planning to actually *attend* mass, not just dream it.

A Hurricane got in his way. Walking through the Quarter, he resisted and passed up one of the entrances to Pat O'Brien's, but around the corner, the second entrance to the famous bar and restaurant lay in ambush. Once attacked, it was easy for O'Brien's to pull John in . . . and, the Hurricane tasted *really* good too. Actually, so did the second and the third. In one of the alleys on the way home, John stumbled on a man even drunker than he was and emptied the poor guy's pockets.

Upon returning to the Shotgun a little richer, John crawled under the house and made good on some of the remaining debt to his unknown benefactor.

Can a person Pay it Forward *with someone else's money?* he wondered.

The next day John was nagged by something else that he couldn't fully grasp. It tugged at the back of his brain, but try as he might, he couldn't bring it forward. For all he knew, it had something to do with the newspaper. From that moment on, every time he had a chance to steal a copy of the *Picayune*, he did so. One day he slipped a copy

In Better Times

out of a newspaper vending machine that hadn't closed properly and checked the date, wanting desperately for it to be from 2006 or seven or anything, but what he found was April 21, 1999, instead.

All the news was about a shooting on the town square in Littleton, Colorado. Some wannabee hunter had killed and wounded 11 folks from a perch on a church tower before being picked off by a police sniper. Paul watched John read the newspaper story of the event and said, "Hey, John. Isn't that where your commune was?" John had no clue for, as far as he knew, he'd never really been to Colorado but, then again, his namesake apparently went to the mountains . . . supposedly.

Perhaps he could've indeed once visited Colorado, so he replied, "Yeah! Great little town! Get it? *Little*-Town, Colorado?"

A month or so later, John was working off community service *part-time* at the *Bon Temp*, a nonprofit bar (John wondered how a nonprofit bar could *make* money . . . and how it could have the goal of weeding people away from alcohol by employing them to serve it). He'd asked the manager about that one day and the man only responded, "Hey man, this is New Orleans! Whaddayawant for crying out loud?"

It was at that moment that John heard the name, Reverend Billy Bob Buckmaster, broadcast over a TV newscast. His hands began shaking uncontrollably as Trip was introduced as the sole $36 million-dollar winner of the Texas Lottery. Billy Bob looked into the camera directly at John, and said, "All my life I've played the birthdays of my kids. Last month I threw a few of my apartment numbers into the mix: 3 – 11 – 16 – 28 – 40 and 44. Winner. Winner. Chicken Dinner! Yee-hah!" John later swore that Billy Bob finished his response by again looking at him directly through the TV set and saying, "Too bad for you, John. *Sucker!*" Either way, the anchors had a good chuckle over Trip's response, one even singing the first few lines of "Amazing Grace" in recognition of Billy Bob's theoretical theological status.

Still, all of America seemed pleased by Trip's *bon chance*. It took a day or so before even John felt good about the big man's big win. That bothered him in itself . . . or something about what happened did. He wasn't certain. He also got an ache in his stomach whenever he thought about missing out on 36 million dollars. *How many zeroes are in that number*, he wondered.

Numbers . . . numbers! That's it!"

XIV

THE CLAIRVOYANT

The first thing next morning, John searched until he found a day-old copy of the *Picayune* in a Bourbon Street trash bin. There was Trip's picture, big as life holding the winning numbers, 3 – 11 – 16 – 28 – 40 – 44. For the next twenty minutes, he sat next to the trash bin trying to piece

In Better Times

together his recent past. He held both his hands to the sides of his head as if trying to keep it from exploding. Tourists passed and laughed at his predicament. "Probably had a rough night on Bourbon, huh bud?" asked one knowingly.

"Not *on* Bourbon," John replied, *With* bourbon!"

Really though, John was mentally pushing jigsaw puzzle pieces around inside his skull, searching for two that fit. That night he was shaken by a violent dream where he was struck by lighting and wandered naked through the city, ending up in a crawl space beneath a dumpster where he found a loaded pistol and an empty bottle of *Chivas* with a worm in it. He woke for a moment drenched in sweat but fell back to sleep almost immediately. Again, in restless sleep, he dreamed that he'd gone back in time exactly one year and had popped up floating in space, staring at the big blue earth only a tantalizing 50,000 miles ahead of him.

In the morning, Paul reacted to John's pale, unkempt appearance, asking him what in the world had happened. John told him not to ask again unless he first came up with a piece of paper so he could write a note. Paul wanted to know why, and John said, "I want to hand it down to my heirs."

Paul laughed but still came up with a mostly used yellow pad of elementary school-lined paper. He made a derogatory comment about what John could do with the paper and laughed again. Later Paul found John outside, on his knees, entering the crawl space under their house. A sheet of paper from the yellow pad was folded and between his teeth.

Paul shrugged and said, "Too bad, John. And I had such high hopes for you."

The following Sunday John recalled his attempt to put himself on the road to success. He headed for the cathedral. He called it an inspiration but he'd had a sudden urge to attend mass. This time he tugged on Paul's elbow and unlike before, the two young men managed to bypass O'Brien's Hurricane Grill and attended mass at the St. Louis Cathedral. It was the first time they'd done so together in almost twenty years. The last time had been with their mother. The priest conducting the Mass was one Paul knew from the time he'd performed *Last Rites* on him two years earlier following a mugging . . . and then performed them a second time on him a couple months back when he was so heavily drug-induced that everyone, including the priest, was certain Paul wouldn't make it.

As they left the Cathedral, Father Boudreaux pulled John to the side and said, "Son, I know you're trying to do right, and I believe you're on the right path. Stay on it. I've called one of our parishioners and he's got a job waiting for you . . . *if you want it*. It's not a great job or even a fun one. The hours are bad, and the pay is too. Worse, the job . . . frankly . . . sucks. Nevertheless John, it's a job. It's a *real* job!"

"Father," John responded morosely, "I'm the all-night manager at *Bon Temp* and I'm staying off the sauce all by myself . . . mostly. Maybe you can convince my brother here to take you up on your job."

"I'll do that, son," said the Father. "And bless you

both." He then told Paul about the possible job.

John stood to the side and wrote down the information about the possible job because Paul showed no excitement about it whatsoever. It was minimum wage and entry-level . . . an all-night, part-time position at the Beiderweil Funeral Home on the edge of the French Quarter on Royal.

It took a fair amount of urging on his part to get Paul finally to respond to the opportunity, but the younger twin had just turned 18 and finally agreed to interview for the job. John helped him spiff up for his face-to-face meeting with the Beiderweils and prompted him with likely questions the owner might ask. Questions like, "Paul, what are your personal goals if you get this job?"

Paul looked at John, and with a crooked smile on his face, replied. "I want to bury you!"

John's eyebrows pinched upward, and he patted his brother on the back saying, "Just tell him you want to learn the business from him, Paul."

Two hours later Paul returned to the Shotgun lugging a twelve-pack of malt liquor.

"$6.95 an hour, two nights a week, and all I have to do is roast some turkey!" Paul chuckled. "I got the job. I start tomorrow night . . . and, I *get a uniform!*"

"What do you mean, *roast some turkey?*" John asked.

"Well, if a stiff comes in and I'm the only one there . . . or if there's a burn-order left over for the night shift, I get to cremate the dude! Can't get any better than that! And I get paid for doin' it!"

And so, both twins entered corporate life: John

managing the *Bon Temp* bar all night on Mondays, and Paul occasionally pushing a body from a morgue-style locker into a cremation oven at a nondescript funeral home located in a less-traveled spot just off the French Quarter. Paul believed that he was destined for management... at least that's what Cynthia Beiderweil, the daughter of the owners of the funeral home, told him.

It became July, and even years after he woke up naked on a golf course, John's memory still was playing tricks on him. Mostly, he had problems fixing on dates. One day while walking down Canal Street, the two brothers passed a magazine stand and noticed a copy in the rack with a headline reading, "JFK, Jr. Talks Politics."

"Can't be," John told Paul. "He died in a plane crash."

"You dummy," shouted Paul. "He didn't die in a plane crash! He was shot in Dallas," and then he laughed.

Two days later though, even Paul was flabbergasted to hear of JFK Jr.'s death a week earlier in the crash of a small plane.

"You, my man, are psychotic!" Paul said to John when John had told him the story of JFK, Jr.'s death without reading the news story. "We need to put you on TV. We could make a million bucks!" The thought started when Paul began seeing value in John's psychic abilities but the Crystal Ball On-Off switch in John's mind seemed to usually be in the *off* position.

Meantime, John began attending AA meetings at the Cathedral and his life clearly began taking a turn for the better. He was promoted to Full Time Bar Manager at the

Bon Temp and was now earning real money for the first time in his life. John was convinced it all began when he met Billy Bob.

John was *87 days sober* and making plans to build a new life for himself and his clueless younger twin brother when he was sideswiped by a cab while lighting a cigarette on the way home from work. The brush with the cab threw him in front of a fast-moving Streetcar, Number 024. It was on the Neutral Ground where John Pope breathed his last.

John's body was taken to Beiderweil's and, as fate would have it, Paul was supposedly on duty alone, holding forth in the creepy old funeral home basement. Interrupted in a delicate moment with Cynthia, Paul nevertheless called a halt to the proceedings and forced himself to deal with the arrival of an ambulance.

"This guy literally got bumped off," the EMT told Paul while chuckling.

"Huh?" asked Paul, not getting the man's attempt at a joke.

"Morgue humor, man!"

It was dawning on the EMT that the man who'd been deposited on the preparation table uncannily resembled Paul.

"Hey, man! This dude looks just like you. If he wasn't a bit older than you, I'd say he could be your twin!"

But Paul wasn't listening. He was in a daze. In front of him lay his dead brother. "I told you that cigarettes were gonna kill you some day, John," he said to the corpse.

The EMT, a bit stunned by the comment, quietly

left Paul alone.

But he wasn't.

Cynthia, lying still and naked all this time . . . fortunately, covered by a sheet on the other preparation table . . . sat up and said in an attempt at a male voice, "Hey, Paul. That dude looks just like you! Get over here my man and finish the job!"

Later, after Cynthia returned upstairs to her parents' apartment, John thought about his situation. He had no savings or insurance with which to bury John. After a moment's thought, he slapped his deceased brother's face and said, "John, you an' me was gonna make it big on TV since you could see the future. Couldn't you at least see that damn streetcar coming?"

Cynthia found herself lonely again and returned as Paul collected John's ashes after the cremation. She assisted. Afterward, Paul placed the ashes in a silver urn and carried them to a seldom-used closet in the Casket Selection Room. There he found similar urns. The one in front had the name, *Pope, John*. Amazed at the coincidence, Paul said to the urn he was holding, "That's exactly what I'm talking about, John! You *could* see the future!" Paul stuck an identity label on the new urn, placed it on the upper shelf, and closed the closet door.

His brother was dead, but something just wasn't quite right with what had just occurred.

Without John's positive influence, Paul went through a meditative period where for several months he committed to following his brother's continuing lifelong desire to go west to the mountains of Colorado or even beyond to California. *I think I'd like to be a Beach Boy*, he daydreamed. All day long, a song stayed in his head. That night he rushed to work and found Cynthia. "Hey girl," he sang, "I'm feeling those good vibrations . . ."

Cajun heritage was hard to overcome. Many Louisiana natives never stepped across her borders for their entire lives. Paul was one of them. Remaining in New Orleans, he soon returned to making poor decisions. A few weeks later, he and Cynthia were discovered by her parents playing autopsy doctor and Paul was fired. But, thanks to living free in an abandoned shotgun, Paul was able to survive financially. He still had no electricity or air conditioning, and his rattrap home continued to deteriorate. Soon, even John's illegal water line failed. Within a month, the house was sold by the city for its tax value. A few weeks after that, the city received the proceeds from the sale and sent Paul packing.

Life was tough for the Popes, again . . . or now it was only *The Pope*, singular.

The next two months proved to be a downhill slide for him. Paul was evicted from a homeless shelter for fighting. He lost weight because competition for the best street corners on which to beg was fierce and he was almost never sober enough to defend the corner he'd chosen. The police were tired of hauling him to Charity Hospital, unconscious and beaten almost to death. Fortunately, upon his latest discharge, Paul managed to secure a spot begging on Lee Circle. Unfortunately, two days before, a crackdown on panhandling had begun. Broke with no options, Paul mulled things over and decided on a return to crime . . . and, *penny-ante* crime would no longer solve his needs. He elected to step up the game. He had regained confidence in his competence.

XV

April 18, 2005

Two days earlier Paul had botched an attempted robbery of a convenience store. Police were actively searching for him. Because he knew they were watching his shotgun home on Waterloo, Paul bypassed it and hiked up Canal Street toward New Orleans City Park and his nighttime palace of safety: a few grubby golf-course restrooms. Paul was crossing Canal Street when he was mistaken for an honest homeless person by a social worker driving home from work.

"Sir?" she asked as she pulled over next to him. "My name is Sarah and I work for the Mission. Can I give you a lift there? We can get you a change of clothes, a shower, a hot meal, and a bed for the night if you like."

Realizing that getting off the street for a while, especially given the scrutiny he'd been experiencing following the failed bodega robbery, would be helpful, Paul grunted, "Sure. Thanks, lady." Within a mile, it occurred to him that police were undoubtedly checking shelters all over the city in their search for him. A trip to the Mission, a shower, a hot meal, and a bed for the night just wasn't going to work. "Ma'am," he said, "could we make a stop on the way to the Mission, so I can pick up my things?"

Sarah knew how valuable personal items were to homeless people no matter how pitiful they seemed. "Sure," she said. "Will it take long?"

"No," said Paul. "Just a few blocks away. I really appreciate this."

"You, sir, are more than welcome!" Her face brightened at the thought of doing a good deed.

Paul guided her a few blocks north toward City Park and directed her to pull over into a poorly lit cul-de-sac where most of the lots were heavily wooded and undeveloped. Sarah assumed he had a tent in the woods at the back of the cul-de-sac, as did many homeless people.

However, for the second time in three days, Paul pulled out his snub nose pistol and this time demanded, "OK Lady. Stop the car. Give me all your money."

Working for the Mission had taught Sarah to be wary. She was wise to the slyness of many vagrants and revved the engine. With a quick shove, she pushed her ride out the open door. Paul landed hard and slid on the gravelly pavement. As Sarah backed up to turn around, the open passenger car door whacked Paul across the head. For good measure, Sara adeptly spun her small car into a 180 and sprayed gravel back as she accelerated. Paul was left bleeding and lying in the street, pelted by flying rocks with a huge gash on his forehead.

The twisted ankle provided an exclamation point to Paul's day. The head wound began to swell, giving him a pair of major head lumps . . . the one from a tiny Asian store manager two days before that still throbbed, and now a second lump from a car door belonging to a petite social worker. As she turned the corner, Sarah glanced into the rear-view mirror and dialed 9-1-1 with her free hand.

NOPD was nearby, arriving on the scene in less than two minutes only to find that the perp had crawled away. "If he was where she described, the guy probably went through a break in the trees over there. That looks like a path," said the first cop to the second on the scene while pointing to a slight break in the heavy foliage. "The description of the perp matches that of the idiot who tried to hold up the convenience store a couple days ago. If it *is* him, he's armed. Call for back up . . . and bring in the dogs!"

Crawling and limping from a crime scene two nights before where he'd been belittled by a small woman, was becoming a habit for Paul. This time his luck was turning. He made it a dozen feet into the woods and happened onto a useable walking stick. It made a real difference.

Behind him, he'd heard the cops call for canines and should have been worried, but Paul knew in the long run that he was smarter than they. That's why he'd asked Sarah to stop her car in an area with which he was already familiar. Supported by a thick crutch but bleeding from the forehead and hobbling badly, Paul worked his way down a narrow path through the trees. Closing in on him even more, the path wove through a thick forest of sticker bushes. Many of them tore at him, finally catching him securely by his already sore ankle. Paul tripped and fell. As he pulled the stickers from his clothes, He was relieved to finally see an end to the forest and, as he hoped. He was relieved because he expected to find smoother going on the apron of a golf course.

Paul left the woods sixty seconds ahead of the two pursuing officers. Meanwhile, more police were pulling into the cul-de-sac including two officers with canines. They were only seconds behind the first two. Dark clouds swirled in the sky and a three-quarters-full moon slid in and out of visibility. It was about to rain heavily.

As Paul crossed the fairway he heard the dogs closing in. Besides his previous wounds, his arms and face were now cut and bleeding from the sticker bushes.

He'd had better nights.

In fact, Paul had been thinking lately about what a total failure his life had become. Now he was at his wit's end, likely facing off with perhaps a half dozen armed cops. He saw himself walking, shackled, down Broadway at the Green Mile, guards on each side of him and inmates whistling and heckling, "Hey, newbie. Get cleaned up 'cause I'd like to make your acquaintance!"

Under a cart path light, Paul looked at the gun in his free hand. He concluded though that even with the situation dire, he didn't have the fortitude to pull the trigger on himself. He settled instead on *Suicide by Cop*. As police flashlights wagged back and forth, more cops, and now dogs, appeared from the opening in the woods.

Paul stopped on the far side of the narrow fairway. To make a better target of himself, he stayed within the circle of illumination provided by a cart path light. Several police flashlights found him as well. He extended his left arm and aimed the 38 at the closest officer. He heard several of them shout, "Gun! He's got a gun!

"You guys better back down or I'll get at least two of you before you get me. I'm an expert shot so drop to your knees and lay down your guns."

"Don't do it, Mister! You don't have a chance!" the first cop on the scene shouted.

"Drop your weapon, scumbag!" yelled another. "You couldn't hit the camera in the bodega an' you couldn't hit me if I was two feet in front of you! I'm not even gonna pull out my gun!" The cop began warily to walk toward him.

That was all it took to set Paul off. The sound his gun made as it fired surprised them all. They hadn't believed that the shabby character standing before them had the testicular equipment to do that. The second cop was right, though. Paul couldn't hit the sky if he aimed up. The round missed wildly, perhaps even deliberately wild. The police reacted by aiming their own weapons with arms locked forward.

There was a short pause in the action. The police were holding their weapons steady when a large bolt of yellow lightning struck the streetlamp above Paul's head. In a flash, it zig-sagged down toward him. For a moment Paul glowed . . . and then he disappeared.

XVI

THE RISEN HERO
April 1991 – New Orleans

The sun pushed its firstborn rays at the horizon. One even caught the top of a tree near the fourth green of the New Orleans City Park Bayou Oaks Golf Course. With a sudden jerk of his body, Paul's eyes flickered open. He immediately concluded three things: a.) He was naked, b.) He was flat-eagled on the apron of a golf course green, and c.) He had no memory . . . nada . . . nothing . . . not even a name. Whoever he was, he was in reasonable shape except for a smoldering burn on his right knee, with smaller burns on each elbow. Other than that, he was only cold and wet with the dew. In the moonlight, he detected wisps of smoke rising from a nearby charred telephone pole that apparently had been struck by lightning.

Wow, he thought! *I guess I'm stunned* and *stewed. I wonder how and when that happened. And to begin with, I wonder how I got out here on a golf course in the middle of the night? Better still . . . who the hell am I?*

In the ebbing darkness, his eyes picked out three small buildings a few hundred feet away. Exploring them, he found clothing in one that served as a small work shed. As the sun came up, now dressed as a Bayou Oaks Golf Course maintenance man . . . at least that's what the logo said. He became Luke, for it was the name embroidered on the uniform. With nothing to do and nowhere in mind to go, *Luke* headed for a few lighted tall buildings in the distance. Eventually, he found himself strolling down a street called Canal.

Everything he encountered was new, but at one point he felt an intense desire to turn down a side street where he stopped in front of the fifth house on the left, a tumbled-down, narrow, white frame building set on piers. The word "Shotgun" popped into his brain but he could see no weapons visible anywhere. It didn't matter. The building was of no real interest to him. What stopped him though was a somewhat familiar-looking young man half-awake on a broken-down couch on the porch. "Can you help me, sir?" My name is Luke and I'm confused, he said, afraid to admit that he didn't even know his own real name. "I'm confused and seem to have gotten myself lost."

The young man shook off his sleep and stared at his visitor as if a joke was being played upon him. Finally, he responded, "Yeah, man. Luke, is it? Come on! Matthew . . . or Luke . . . or *John*, or whatever the hell you want to call yourself today. It's about time you came home, son. You look like shit!"

Months went by. Paul the Older – alias, Luke, the former Golf Course Naked Man – soon evolved into the long-lost, John, identical twin brother to the man on the porch, Paul. Paul the Younger was ecstatic to have John back in his life. *John . . . Luke . . .* the amnesiac, relearned who he was . . . or perhaps . . . *who* he was supposed to be. Something though wasn't quite right about the whole thing but most of the pieces to the puzzle seemed to fit. *John* believed that, given time, everything would sort itself out and become clear.

When he sleep-talked about time travel, Paul repeated the words his father had taught him years before. "It just ain't possible, John! Or is it *Jean-Luc* now? If it was, you'd be floating' in space right now, or you would be on the Bridge of the *Enterprise*! You ain't, are you?"

John ain't, but he sure wasn't certain when or where he actually was. Committing to regain his full memory and senses, John began to make a life in his new brother's Mid-City neighborhood which was populated by numerous equally dilapidated *Shotgun Homes*.

Life though was tough for the Popes.

* * * *

Two years later, in May, John attempted to take advantage of water issuing from broken piping in the alley behind their shack by digging a shallow trench and rerouting it using stolen PVC pipes from the city main to a connector in the crawlspace beneath their house. While there, he found an empty brandy bottle with $100 in it and a note reading: "If he says his name is Billy Bob, give him the numbers below and then tell him to keep playing them no matter what." A string of meaningless numbers scratched in a barely legible hand followed.

Skyrockets were going off inside *John's* head. He recognized the terrible handwriting on the note but couldn't place the author. Drums still *rat-tat-tatted* in his brain whenever he tried to unravel his past. Ultimately, he explored options on what to do about the note and the money from the bottle and decided on attending Saturday Evening Mass.

John had planned to put the money he'd found into the collection basket. Of course, he was waylaid by drums in his head steering him to a bar where a two-piece band was playing. The band was called *The Time Bandits* and they claimed their third member, the drummer, was lost in time and maybe in another dimension. Appropriately enough, the bar was called the *Time Zone*. Some of his leftover crawl pace money went for a shot and a beer. An hour later in a moment of nowhere-near-sobriety-but-total-generosity, John, held a beer out, and said to a large man sitting next to him wearing a cowboy hat and a clerical collar, "Big mon, 'dis Bud's fo' you!"

XVII

"Brother," Reverend Billy Bob Buckmaster said, happily taking the fuller of the two beers from John's other hand, "Thanks. I'm Trip B."

"Say again?" asked John, but he smiled after a recurring blurred memory exploded in his head in full color. *Where did that come from?* he asked himself, but instead, after a moment to cogitate, said aloud and with the extra precise pronunciation that drunks often attempt, "Mr. B., How do you do? I am John Pope." The multicolored cloud in John's head then disintegrated and conscious reasoned thought, or at least as much of it as he was capable of at that moment, returned. He looked straight into the man's eyes . . . mostly.

Extending a baseball-mitt-sized hand, the big man replied, "Trip B . . . Triple B . . . Billy Bob Buckmaster, formerly of Waxahachie, Texas! But now I call Dallas home! Good to meet you, soldier!"

Trip B slapped John on the back and Augustus Busch's bestselling beverage sloshed over the mug's rim spilling into the cleavage of a hard-looking lady parked on the stool next to John. He had deduced earlier that she was a hooker but also thought that if he played his cards right, he might have a chance with her. Hell, he might even be in love.

For a fraction of a second John also considered leveling Billy Bob for spilling his beer into the enticing cleavage. The thought then occurred in slow motion that he could lick the beverage up before it dropped further. Before he could act on that thought though, the woman fled the bar, swearing at them both.

Unimpressed, Billy Bob got right to the point and slurred, "Do y'all have a lottery in this state, John? I *love* lotteries and I've still got fifty bucks. I like you, man, and," he broke into song, "*I got a feelin'!* Gimme' some numbers, boy, and we'll light up the piñata."

John's mental cloud was settling in again and he took a moment to make certain he understood Trip's request. "If you got $50, how 'bout you buyin' *me* a beer, will ya' ole buddy . . . *Crip*, was it?"

The same sense of *déjà vu* returned that on several occasions before had stopped him cold – actually, this time it was a sort of *déjà vu, déjà vu*. Unable to fix the vertical hold on the vision in his frontal lobe, John finally translated Trip's message and recalled the note in the bottle. "Billy Bob is it?" he asked with the tiniest bit of trepidation.

"Damn straight, son. Nice to know you."

John reached into his pocket and pulled out the torn slip of yellow paper he'd kept from the bottle. He read part of it to his new drinking buddy, "Trip, it says here that a man named Steve is coming back to his old job. Buy all the stock you can find in . . . the paper's torn right here," he said, "but I think it must be a fruit company because it says . . . Apple?"

"I need numbers, man," said the man called Triple B, "I don't want no *fruit*, for crying out loud!" Bob drained the rest of his Budweiser and slammed the can into a pancake on the bar top. He spun his big frame on the bar stool, expertly performing a 540, and stormed from the bar looking for the woman wearing John's beer.

* * * *

John made his way back to the Shotgun, mulling the message he'd passed along to Trip. It wasn't the same one he'd read while under the house, was it? He dug around in his jeans to see if there was another piece of yellow paper in there besides the first one buried along with all the crap he normally carried around. Instead, he found a twenty-dollar bill. He'd forgotten about it about the same time

In Better Times

Trip spilled his beer on the hooker. It was the last of the money he'd found in the bottle buried under the house.

No other note, though. He couldn't understand how the piece of paper with numbers on it could have disappeared from his pocket, or where the other one came from with the message about somebody named *Steve*. Puzzled, he studied the crumpled note again and it occurred to him then to flip it over. Sure enough. On the other side, he found the missing numbers: *3 – 11 – 16 – 28 – 40 and 44*. John swore to himself and rushed back to Bourbon Street and to the *Time Zone* to find Trip, but Billy Bob was long gone.

For the next five hours, John searched every bar and brothel on each side of Bourbon Street but found no trace of the former Pentecostal minister from Texas. As a last option, he spent twenty minutes in the downtown casino looking for the fat man before being thrown out by security. In disgust, John crumpled the note and tossed it in a sewer.

A voice in the back of his head, sounding an awful lot like his mother, told him he'd failed the biggest mission of his life. All the way home he repeated, "Damn. Damn. Damn!" Before he climbed the porch steps on Rue Waterloo, he tossed a newly emptied brandy bottle back into the crawl space. He'd slipped in the ten dollars and change leftover from the twenty after he'd purchased a new bottle of brandy.

Sunday found John in the pews of St. Louis Cathedral, cradling his head from the loud organ music *and* a monumental hangover. Recalling his incredibly bad luck while at the same time trying to follow a sermon on greed from a priest named Sue, John shed tears whenever the face of the Reverend Billy Bob Buckmaster flashed in his mind . . . which was approximately every twenty-seven seconds. He wasn't sure why. *Trip is gone!* Still, something told him that the episode with the Texas preacher *wasn't* over, and the finale would not offer a happy ending.

As John feared, a month later while cleaning tables at *Bon Temp*, Trip reappeared like a bad penny. He heard the name *Billy Bob* coming from the *Bon Temp's* TV. Tears formed on John's cheeks as the $36 million-dollar sole winner of the Texas Lottery was introduced. Billy Bob looked into the camera and said, "All my life I've played the birthdays of my kids. This time I drew numbers from my ten-gallon hat: 3 – 11 – 16 – 28 – 40 and 44. Winner. Winner. Chicken Dinner! Yee-hah!" The anchors cackled so hard *they* too shed tears. By now, John's own tears had formed a veritable river. He ended them by throwing a beer glass through the *Bon Temp's* television screen.

In never-ending misery, John attended Mass at the Cathedral for the second time in a month. Just before it began, the priest – *Or maybe the word is Priestess,* John thought. *Do I call her, father?* – told John she'd like to meet with him for a moment afterward. John found it difficult again to concentrate on the sermon, this one also on the subject of greed. He found himself irritated at the priestess for no real reason. When Mass was over, he waited for the parishioners to receive their, *Bless you my* *child*s from her. At last, he was alone with Sue. John said, "Father . . . or is it 'Mother' now? Reverend What-Ever-the-Heck-Your-Title-Is, give me the note you're holding, and I'll give it to Paul."

Confused by the exchange, the priestess paused for a moment before extracting a note she'd written for John. "Do that," she said, handing it to him and . . . the name is *Father Sue*. Like the Johnny Cash song. Please give this note to your brother! And bless you, my son."

Maybe he should call her Mom, then. Father Mom? *Naw! That wouldn't work!*

It took intense urging to get Paul to respond to the job opportunity at the Beiderweil, but he finally agreed. "I will, John, but you owe me . . . *big time!*" Among his arguments to convince Paul to apply was his suggestion that Paul might get an employee discount. Paul's eyes lit up. "What if it's a casket? If it is, maybe I can sell it at the Flea Market?"

* * * *

The next afternoon Paul cleaned up as best he was able and set out for the funeral home for the job interview. A few hours later he returned with two Abita Ambers and a frown on his face.

"Only $5.65 an hour, I have to work two nights a week, and there ain't no employee discount . . . but, I got the job!" He broke into a big grin. "I start tomorrow night. I think it's a dairy store or maybe an ice cream store. What do you bake in a creamery oven anyway?"

And so, both twins stuttered through corporate life: John cleaned tables and played the drums Friday nights at the money-losing non-profit *Bon Temp* bar – John called it a *No Profit Bar* – and Paul occasionally shoved bodies into the oven of an old funeral home and crematory. He roasted peanuts in the oven on the side and sold them on the streets in the French Quarter for . . . *peanuts*.

Over the next few weeks though, Paul's life improved after he met Cynthia Beiderweil, the owner's daughter. She helped him believe that he was not only Houdini reincarnated but was destined for eventual Beiderweil upper-level management.

"With a little work on your part, and with me giving my mom and dad a few hints," she told him, "you might even become president of Beiderweil someday!" Paul laughed off the idea, but the thought stayed with him for weeks. He'd known all his life he was management material! His father had told him so.

One morning John was awakened from a sound sleep by Paul returning from a salvage job . . . salvaging someone's color television from an unlocked house on his way home from Beiderweil. He also brought with him an orange fifty-foot extension cord and suggested to John, "We got a new TV, Bro. Now we need electricity. You're the handy one, dude. Wire us up!"

With nothing better to do, John obliged and crawled under the shotgun, running a split of cable from the home next door. Burying it and the necessary AC line below yard debris, he crawled back under the house to finish up. While he was there, he saw his empty brandy bottle and, in a gesture of goodwill, restocked it with cash but wasn't certain why he did so. In the end, he reasoned it seemed like the fair thing to do.

In writing a note to replace the one he'd thrown away, he worked from his memory which was much better at recalling numbers and recent events than it was for anything going back a few years. The note he wrote recalled the words of the original that had been on some yellow-lined paper. He stuffed the note in the bottle with the money.

It seemed odd to have no electricity in the house and yet have a fully functional 32-inch color television. Now that they were hooked up to cable and to the world, the two men camped out and binged on endless television. They became hooked on a new show called *Survivor* and made bets on who would win, Paul chose Kelly Wiglesworth and John picked Richard Hatch. In the series finale, Paul won the bet. John was required to steal the next bottle of whiskey.

* * * *

John was sleeping peacefully in a gutter on Bourbon when a clean-up crew asked the New Orleans police to arrange wake-up service. The next morning, the cops kindly offered John two options. Of the two, he chose to attend AA meetings at the Cathedral and to fully commit to sobriety. John told the police from his knees in the drunk tank, "My lips will never touch alcohol again. I promise! I swear!"

Twenty-two hours later John slipped from a stool at *Bon Temp* and fell to the floor. This time an ambulance, called by the bar, dropped John off at the same place where he'd slept the night before. The place offered free lodging and meals ... and, it had a bar ... actually, thousands of them.

Things weren't looking good in general, but John finally realized after 30 days residence in the Greybar Hotel that he simply must eventually become "a man." He went back to AA and climbed aboard the wagon. Other things turned positive as a reward. He got a full-time job working at a local hardware store and won $1,800 after investing a dollar on a scratch-card. Even Paul absorbed John's good luck and began dressing better for, he'd found where John hid his winnings and earnings.

When he looked back on it, John began to be convinced things were improving after he'd paid back the brandy bottle. Or maybe it was meeting Billy Bob. Or maybe it was AA.

He was 74 days sober – it seemed like a decade – and was walking home from the hardware store when a mugger stopped him. When John told him that except for his cigarette, he was broke. The mugger took his cigarette and buried it in John's palm. As John howled and danced in pain, the vagrant, still angry because he'd not found any money, shoved John in front of a passing Canal Streetcar, Number 024. Arriving EMT workers not only declared John dead on the spot, or more accurately on the rail, or even more accurately, on both sides of the rail, and transported what was left to Beiderweil.

In Better Times

Paul was alone in the funeral home and in a foul mood because Cynthia was entertaining a male friend in the apartment upstairs. After the EMTs dropped off the various parts of their latest customer and left, Paul noted the man's burned palm before he recognized its battered face. Preoccupied with Cynthia's absence, his instant reaction to identifying the body of his brother was, "Remember John, Smokey says only you can prevent forest fires!"

Less than two hours later a grim-faced Paul had filled an urn with John's ashes. Still, he brightened a bit when Cynthia came downstairs to say hello. He told her what had happened and together they carried the urn to a closet in the casket display room, affixing a small label to the urn before placing it on an upper shelf. There were similar urns already in place, but both had other things to do and didn't dwell on any potential coincidences.

Over the next few weeks, Cynthia appeared in Paul's life fewer and fewer times because she'd found a friend who visited whenever he was in town. Cynthia replied a bit testily when Paul quizzed her about the frequency of the visits, saying "He travels here on business from out of town and I feel obligated to give him some time."

Paul asked her where the guy lived, and, after a moment, she replied, "Covington. I think it's across the river from Cincinnati."

* * * *

While blasé at first over the loss of his brother, in short order, Paul grew depressed . . . or perhaps it was because of the loss of his girlfriend. His increasingly lackadaisical attitude toward his duties got him fired from Beiderweil within a month. He returned to Rue Waterloo disconsolate.

XVIII

April 16, 2005

While scavenging for food scraps in a dumpster behind an Italian restaurant on Canal, Paul pulled out a bag of garbage that had a hard, metallic lump of something in it. Wrapped within a paper towel inside the bag he happened on a slimy 38 auto with most of a full clip in it. After checking to see if any neighbors or passersby had witnessed his find, Paul quickstepped two blocks to the nearest convenience store, entered it, and fired a round into the cash register. At the recoil, the slimy automatic slipped from his grip and fell to the floor where it fired again, wounding him in the ankle.

Instead of yelling, "This is a hold-up!" as he'd practiced, Paul doubled up in pain, screamed, "Holy Crapperooni!" and fell to the floor swearing even nastier swear words. He still had hopes of standing and completing the robbery, but intense pain kept him from remembering the exact phrase to use when robbing a convenience store.

Unwilling to give her would-be robber the time to get his head straight, the small European woman manager wearing a babushka yelled, "Arschloch!" and hit Paul over the head with a small fire extinguisher. Now he was hurting at both ends and compounded his humiliation by urinating in his pants. "Mein Boden ist du unordentlich!" the woman screamed at him, so, she hit him again.

Paul was red at the top, red at the bottom, and yellow in the middle. The woman looked down at him with fire in her eyes and kicked him where the pee never sparkled. Paul screamed, this time in an unnaturally high-pitched voice. Shoving the gun into a pocket, he literally rolled out of the store, leaving three distinct trails of liquid in his wake. In a mocking tone, the bell on the store's door tinkled as it swung shut. At the sound, the clerk calmly picked up the phone and said in a perky, but heavily accented voice, "Nine-vun-vun, please. Danke!"

By the second night after the attempt on the bodega, Paul had limped most of the way up Canal Street. That's when Police tracked him to a ten-block area. He'd spent the last two evenings sleeping between the tombs in the Masonic Cemetery and was in no mood to be hassled. He limped north as best as he was able and for the next two hours successfully dodged in, out, and around, above-ground graves in several more Cities of the Dead before arriving at an overgrown path that meandered a bit through a forest of trees, eventually leading out and on to a putting green on the Bayou Oaks Golf Club, his destination and overnight home on several previous occasions when he'd been on salvage runs and too far away to stagger home. Dark clouds swirled, and the nearly full moon peeked in and out of them. Thanks to police dogs that traced Paul's scent, the cops closed in.

Yellow lightning struck. A big boom sounded.

XIX

THE TATTOO
EARLY MORNING, APRIL 19, 1995

Paul groggily regained consciousness. He'd lost his memory and, because it was dark, didn't really care that he was naked. Totally nude, he followed the cart path to the Club House where fortunately the pre-dawn glow placed him mostly in silhouette. Golf course groomsmen were setting out to keep all 18 holes of the Bayou course in pristine condition. The first worker to catch sight of Paul was an elderly Mexican man who was rightfully shocked. Aboard a maintenance version of a golf cart, he lost control and drove directly into a ten-foot-deep water hazard adjacent to the cart shed, all the while screaming, "¡*Ay, caramba!*"

A more thoughtful response was that of another worker who grabbed a handful of newly laundered golf towels and threw them to Paul, who struggled to catch them with both hands, leading to several more of the groomsmen yelling versions of, "¡*Santo* Mierda! ¡Ay, caramba!" Paul saluted them and looked around in the cart storage barn for a moment before finding a short piece of twine, and tied everything together, covering himself.

"Thanks. I'll bring 'em back tomorrow," he said to one of the workers as he walked off.

"Eeewuu! Por favor no moleste señor!" one worker yelled, making a lemon face.

Approaching the clubhouse, Paul chose to turn toward the course entrance which led in the direction of the downtown skyline.

Despite the early hour, 9-1-1 became quickly inundated with colloquially correct callers who swore that a dirty, pale all-over Native American was walking down their streets in the northern part of the city *au naturale.* Police responded and quickly took Paul in, charging him with suspicion of public drunkenness and *Attempting to Impersonate an Indian (New Orleans ordinances had not yet caught up to politically correct America.).*

They threw him into a cell that normally housed rowdy Mardi Gras revelers but didn't charge him with nudity because, after all, this was New Orleans, and hey, he just might be one of the Village People heading for a gig. They were unable to determine the man's identity but suspected that his amnesia act was just that. He was issued prison clothing and, after a day in the Greybar, was released, dressed in the height of fashion in alternating black and white striped coveralls.

Freed from the city jail, the amnesiac wandered down Canal and turned onto a familiar street, stopping in front of a dilapidated shotgun home. He was forced to shake the arm of a young man sleeping on the floor next to a fallen porch swing. Failing to bring the young man to consciousness, he shook the arm harder, finally getting a telltale eye-flutter. Paul told him he was lost and remembered nothing before the previous morning when he'd found himself naked on a golf course. He asked for help and the young man instead responded, "John, is that you? Man, you look a little on the heavy side. You need to stay away from stripes in the future! Or is this for a class picture? When will you graduate? Five to ten?"

XX

Soon, Paul-the-Older became *John* the long-lost identical twin to Paul-the-Younger who had immediately accepted the stranger's identity as fact. Paul the Older thought, *there's something about my supposed younger identical twin brother that just doesn't jive.* Working past their age discrepancies, the two men decided to try to make a life living in the Mid-City shotgun home where they'd, perhaps, reunited. While they bonded to a degree, daily life continued to be a challenge for each.

To Paul's absolute contempt, the man . . . the newly *renamed* man . . . *John* . . . took a full-time job at a Canal Street hardware store that to him seemed vaguely familiar and, except for an insatiable hunger for alcohol, began to straighten out his life. Having access to home repair materials at an employee discount, John began to repair broken things around the shotgun and at one point was attempting to fix faulty plumbing in the crawlspace beneath their house. There he found a brandy bottle containing

$100 in cash and a two-sided hand-written yellow note in barely legible penmanship. Among other things, it predicted that he'd soon meet a man named Billy Bob.

John pocketed the note to try to figure out its message at a later time but was absolutely delighted with the money. Making his way to the *Time Zone,* he quickly put any thoughts about the *12 Steps* to the back of his mind because, after all, *it was happy hour,* and *this was New Orleans!* In a moment of unusual generosity, he gave a Happy Hour bonus beer to a heavy-set man wearing horn-rim glasses who had just joined him at the bar.

"Thank you, my friend. Hi, there! I'm Triple B," the man replied extending his fat hand.

"Bridget Bernadette Bardot?" asked John, attempting a poor comeback to what he perceived to be a poor attempt at New Orleans humor.

"Oh, come on now!" responded the heavyset man who was not happy at often being the butt of jokes.

"Is your name your apartment number . . . and you're lost?"

"Yeah. Whatever. Heard 'em all before. I'm Billy Bob Buckmaster," the man finally said, extending his hand, "Call me Trip."

"Anything you say, B-Master," responded John, his short-term memory rattling the chains in his skull.

Trip came around and laughed at the new nickname and slapped John hard on the back. Most of the beer in Trip's hand – actually John's Happy Hour beer – sloshed out onto John's brand new, hard-earned, expensive Polo shirt. For a moment he considered throwing a punch at the fat man but something in the back of his head stopped him. Maybe it was the glasses, but John concluded it was more likely Trip's clerical collar.

The men settled in at the bar and talked about livin' the life. They began to share ideas on how to strike it rich. John's head was squeaking and clanking the more they discussed making fast money. When the subject of lotteries came up, Billy Bob said, "I like you, John! Gimme' some numbers to play!"

Squeak, squeak, squeak, clink, clink, clink!

"I'm reading your mind, Trip!" said John, pulling out the hand-written note from his back pocket and studying it. "3 – 11 – 16 – 28 – 40 – 44! Keep playin' those numbers for at least two months," he said. "They're sure bets! I've got the fix in, Billy Bob," which was also a prompt taken directly from the note.

* * * *

John owned no hatching chickens but wouldn't consider taking the time to count them even if he had. The excitement over meeting Trip in person was just too much to bear. With something possibly good in the wind, the twins that evening discussed changes John felt were needed in their lives. He pressed for a sign of reversal in their fortunes if *each* secured meaningful full-time jobs. Paul replied," I don't know, John. What you're proposing, sounds like a lot of work!"

In the end, only John committed to serious self-improvement. Accordingly, over the next three months, relations between the two "brothers" soured much as they had years before over a police matter concerning a robbery and then a mistaken identity. Fortunately, thanks to their different schedules – John worked all day; Paul stole all night – they rarely saw each other. In memory of their mother, John began attending Mass at the Cathedral, and the priest, Father Hippolyte, convinced him to come back each Tuesday for AA meetings. "Bring your brother, my son." John promised to do so but wasn't confident.

Paul lived up to John's lack of confidence in him.

Six months later John ran into a new friend who'd moved to the Big Easy after living all his life in Dallas. He asked him if he'd ever heard of a community church preacher back in Texas named Billy Bob Buckmaster.

The friend said, "Yeah. That was big news for a while. Stuck a shotgun in his mouth about two months ago. Apparently, he had the winning numbers for the big state lottery and forgot to play them. Turns out his congregation didn't know he was enjoying the lottery with the collection money."

* * * *

Paul had scouted a home in the Garden District for several weeks and when the owners left for vacation, broke in, intent on making a withdrawal of its pawnable items. However, the *living room bar* caught Paul's attention first and when the owners returned early, they found him splayed out unconscious on the floor. Paul was given a free ride to the hoosegow to sleep it off. Assuming he regained consciousness, he was to meet with a judge the next morning about his future and perhaps an improvement in his living conditions.

The judge, a recovered alcoholic, felt sympathy for Paul and ordered him to do *time* in the form of Community Service. A priest who was a friend of the judge and also a recovered alcoholic told him about an entry-level position available at the Beiderweil Funeral Home. Paul was offered a chance to either clean floors for thirty days in the Beiderweil prep room or clean bathrooms in the parish jail for ninety. *No question.*

One evening at about 10 p.m. as he was polishing the floor of the old mortuary, a television set mounted on the wall of the prep room showed live coverage of an accident in Paris. British Princess Diana had been killed following a fall from her horse *Charley*, her head striking a rock. Paul, who'd had a crush on the princess, was caught by old man Beiderweil watching the coverage instead of working off his community service. The old man threatened to end the job then and there, which would send Paul back to jail. Paul begged for mercy. A good old soul, Walt extended Paul's community service sentence by three more months, assigning him to all-night duty, and to be supervised for the first few hours every night by his daughter, Cynthia.

* * * *

A month and a half later, a bit after nine at night, John was walking home down St. Charles Avenue from

In Better Times

his hardware store job. A few minutes earlier, Streetcar Number 024, empty of passengers, had picked up an inebriated man who, as it developed, was armed with a knife. The man, either high or intoxicated, threatened the driver, finally pushing him down the steps and out onto Neutral Ground.

Taking over the controls and learning streetcar-driving OJT, the drunk throttled up to maximum speed and zoomed past four stops on the St. Charles line, running at least at 11 miles per hour. While attempting to light a cigarette, the hijacker encountered a pedestrian named John Pope crossing the tracks, nailing him front and center.

John had been hurrying to cross the tracks so he could be picked up by the same street car that would soon dissect him. In his statement, the hijacker told police, "I tried to steer around the guy but when I turned the wheel, nothin' happened!" He later told the officers as they stared at the body parts, "It wasn't my fault. As you can clearly see, he was comin' at me from more than two different directions."

Paramedics tried to revive most of the upper half of John but in the end, the coroner arrived and stopped them. Making his formal declaration, the coroner pointed to John's body lying on either side of the tracks and said, "These two shall pass." Paul's body parts were transported to the nearest funeral home.

After an hour, most of the body lay face down on the preparation table so Paul asked Cynthia to help him turn the parts over. They then began assembling the mangled body parts in different ways. It was while playing that game that he and Cynthia became distracted by finding a blurred tattoo of a fleur-de-lis on the body.

"It's you, Paul!" she declared. "You're dead!"

"Oh, my God! I am dead, Cyndy! I'm dead!"

The tattoo on the body was an exact copy of one that Paul carried on his own rear end . . . and in exactly the same location. Both Paul and Cynthia were clearly disturbed at the sight of Paul's tattoo on the just-arrived corpse in the exact same location. While Cynthia took his pulse to make sure he was alive, Paul cleaned up the dead man's face. It was also Paul's.

Cynthia, a bit more mellow than Paul, told him, "Naw. Can't be. You can't be in two places at the same time. Must be your twin. What's his name again?"

"John. Oh, my God. It is *John*! John, what're you doing with my tattoo on your butt? Is nothing sacred?"

Confused, Paul left Cynthia to mind the body. He walked to a bathroom mirror and dropped his pants, attempting to see if *his* tattoo was still on *his own* backside. Because, if it wasn't, he was dead and should instead be out in the work-up room on the table. In shock, he concluded that both tattoos were identical, even including how blurred they both had become over time. Paul sat down on a stool in the preparation room too stunned and confused to turn his late brother into an urn full of ashes.

Cyndy, however, was only too happy to do the deed for him. In the end, she placed the one containing John with others on the upper shelf of the closet in the casket display room. She'd grown especially fond of that part of

In Better Times

the process. She returned to him and said, "Now you're alive Paul. It is only you with that blurred tattoo on your butt. You should be happy!

* * * *

Three weeks later, John's passing continued to puzzle Paul. He couldn't get over the fact that he'd cremated a body with the exact, same, blurred tattoo on its butt as his own. He still felt though as if he'd cremated himself and went to the mirror to inspect himself for charring.

On the other hand, the death of his twin became an inspiration, because Paul now felt an obligation to carry on where John had left off. Paul had spent all his life trying to *avoid* self-improvement, whereas, John had tried and tried to convince Paul to join him in bettering their lives.

Now, with his death and the discovery of the no-longer unique tattoo, Paul committed to following through on what would likely have been his brother's *final* wishes. Or . . . was it really his brother who'd been toasted? The tattoo had him wondering who the guy he called *John Pope* really was.

A week later Paul went to work early and knocked on Walt Beiderweil's office door.

"Come in," said Beiderweil, buttoning the top button of his shirt before tightening his tie. He'd been expecting a customer, and the knock on his office door by one of his employees was unexpected. He'd hoped someone had died, and now instead of a new customer, it was just an old and mostly incompetent employee.

"Oh, it's you, Paul. What can I do for you?" Beiderweil said in disappointment.

"Mr. Beiderweil, I've been working for you doing community service now for almost three months. I know I haven't always been a great employee. At the beginning I . . ."

Beiderweil interrupted, "No, Paul. Frankly, I've been unhappy with your performance for quite some time now. And to be truthful, I think you've been growing more lackadaisical every day. In fact, I think . . ."

Paul was irritated at Beiderweil's interruption of his memorized mini-speech for several reasons: a.) Ole Man Beiderweil had always been very negative to him so this probably wasn't going to be a pep talk, and b.) he'd worked on this speech for two days, and now he'd probably have to start over.

He paid Beiderweil back with his own interruption.

"Well, yeah. Perhaps," edged in Paul. But I think I've learned a lot since I got here, and if you hire me full-time for your overnight slot, I promise you won't regret it!"

Beiderweil had been postponing letting Paul go for exactly that reason. For weeks he'd been unable to find anyone interested in doing custodial work in the creepy old mortuary, especially at the pay he offered. He backed off from his intention to let Paul go. "Paul, I'm due to meet with a customer in a few minutes. I'll tell you what: I'll think it over, but don't get your hopes up."

Paul stepped out the office door with a worried grin on his face and headed for the Preparation Room where he found Cynthia playing doctor on their newest customer. She turned and said, "Well? Did he go for it?"

"I dunno', Cindy," he replied. "I don't think your father likes me."

"Don't worry about it. I'll get him to change his mind. He's a sucker for me. I can get him to do anything I want! Until I do though, *work your ass off!* Make him think you really love it here. On another subject, let's do it in the hearse tonight!"

* * * *

Two days later, after having wrapped up a very expensive funeral, Walt Beiderweil pulled Paul to the side. "I was ready to let you go, young man." he said, "but Cynthia told me how hard she sees you working . . . and, to be truthful, we've had a good week. I'm giving you a raise to $7.15 an hour and will guarantee you 30 hours a week . . . but you gotta work nights, son, and you gotta improve."

For the first time in his life, Paul concentrated on doing a good job. Besides, if Cynthia told him he did well, sometimes there were benefits.

* * * *

It took three months, but Beiderweil eventually made Paul *full-time time* which qualified him for medical insurance. Old Walt threw in a 25-cent-an hour-raise on top of that.

Before his passing, John had been spending a portion

of his earnings fixing up the shotgun, and now Paul began following John's example. Soon the former shack-of-a-shotgun showed signs of almost resembling a home – one that the neighbors could be proud of.

They weren't.

A week after completing a full repainting and repair of the crumbling exterior of the house and porch, in a conversation with a neighbor, Paul told her that he was bringing in a professional landscaper to draw up plans for beautifying the front yard.

The next morning Paul returned from Beiderweil's to find the shotgun covered in graffiti with broken windows and ransacked rooms. In spray paint on the living room wall was a message: *Don't change things. We liked it the way it was!!!!!*

It turned out that a few of the neighbors were worried that Paul's efforts toward gentrification might bring in yuppies who, rather than buying drugs, just might want to renovate their new acquisition. If that were to occur, the old neighbors might be forced to find other locations in which to ply their drug and prostitution trades. That meant, among other things, that their regular customers would probably seek other closer-at-hand dealers rather than track their former providers to their new locations.

"Yeah, I guess I can understand that," Paul said to the neighbor.

But Paul was depressed to see his hard work trashed. He went into a funk lasting weeks, always wondering how John would have handled the conversation with the neighbor.

Worse, because John had always paid the few bills they owed, Paul was clueless about required property taxes and other recurring expenses. And so, thanks to his efforts to fix up the place, even with graffiti now decorating it and the windows shattered, the Shotgun had sufficient value that the city took interest in it and gave Paul six weeks before evicting him for failure to pay.

Six weeks to the day, Paul found another abandoned home a few blocks away. By this time, the continuing barrage of bad news had taken a near-fatal toll on him, a *once-recovering ne'er-do-well*. First, he'd begun a reversion to his old self and was soon let go at Beiderweil. It didn't help that Cynthia had taken up with one of the EMTs who occasionally brought in customers who were beginning their exploration of the great unknown. She also enjoyed having fun in the back of the ambulance as it screamed down the interstate with its siren yodeling. Since they were below sea level in New Orleans, it was sort of like joining the Mile Low Club.

Still, for Paul – *a person who'd once tasted the good life* – a part of him yearned for a return to his old life. Like an addicted smoker who had tried to quit, he began to fail with enthusiasm. Sometimes though, things accidentally looked promising.

During a longer-than-normal period of sobriety, on September 9th Paul enlisted in the Air Force a few days after terrorists hijacked two tourist trains, crashing one into the big lagoon in Disney World, and another into a pie-stand at Dollywood. A third, a streetcar, took out Chubby Checker's front porch in New Orleans, and a fourth found the earthquake ride at Universal Studios California. Three persons were slightly injured including a homeless guy who normally lived in the right field bleacher restrooms of the House that Ruth Built but was vacationing in Los Angeles.

It was a rough enlistment. Five weeks into basic training, four Drill Sergeants and the Company Commander unanimously selected Paul as the *Enlistee Most Likely to End Up in Fort Leavenworth*. He was discharged from the Air Force *without honor*. Paul returned to his shack less than three months after he left it - *a failure, even as a patriot*.

XXI

April 18, 2005

Paul immediately returned to burgling, dealing, injecting, over-imbibing, pickpocketing, and raiding dumpsters for food. On a cloudy afternoon in mid-April, he found a pearl-handled 38 caliber pistol in a dumpster and bought a stolen box of ammo from a neighbor to test out his new weapon. There of course were no shooting ranges nearby, nor any place, in fact, willing to allow a person like Paul to practice his pistol skills . . . so, a convenience store robbery attempt went comically bad.

Humming a Manfred Mann oldie, at ten one night,

In Better Times

Paul entered a convenience store at ten p.m. and fired all six shots at a video camera and, missing from three feet, and realized that his neighbor had sold him blanks instead of real ammunition. At that point, a grandpa with trifocals standing behind the register pulled out a sawed-off double-barreled shotgun from beneath the counter and let fly in Paul's direction. pulling the trigger. Incredibly, Paul wasn't hit but slipped and fell. The old man though went back on his heels at the recoil, unloading the second barrel into the ceiling causing most of it to drop to the floor.

Still humming the tune, Paul was blinded by the dust and tripped over blast debris, badly spraining his ankle. With the alarm now going off, he stumbled out the doors and wedged himself between the exterior wall of the store and the sticker bushes next to it. He followed the wall and found what appeared to be the old man's unlocked 1975 two-tone AMC Pacer, white over red, that was parked out back. The keys were in the vehicle and soon Paul was cruising north toward safety. A stroke of lightning flashed in the skies. Thunder rolled. A light rain began to fall. As the car accelerated, Paul fumbled for the car's wipers and ran over a curb, blowing the right front tire.

With police zooming past him in the opposite direction toward the bodega, Paul hung on as the Pacer continued to clump-clump-clump heading north. Soon he was relieved to find a familiar cul-de-sac in which to turn. It was walled with dense tree stands on both sides. He'd been there before. Three hundred feet in he passed the only home on the short street and came to a halt just past it. Fortunately, the house appeared dark and uninhabited. Either that or the owner wasn't home.

Thick trees provided a background for realtor signs that fronted each of the other lots. Paul, now an injured and failed robber but a successful car thief, *if* one could call a Pacer an *actual car*, squinted his eyes as he searched for a familiar opening in the wall of trees, one he'd explored previously.

He found it.

An eighty-eight-year-old woman who owned the only house on the street was extremely cost-conscious. She kept her home deliberately dark. She was also unused to any traffic on her short street. To save on the utility bill, she was reading Kirkman's *The Walking Dead* using a small battery-powered reader's light modeled after a miner's lamp. It was attached to her head. Minutes earlier she'd been so enthused at the story that she told herself that she wouldn't put the book down except for an intruder . . . and now one was driving furtively down her street.

She turned off her headlight, rose from the chair, shuffled over to the bay window, and watched as the intruder came to a halt, paused for a few seconds, and then, oddly, backed up past her vantage point. Carefully pushing her lace curtains aside, she picked up the handset from a pink Princess Phone on the table – *That table fits my bay window so well,* she thought as she dialed 9-1-1.

The rain was falling heavier now. Alarmingly, before her very eyes, the driver pulled his vehicle into her *very own* driveway and got out. "Hurry, please," she calmly and politely told the 9-1-1 operator, "A man has pulled his strange-looking vehicle into my driveway, and he's gotten out. I'm alone and it looks like he's holding a gun. I think he's coming to rape me."

As soon as she hung up though, the invader limped back into the street, stepped across growing puddles of rainwater, and disappeared through an opening in the trees at the end of the cul-de-sac.

Paul was in no real hurry because the forest immediately shielded him from the rain and from anyone who might be watching just like he expected. His stolen car was parked innocuously in the driveway of what he believed was an empty home near the end of a mostly empty tree-filled cul-de-sac. In less than a minute he had vanished into the dense foliage.

Thanks to his observer though, Paul soon heard sirens for the second time in twenty minutes, and in each case, he assumed correctly that they were coming after him. Brakes sounded behind him as more than one police vehicle careened into the cul-de-sac where the elderly woman, now dressed in a pink flowered house coat, was pointing at the trees and waiting calmly to explain, "Officer, he went in there, and he has a gun!"

Paul uttered obscenities over the sirens but hoped they were nothing but a coincidence. As more were heard in the distance, and now hearing muffled shouting, Paul realized the growing threat and limped up his pace.

The senior cop on the scene didn't believe in coincidences either. He put the convenience store robbery, the report of a stolen car, and a vehicle fitting the description of a Pacer parked in the woman's driveway, all together. "We have an armed robber and car thief who is on the run on a path leading into the woods just off the cul-de-sac on Swan" he radioed. "Be alert. He could be hunkered down along the trail waiting to ambush us!"

His sprained ankle was now causing Paul real problems, plus sticker bushes slowed his forward motion. Paul wondered, *How did they find me so quickly?* He shuffled faster, tripped on a root, and went down, spraining the other ankle. But, having heard the withering sound of a radio report of a suspected ambush behind him, he said aloud, "I'll fool 'em!"

Picking himself up, and mostly out of breath, Paul limped into a clearing featuring a beautifully manicured and very large lawn surrounded by forest on all sides but one. The moon emerged from behind heavy clouds. The rain slackened for a moment. A typical Louisiana short-lived drencher appeared to be moving on.

Paul found the narrow-paved path he was looking for. The area was lit by a golf course-style streetlamp. Lightning flashed again and thunder began to roar almost immediately. The bright flashes allowed him to see several out-buildings on the far side of the smooth lawn. There were shelters over there. He'd been seeking them to get out of the rain and to hide from any followers. As the rain restarted, he turned and shuffled toward the buildings.

Lightning and thunder now were occurring simultaneously.

In Better Times

Several police officers emerged from the forest and saw, thanks both to the lightning and the streetlamp, a figure moving before them and about to reach the path. "Stop! Police! We gotcha'! Freeze or we'll shoot!"

Exhausted, Paul turned to face the officers who were still 50 or 60 feet away. Blood from multiple brushes with bushes, mixed with rain, streamed down his bare arms. His ankles hurt like blazes.

"Don't move, dirt bag or you're goin' home in a box," shouted a cop, newly arrived from the forest.

It occurred to Paul that he really didn't have a home to return to. He wanted to tell the guy that but without realizing the consequences, pulled out his own gun. He checked the cylinders, but found only empty cartridges – *and those were from blanks*!

SOB! He thought. *I'll never buy anything from him again!*

Four well-armed policemen were facing him with more cops pouring from the forest.

"Gun! Gun!" shouted a newcomer. As one, four officers dropped into firing positions, both hands holding their weapons straight out, aiming at an unsub who was standing in a puddle of light holding his own weapon, and wearing a Pink Energizer Tee Shirt and jeans . . . with spangles on the butt.

Paul's vision was obscured by the falling rain, but he could see flashlights coming through the woods as even more police were emerging. He knew his gun was empty – even of blanks. He knew he was outgunned by at least fifteen to one even if he had bullets. Lifting the weapon he chose not to point it at them but began to cock it toward the side of his own head.

"No! No! Don't shoot," screamed one of the cops. There was a flash of light and a loud boom.

Lightning struck hard, and for several seconds the cart path streetlamp went dark before flickering back to life. Those officers with flashlights re-aimed them toward where the man in the pink shirt had been standing. A heavy smell of ozone filled the air.

Nothing. Nothing! The man with the gun had slipped into the vapor.

XXII

THE NOTE
APRIL 19, 1995

An hour after dawn, two golf carts approached the fourth green of the Bayou Oaks Golf Club on the north end of New Orleans, each with a pair of ministerial golfers aboard. Each of the men had miraculously placed his third shot on the green, or in one case, on the apron. It was a par four hole, so they were all in great spirits.

The rabbi appeared to own the closest lie. From where he'd taken his third shot, his ball bounced and rolled to a stop perhaps 18 inches from the cup. It helped that the flagstick that day sported a red flag because the fourth was a big green and he probably couldn't have hit it much further with the club he was using. From a foot-and-a-half away, he'd probably take this hole . . . not only a par, but his first winning hole of the morning earning him a dollar from each of his companions. More importantly, thanks to that last shot, the hole would *at minimum* cost him nothing. To him, that was even more important.

The Methodist minister had taken the first hole with a nice escape from a sand trap and then nailed a long putt. But he'd come in second since then. On Four, he lay furthest out. Long putts though were his specialty, so he couldn't be counted out.

The older of the two priests wasn't a great golfer, but he played well enough to get by. His "three-and-on-the-green-with-a-chance," was probably going to be his best bet for par over the course of the morning.

The newest addition to the weekly outing, the younger priest, had yet to win a hole . . . and it was worth a bet given the talents he'd exhibited so far, that he'd be lucky to take even *one* today. Perhaps on six as it was only a 110-yard, par 3. The young priest's game was by far the weakest of the four. Even so, on this the fourth hole, he'd had three good swings.

Although the Bayou course was new to three of the men, they'd been meeting like this nearly every Wednesday at dawn for several years running, mostly playing on less expensive courses. It was a real treat when a parishioner treated them to a round at a country club. This morning there were no freebies and no discounts. Even the dollar-a-hole bets were serious money.

The neophyte to the group was the younger priest. As such, his punishment, assuming his play today landed him in last place, would be to buy a round of drinks at the 19th Hole or, coffee in the case of the older priest who'd not only battled the devil all his life but had some issues with the bottle too. If the timing worked out, drinks and coffee should occur about noon which was about four hours later than necessary for many of the residents of New Orleans including the first three golfers to begin the day's consumption of "tea".

Late the night before, the younger priest, who technically was an *assistant* to the older priest, had taken a call from him complaining that *The Baptist*, who was usually the most temperamental of the weekly foursome, and who *also* was a coffee drinker, had canceled complaining of stomach issues. On the phone, the old priest pressured his young assistant, suggesting that there were months of Sunday 6 a.m. masses waiting for him if he didn't join the other three at dawn the next morning. The younger priest had declined anyway.

"Oh, come on! I was just kidding. You'll have fun. The rabbi and the minister are always telling jokes. And, truth be told, we have to have a foursome!" the old priest said. "We get free cart rental if there are four of us!"

The two carts – each containing a priest – moved up the fairway where they'd eventually end up parking close to the green. The young priest was piloting the second cart. His passenger, the rabbi, turned to him and said, "I have a joke for you. . . Father George said it would be okay." The younger priest nodded apprehensively, and the rabbi continued:

"Miss Elsa, the church organist, is in her eighties and has never been married. She's admired for her sweetness and kindness to all. One afternoon the pastor . . . uhh . . . no. Let's make it the *rabbi* since you're new to this group . . . *The rabbi* comes to call on Miss Elsa and she shows him into her sitting room. She invites him to have a seat while she prepares tea. As he sits facing her antique pump organ, he notices a cut-glass bowl sitting on top of it. The bowl is filled with water and in the water floats, of all things, an unopened condom. 'Miss Elsa, I wonder if you would tell me about this?' he asks, pointing to the bowl. 'Oh, yes,' she replies. 'Isn't it wonderful? I was walking through the park a few months ago and I found this little package on the ground. The directions said to place it on the organ, keep it wet, and it would prevent the spread of disease. Do you know, I haven't had the flu all winter?'"

The assistant priest nearly lost control of the cart, laughing, and narrowly missed a tree. He was feeling better about this outing despite his early ineptitude with a two-iron and putter.

The cart path they were heading down was on the same side of the fairway as an incredibly large, beautiful, and ultra-modern home ahead and to the left, overlooking the green. It drew the attention of everyone. "Oh my," said the minister in the first cart, "If he isn't Methodist, I need to convert him."

The old priest next to him responded, "Too late. I

got him, and he's a *regular* for ten o'clock Mass at the Cathedral. I'll see him tonight at the funeral home he owns when we wake Councilman Forge'. May I tell him you'd like to convert him to Methodism when I see him?"

The minister laughed and said. "George, you got 'em *all* locked up!"

"Hey, this is New Orleans. Why do you think that counties in Louisiana are called Parishes? They're almost all Catholics here. It's in my contract!"

They both laughed.

As the second cart approached a huge Live Oak that forced a portion of the path out a bit to circle it, the minister said to the old priest, "Hey, I got one for you, George. Bet you haven't heard it: Two atheists, a pagan and an agnostic are in a boat, fishing, when the pagan falls overboard . . ."

As they rounded the tree, the cleric stopped in midjoke. Something large and dark was blocking the path ahead. "Holy Moly!" the old priest said, crossing himself.

"Cheese and crackers got all muddy!" said the minister.

From the second cart, the rabbi exclaimed, "Oy vey! Some poor schmuck bought the escalator!"

And the younger priest simply said, "Oh my God!"

A man lay on the cart path, unmoving.

The rabbi gave him CPR, the priests gave him last rites, and the minister called 9-1-1. The man on the ground was collectively declared by all four who'd seen their share of dead people, to be on his way to eternal life, either up or down.

An ambulance arrived minutes later, followed by a pair of policemen. The cops shook their heads, noted that there were burn marks on the ground and that a charred and broken limb from the tree lay near the man, *still* smoking.

"Obviously lightning," said one cop. The second agreed. They too had seen their share of dead bodies. They were either so certain of their diagnosis or so unwilling to touch the body that neither bothered to check its carotid.

The paramedics did though, checking for life despite all the amateur diagnoses. They were astounded to detect a tiny, occasional flicker of a heartbeat. The other six present, the two cops, two priests, a rabbi, and a minister, then took turns checking for themselves. They concluded again . . . for their professional reputations were at stake . . . that as stated previously, *this guy was toast* – literally – and they were certain again, that this time, he was indeed gone.

The EMTs had never really been certain they'd detected a tiny beat of the man's heart in the first place, and they were unable to replicate it. Unhurriedly, they discussed whether racing to the hospital down I-10 during rush hour might be an act of suicide in itself.

"My sons, there's no reason to risk your lives driving at twice the speed limit to try to save a dead man," counseled the older priest who'd taken upon himself the role of senior spokesman for the foursome. Having heard the clerical declaration of death repeated, the EMTs relaxed and took their time packing the death-by-lightning victim for delivery to the nearest hospital morgue.

The cops didn't object, in fact, they were already off

on other police business. Their sirens wailed as they peeled out. The clergymen had moved on as well, for the rabbi was now standing between two small white cones getting ready to tee off on the fifth. They'd steered well around the dead man, each priest crossing himself for the last time, and were soon talking congregational gossip.

They'd decided it would be in poor taste to complete play on the fourth and had mutually agreed that the rabbi had taken the hole and would have honors, but all would score par. "

Schickzas!" said the rabbi under his breath, but his non-Jewish partners failed to hear the mild insult and so the rabbi settled for gritting his teeth and shaking his head from side to side.

For the dead guy though, lightning seemed to have scored a hole-in-one.

A few minutes later, the ambulance departed the scene traveling at less than the speed limit. It arrived at Central City Medical Center just off the I-610 connector where emergency room personnel were surprised to find a solid and steady pulse.

When ten days at Orleans Parish expense had passed and the patient, who was signed in as John Doe, displayed no memory of how he got to where he was found, who he was, or more importantly, who was paying his bills, CCMC Social Services and the man's assigned doctor ordered him released on his own recognizance, suggesting that he visit a nearby church offering emergency shelter.

The shelter was operated by a small independent

community church. Had its pastor been one of the members of the foursome the morning when Mr. Doe was found on the cart path, she would no doubt have been stunned to find that the presumed victim – dead from a lightning strike – had signed into her shelter alive and well.

There, Mr. Doe spent another ten days, the maximum stay allowed. Given his continuing lack of memory, John Doe, who'd readily accepted his new name, was counseled and given information on services available elsewhere. In the end, he was escorted out the shelter's front door.

Doe walked from the shelter as clueless and homeless as he had been when he arrived in the emergency room nearly three weeks earlier. Wandering the north end, he spent a cold night in the Masonic Cemetery where it seemed even the residents there wanted him gone. That didn't bother Doe. He slept the sleep of the once presumed dead.

In the morning, Doe began what turned out to be a long walk, aiming for the downtown skyscrapers. Halfway down a street called Canal, as he began to cross another called *Rue Waterloo*, a sort of supernatural force guided him left.

Four homes past the corner, the hairs on the back of his neck came to the fully upright and locked position. It wasn't because the neighborhood looked like a combat zone, although it did. It wasn't because two young boys, one on each side of the street, were anxious to introduce him to men who currently made their offices in two of the abandoned homes on the block and had something to sell him, although they did. It wasn't because four ladies who claimed this block as their own all propositioned him, because *they* did. They did this not only because he seemed clueless as to his whereabouts but, thanks to the hospital's thrift shop, this potential *John* was dressed very well, and so, the women adjusted their prices upward.

The supernatural part of the moment though occurred within two minutes of turning down the street. John Doe found himself before another poor excuse for a home that somehow looked familiar. *This house had seen better days . . . perhaps back in the 1770s,* he thought. Then he wondered how he'd even know that because he didn't even know for sure what year it was.

A man, perhaps young enough to still be a teenager, was sleeping in a sitting position – slouched might be a more accurate description – against the wall of the front porch, a mostly empty bottle of vodka cradled in his left arm.

Doe called out, "Hello!" and then approached the porch because the young man hadn't responded. When he put his weight on the first of three steps leading up to the porch deck, it collapsed with a loud crashing of old rotten timber. Doe was unhurt but stood awkwardly with one foot on the sidewalk and the other on the ground inside the shell of the step.

"Not my fault! Not my fault! We're not liable!" came a strained almost automatic reply from the suddenly awake teenager on the porch. He was stretching and yawning and was about to offer another disclaimer to liability.

The legality stuck in his mouth as the image of the visitor began to focus before him. His eyes grew wider and more dilated, his mouth opened in wonder as his chin dropped, and while he'd first appeared leery, his facial expression now evolved into one of absolute astonishment. He rethought the next disclaimer he'd been ready to offer. What came out of his mouth instead was a less-than-original, "What's your name, dude?"

"My last name's Doe, or so I've been told," said the visitor. "How 'bout you? Who're you?"

"Bond, James Bond," said the young man . . . and suddenly, the formerly sleeping young porch dweller was wide awake and cracking jokes. He laughed and jumped to his feet, which apparently was not the best thing for him to do given his previous activities. The young man immediately staggered on the broken steps, closed his eyes in pain, and grabbed his head with his hands. "Oh, my God!"

Whatever pronouncement he was about to make was put on hold. He held his head with both hands in a classic hangover pose and moaned, "Oh God, my head!"

Finally, the pain seemed to drain away and his grimace relaxed. After working his jaw down and around, he squinted his facial muscles into a more normal appearance. Disjointedly he shouted, "John is that you?"

"How'd you know my name is John?" asked Doe. His intonation was one of excitement. Had he found someone who knew him?

"Well . . . for crying out loud, John, we're twin brothers, man!"

Astounded that he may have accidentally found a

close relative, the visitor asked, "Really? Is your last name Doe too?"

"Hah! Good one, John. We're Popes, you joker! Welcome back, my man! How many years has it been anyway? Where'd you come from? At different times people told me that you were in the Appalachians, the Rockies, and the Ozarks . . . always with a woman. Is it true?"

The young man changed course again, not giving John a chance to respond.

"Are you gonna keep that awful beard? Why aren't you talking? Are you deaf? Are you hungry? Oh man . . . are you thirsty? Let's go get a beer. Man, oh man, oh man!"

John Doe was totally flummoxed. Out of the blue, he'd found someone who recognized him, but one who wouldn't give him time to ask any questions such as, 'Who are you really? Who am I? Where are we? What year is it? Are we part of a family? Where's the bathroom?'

But beer seemed to be the best starting place for all these questions and that led to more beers . . . and more beers. By the time they returned to the Shotgun, John was convinced that his first name *was indeed John.* But whether his last name was Doe, Pope, or Van Winkle was the question of the day.

By the next morning, both men could be found resting with their backs to the same wall on the same front porch with the same broken steps on which their reunion had occurred twenty-three hours earlier. Their heads hung to the side and both were unconscious. A case of crunched-up Old Milwaukee empties lay between them.

In Better Times

They were awakened finally by a small crowd, neighbors it turned out, pouring into the street from their homes where a man holding a blaring transistor radio was sobbing. The former *John Doe* noted with alarm that some of the folks in the street were armed.

This time the *two* men who'd been sleeping it off on the porch, staggered to their feet, tripped carefully down the broken stairs, and made their way to the crowd in the middle of Rue Waterloo.

"They did it. Those bastards did it!" a man brandishing a shotgun said between sobs.

"Who did it?" asked another. "Last I heard they *didn't know* who did it. Have they caught him?"

"Maybe it wasn't a bad guy who did it at all! Maybe it just blew up, or maybe it was a *bunch* of bad guys that blew it up," said a woman who'd just returned from working the night shift and was dressed for it. "That's what I'd guess."

Another neighbor brought out a battery-powered television with a four-inch black and white screen. The crowd surrounded him as if he were an old-time newspaper seller waving his last copy of the paper declaring that Dewey beat Truman by a landslide. The Mini TV Man though was attempting to hold the small set up so that everyone surrounding him could see it. Consequently, with his movement, only a few could see the picture.

Those who could get close enough, perhaps two of the people out of a crowd of a dozen or so, barely made out the small image, obviously shot from at least a block back from its target. Smoke was pouring from a building of some kind. Fire trucks were seen spraying water over the remains. At the bottom of the tiny screen, even tinier emergency personnel milled about. Up closer, a silver-haired reporter held a mike in his hand and reported in his announcer voice, "We're being told that there was no warning before the explosion occurred. This *is* terrible..."

A voice interrupted the coverage belonging to an unseen announcer back in the studio, "Tommy, do the authorities have any idea what caused the explosion?"

Tommy was speaking but was drowned out by Paul's few neighbors who were standing close enough to actually see the mini-TV's screen. "Holy Enchilada folks, that's CBS and they're carrying live coverage from Channel 12 right here in Nawlins. It must be the Superdome that blew up 'cause that's Tommy Tijon!"

"Hey... *What* happened?" asked Paul Pope, as he and the former John Doe joined the small crowd of neighbors crowding around the guy with the TV.

"I think they blew up the Dunes in Vegas!" confided one man who'd just joined the crowd and who was possibly even more hungover than either John or Paul. In fact, the newcomer won because he was still drunk, and Paul was just hungover.

Paul recognized a comrade in booze, showed some compassion, and said, "Naw, that was last year. This is this year."

"It was the Superdome, you idiot!" said another neighbor. "It's probably what woke you up from your siesta on your porch. Didn't you hear it or feel it? Look at the smoke. I can see it from here!"

Paul turned around and looked behind him. Sure enough. Here they were trying to look at a four-inch screen from four or five feet away when the big show was live and in color right behind them. Now that he'd become aware of it, he could even smell it. But it wasn't the Superdome or even the Arena next to it that was burning. A monstrously huge black cloud of smoke was climbing into the sky from a structure north and slightly west of the Superdome. It may have even been a building across the river in one of the refineries in *Oil Town*.

XXIII

Following the explosion, time seemed to fly by for John. As ultimately reported by the local TV news stations, a grain silo at the riverport in Avondale had exploded into a giant fireball. Fortunately, when all the damage was tallied, no one had been killed and the few minor injuries that had occurred were limited to minor burns and smoke inhalation, and even these were sustained only by emergency response professionals.

John and Paul had spent their time since then getting to know one another better. John had happily accepted the last name of *Pope* since Paul was such a strong believer in the theory that they were twins. But he still remembered nothing before the morning he awakened in Central City Hospital. And while it seemed credible that he and Paul *might* be brothers, could they actually be twins? *I'm way older than he is,* thought Paul. *How can that possibly be?*

Paul explained the anomaly to him by recalling that John's last few years had been spent wandering the country in a drug-heavy environment, mostly in a Colorado commune, and his memories were likely erased by chemicals. Anything could have happened!

"You're probably going to get *meth face*, John! Too bad for you."

John tried incessantly to pry the missing history from his brain, but his memory was still three passengers and a dining car short of an express. Meantime, he was just happy to have a birthday, an identity, and a family . . . if one believed that a single brother constituted *a family.*

The twins settled into a routine where Paul tried to introduce John to the dark arts and there was some success: petty thievery, dumpster diving, begging for food/drink money, pick pocketing, and even some small-time burglary. While Paul was an expert at all these skills, John wasn't and found them to be most distasteful, unnerving, and in most cases, illegal.

His *talents* seemed rather to lie more in the vein of handyman and home repair. To eliminate the need for twenty or so buckets and rusty wastebaskets scattered about the Shotgun to catch leaked-in rainwater, John's solution was to be proactive. He spent considerable time trying to seal the roof. One day he realized that either he had inherited basic carpentry skills or, as Paul said, "John, I think you learned some handyman skills in the mountains before you lost your memory."

To Paul's dismay, John decided to take a job as a novice member of a construction gang because he was feeling the need to bring in honest money. Paul just stared at him dumbfounded when Paul mentioned that. Because of his inherent skills and talents, John was accepted as a semi-skilled worker and began bringing home real money. The Shotgun soon began to appear like a pilot effort toward Rue Waterloo gentrification.

Nearly a year went by.

"Hey, Paul," said John one morning as his brother came in carrying a large box, but staggering as well from a hard night on the town. "Let's go for breakfast at Mother's."

"Oh God, John. How can you even think of eating? I think I'm gonna puke." And he did.

John had grown tired of this routine and the cleanup it necessitated. He asked, "Paul, how'd you find the money to get drunk? You were broke yesterday."

It was then that reality set in. John grabbed his wallet from the dresser top and inspected it, finding it empty. Paul had cleaned him out . . . *again* . . . this time of all his previous week's pay.

"Gimme' what you got left, man!" he demanded of his brother.

Paul gave him an *I'm Guilty* smile and turned his hands, palms up. "Sorry, dude. It's gone. But I'll pay you back. I promise!" He reached down and picked up the large box he'd just brought in and, from it, pulled out a 32-inch semi-flat screen. "You want a slightly used TV? Bet you could get a hundred bucks for it!"

This scenario had occurred too many times. It became the final straw for John who was trying his best to live a better and more honest life than the one his twin had made for him. *Apparently*, he concluded, *Paul is someone who can't seem to mend his ways or pay the consequences for his actions. There must be something better out there for me than this.*

It took nearly a week though before John acted on the thought. He would move out.

Having repaired most of the problem areas of their shotgun, John felt better about moving out on his brother. At least he'd be leaving him better off than he'd found him. He grabbed his few possessions and told Paul he was hoping to find a *room for rent* in the Magazine District. To help his brother stay on his feet, John paid the water and electric bills in advance. He did that himself because he'd learned not to trust Paul with cash. He found a monthly single Room-and-a-Bath just off the Magazine District at a price he could afford, paid for a month's lodging, and moved in a day later.

Paul was left on Rue Waterloo helpless. He continued living hand to mouth . . . *someone else's hands to his mouth*. He mourned the loss of his brother for a second time and vowed he'd reform, get sober, and start over . . . *someday soon*. A week later he made good on part of his vow and attended a twelve-step program meeting.

Three months later, Paul celebrated having been on the wagon for several weeks, but by that time John had long since moved on. Then, after missing AA for two weeks following benders, Paul returned on a Wednesday to the church hall where the 12-step meetings were held. He didn't go in though. Instead, he rifled through the cars in the church parking lot and headed back to the Shotgun with the loot. There he discovered the hard way that his electricity had been turned off by the city. Water was the next to go a week later.

Before that, John had begun to make a real difference in their lives simply by keeping clean and showing up for work on time. Since their father's disappearance, the boys had never really had a male presence in their lives. John Randall Pope had never held a job for more than a month or two even for the short period in their lives when he was around. When he concentrated on it, Paul ran out of fingers when he tried to recall how many times, like his father, he'd pledged to reform, but failed. But there was always an eleventh.

Paul tried sobriety again and this time mostly succeeded for most of a year. He *generally* stayed sober and actually found a few short-duration manual labor jobs. Like his father before him though he didn't like any job where he was asked to work outdoors in the heat and humidity. And he wasn't too fond of those jobs that were indoors in air-conditioned comfort either. And truth be told, he wasn't in shape to do any heavy lifting. He'd told that to a prospective employer who wanted him to wash dishes in a restaurant.

One day John surprised Paul by stopping by the Shotgun carrying bags of groceries and clothing he no longer needed or wore. Paul seemed genuinely happy to see him and hugged his brother closely. John took that moment to pass along a job opportunity he'd received from Father Clementine down at the Cathedral.

By this time, Paul was ready to try working for a living again. He cleaned up, put on the clothes John had brought for him, and applied for what turned out to be a custodial position at an old mortuary within walking distance. It was an all-night job and the owner lived upstairs. Help, guidance, and perhaps mentorship would be close at hand. *What more would I need?* Paul asked himself.

The new job included cleaning, dusting, and vacuuming the entire main floor of the funeral home every night. He could also earn extra money doing odd jobs like trimming the bushes and mowing the lawn. If wakes were going on, he was required to stay out of sight and to do his cleaning after the family of the deceased had left for the night. The toughest . . . and creepiest part though, was cleaning the preparation room with its morgue-style lockers. He called 'em, *Cold Meat Coolers*.

One morning about two a.m., he got up enough nerve to open one of the drawers, roll back the sheet, and view the body. It was of an older man who'd been a victim of a small plane crash. The body had been badly disfigured and the resulting fire made everything even worse.

Rather than being horrified, disgusted, or squeamish though, Paul found the experience fascinating. When the owner of the funeral home, a man named Walter Beiderweil, unexpectedly opened the Prep Room door. Paul jumped, embarrassed at being found out, expecting to be fired on the spot. Beiderweil, however, understood Paul's curiosity and appreciated both his accepting attitude, as well as his ability to maintain composure. The mortuary industry was populated by a singular kind of personality and Beiderweil sensed it in this raw young man.

"Would you be interested in learning the business?" he asked Paul, who actually was ten seconds from bolting through the delivery doors and twenty seconds from vomiting . . . not necessarily over what he'd witnessed, but the fact that he'd been found out doing something forbidden.

"What do you mean, sir?" asked Paul swallowing hard.

Beiderweil liked the response, the courtesy, and the willingness to ask questions! "Easy son. If this is your first time seeing a body, you're handling it very well. I'll tell you what: You start coming in every night as usual, but don't show up 'til midnight. Either I, my wife, or my daughter will handle the wakes and any deliveries that come in before then. You just keep doing the job you've *been* doing, and when I come downstairs around 5:30, I'll start teaching you the trade . . . if you think you can handle it . . . and this . . ." he said pointing to the open drawer containing the body ". . . is a real test of manhood. You passed, my boy! You passed! What do you say to my offer?"

"You bet, sir. I'll do it. Thanks. Can I start tonight?"

"Right on, Paul!" said Beiderweil slapping Paul's shoulder. In reality, it took all Paul could do to keep his cookies in their package, and while that may have been obvious, the old man said nothing. Beiderweil appreciated it. "It'll pass, son, he said patting him on the shoulder, "and, starting *now*, you've got a retroactive pay increase of a dollar an hour. You're now earning $7.65!"

Still, there were some steep hills for Paul to climb on the roads to sobriety, independence, and a calm stomach. On numerous occasions Paul slipped off the 12 Step Wagon, causing problems both at home and at work. Generally, though Paul was stepping up to the plate . . . plus his self-esteem seemed to be on the rise.

But of course, and as always had been the case, Paul managed to find a tall cliff, climb it, and then step off into the void of bad behavior. Another cliff followed, and another.

It was inevitable. Paul was eventually let go from Beiderweil's. Old Walt had seen too many of his fellow practitioners find sobriety difficult given the job a mortician is forced to perform. Perhaps the firing would become a lesson learned.

A month went by. It was the first of May.

Two weeks without electricity and Paul's decline had been faster than John could imagine . . . *or remember*. To compensate, one night Paul connected a 40-foot heavy-duty extension cord from a neighbor's house to his. He'd pilfered it from a pickup parked in the church parking lot where the 12-Step meetings were held. Paul originally planned to pawn the utility cord but he'd had second thoughts when the electricity was shut off. Months back, John had tried to teach him the basics of electrical wiring but nothing stuck.

Almost at bended knee, Paul knocked on John's door and begged him to visit, and while there, correctly hot-wired the shotgun to the one belonging to his bill-paying neighbor next door.

Suckered again by his brother, John planted it, wired the shotgun up, and covered the exposed extension cord with dirt and leaves. Next, he worked his way through the crawl space below the Shotgun to complete the connection.

While in the cramped and humid space, John spotted a brandy bottle poking its head from one of several trash piles and picked it up. *Can't keep a pig from his old tricks,* John thought and felt shame. But there was no Brandy in it. Instead, he found the bottle filled with several twenty-dollar bills plus a wad of ones, a note, and a piece of old yellowed newspaper dated *the 29th of June – almost two months into the future.* The story described a Dallas minister who'd won the Texas Lottery for $36 million. John was too impressed with the money to notice the incorrect date.

John had a tipping point too. He had lived by the adage, *Never look a Gift Horse in the Mouth.* Stopping in the middle of his project, He pocketed the cash and the note and set out for a friendly bar to invest it in liquidity. Sobriety was only good for so long. The empty brandy bottle made him want the real stuff. *It was a bad sign,* he knew.

They greeted him at *Bon Temp* like an old friend or maybe because they just confused him with his brother. His former favorite bar stool at *Bon Temp* was occupied by a big man wearing a cowboy hat and the stools on either side of the cowboy were taken as well. John was a creature of habit. Even though he'd not been through the doors of this fine establishment in months, *that* was still *his* stool!

He turned and walked out the door.

John paused for a moment outside *Bon Temp*, tempted to go back in and throw the big guy out, but then grimaced and reminded himself that he was on the wagon and had been sober for nearly a year. Instead, he decided that a bit of alone time was needed to celebrate his find. He turned and headed for his second favorite liquid palace of repast, *The French Quarter Round*.

XXIV

While working on his third shot and beer at the *Round*, John was joined at the bar by the same cowboy wearing bib overalls and a blue flannel shirt who'd taken his stool at *Bon Temp*. The cowboy pulled up next to him and in doing so, clumsily jostled John and John's cup of *Stallion Pale Ale*, a prized local beer brewed in Kenner, a good portion of which puddled on the bar in front of them.

The newcomer stared at the puddle, gave it a proper hand salute, and slurred, "Never look a gift mouth in the horse," bent down, and with a loud sucking sound, began to lick the bar clean. John's temper was building and he loudly shouted, *"Holy explicative!"* In disgust, he watched as the cowboy continued to slurp the bar spotless . . . of *his beer*! When he could take no more, John growled, "Hey,

In Better Times

Cisco . . . If you haven't figured it out, that was *my* beer you just inhaled . . ."

The astute bartender, sensing trouble, quickly filled fresh drafts of *Stallion* for each of them. The guy in the bib overalls sat dopey-eyed, dumbly licking his lips and burping. Finally, he turned to John and said, "You want I should give it back, Pancho?"

The man belched, triggering a reflex, and did indeed give it back, and then some. A fair amount of the effluence landed in Paul's brand-new untouched cup of Stallion.

Really angry now, John slid back from the bar to avoid the mess and said, "That's it. I'm off the sauce for good!" He stood up and turned for the door.

"Clean up on Aisle Five," yelled a man sitting at the far end of the bar, who then laughed.

Having lost his second *Stallion* in less than a minute, plus his appetite, John was halfway to the door as the bartender swore at the cowboy and began cleaning up the mess. "You're outta' here fat guy," he yelled, "and don't come back . . . ever!"

Waving at an off-duty cop sitting at a booth in the corner, the barkeep said, "Tony, can you give me some help here?" Within two minutes several NOPD officers arrived and escorted the now barely conscious cowboy out the door.

All told, the ruckus took about five minutes. The bartender pleaded with John to stay while he cleaned up everything. Attempting to keep from losing the other five remaining customers, he pounded the bar and said, "Sorry about that, guys. Everyone gets a refill on the house!"

John had the bar's door handle in front of him. A voice in his head was warning him that just the day before he'd vowed continued abstinence according to the twelve steps. He'd *almost* broken that vow. The "intent to drink" had been there though and that in itself was a violation of the code, so he turned back, deciding to stick around. Staying far away from the area of the bar where the action had taken place, he walked over and introduced himself to the customer who'd called for *clean-up on aisle five*. "Funny line," he said to the man.

The man returned the handshake as John's eyes locked on his priest's collar. "Father Bill," said the man by way of introduction, but you can call me *Billy Bob*. I'm visiting from Dallas, my friend. An, y'all look like you need a *friend*."

John felt an alarm going off in his brain and knew he hadn't had that much to drink . . . yet. He coughed a couple times and said to the man, "Uh, Father, I . . . uh . . . I really just want to drink in peace and move on."

The Padre grabbed his arm and said, "Look amigo, I won't keep you long. Have a seat and I'll buy another round if you'll help me with my hobby. By the way, just call me Billy Bob."

From his youth, John had adhered to only two rules in life: *1. Never turn down free beer*, and, *2. Always accept a free beer when offered.*

"What hobby can I help you with, my man? And, thanks. Don't mind if I do."

In Better Times

John got the bartender's attention and held his left hand up in the internationally accepted *Get Me a Drink and One for My Buddy Please* gesture. And that, thanks to a different cowboy's brief appearance and indentured departure, was the beginning of a friendship John promised he'd remember forever, or at least for as long as the free beers kept coming.

It turned out that Billy Bob was, or perhaps *once* was, a minister, not a priest, and he hadn't missed playing the Texas Lottery since it had begun six years earlier. He'd tried every number combination he could think of, birthdays, ages of his kids, prime numbers, religious holidays, hymn numbers, various combinations of the estimated ages of the twelve apostles at their death, and so on.

Three weeks earlier, he'd gotten lucky and won nearly two thousand dollars and so he was currently in Louisiana touring her family of casinos. "I'd play blackjack in Texas," he told John, "but we ain't got legalized gambling back home. Just the lottery. Blackjack's why I'm here in the Big Easy."

The Reverend Buckmaster, as it developed, was willing to allow his new friend in on a five percent share of the big pot back in Texas the next time Trip played, if only John could come up with the winning numbers, plus $20.

"My creativity with numbers goes only so far," admitted the former circuit-riding minister.

Thinking about the stash of money in his pocket John realized he hadn't even counted it yet. *There must be another thirty dollars or so*, he imagined. "Okay, Father

B, I've got twenty. What's next?"

"Show me the money!" said the Reverend Former Father Billy Bob Buckmaster. Exhibiting his strong faith in mankind, he held out his hand, waiting patiently.

John fished around in his pocket and came up with a green and grey piece of wrinkled paper, one with a drawing of Andy Jackson on it.

Buckmaster took the money and said, "Bartender, give this gentleman another beer!" Turning back to John, he said, "Now for the tough part: The numbers, son. Give me the numbers."

"How many numbers do you want?"

"Six. Six is all I need."

"Six. Okay, if you already got the *number 6*, how 'bout a seventeen?"

"No, son. Six *different numbers*. Not just a *six*. An', I'm gonna be suspicious if one of 'em's a six."

"Oh. Okay. Let's see. How about a 7, a 63, 116, a 98 . . ."

Billy Bob interrupted. "Wait just a second, son. Can't be nothing bigger'n a 50."

"Whew. This is getting tough, Hoppy. 3, uh 11, 16, uh, let's see, 28, 60 . . . no, no, *40* . . . 44, an, uh . . . 48. Is that six of 'em?"

"No. One too many. Which one should I dump?"

"The first one. What was it?"

"Three."

"Yeah, that's it. Get rid of the three."

"Perfect my man. Lemme' make certain I've got 'em

correct: 11-16-28-40-44 and 48."

"Sure, I guess. Whatever you say."

XXV

John couldn't wait to find Paul and tell him what had happened. He'd told Paul he might be coming over that evening anyway to watch TV if the electrical project worked out.

Between finding the bottle of cash, the barfing Cowboy, the cops showing up, and the beer-buying, lottery-playing Rev. Billy Bob, it had been an afternoon and evening of hands-on frivolity. But, as he walked home up Canal, the more he thought about it, the more ludicrous the whole story sounded. He'd barely ever played the lottery – there were other more important, and liquid uses for that kind of cash – and now he'd entrusted $20 to an absolute stranger who lived maybe a thousand miles away.

Sure enough, he found Paul sitting on the porch in one of their *Dollar Store* $5 plastic chairs waiting for him. When John poured out his story of the encounter, Paul grew irritated and stood up, looking down at his brother in the other chair. "By my estimate brother, you blew thirty or forty dollars on drinks and a fishy-sounding lottery scheme. Isn't this the same kinda' crap you been tellin' me to avoid? Worse, you spent them on a guy you'd never met before. Now, you have *no* way of getting your money back even if this guy hits it big . . . and the odds of him ever hitting it big are a couple million to one *if* they're *that* small."

Rather than be upset at the rebuke, John found himself proud of Paul. His younger twin brother was making real headway toward becoming a person who valued honest money and sobriety.

Paul's sermon continued. He was in a full-grown Pacific Ocean-sized fit of self-righteousness. "John, taking money that you found . . . money that rightfully belonged to someone else who perhaps mistakenly buried it in a brandy bottle under the house is wrong . . . just wrong!"

The pontification continued. "You've taken somebody's treasure . . . maybe not by fingering it from a mark's pocket or by selling a TV you heisted . . . and you don't even know the person who buried the bottle, or who the person is to whom you gave the money! Worse, you didn't even think of other uses for the cash, you just decided to go out and get drunk! Wake up, man. How many times have we talked about this?"

John pretended to be hurt by Paul's comments, but he was incredibly proud of the way Paul seemed to be maturing right before his eyes. "Yeah, but Paul," he said. "if Billy Bob wins it big, we get five percent!"

"Uh, huh. And how is he gonna track you down to pay you your share even if he's honest about it?" Paul continued. "And the odds are astronomical that he *won't* be honest with you, that he won't win, and even bigger, that if he does win, he'll never consider sending any of the winnings to you!"

Finished with his mini-sermon, Paul sat down in his

In Better Times

plastic porch chair much calmer than he'd been a few minutes earlier. He fell silent for a minute.

John meantime, remained slouched in his matching chair, pretending to be sulking.

It was a real switch for the brothers. For almost the first time ever, Paul felt guilty for yelling at his brother. He changed the subject and said, "Okay, John. Lost cause. We won't look back. But I'm asking you to put the cash back in the bottle tomorrow . . . all of it!"

"*All* of it?"

"Yes. All of it."

"Alright," and John sighed heavily. "I will. What about the note?"

"What note?"

"There was a note in the bottle when I found it."

"Show it to me."

John fished around in his jeans pocket and pulled out the crumpled piece of yellow paper written with two different kinds of barely legible penmanship on it. He handed the note to Paul who read it, and then reread it.

"Listen to this, John!" Paul said suddenly with enthusiasm, "The note . . . if I can read it, and believe me, it's really tough to make out the printing." He un-crumpled the note even more and struggled while reading aloud. "The note says . . .

'Here's some money. Go to the Time Zone, or where it leads, and meet a man named Billy Bob. He'll call himself, Trip. He needs the following numbers: 3, 11, 16, 28, 40, & 44!

"The rest looks like somebody else's handwriting."

A man named Steve is coming back to his old Job! Invest all the money you can get hold of in Apple Tech. Pay it forward, brother.

Replace the money in the bottle along with this note and put it all back where you found it. THIS IS NO JOKE!"

Paul flipped the note over saying, "Wait, there's more. On the other side, it says:

Give Trip these numbers: 3 – 11 – 16 – 28 – 40 – 44. Tell him to keep playing them no matter what.

Paul sat down on his plastic chair and said, "Holy Crap!" What did you say the guy's name was, you know, the guy you met at the bar?"

"Billy Bob. Billy Bob *Bushwacker*, or something like that. Wait, it's here in the note."

Paul fumbled with the note again and said, "Buckmaster! His name is Buckmaster.

"Listen, John. This whole thing doesn't make sense. Some of the writing is printed and some of it's in cursive. Some of it's repetitive. And it looks like some of the writing's older than the rest. And John, the bottom line is, you *found* this Buckmaster guy at the bar today! We need to find him again and give him this note!"

"But I didn't go to the *Time Zone*."

"Yeah, but that's where you went first so I think it still should work! We gotta find this Billy Bob guy. My gut tells me that something big's gonna happen if we do. Let's talk strategy on the way to the bar. When we get to the *Time Zone,* we'll find him. Boy! Have we got a lot to

In Better Times

talk about!"

As they stood up from their porch chairs, a slammed, yellow-over-green '51' Mercury with blacked-out windows, slowed just before their house. A rear window rolled down and a three-round burst from an automatic weapon rang out. No sooner had the echoes of the shots died down, then a man emerged from the shack next door, ran into the street, and emptied a pistol at the car as it began to accelerate away. A voice from within the car yelled, "Shit, Tony! We got the wrong house!"

The Merc burned rubber and was nearly gone from view as John slumped slowly to the porch floor. Not noticing, Paul yelled out, "I got part of the license number! It ends in *024*!"

An ambulance and police cars arrived within four minutes, but John wasn't present to see them. Father Clementine, the assistant to an older Parish Priest, showed up from the Cathedral and administered the last rites.

XXVI

The story of the drive-by shooting made all the TV news strips but not because of John's death. The event became *news* because it was the third drive-by shooting in New Orleans that week in which someone had died, and in one of the others, the same yellow-over-green '51 Mercury with a license plate that included the numbers 0, 2, and 4 were involved.

Paul's appearance was sufficiently pitiful on the best of

days. The loss of John, just when things were starting to look up for the two of them was devastating. He blamed himself for not shielding his twin from the gunfire. The news coverage, including interviews with Paul, highlighted the plight of impoverished people in the city.

Partly because of the newspaper story accompanying a photograph of Paul in obvious misery, a fund was created to defray burial expenses. Beiderweil Funeral Home offered to cut most of the expenses anyway because of Paul's previous employment, and also because doing so put the name of Beiderweil in every news story running. Paul was rehired a week later. That made the news too.

Paul elected to cremate John's remains rather than bury them. It was a Beiderweil suggestion that ended up being much less costly as well. When the oven had done its job, an appropriately somber Walt Beiderweil handed Paul a small cardboard box containing John's cremains and left him alone to grieve in the *Family Members Only* waiting room.

Paul really didn't know what to do with the cardboard box of ashes so while on duty a few nights later, found an extra urn and poured what was left of John into it. Then he placed a hand-written label on it and stuck it up on a shelf in a small closet in the casket display room that was rarely if ever, used. There were some other similar-looking urns there anyway so he reasoned it must be okay. Then he waited for Cynthia to come downstairs.

That was the old Paul. Things were about to change though.

* * * *

The first thing Paul did with his Beiderweil paycheck was to fill an empty brandy bottle with two twenties and 60 one-dollar bills . . . just as John would have wished. The crumpled note followed. He also crammed the newspaper story of John's shooting into the bottle and placed everything in the same trash pile under the shotgun where the original was found. There was a lot of stuff in that bottle. Paul had to test three of them before finding one large enough to hold everything.

Well, okay. Some things weren't about to change.

Paul paid *back-due* bills for electricity and water with some of the money left over from the fund. With the remainder, he went on a bender that angered Walt Beiderweil so much that he threatened to fire him again. In the end, fearing negative publicity from firing a grieving, down-and-out semi-homeless man, he elected to keep Paul on. "But this is the last time," the old man warned.

XXVII

The weeks and months flew by and Paul, missing his brother, once again regressed. He recalled his father once saying, "You can't teach an old dog new tricks." Soon he was again without a job and the city posted an eviction notice for failure to pay taxes. By then the electricity and water had been turned off. The funeral fund had long since been exhausted on beer. Paul's *Andy Warhol 15 Minutes of*

Fame was over and public sympathy moved on.

Paul reverted to his previously well-honed skills: dumpster diving, petty thievery, pickpocketing, and all the other things that had gotten him in trouble before. Hungry and sleeping in restrooms on a golf course on the city's north end, Paul emulated John Dillinger and fashioned a fake revolver from a bar of soap, staining it black with shoe polish. Brazenly he charged into a convenience store announcing a holdup. "Gimme all your money!" The small Vietnamese woman-manager pulled her huge .44 Magnum Smith and Wesson from below the counter, pointed it in his direction, and in a tiny, accented voice asked, "Do you feel lucky sucker?"

The powerful weapon had a hair trigger and it went off. Dirty Harry would have been proud . . . proud that is until the huge bullet merely nicked Paul's ear and took out a fire extinguisher mounted on the wall. It exploded, showering Paul with acidic foam. Covered in the stuff, Paul screamed and tripped, falling flat on his face and spraining his ankle. Fortunately, he managed to limp out the door and make a successful, albeit embarrassing escape. The entire episode was caught on tape by several security cameras.

The quality of the image was perfect, and Paul was identified within minutes. The city was outraged that a person who'd been a recipient of charity money not many months before, had apparently turned bad. Before he'd limped a mile from the scene, the entire active-duty NOLA Police Department was reacting to his BOLO.

The video of the attempted robbery eventually made it to the finals of America's Funniest Videos and the little Vietnamese woman won $10,000. She planned to retire from her career in the convenience store business. "Good Comes from Evil," read the headline in the *Times-Picayune*.

Before that all happened, however, Paul was able to make his way to the Bayou Golf Club. He'd just opened a door to an outdoor restroom when lightning struck.

XXVIII

THE POPE
7:00 A.M. – CLUB HOUSE FOR THE CITY PARK GOLF COURSES – NEW ORLEANS

Terrance Gerald Lewis, who was called "Gerry" by his friends, sat with his back to the Clubhouse windows. Had he turned around in his chair, he could have watched as a foursome teed off less than thirty feet away on the other side of the big plate-glass windows of the clubhouse bar. It was chilly today and the four golfers beginning play all wore jackets. In another hour or two, it would be another fine day but at this hour of the morning, the weather in New Orleans was cool . . . cooler than normal for this time of the year. Still, that was one of the many reasons Gerry had retired to New Orleans from northern Michigan . . . the weather.

Gerry Lewis wasn't in the clubhouse this morning to

golf though, although he did that frequently. Today was Wednesday, and this was the morning he reserved for his weekly gathering with three other veterans, all from the 1st Marines in Vietnam, and the group's quasi-leader.

They'd met accidentally in Dallas at a reunion for members of the Division, most serving in the country's I Corp Region. None had known each other *during* their time *in-country,* although two had served at the same time at the same big Marine base near Danang. They'd all met for the first time at a reunion and, partly because they discovered they all were now living in New Orleans, became fast friends and literally, comrades in arms.

Gerry was the only one of the four who'd not won a Purple Heart. Oddly though, he carried a Silver Star, and at one point had been considered for a Congressional Medal of Honor. He'd served as a Door Gunner on a Huey gunship that had been shot down in *one more battle for another meaningless hill* in the jungles near the Cambodian border.

The chopper was on its way out of a *Hot Extract* mission and carried two wounded plus three other marines at the moment that it took one too many 50 caliber rounds to the turboshaft. Sergeant Lewis pulled everyone from the crash to safety, including going back into the burning chopper and then back out of it into more fire, both from real flames and those from enemy weapons, before returning to retrieve the body of the dead pilot. He then led the holding of the crash site until rescue choppers arrived thirty-five minutes later, gaining three kills, including that of the VC sniper who'd started the whole ruckus. He never talked publicly about the experience, but his wife had heard the play-by-play many times over when Gerry Lewis talked and thrashed in his sleep.

At the clubhouse table to his right sat Thomas Dewey. Dewey wasn't related to the former Governor and presidential candidate – at least that he knew – but he never bothered to correct those who responded to his name with the question. To his golfing buddies, he was known as an occasionally irritating winner who, more often than not, would yell out on the way back to the clubhouse for drinks, "Dewey Wins in Landslide!" While that wasn't exactly the headline from the November 1947 *Chicago Tribune*, most people remembered it that way.

Dewey was the youngest of the group and had been a Company Clerk in Vietnam, serving conscientiously. He and other *Transition-to-Home* mates had been rocketed by the VC on their second to last day in-country at Cam Ranh Bay's transport compound which lay immediately next to the airfield. It was then that Dewey was clipped by shrapnel, earning a Purple Heart. He was more than willing to talk about the experience, laughing and denigrating the fact that he'd "*earned*" recognition. "I didn't *earn* it," he'd say while laughing, "but if it was gonna happen, why didn't it happen on Day One instead of Day 364!" The reality though was that Thomas Dewey was deeply in awe of those who'd paid the price *for* him, and he'd sometimes shed more than a single tear for them. He was incredibly honored to have received the award.

Next to Thomas and across from Gerry Lewis sat Huey Pierce Landry. A native of Houma, Louisiana, where the local sports teams were all called, *The Braves*. Huey was, indeed, named *after* the late Louisiana Governor and former Presidential Candidate, Huey P. Long, an icon in the state. Huey Landry's claim to a Purple Heart lay in Tay Ninh Province and came by way of *friendly fire*. A Claymore mine that a friend was planting, detonated prematurely, killing the young marine putting it in place. Lewis had been standing guard ten or fifteen feet behind the mine and was partly shielded by his teammate's body.

The concussive sound the Claymore made as it exploded permanently damaged Huey's hearing, and he was severely burned by the blast. After recovering, Huey returned to his unit and fought in a half dozen battles, winning a Bronze Star for Exemplary Conduct Under Combat Conditions." He was the kind of hero and person who also refused to discuss the conditions for which he was awarded the Purple Heart. It was his sad penalty to see his friend the very moment the friend had died and he'd been saved. The moment recurred in his dreams at least once a week.

By 7:08 a.m. each of the three men had finished his first steaming cup of hot black coffee. Lewis turned to the other two and said, "I wonder where Scrooge is? He's always the first one here, and if not, he's at least always, *exactly* on time."

Scrooge was a retired two-star, better known in military circles as a Major General of the U.S. Marine

In Better Times

Corps, a.k.a., James R. Scrogg. He'd been a Lite Colonel Battalion Commander in the late 60s in the I Corps Region of Vietnam but was a grunt at heart. He'd also earned a Purple Heart and had dozens of other medals attached to a uniform that he brought out only on special occasions. Discussing his medals was *verboten*, but *Scrooge* walked with a cane and each of the others in the small group knew not to question why.

Their regular waitress, Zoe, a thirty-something single mom of one, brought fresh coffee to the table. She'd been their regular waitress for more than two years now. Without any sort of greeting, she began refilling their cups, asking, "Hey guys. Where's Scrooge? You don't normally find Huey, Dewey, and Lewie without Scrooge!" The guys shook their heads. No one had an answer.

They loved their nicknames. They'd had them for years, except for "*Gerry*" Lewis who was better known in other social circles by that nickname rather than as 'Lewie'. It took one of their wives to realize that the four veterans, coming home from a Dallas reunion as pals, could be identified as Huey, Dewey, Lewie, and Scrooge. Lewis though, often congenially griped that his last name should be pronounced the way it was spelled: L-E-W-I-S, not *Lewie*.

General Scrogg originally had chosen the nickname *Corporal* for himself, rather than *Scrooge,* since the others were all enlisted men who often called each other by their military ranks. It was a nice touch, but Huey, Dewey, and Lewie insisted on their own in calling him Scrooge, but *sir* within the setting of the group. They loved the old man. At first, they'd wanted him to remain known as "The General" but Scrogg said he thought that it didn't match the other more friendly nicknames in the group. Outside of military circles though, he most wanted to be known as a *citizen*.

In the end, they'd all agreed on *Scrooge*, a bit of acceptable enlisted mockery given his real last name because the General was notoriously cheap when it came to paying up golf losses. Despite this morning's weekly social gathering, the men were also a foursome most every Monday a few miles away at the Country Club course where their fees were waived and paid gratis, thanks to the generosity of the General who held a membership there. Here at Bayou Oaks, the general was *never* asked to pay.

By 7:20, and beginning their third cup of coffee, they asked Zoe to find out if she'd heard anything yet about the General's absence. A few minutes later she came back to the group and said, "He's on his way. The police are leaving now." With that, she turned and walked away as Huey, Dewey, and Lewie sat holding their coffee cups frozen in midair.

When Scrooge finally showed up about 7:35, Zoe promptly appeared with a fresh pot of coffee and stood silently while they performed their regular mini-ceremonial greeting. The first three rose and joined the General in a huddle. The old man led the moment, concluding with, "Semper Fi, Gentlemen."

"Hoo-Rah," came the reply, "Semper Fi!".

In Better Times

The regulars in the clubhouse breakfast bar ignored them. They'd heard Huey, Dewey, Lewie, and Scrooge go through the same drill for years. The men sat, and Zoe quickly presented the Two-Star with a personalized mug the men had presented to him – saying irreverently, "Mornin' Scroogie!"

General Scrogg smiled and air-kissed Zoe. He appeared a bit frail but was ruddy in complexion. After all, he was older by fifteen years than any man in the group and easily admitted to being cold. "Thanks, Zoe. I really need this. It's been an interesting morning."

"Where's your jacket, sir," Huey asked? I've never seen you go without it on a day this cool."

"Gave it to a friend. God rest his soul. And the police never returned it."

"What?" asked Lewie. "What do you mean by that?"

They each knew a good story was coming. It was going to be a great morning.

"Well, you know, I get up at four and take a walk every day, right?" asked Scrooge.

The others nodded. They knew that, even with a cane, rain or shine, the general was committed to early morning seven-mile walks. "Well, this morning I was walking backwards down the Bayou Oaks fifth fairway..."

"Backwards, sir?" asked Dewey. "Why would you do that?"

"Okay, I wasn't *walking* backwards, I was walking down the fairways, from eighteen down to one. I was walking the *course* in reverse. That way you know if a player is hitting toward you and you can get out of the way. *Backwards!*"

"But who golfs at four-thirty a.m.?" asked Huey.

"Point taken. But that's what I'm accustomed to doing and I find it hard to change a habit ingrained over a lifetime."

"So, what about the police?"

Huey, Dewey, and Lewie almost chimed the question together.

"Alright. You'll recall we had a bad storm overnight?" The men nodded in agreement. "I came across a lot of tree debris along my walk. Had my trusty Life Saver Four Cell Flashlight with me like I always do." He held it up, turned it on, and shined it into the eyes of each of his table mates. "Must be prepared, right?" The three men nodded again, smiling.

"As I walked past the fifth tee of the Bayou Oaks Course, my light here caught sight of a large tree down and lying across the path ahead of me near the fourth green. At first, I thought I might be mistaken, but it looked as if there was a body lying across the path near the downed tree."

The men hung on every word.

"I hobbled up to the form on the ground. It was that of a nearly naked young man who'd obviously been felled by lightning sometime during the night, probably in the early morning."

"It is *still* early morning," responded Dewey wondering how any living being could rise at four a.m. to walk seven miles. He'd always had trouble making it to the clubhouse for their seven a.m. breakfasts.

"Was he hit by the tree limb?" asked Huey.

"Was he dead?" asked Lewie.

"No, not the tree, but I did believe him to be dead at first. He was blackened by soot the way some of the meals in this damn clubhouse are cooked!" Scrooge said this looking back toward the kitchen, and then coughing because Zoe was approaching with more coffee and she'd no doubt heard his minor insult directed to the kitchen.

Scroogie continued. "Kneeling down, I took the man's pulse and almost missed it... but it was there. I can't really kneel down well because of this damn knee, you know," he said as he patted the knee. "So, I started pushing in on his chest. You know, trying to do some CPR. Tried to remember that song you're supposed to do CPR by... by the BooBoos, or someone. Whatever! Anyway, after a while, the guy came around."

"So, what did you do then?"

"Well, dammit! I called 9-1-1 naturally."

The men nodded in agreement again. It was the right thing to do.

"It wasn't long before police and a medical team arrived. By that time, the man was sitting up and shivering, so I gave *him* my jacket."

"You gave him your favorite jacket?" asked Lewie.

"You mean you gave him your brother's field jacket from Nam?" asked Huey.

Scrooge grimaced and then nodded, *yes*.

"Who was he?" asked Dewey.

"Don't know . . . and he didn't either. Said he couldn't remember anything, even his name. Came close apparently to being struck dead by lightning."

"What was he doing on a golf course, in a storm, in the middle of the night?"

"I don't have an answer to that. He asked where we were, and I told him that we were near the fourth green of the Bayou Oaks Golf course which didn't seem to help him any. When he looked puzzled, I said, 'We're in New Orleans, of course.' With nary a word, the man stood up, maybe a bit shakily, and walked off heading toward the downtown skyline, which, at that hour was only lit by lights in a few of the skyscrapers. Never even thanked me for my jacket. I loved that jacket!"

"A few minutes later, the police and an ambulance arrived, and I was alone, standing next to a tree that was still smoking. You know the son of a gun walked off with my damn jacket?" Scrooge repeated.

"Your Vietnam Field Jacket, sir?"

"Yes. Well, my brother's Vietnam Field Jacket! Dammit! I've had it almost forever."

At that point, a small commotion occurred in the clubhouse. A tall thin man walking with a bit of a limp came through leading an entourage of four officials from the Bayou Oaks courses. Applause began.

The man leading the group spotted General Scrogg and immediately headed over, greeting him with enthusiasm and a hug – not something the General normally would allow.

"Gentlemen," said Scrooge, "This is an old friend of

mine you've probably heard of before. Meet Pete Stickney, fresh from the Masters where he placed in the Top Eight, he did. "Well done, Pete!"

The guys, and most of the clubhouse, nearly slavered to reach out and shake Stickney's hand.

"I thought you'd be on the circuit?" said Scrooge to *The Stick*, as he was known.

"No," said Stickney. "I'm taking the week off, and while I was in the neighborhood, so to speak, the officials here at Bayou asked me to walk the course and look for possible improvements that might better help them attract a tour stop for either the PGA or the LPGA.

All sense of clubhouse decorum had ended with the arrival of the celebrity. The General's interaction with a lightning victim near the fourth green earlier that morning was forgotten in the rush to meet the celebrity.

XXIX

As he headed down the cart path generally toward the course entrance, the slightly injured amnesiac found pants for his outfit in a maintenance shed and then began a hike toward the city. The air was cool. The marine field jacket made a real difference.

As he walked, he searched his memory for anything that might give him a clue to who he was but could only remember that he thought it was the spring of 2005, his last cogent memory. He guessed he was nearly 40 years of age and decided to take inventory of himself and perhaps bring out any clues that would help him identify himself.

He wore his hair long with a heavy growth of beard. His hands were calloused, and one of them hurt like hell. It appeared to be a bit charred. On closer inspection, he realized that he was severely underweight and carried a load of deeply ingrained dirt just about everywhere on his body. "I really need a shower," he said aloud, but since he was alone in the predawn hour, he directed the comment only to himself. *Maybe I just look like I'm 40. Maybe I'm younger than that.*

Something wasn't right with him though. He tested his voice again, calling to an early morning squirrel out for a walk. "Hey, buddy. How ya' doin'?" His voice was deep, scratchy, and sounded hoarse from heavy smoking. He coughed and was a bit disgusted with the result. Passing by a closed liquor store, he felt a magnetic pull. "Hmm," he said. "I'm not sure I like who I am . . . *whoever that is!*"

A few early joggers detoured around him. One shouted, "Get a bath, old man. You stink!"

He called back, "Yeah. Okay, man. Sorry," and heard that same scratchy voice come out. It was totally unfamiliar to him.

Tiring and hungry, he turned down a street and found a young man sleeping in a hammock on a front porch. A broken porch swing sat on the floor at one end of the porch. It was a strangely narrow building, maybe a dozen feet wide and it had obviously seen better days.

Sensing that the form on the porch was beginning to awaken, he climbed the steps and said, as gently as possible, "My friend, could you spare me some food, and especially a cup of water?"

"Is that you, John?" asked the form stretching its arms.

"Maybe," said the man hopefully."

"Maybe, shit!" It's *you*, you son of a gun! How the hell are you, brother?"

With that moment of recognition, at least on the part of the resident of the dilapidated home, *John's* recovery began. As the younger man Paul, told it, he – *John* – had been away for a couple of years exploring the hippie life, probably in Colorado. Something had apparently happened along the way. *John* did have a minimal memory of taking a severe beating which might account for his amnesia.

In truth, *John* didn't honestly recognize the other man as his brother . . . or especially as his *twin* brother. Nevertheless, he spent the next month posing as such and learning Pope Family History – *or perhaps relearning?*

He also learned the ways of the real world: panhandling, pickpocketing, begging, dumpster diving, small-time burglary, and all the other fine arts of homeless living. Actually, the two men weren't technically homeless. They had a home, but it was the closest thing to being homeless.

One early morning a few days later, Paul and *John* were taking a content inventory for a vacationing homeowner in the Garden District. They'd just found an open gun safe and were checking out the homeowner's weaponry when police officers broke down the front and back doors of the home. "Gentlemen! Please present yourselves with your hands held high." The request came from a very polite member of the NOLA PD. Her service revolver was pointed at John's chest.

John and Paul were booked on charges of attempted burglary and spent several nights in jail. When the homeowners returned from their trip to a fishing camp near Bayou Pigeon, they could find nothing missing or even disturbed. Good hearts, they chose to not file charges, and the two men were released, each having enjoyed showers, shaves, and decent meals for most of a week while in jail.

Their processing had required the submission of DNA samples and fingerprints. The fingerprinting had occurred upon booking, but both men's hands were so filthy at the time that the prints were largely illegible and forgotten. A month later when the DNA analysis arrived though, it proved extremely interesting. Both men . . . incredibly . . . appeared to have the same DNA.

"Yeah, I think they're identical twins," said one of the technicians. I suspect it could happen on occasion. Their DNA's gonna be close anyway."

"They can't be identical twins! One of 'em's at least ten years older than the other!"

"It can't be!" said her boss as she shook her head in exasperation. "It's not theoretically possible!

"It's an anomaly." Repeated the subordinate, "I tell you; it *can't* have happened! It's a scientific impossibility!"

Closer examination of the results created more problems. One of the men indeed did test about ten years older than the other. How could that be if they were identical twins?

In Better Times

After they were cleaned up, fingerprints were taken and compared a second time.

"Identical!"

"Impossible!"

Thinking he might get a research paper published out of this, the senior technician sent samples off to the National Institute of Health in Atlanta. The NIH had the equipment to resolve the apparently, conflicting test results. Still, if the case proved unique, it would be a slam-dunk scientific *Hit Record*, rockin' the charts in the labs of Nobel Prize-winning scientists around the world. The individual discovering this uniqueness and postulating a plausible explanation for it would join his or her peers in Stockholm in the very near future and would ride the Nobel Prize escalator of fame for the rest of his or her life.

By the next May, a closed-door meeting took place in Oslo. The results of the testing of John and Paul Pope's DNA produced totally unexplainable results. Not just unexplainable, but unique and unreproducible in all of scientific history.

Afraid to admit an impossibility, all records of the event were destroyed, as well as the DNA samples held in NIH lockers.

It never happened. Case closed. Fini, fidi, fici!

* * * *

Time passed. John and Paul coalesced and made the best of their uneducated, impoverished, and often criminal lives. Paul the Older took on the character of, and learned to believe to some extent that he was indeed, John, Paul the Younger's formally AWOL brother.

Deep down, *John* knew he really wasn't *John,* but he was so confused with so many competing memories bouncing around in his head that it was difficult to decide how or when to act. There were mornings when he didn't want to get off his cot on Rue Waterloo.

* * * *

More than two years went by after their reunion. Paul grew openly antagonistic toward the man he believed to be his brother. John's inability to move on with his new life always lasted another week, and then another, and another...

Long enough, Paul thought. *One morning soon, he will just roll over and simply decide to become the John Pope that we all want him to be.* But he'd been saying that now for the past two years.

"Come on, John," Paul whined, "If you don't get with it soon, I'm just gonna have to shoot you."

It was meant as a joke of course, but John took the remark with some seriousness. In the two years plus since their reunion, he'd accompanied his "brother" on forays into other people's homes late at night where, had the occupants awakened, there easily could have been confrontations. John had seen how quickly Paul was ready to resort to violence.

When he'd suggested that he was willing to *shoot him*, the threat may have been made in jest, but it seemed to

In Better Times

John that Paul had it within him to make good on it. He began to sleep less well and tried to keep an eye out for any brewing trouble.

In one of many family teaching situations that Paul conducted, the subject of the suicide of their father would occasionally come up. Slips of the tongue by Paul convinced John that their *old man* had not just left home and done himself in, as the family told the tale.

Too much indicated that their father had been murdered – pushed off the roof of a seven-story hotel near the French Quarter. Still, John's memory of events back then was so confusing that it was possible *he* could have done the deed, not Paul. How would he have any knowledge of why his father had not survived the night if he'd not been involved?

The stories that Paul told of their father's musings about science bothered him as well. *Could matter really come to exist from nothing? Did space have a finite end? When did time begin? Could a spacecraft exceed the speed of light? Were there multiple universes operating side-by-side?*

John knew that intellectually he was not the person to think through these problems or to even guess at the answers. And Paul seemed oblivious to all his concerns about them. The best he could do, he reasoned, was to concentrate on what his talents and skills could do to provide *meaning* to their pitiful lives.

"Hey, guy," John asked Paul one morning. "I'm gettin' tired of getting rained on in the middle of the night. What say we fix the damn roof?"

"Yeah," agreed Paul, "Let's steal us some tar and shingles and get to work in a month or so!"

"No, Paul. We've got enough troubles. I'm goin' out and gettin' a job today and the first thing I'm gonna do with the money is fix up this shack! How 'bout it? You want to help? You could get a job too, you know!"

"Wow, John! That sounds like a lot of work! I dunno . . ."

But Paul was bored, and it wasn't Mardi Gras season so he went along with the idea. Manual labor was often in demand in New Orleans as construction workers tended to go where the work was, and for several years running now a hurricane or tropical storm had struck somewhere along the Gulf Coast. Construction workers knew that incredibly lucrative wages were often paid during times following a bad storm. Remodeling and the usual new home construction would usually fall behind in the workers' home communities because of it.

Each of the young men signed on to construction gangs because their skills were very primitive, similar to those of the workers who hauled materials around job sites. The money was usually entry-level, but even entry-level wages were hundreds of times more than they'd been bringing in.

One day, Paul came to John and said, "Hey, bro. How 'bout I treat us to dinner and a beer?"

John was adequately dumbfounded. His brother was sober and had enough cash to treat him to dinner? And this occurred after they each had sunk some money into home improvement! The roof was patched, the porch and

In Better Times

its swing repaired. They'd even replaced a few windows which allowed the inside of the small house to hold heat better in the winter.

"Yeah, man! Where are we going?"

That night over take-out barbeque and Abitas on the front porch, they began a serious discussion of their father's scientific theories. The topics were always on both men's minds anyway.

"You know John," Paul began, "I think Pop was onto something. I think Time Travel *is* possible. I remember him saying that ole Doc Anderson had offered to show him an actual time travel engine, he called it a Time Control Machine. Pop was gonna go over and see it work but he got drunk that afternoon and trashed a bar instead. Cops got him an' he spent two nights in the tank.

"By the time he got out and went over to the Doc's house, the man was gone. Gone! There was no time machine in the house or his workshop in the garage. His house looked the same, still full of all his personal crap, but no machine . . . and no Doc Anderson.

"*I think he went to the future!*"

* * * *

A long luxury car passed the house slowly on a chilly February day. John was wearing the old green army field jacket he'd been found with some time ago on that golf course. He was doing some early planting of flowering plants along the front porch. The Lincoln Town Car pulled to a stop in front of the house and an older gentleman got out and, walking stiffly with a cane, approached him.

"Hey, son. Can I talk to you for a moment," the stranger asked.

John didn't respond but put down his small hand shovel, got up, and walked over to the man, brushing his hands as clean of dirt as possible. "Yes sir, what can I do for you?"

"Please don't call me, sir. Had enough of that in the Marines. I'm an old man now. Just call me, Jim."

"Well, Mr. Jim. Again, what can I do for you?"

"Do you mind me asking where you got that jacket?"

"What this old thing? I don't rightly know. I think I've had this as long as I can remember."

"It says, 'Scrogg' over the pocket and has E-5 Sargent stripes on the sleeves. Do you mind if I take a look at the inside collar?"

"Sure. Go ahead. "John took off the jacket and handed it to the old man.

"If I'm right about this, I'll find the name of my brother, William Scrogg across the inside pocket."

"I'm sure you will, too, sir . . . I mean Mr. Jim."

"Sure enough. There it is. See? Do you know where this jacket came from, son? It was my brother's, and he wore it when he shipped out for Vietnam quite a few years ago."

"Wow. Imagine that," said John. "I can see it has serious meaning for you." John paused for a moment and made an uncharacteristic decision. He'd liked the old man instantly. There was a ring of familiarity to him that he couldn't pinpoint though. "Sir . . . Jim . . . I want you to have it."

"You sure you don't remember where you got it? Do you remember me helping you up on a golf course a year or two back? You'd been hit by lightning, or close to it. I can still see the scar on your hand from the burn you got that morning."

"Yes," said John as he squinted his eyes in recollection. "I think I do remember you now. At least a bit. Those were some tough days for me. I didn't know who I was then or how I got there, but I remember you. I'm certain I never thanked you for what you did for me that morning. I'm indebted to you, sir."

"Please, don't call me sir."

"Right."

"Here's what we'll do. I'll pay you a hundred dollars for the jacket. You see, my brother was killed in the Tet Offensive and his jacket here means a lot to me. Some things come full circle you know. He died wearing that jacket and, judging from how you're fixing up my old house, you . . . or he . . . may have been reborn in it."

"*Your* old house?"

"Yes, son. This was my house when I was a kid, and I drive past here every so often to check it out. The house has been pretty run down for years, but recently I've seen you out here working on it. You're doing nice work, son. I didn't realize who you were until I saw you wearing the jacket a few minutes ago." The old man paused for a few seconds and continued. "I see you painted the old house. Why purple?"

"Well, it really needed painting but the best we could afford was 20 gallons of purple that Sherwin-Williams had brewed up for someone else . . . someone who ended not wanting it. Almost got it for free!"

"Uh-huh. I see." He paused again. "Can I treat you to lunch?"

"Oh, no thanks, sir. I mean, Jim. I just have a few more flowers to plant before I head for work."

"What do you do?"

"Well, I'm workin' off some community service over at a bar called *Bon Temp* an' I'm due there in half an hour."

You look like you know what you're doing with tools. I own half interest in a small hardware store in the Magazine District. How'd you like to come to work for my partner?" Another pause. "Full time. Medical benefits. $12.50 an hour. Start tomorrow morning. We open at O-700. Be there at O-six-thirty."

"I don't know what to say?"

"Tell me your name, son."

"Uh . . . John. John Pope."

"Just say, 'Thanks', John, and I'll see you in the morning."

"Sure thing, sir. What'll I be doing?"

"Well, my guy will teach you the ropes but mostly you'll be unloading and stocking supplies. I'm sure Tim will eventually work you into sales and then you'll get a commission too. By the way, John. My name's Jim Scrogg. Here's my card with the address of the store.

John took the card and examined it.

"By the way, tell Tim to give you all the best white exterior he's got and to send me the bill. Have my old house professionally painted, John. My gift to you, to my brother, and to my old home!"

"Damn!" John said it as a southerner. It came out, "Day-am! Thank you, sir. And I'll make you proud at the store."

"I'm sure you will, son. And don't call me sir." Nobody ever called my brother, sir, and he's the one who deserved it." The old man smiled, and they shook hands. "See you in the morning. I think I'll be there to introduce you to Tim."

Scrogg headed back to his car reverently carrying the worn and dirty field jacket. John heard him say, "I'll take care of you, Sargent," as he laid the jacket gently on the back seat.

* * * *

From that moment on, things improved at a rapid pace at the Shotgun on Rue Waterloo. The front door was replaced, the small back porch was repaired, air leaks were patched, and a fresh coat of exterior white paint made a huge difference in the building's appearance. It took three coats to erase the purple. While it wasn't historically accurate, at least the place looked, well, comfortably livable. Paul had even helped with the painting since John was now working five days a week at the hardware store, including weekends.

The twins were proud of the work they were doing. *A new leaf has turned*, John thought, or at least hoped.

At John's urging, Paul talked to a friend who'd taken a job emptying trash into the city's fleet of garbage trucks. He was soon added to the waiting list of people seeking to work these surprisingly well-paying jobs. Meantime, Paul was placed on a crew that worked 24/7 keeping the French Quarter clean. The job started at three a.m., which worked out fine with his other schedule.

One morning, Paul returned home after putting in a solid eight hours. He told John that the manual labor reminded him of their mom, and the two began retelling stories about her. The tales of a mother's love under difficult circumstances inspired the two men to attend Wednesday night Mass in her honor. Afterward, the priest, Father Noël, sensing their willingness, invited them to become more involved in the church. They agreed to come to the fellowship hall for the Tuesday night *Suppers for Sinners*, a terribly prejudicial name for an event, but one that guaranteed the attendees would show up in the correct frame of mind. The food, while bland, still tasted better than anything they were dishing up at home . . . and it was free! Since they knew for a fact they *were* sinners, John and Paul felt qualified to attend a dinner named for them. The free hot meals weighed heavily on their decision.

Through friends they made at the dinner talks, Paul quit his city trash job and began working for a nonprofit whose goal was to give homeless men a purpose in life. The charity operated a bakery called *Half Baked* which was located near the Audubon Zoo. *Half Baked's* employees were mostly former convicts freshly released from prison, but they also counted numerous homeless men who agreed to follow the strict House Rules regarding abstinence. Paul's duties included spending a night or two a week as a house supervisor. Still loose in his personal off-hours behavior, Paul chose to overnight at the *Half-Baked Halfway House* sometimes when he needed to scout out its Tulane neighborhood for his less-than-legal forays.

An old dog can't shake his fleas, thought John.

Affiliated with *Half Baked* was the non-profit bar and grill called *Bon Temp*. There, the Program Director's theory on rehabilitation was put to the clients to the test, deliberately placing alcoholics behind the *Temp's* bar to test a person's commitment to give up intoxicating liquors. It was trial by fire, and it often was successful. Even when it wasn't, the method quickly separated those who failed from those with a solid commitment to make it back to normal life. The failed souls became lessons to the others to stay the line.

For the first time in his life, it was at *Half Baked* and then at *Bon Temp* that Paul moved from part-time to a full-time, regular, FICA-paying employee. But history is difficult to overcome. Within a few months, Paul again found himself out the door.

For being late, smelling like booze, being insolent to his supervisor, and so on, Paul had been let go. Again. Still, it had been a basic learning experience for a person who'd never worked a full-time job for a single day in his life. After his dismissal, Paul apologized to *Bon Temp's* manager, and then to John. Paul told him he'd learned his lesson and promised to find another job where he'd again test those newfound values against his lifelong poor behavioral instincts.

John smiled because he knew *Bon Temp* had paid Paul two weeks' severance on his way out the door . . . more honest money than Paul had ever had in his pocket in his entire life. He hoped that the big payday would prove cathartic. He helped Paul find another job, this time with a construction company doing manual labor.

After three days, Paul appeared to have found his calling. He returned home tired and sweaty but with improved health and self-confidence. The twins even opened a checking account with debit privileges. Unfortunately, after withdrawing twenty dollars from the account as a test, Paul's first instinct was to first consider how difficult it would be to take an ATM home with him.

There were still miles to go before the dawn.

Months went by and the Pope Family's Standard of Living rose. Improvements were being made to the house every week. As well, both men purchased inexpensive but decent clothing.

Sometimes good intentions and works have a way of turning on those who own and perform them. Their neighbors considered the changes going on next door and suspected the boys were dealing. That was alright with them, but the city noticed the improvements that were taking place at a formerly abandoned Mid-City shotgun home. An inspector confronted Paul about ownership and the work going on. It quickly turned into a shouting match between Paul and the inspector.

John made it home from work just as the police arrived. Social workers were called to mediate. The city had been concerned for many years that it *owned* too many abandoned houses which were deteriorating faster than could be repaired at city expense. One of the Social Workers realized that something good was going on at the *Shotgun on Rue Waterloo* and convinced her boss to create a new charitable program helping impoverished people move toward home ownership. The *Shotgun on Rue Waterloo Project* was born thanks to the many years of *squatting experience* of John and Paul Pope.

Through it, a compromise was offered by the new charity. All parties agreed to the following: If improvements to the home continued and met code, the two men could stay there . . . providing they signed an *intent to purchase* and a *liability release*. The agreements were shepherded and guaranteed by the agency proposing the original concept. John and Paul also agreed to pay taxes – *not back taxes, but current taxes* on the property. Back taxes were forgiven by the city providing the men held to the agreement. The nonprofit even fronted a loan to do this. John and Paul signed on the dotted line. It was the first time in their lives they'd taken on debt and actually intended to repay it.

The potential for home ownership spurred them on even more. Access to employee discounted building materials and John's close association with knowledgeable home repair experts impacted their living conditions. Previous repairs had been relatively superficial. Now they were pouring cement and replacing windows . . . and, they were having a ball doing so. Part of the requirement for future home ownership was replacing the home's dated and unsafe wiring. They worked on this project together.

The day the electricity was turned back on was one for celebration. John and Paul sat in front of a used television all night drinking bottled iced tea chilled by a second-hand refrigerator they'd purchased for next-to-nothing from a Habitat for Humanity *Re-Store*. They celebrated again when they plugged it in and opened the door and . . . an interior light came on. Within a day, they'd purchased other lights and lamps to turn on. An old heating system in the home was repaired, partly with donated funds from an HVAC company that supported the charity. It was now functioning.

Sleeping in a heated home of their own in January made life immensely more enjoyable . . . and safer. With heat coming from the new vents, they donated an old butane heater that Paul had stolen years earlier. The repair work became a bit sporadic though, for both men were still working full-time. John had to ride the streetcar carrying lumber, tools, and other construction materials home. Often, he was refused boarding and had to walk home with his load.

They attended Mass at the cathedral. Most times when they heard the liturgy, they'd tear up at the memory of their mother herding them through those same doors, prompting them to join in. They sat in the third set of pews to the right of the altar, exactly where she'd sat with them years before.

Sensing rehabilitation for the two long-time ne'er-do-wells, Father Noël told Paul about a somewhat distasteful but well-paying job with one of his parishioners, a man named Walter Beiderweil. He gave Paul the contact information but called Beiderweil himself and arranged for an interview. When Paul returned to the shotgun and told John that he had an interview scheduled for the next morning for a potential internship in a funeral home, John was not impressed and said, "I hope it isn't that Beiderweil place off Tchoupitoulas. I hear the work there is disgusting."

It was, but Paul took the job anyway and it wasn't an internship. It was a full-time job, working nights. In a grim sort of way, Paul looked forward to his work as Assistant Crematorium Technician. Perhaps owing to its perceived distasteful duties, the pay was well above average. Paul worked nights, especially after meeting Old Walt's daughter, so the two men now saw less of each other than before.

Life wasn't so tough now for the Pope family.

On the national front, war clouds were building after an attack on the Twin Towers in New York and both the Pentagon and the Capitol Building in the District of Columbia. With either war or potential combat in a foreign country imminent, John frequented the crawlway to repair a recurring problem with the cable connection so they could better follow CNN's war coverage. They cheered as U.S. Troops took Baghdad and eventually captured Saddam Hussein. Paul considered enlisting –

after the war was over – to help the U.S. win a War on Poverty. Discouragingly, John caught him selling stolen ammunition as *war souvenirs* and admonished him. In his heart, he was concerned that Paul might be regressing to what his mother had once called Paul's *evil nature*.

In May, John was again in the crawlway, this time to repair a disintegrating foundation support. There he found a dirt-encrusted peach brandy bottle containing a hundred dollars. A note in the bottle suggested that it would be personally beneficial to the finder if he chose to invest his money in *Apple Tech* and urged the finder to announce a series of six listed numbers to a Dallas Community Church preacher named Billy Bob. A line at the bottom read: "THIS IS NO JOKE!"

The note and the cash hit John like a ton of bricks. Old memories of a man named Billy Bob came back and attacked him in his sleep. By daylight, he was physically ill but didn't know with what, or why. Despite his queasiness, the money, coupled with the strange memories pounding in his head, burned a hole in his pocket. Things were changing again. He felt as if he was falling under someone else's control.

Paul hadn't come in yet from his night shift, which was beginning to happen more and more often. Finally, by 9:30, John succumbed to his fears and headed for Paul's former place of employment, *Bon Temp*. Arriving by 10:05 he wasn't at all surprised to find it full of drinkers, after all, this *was* New Orleans. By eleven in the morning, John himself had tripped on all Twelve Steps and was unfit for

In Better Times

company. He bought drinks for everyone in the bar with what was left of the hundred dollars.

"Brother," the Reverend Billy Bob Buckmaster said, extending his hand, "Thanks for the Coors. I'm Triple B.

"Say again?" asked John, but he smiled crookedly, and his slur was a bit practiced, "Howduhyuhdoo? I'm John Pope."

"Trip B . . . Triple B . . . Billy Bob Buckmaster! *The* Reverend Billy Bob Buckmaster . . . but, Trip B to you." Trip B slapped John on the back and John's beer sloshed out of the glass and onto his lap.

Billy Bob didn't apologize but instead said, "Gotta be more careful, my friend." And then a non-sequitur: "Hey, do y'all play the lottery here? I like lotteries and I like you, man! Got some winning numbers, huh? Give 'em to me and we'll light up the Christmas Tree."

For a moment John considered the intricate moves he needed to do to lick spilled beer from his own lap . . . and the looks he'd get from the other patrons if he did. Then he took another moment to make certain he understood Trip's request. Full sobriety was returning in a rush. The instant Billy Bob identified himself, John's spinning mind slowed down. It had been whirling since the night before with the discovery of the brandy bottle and the note.

The liquor at *Bon Temp* hadn't helped, but a sense of *déjà vu* collated his memories. He squinted as he translated Trip's request, and while fumbling in his pocket said to Trip, still deliberately slurring, "I gotta piece of paper here an' I think it says that Steve wants a job . . . at an apple cider mill!" His attempt at a hiccup didn't really sound realistic, even to him. Finally, though, he produced the torn slip of paper from the depths of his pocket. It was badly crumpled. He tried to straighten it out and read it for Trip, but all he managed was, "Uhh . . ."

After twenty seconds, Trip responded – a bit frustrated with the process: "Well, what is it, man?"

"No. No. Wait," John slurred, while still fumbling with the crumpled note, "here's what it is. It says, *'A man named Steve's coming back* . . . I think it says, *to his old Jobs.'* That makes no sense!"

At this point, Trip was ready to give up and move on. "You're right! That don't make no sense at all," he said to John, "and I'm not Steve! I don't want no apples; I don't want no apple cider. I want numbers."

Billy Bob was irritated at the waste of his time but did his best Lawrence Welk imitation, singing, "Gimme' a one, An a two . . ." There was no response from John. Trip chugged his beer and turned to leave.

With John seemingly lost in a drunken fog and unable to communicate, Trip gave up and left the bar wobbly, leaving John behind. John, still caught up by the memories and messages bouncing around in his brain, knew in his heart that an opportunity was passing him by. He concentrated on sobering up as much as one mentally could do without medication. But he succeeded.

John nearly fell off the bar stool in his haste to follow.

Out on Magazine Street, John caught up to Triple B and said, "Here. I got this paper with your winning numbers on it. You can have it, Reverend Bob. Just remember that you got these numbers from me, John Pope!"

Billy Bob looked at the piece of paper and asked, "Who the heck is this Steve fellow anyway? I don't want names, I want numbers!"

"Flip it over, Billy. Flip it over."

"Oh, yeah. Okay, John." Turning the slip of paper over, Billy Bob read the numbers, thought for a second, and then said, "I'm only gonna do this 'cause I like you, son, and . . . because . . . I see you got an angel sittin' on your shoulder! Yeah, For *real!* I can see 'em, cain't you? You know that, don't you son . . . *John?* An', I *like* angels!"

"Yeah, Pastor Bob. Remember, I'm *John* . . . John Pope. When do you think you'll get a chance to play the numbers?"

"Tell you what, Buckeroo. I'm due back home in Big D next week. Today's June 15th so I'll probably play 'em first thing I get back to Texas, probably the 20th an' I'll cut y'all in for five percent if these *numeros* win the big pot!"

"Promise?"

"Promise, partner!"

They shook hands.

* * * *

Somewhat confused by what had just happened, John made his way back to the shotgun. On the way home, he purchased a pint of apple brandy and, rather than waste it, finished it off just as he turned onto Rue Waterloo. He stuffed a dollar bill in the empty bottle and added any change small enough to fit in the bottle's mouth, finally tossing it into the crawl space under their home.

The moments in the bar replayed themselves in John's mind over and over. It was after midnight when he remembered that he'd given his only copy of the note and the numbers on it to Billy Bob.

Sober, John stayed awake the rest of the night planning his next move.

The next morning the two brothers discussed the ramifications of John's meeting with Buckmaster. Paul, the practiced scammer, told John he thought Trip B shouldn't be trusted and the more John thought about it, he agreed. He decided it was time to be proactive.

The truth was, John had begun to be *distrustful* of what Brother Paul was doing behind his back as well.

His memory was improving. He stayed up again the next night to finalize plans. When he saw Paul the next morning though, he kept his plans to himself.

THE TICKET

I

Mid-June 1997

Paul was out almost all night, returning about five a.m. He was hard asleep when John walked out the door carrying his few personal items packed in an old and beat-up duffle bag. Leaving a note for Paul, he told him he was on his way back to Colorado, that he'd realized he missed the cooler weather, the family he'd left behind, and even the snow. The move wasn't expected to be permanent. He'd likely return to New Orleans in a few months . . . then again, maybe never. He said he hoped that if he did return, he'd find a *permanently* reformed twin.

While he could now afford to take Amtrak to his destination, John chose a freight train for old times' sake. It was heading to Dallas after stops in Baton Rouge and Shreveport. There were no Amtrak trains that left from New Orleans, traveling directly to Dallas. There were connecting routes, of course, but changing trains in Houston or even Chicago wasn't really practical for him from a time standpoint. That process would consume too much time, and John was on a schedule.

His train didn't even slow down for Dallas, but fortunately for him, it eased up and came to a halt for a change of equipment in familiar territory. John detrained in the big rail yards of Fort Worth 36 hours after leaving the Big Easy. He'd actually enjoyed being on the road again – or really, *on the rails again* – away from the rampant poverty of New Orleans and away from his habitually malevolent brother. For old-time's sake, he had lunch in the John Peter Smith Hospital cafeteria only a few blocks from the yards.

Downtown, he rented an inexpensive Honda Civic and made the short trip to the Stock Yards area of Cowtown to visit a Cavender's Western Store. He didn't go into the store, however, just checked around out back and got lucky. John had brought very little cash with him and was relieved to find that men's stores in Texas, or maybe just western stores in general, were much less picky than those in Louisiana. They threw out clothes with even the slightest imperfections.

Packing his new western wear in a trash bag, he stopped at a grocery store and picked up enough water and munchies to keep him going for a couple of days. He then drove the Civic to the Dallas suburb of Oak Cliff where Billy Bob lived on East Suffolk. On the afternoon of June 25th, he began to stake out Trip's house, observing it from behind the walkway bushes in front of a vacant home across the street. For a day and a night, Trip's home remained dark.

John was rewarded on the third evening at about eight as a beat-up 1985 Oldsmobile F-85 with only one working headlight, pulled into Billy Bob's driveway. It came to a halt partly on the front lawn. Sure enough, the

Reverend Billy Bob Buckmaster emerged, worn suitcase in hand, and commenced a serious bit of weaving as he made his way to the front door. There he spent nearly five minutes in the darkness sorting through a handful of keys he found in his pocket before finding the right one and finally letting himself in.

Over the next 48 hours, John followed Trip everywhere. On the evening of June 27th, the good reverend pulled into a convenience store parking lot. John parked next to him and followed him in. By then, he was wearing brand new, but mismatched boots – *at least they were both brown,* a beautiful, formerly crisp western shirt with the imprint of the Texas flag taking up front and back, a pair of too-tight-fitting jeans, and a giant silver belt buckle that read *Rodeo* on the front. He topped the outfit off with a genuine Stetson cowboy hat with only a slight smudge near its crown. While rummaging through the pile of discards behind Cavender's, a day or so earlier, John had discovered a red and blue bandana to tie around his face and use as a disguise, if needed.

The bodega was brightly lit and John considered whether he ought to pull the bandana across his face so Trip wouldn't recognize him, but then realized the clerk might take him for a robber. Instead, he pulled his cowboy hat down low and sauntered into the bodega, hands on his hips less than a minute after Buckmaster. John slapped his side as if looking for a sidearm playing the role a bit too strongly, and moved behind Trip as the preacher purchased a single lottery ticket using a *Pick Your Own Numbers* form.

John pretended to complete a *Pick Your Own Numbers* as well as he peeked over Trip's shoulder. Sure enough, Trip entered the numbers he'd given him the week before in New Orleans. As Buckmaster left the store, John crumpled his blank ticket and tossed it in the wastebasket.

He'd honestly hoped Trip would live up to his word about splitting the proceeds of a lottery win but this was exactly why he'd made the journey to Dallas. He didn't trust the man. In the bodega, he'd watched as the *only* name Billy Bob entered on the Pick Your Own form was that of one William R. Buckmaster. John had come mentally prepared for a complete deception, but still!

As John drove away from the store, Billy Bob's decision continued to puzzle Him. He'd really hoped Trip would throw him a chip from what was likely going to be his big payday.

"Okay," he later told himself aloud, "I'm disappointed that the Big B made no effort to add my name to the ticket as he'd promised. Here, I'm the one who provided the SOB with winning numbers worth millions of dollars! He promised me a five percent share of the winnings and that'll be a lot of money, but his take would be seven times that much! Seven times! Whew! Damn!

John drove around Dallas for an hour venting and considering his options. Of course, the very possibility of Trip double-crossing him is what drove him to stake out Buckmaster in the first place. Finally, he made his way to the parking lot of a big chain motel just off I-30 and waited. The motel had left its lights on for him, but for what he was about to attempt, John needed to remain in the shadows.

Nearing nine p.m. an elderly couple approached him walking back to the hotel from a nearby IHOP. As they stepped out of the circle of light coming from a streetlamp and into darkness, John jumped from the shadows and menacingly accosted them, demanding $40. The old man gave him a hundred-dollar bill and pleaded with him not to harm them.

"Give me your name and address and I'll pay you back, I promise," John replied and he meant it. But the older couple assured him they'd rather not ever see or hear from the bizarrely dressed cowboy again and quickly walked off into the darkness.

John was already late in returning the rental Honda and he needed to get away from the hotel before the couple brought in the police. He abandoned the car after wiping it down a block from the downtown Dallas bus station. Inside, John bought a ticket for the town of Waskom, near the Texas-Louisiana state line. He didn't have long to wait. Because most buses from the west and north stopped in Dallas while making their way east, they rotated through the terminal with some regularity.

The next bus out for Waskom was due in an hour. Killing time, John found a restaurant near the station. Even though it was early morning, he spent $18 on the best ribeye he'd had in a decade. Deliberately, he drank only water.

* * * *

In Better Times

Late that afternoon, exiting the bus as it made its brief stop in Waskom, John hurried to a nearby combination convenience store and gas station advertising the Texas State Lottery. Except for the cashier and one other person purchasing coffee and a donut, John was the only one in the store.

At the counter, he purchased a single Texas Lottery ticket for the coming draw entering the numbers 3 – 11 – 16 – 28 – 40 – 44 on a *Pick Your Own Numbers* form. Carefully he pocketed the ticket. A block over from the convenience store he found a cheap motel where they too had left the light on for him . . . this time for only $14.95 a night. He hoped for a comfortable and bedbug-free night's sleep.

But it was not to be.

On the night of the 21st of June 1997, from luxury accommodations in Waskom, Texas, John Pope peered at a beat-up black and white television anxiously. Completely ignoring the folderol coming from the announcer's mouth, John Pope was finally rewarded with an announcement of the drawing of the winning lottery ping pong balls. He took out his ticket and was ready to check the numbers off against the draw to make certain they were the ones he wanted. His fingers, toes, and eyes were crossed in anticipation, just as his Mom had told him to when he was a kid.

One by one the balls were sucked by the machine into a tube that spit them out onto a slotted display stand where a model's hand made an appearance to make certain the balls were turned right side up.

Thonk. The first ball was a sixteen. *Thonk.* Then a three. *Thonk.* Then a forty-four. John wiped his forehead with his bandana. *Thonk.* Twenty-eight needed help and had to be rotated into a proper viewing position. *Thonk.* Forty whooshed into place requiring no floating hand to set it upright. John took a deep breath as the last ball popped into place. *Thonk.* It was a 1. "Oh, crap!" he yelled at the television. Just then the disconnected hand came back into view and rotated the last ball to reveal an adjoining *one*. Eleven!

The image shifted from a close-up of the lottery balls to a long shot of a man holding a hand mike with one hand and a slip of paper with the other.

"Your winning numbers for the 36 million-dollar Texas Lottery are 3 – 11 – 16 – 28 – 40 and 44!" announced the announcer. A woman, presumably the one with the hand, entered the frame holding a slip of paper. In his booming announcer voice, the announcer said, "Our results are in! Sorry if these weren't the numbers on your ticket, but if not try again. Next time *may* be your time to," he paused dramatically, "win the Texas Lottery!" This time only a minor pause ensued. Then a drum roll sounded.

Looking into the camera, the woman smiled a completely insincere smile and handed the slip of paper to the host.

"Our computer has checked all the numbers entered and two winning tickets will share the biggest grand prize the Texas Lottery has ever awarded! Congratulations! You two lucky folks will share 36 million dollars! I see one of our winners is from Dallas, and . . ." the announcer paused again with deliberate drama . . . "the other winner is from the big east Texas town of . . . Waskom!"

There was a scattering of applause from the TV station studio crew.

"Yee-hah!" screamed John at the top of his lungs.

A hand pounded on the wall in an adjoining room. "Shaadup in there or I'll call the manager!"

If the hand that knocked on my wall was attached to another lottery ticket buyer . . . a loser, thought John . . . *I may pay for his room!*

Following the announcement of the winning numbers, there was no possibility at all that John would sleep a single wink that night. In fact, he not only didn't sleep, but he also didn't take a drink, save for a glass of water. There was simply too much at stake. He wanted nothing that might impair him from the tasks he'd planned for the following morning. That's when he expected to appear at the Waskom convenience store as soon as it opened and claim his 18 million dollars.

While the store didn't open until six, John was there at five.

This wasn't a chain store, so it was the owner himself who arrived, delighted to have a customer waiting for the store to open. Unlocking the door, he quickly learned that his customer was a major winner from last night's lottery drawing. That made him even happier because his store would share in the windfall.

"Unfortunately, however," he told his cowboy customer, "any win of a hundred dollars or larger must be claimed at one of the regional lottery branches. The nearest is about a half an hour up the interstate towards Dallas in Marshall."

John was perplexed for he hadn't wanted to jinx the numbers drawing process by pre-planning an aftermath for the announcement of the winning numbers. In truth, he hadn't prepared for this eventuality. Then he recognized a younger guy coming into the store. He'd seen him before . . . last night, in fact, purchasing a cup of coffee at the same store.

The man must live on coffee because here he is again! he thought.

John put his thumbs into his britches and said in his best Texas drawl, "Hey son, I need a ride to Marshall, and I'll pay you $50 to take me there." The man apparently knew the owner for he threw a questioning look at him. The convenience store owner nodded his head in approval.

"Show me the money," said the man to John in his best Cuba Gooding drawl.

"Sorry, there's a small rub. Here's a twenty," said John. "That'll cover your gas for both legs of the trip. Plus, I'll give you *eighty* more when I come out of a building there. Probably be inside there for ten minutes. An hour and a half round trip for $100. What say, my man?"

The guy wondered if he was being taken but he'd already received $20 for his trouble and had nothing else to do. He looked questioningly again at the store owner who then whispered something to him. The man turned

In Better Times

to John and said, "Congratulations, Mr. Dillon! Let's go then! All aboard for Marshall!"

John was a bit embarrassed to still be wearing his wrinkled Texas flag shirt, jeans, huge belt buckle, and cowboy hat. The hat got knocked off his head anyway as he wedged himself into the guy's tiny automobile.

They made the trip to Marshall and easily located the office of the Texas Lottery there. It was just past seven in the morning when John entered the small office and was quickly allowed to claim a bit more than eighteen million dollars before taxes. He trembled as he presented his lottery ticket for verification.

The small office operated with a staff of only three and there were several minor winners in the office already awaiting payoffs. John held on nervously as the clerks waited on them and paid their winnings. Then he ran John's ticket through the machine to verify its authenticity. It turned out that at that location they'd never before had a winner of more than $5,000.

The clerk began shouting. "Hey, hey! You, sir, are *definitely* one of the big winners!" He said this to the ceiling while waving the printed declaration.

The chaos in the small office was instantaneous. There was applause and everyone present slapped John on the back, offering congratulations. Five minutes later John finally had a moment to interrupt the celebration and ask the clerk if he could get his money and leave. "I have a ride waiting for me."

"I'm sorry sir," the official said to him. "The most I

can give you now is $50,000 and I'll have to get most of *that* from the bank . . . and, I'm sorry, but no local bank will open for two hours.

"Anyway, there're things you must do before you can get your money. For example, you need to choose whether you want a lump sum or an annual payout for life. There are federal income taxes to account for too. It'll take time to fill out the paperwork for both. Plus, if it's "lump," then we're required to deposit the remainder after taxes into a bank account because we certainly can't have you walking the streets with that kind of money on you! You'd be dead within an hour."

Whoo! Grim, thought John.

But, before he could object, the clerk said, "First, I've got to call the main office in Austin for instructions. We've never had anything like this happen before!"

John realized that a.) this process was going to take more time than he'd planned, and b.) he had a guy waiting for an $80 payoff outside. "Sir, I need a couple hundred dollars right now to pay off my ride outside. Can you loan me that? I can assure you that I'm good for it and that I *will* pay you back."

The official had seen things like this occur before, albeit on a much smaller scale. Against the rules, he pulled ten twenties from the cash drawer and said, "This is coming off the $50,000, you know."

John smiled and nodded in agreement. Stepping outside, he gave $100 to the fellow who'd driven him there. "Thanks for the ride. You can't imagine how much

In Better Times

I appreciate it."

The driver thanked him and said, "I take it you just won a bundle. Do yourself a favor and get some new clothes. You look like you've been riding the range with Roy Rogers!"

The man smiled, jumped in his car, and drove off. Later that day he'd regretted that he hadn't hit up his western-themed fare for more than $120 after he saw a photograph of him holding a large facsimile check for a lot more money than $120 on the evening news. Still, he now had a story of a lifetime to tell his friends. He was genuinely happy for John.

John stepped back into the lottery building and entered the private office of the manager of the Marshall Branch of the Texas State Lottery. The two men argued gently about whether John would or wouldn't – *even at the lottery's expense* – fly to Austin to accept his winnings publicly. John won the argument, providing the Lottery could complete the necessary paperwork in Marshall. Part of the agreement was that the lottery folks would be allowed to choreograph a few promotional moments there in Marshall to get a little PR from the big win.

John chose *lump sum*. The manager did the calculations to determine the final amount and then calculated how much to withhold for federal taxes. John asked about state taxes and was delighted to learn that there were none in the Lone Star State.

Nearing 9 a.m., the staff helped John open savings and checking accounts by phone with the PGT Beauregard

National Bank of New Orleans. Together, they then completed the rest of the paperwork and wired off $13,627,892.49 to John's new account at PGTBNB.

When the Marshall Bank and Trust next door finally opened *its* doors, the lottery manager literally ran to it, was its first customer of the day, and fifteen minutes later returned with $50,000 traveling money for John Pope.

John looked at the wad of cash in his hands . . . *his* cash. He signed for it, paid back the manager for his $100 loan, and then extracted three more one-hundred-dollar bills, giving one to the manager and one to each of the assistants for their help. Then he thanked them all and walked out the door as the country's newest multi-millionaire.

Before he left town, since he'd refused to go to Austin for the presentation ceremony, John and the manager were photographed in front of the small lottery office holding a Texas-sized check with a large state lottery logo on it between them. The huge blank faux check had been stored in a back room for just such an occasion. In hastily handwritten magic marker, it showed half the total winnings from the lottery draw before federal taxes were withdrawn. John's name and the date were also handwritten onto the big fake check with a Magic Marker.

In the photograph, the lottery manager and John each hold an end of the large check showing a winning total of $18,237,189.32 – *all before lump-sum-reduction and federal taxes to be withdrawn, of course* – which worked out well for the television and newspaper stories.

The facsimile check was four feet long and, with

his Cowboy hat perched on his head slightly askew, the approved photo would be preserved in lottery memory banks for a long time. Every TV station in Texas showed it on its newscasts that evening, and every station regretted that John hadn't been available for an interview.

That same afternoon back in Dallas, Billy Bob saw the same photograph on the local news. He was suffering from a monumental hangover that had begun with the announcement of the winning numbers the night before. Later that day he planned to fly at lottery expense to Austin to accept his own facsimile check for the same amount as John.

Billy Bob's gratitude went over well with the media, especially when compared to the still photograph of the strangely outfitted cowboy who was the co-winner, but who was unavailable for comment. John's story slipped quietly into a small article on the back page of section three with the small photograph of John, the manager, and the mocked-up check.

To say that Billy Bob regretted not planning to pay off the crazy drunk back in New Orleans with his five percent would be stating the obvious. When Trip saw the smaller photo of John in a cowboy outfit, he knew he'd made a huge mistake. But he also knew he couldn't complain that John stole numbers from him for if anything, he'd stolen them from John. That decision would haunt Billy Bob until the day he stuck a shotgun in his mouth five years later. Nevertheless, as *his* photograph was taken, Billy Bob Buckmaster shouted, "Yee-hah! Winner, Winner, Chicken

Dinner!" and everyone at the photo session laughed hard.

On his way out of Marshall, John paid $900 for a used 1972 baby blue Cutlass Convertible with 139,000 miles on it and headed east on I-20 for Shreveport, Louisiana. The Bojangles Hotel and Casino put up the country's newest millionaire in its Penthouse Suite for free, and for the next three weeks, John lived the high life.

II

SHREVEPORT, LOUISIANA – JULY 20, 1997

As the Bojangles Casino Hotel Manager personally escorted a dead broke John Pope from his gaudy casino hotel, a few local newsmen in Shreveport were on hand to photograph the former co-winner of the Texas State Lottery. No interviews were necessary when readers and viewers saw the look on the loser's face.

A day later, John climbed down from an empty Cotton Belt freight car in the Big Easy's downtown rail yards.

The suite at the Bojangles hadn't been entirely free because the night before he was escorted out, he'd trashed it after a few too many Gin Fizzes. His 72' Cutlass had been confiscated by the hotel to help pay the damages. Since it was the first and only car he'd ever owned, John mourned its loss as if it were his lifelong pride and joy.

"She was a great car. I only put 143 miles on her," he lamented to a fellow traveler while riding the rails somewhere between New Roads and New Orleans, Louisiana.

Climbing down into the yards of the Big Easy in the early hours of a New Orleans morning, John was again dressed in his *Cowboy Bob* duds. The newer and more stylish clothes he'd purchased in Shreveport were packed neatly away in a fancy set of luggage. But, as a cowboy, the only things about him that made him identifiable to his friends were the beard, which he'd still not shaved, his empty pockets, and a hangover that lasted for the entire two days it took him to travel home Hobo style. John struggled with the luggage, walking from the rail yard, then staggered over to Canal, finally lugging the heavy suitcase up to Rue Waterloo.

* * * *

"Bro! I thought you was goin' to Colorado to stay! Whatcha doin' back so soon? And, where'd you leave Robert Redford's body when you stole his *Electric Horseman* outfit? Hey, Wyatt! You look like shit!"

III

John hadn't spent *all* the money though . . . just $45,000 and change. He still had $200 rolled up in his socks and more than $4,000 in cash scattered about his cowboy duds with some of the money hidden in the lining of his luggage and even more in his underwear.

Returning to New Orleans . . . and partly to sobriety,

the first thing John did was crawl under the house and push $100 into an empty brandy bottle. He added a new note that he'd written on yellow-lined paper, just to be sure. *This is getting out of hand,* he thought. *I definitely need a larger bottle!*

Over the next two months, John negotiated with the city to purchase the Shotgun on Rue Waterloo for $700 cash, plus $1,000 for the lot. He paid $1,800 in back taxes. That pretty much cleaned him out after his wild month of partying in Shreveport.

Of course, he still had the bulk of the winnings tucked safely away in the Pierre Gustave Toutan-Beauregard National Bank. When John thought about the parties and the lost forty-five thou, he heard his mother's voice saying something about "*. . . a bad penny . . . just like your father.*" Her voice haunted him, but he knew if he kept to the course he'd laid out, the voice would return someday to congratulate him.

Recovery from a $45,000 month-long party was sobering, both figuratively and literally, but it didn't take long for John's survival instincts and basic good intentions to percolate. In a few weeks or a month at most, he planned to invest almost everything he'd temporarily stored at the Beauregard bank.

John spent the time until then investigating local brokers. Ultimately, he found one in the city that he felt he could trust. Through him, he invested ten million dollars in Apple Tech. When he did this, he was again dressed in his subdued semi-homeless attire. The broker was astounded to confirm with PGTBNB that a person of John's appearance and demeanor had the wherewithal to have that much liquid cash available . . . ready to invest.

"I'll tell you a secret," said John, deliberately slurring his words, "I earned this money based on directions I found on a note stuck in a bottle hidden in a crawl space under an old shotgun house in Mid-City!"

The broker asked no questions, but his face said he was dubious. Paul added, "You need a tip? . . . Steve is coming back to his old *jobs*."

With that mission accomplished, and with a renewed zest for life, John went 37 days sober and was making plans to create a new life for himself and for his younger self, Paul.

Paul never had been one who kept up with the news and he hadn't followed any from Texas. In point of fact, it was unlikely that anyone in New Orleans would connect the older twin to the cowboy from Texas who'd won all that money. Even then, he was barely recalled in Texas outside of Waskom and Marshall.

On the 38th day of Paul's sobriety, John and Paul discussed the changes occurring in their lives. John's part of the conversation centered on what they would do next, while Paul's comments were more about their appearances: They had always looked exactly alike. After John came home following his *first* trip to Colorado though, the twins only resembled each other.

"The unusual thing," he told John, "is that, you come back from Colorado a second time now, and we look exactly like twins again. Is that where the Old Faithful Fountain of Youth is? Crazy, ain't it?"

John responded, "What Colorado trip?" then paused with raised eyebrows. In a conspiratorial voice, he said, "Paul, have you ever wondered if perhaps we're not really the same person . . . just in two different bodies, one a few years older than the other, thanks to time travel?"

Paul nearly fell from his chair laughing. "Boy, you sure are a chip off the old block! You and Pop! Wow." John dropped the subject, but the concept continued to intrigue him.

With a surprising money stream now fueling their lives, at John's insistence, Paul joined his brother and cleaned up his act. John made certain the two men didn't let the newfound money go to their heads because he demanded that each of them take jobs, John working part-time as a custodian in a branch of the Beauregard Bank, and Paul learning the mortician's trade in an old funeral home just behind Jackson Square. The owner, Walt Beiderweil, had taken a liking to Paul now that he'd cleaned up, was dressing better, and appeared to be off the sauce. Even that didn't *really* bother Walt because many of the morticians he'd known in his life tended to liquidly fortify themselves each morning to do the kind of work they were forced to, *literally*, undertake.

It wasn't long before Paul realized that somehow John had come into big money, and he was a fortunate beneficiary. Paul's tastes improved and he began dating. Cynthia became jealous and told him that he'd changed

In Better Times

for the worse. With improved work habits though, both John and Paul began receiving regular promotions.

John was especially proud and more than pleased to see his brother succeeding in *real life*.

Over the next year, Paul concluded that he had a knack for his job at Beiderweil and told John so. Through his contacts at the bank, John did some digging and learned that Walter Beiderweil was considering selling the business in a year or two as he planned to retire to a fishing camp near Monroe. As a surprise for Paul, John worked up the numbers in secret and made Old Man Beiderweil a *cash-on-the-table* offer for both the business and the building which, after a bit of give and take, Beiderweil agreed to. Among the amendments attested to by all parties, was that the Beiderweils could take as long as they wanted to find a new home before relocating permanently.

John brought in his lawyer, a man named Baron LeBlanc, and the deal was consummated on the spot. All paperwork was filed before the day was done.

As they shook hands over the deal, Walt said to John, "First I need to tell you how much you do . . . and strangely . . . how much you don't . . . look like your brother. Secondly, you know, I've always tried to interest my daughter in business, but she's always been repelled by it. She's a free spirit anyway so I think I'll just let her be surprised one day when her mom and I pass and she finds out how well off we really were. Maybe that'll change her mind about the funeral industry."

Walt held his hand beside his mouth and in a mock

whisper said to John, "I think she's found someone anyway. Maybe with this behind us, she'll tell us who he is." *Wink, wink.*

A week later, John was notified by the law firm, LeBlanc LeBlanc LeBlanc and Blois that all proceedings in the sale of the funeral home had been finalized. Over a late breakfast the next morning at their favorite breakfast spot, *Mother's,* John told Paul that they were now the new owners of the Beiderweil Funeral Home and that its new name would be *Beiderweil and Pope Mortuary. . .* and, best of all, *he* – Paul Pope – would become its General Manager.

Paul was stunned but obviously delighted at the news. Before he could respond though, the television, which was turned to the morning news, filtered through their conversation. A woman reporter said, "We have late-breaking news. The NTSB has released the names of the two victims of a small plane crash early this morning at the Monroe, Louisiana airport. They're Walter and Emma Beiderweil, owners of the Beiderweil Funeral Home here in the city . . ."

Paul slammed a fist into the palm of his hand at the news and said, "Oh, my God!" To John, the response seemed a little practiced.

A few weeks later, a representative of the National Transportation Safety Board released a preliminary report on the crash: "The Beiderweils had apparently been on their way from New Orleans to Monroe for a short fishing vacation. The pilot, Mr. Walter Beiderweil, was an experienced veteran pilot, having flown P7s during the Korean War.

"The accident and the subsequent deaths of the pilot and passenger," reported the NTSB, "occurred while attempting to land the aircraft at the Monroe, Louisiana airport. The airplane was seven years out from construction, certification, and testing. Its last full inspection had occurred only three months earlier. Prior to the crash, the Cessna 152 had operated for 1,827 hours and had experienced no problems whatsoever prior to the event.

"Preliminarily it appears that the nose wheel disengaged from its strut sometime during the flight from New Orleans. Eighteen feet after touchdown in Monroe, the empty strut collapsed, and the small plane nosedived into the runway at approximately 92 mph, coming to an immediate halt.

"Subject to final autopsy results, the occupants appear to have died from blunt force trauma. NTSB inspectors will conduct further tests to determine why the nose wheel disengaged.

"A search is underway, and the public is asked to report the wheel and the assembly's location if found, probably along the plane's logical route from New Orleans to Monroe. If you find this wheel, please photograph it in situ. Do not touch or disturb it. The wheel and any other portions of the aircraft are part of an ongoing investigation.

"It does not appear at this time that pilot error contributed to the crash, however, metal strength test results and final autopsy results remain unavailable to permit us to reach a final conclusion on the matter at this time. It should be noted that in the forty-seven-year life of this model aircraft, no such similar accident has ever before occurred."

IV

SMOKE SIGNALS

The lives of John and Paul Pope changed dramatically over the next three years, especially for Paul. John meanwhile found a nice fixer-upper in the Garden District to rehab as he went along and became quite the recluse. His long grey beard added to the image. An avid reader and a serious financial booster for the city's library system, John appeared in public mostly as a volunteer and advocate for homeless and cancer causes. In the background, he pushed for and provided funding for improvements in the public-school curriculum, improved quality of city teaching staff, and the repair of the city's crumbling buildings.

While generally avoiding the limelight, his behind-the-scenes efforts to increase state funding for schools were high-level and effective. In Louisiana, this meant funding a Public Education Lobby. After only three years, local and state school officials longed to publicly honor John Pope for his work and for his financial contributions, but he preferred to stay in the shadows. John confided to Paul though that he was especially pleased as the city's student retention rates began to climb.

While John did his work in the background, Paul, perhaps because of the darkness that surrounds the funeral industry, worked hard to be visible in projects that centered around fun and physical activity. Beiderweil and Pope sponsored numerous youth football, basketball, and baseball teams, plus annual 3k, 10k, and 15k races, and of course, the city's premier race, the Big Easy Marathon, all of which found a way to wind around the corner of Royal and Nichols, passing the front doors of Beiderweil and Pope's main facility in the French Quarter ... almost always concluding at the 50-yard line in the Superdome.

Paul joined a Mardi Gras Krewe and didn't stop until he was accorded the rare honor of serving as Bacchus, King of Mardi Gras – not only the youngest King ever, but the first non-celebrity to be so honored since 1969. Paul was active with the Chamber and he and his wife Sherrie were known and welcomed in every social circle in the city.

V

April 2, 2005

In his company car, Paul pulled up to the gates of his property and punched in his four-digit security code. This gate and the fourth green offered the only public views of his massive new home unless one happened to be sailing past the Pope dock on Lake Pontchartrain. From everywhere else, the view of the home was blocked by six-foot hedges situated just behind an iron fence of the same height. A security system was in place mostly to *dissuade* peddlers and busybodies, as both the fence and hedge ended at the City Park property line.

As his private gate slowly swung open, Paul crowded it, anxious to get home. Today he felt vulnerable and mortal. He parked the Spyder on the garage apron and stepped out, taking a second to admire the beautiful automobile. Paul was dressed, as he almost always was, in a black suit, and, while not a requirement for his line of work, it sent the correct message. His hair was conservatively groomed.

Once away from Beiderweil and Pope, his demeanor changed . . . mostly. Despite driving home with the Spyder's top stowed, Paul's hair still obeyed orders. Not a single strand deviated from its assigned location no matter the speed or wind.

Parking the vehicle, he slithered out of the Spyder and headed toward the home's front door, opening it. It was unlocked, and that irritated him. "How many times do I have to . . ." he said aloud, and the rest of the sentence bounced around inside his head unfinished. Fifty yards to his right, golf carts scurried down the fairway toward the fourth green. A foursome was at the fifth tee another 20 yards further away. Inside the foyer, Paul called out, "Babe, I'm home. Have you heard the news?"

Sherrie's voice came back from another room immediately. "The Pope died, right? I knew it would mess you up, Hon."

"Yeah," He spoke loudly enough to be heard on the

other side of the house where she was presumably getting herself ready to greet him after a hard day socializing. "You know, I was born almost to the minute he was crowned. I wonder if..."

"Don't even think about it, Paul. *Don't even think about it!* You are your own person. Well, actually..." she chuckled as she entered the room carrying two vodka tonics, "...because you and *John* are identical twins, you are both your own person!"

Paul grimaced at the name and the singularity of the phrase. "With luck, maybe my bearded brother will trip and fall in front of a streetcar... and then I'll be the *only* Pope."

"Don't ever say things like that, Paul. John is simply a lost and wandering soul... unlike you. You are the most handsome, most charming, most intelligent person in the world and someone who is a..." whispering now, "world champion in bed!" She kissed him. "Welcome home. How was work today?"

"Uneventful," he said. "No surprises. Just the way I like it!"

Switching subjects, she replied, "Okay. You know I gotta ask. Given your name, you must be an expert. So, what happens now with the selection of the new pope?"

Paul's smile returned a bit.

"I've got it all down right here," Paul said tapping his forehead with an index finger. "Pop taught us the whole sequence when we were kids. It's *the most* enduring memory I have of him.

"Here it is: First, they have to get all the Cardinals to show up in Rome. That'll take some time. Plus, they have to stage an official period of mourning. That'll take nine days if they hold to the traditional schedule. That'll probably end on Monday the 18th.

The nine days of official mourning will be over at that point. Those nine days are called the *Novendiali* . . ."

"I love it when you speak Italian, Paul," Sherrie interrupted, flirting.

". . . and the Cardinals will then begin their secret meeting in the Sistine Chapel," he continued, ignoring her flirt. "It should only take a few hours, maybe twelve at the most if there's no controversy . . . and then the white smoke will pour forth and we'll have a new pope. I wonder what name he'll take."

"Or *she*," said Sherrie with a grin. She paused, her drink halfway to her lips. "You know Paul, you ought to be a reporter, or at least a consultant on this for the news coverage. Maybe if I called CNN or Channel 12 and told them you were available . . ."

When Paul didn't have a come-back, she changed the subject, saying, "Speaking of the 18th, have you picked up your new tux for the big event? You really need to try it on beforehand so there's time to tailor it if necessary. We'd hate to have New Orleans's latest *Entrepreneur of the Year* showing up in an ill-fitting tuxedo!"

"It's not *Entrepreneur of the Year* . . . that's the name of the magazine," replied Paul as he held up a copy from a stack of a dozen he'd brought with him from the office.

His photograph as one of the three finalists for *Three Under Thirty* was front and center on the cover. "Hot off the presses! I am now, officially one of *New Orleans's Three Under Thirty*."

"Look at you!" Sherrie said. I've never known a Cover Boy before! Congratulations!" On tiptoes, she kissed him lightly while holding her vodka tonic high.

"Oh, and thanks for the reminder but I picked the tux up this afternoon. I left it in the Spyder. Better get it before the weather turns nasty."

VI

THE FIRE
9:40 P.M. - APRIL 18, 2005

It was fully dark, and people were exiting the Superdome in droves. The *Three Under Thirty* event had been both a spectacular success and a financially lucrative event for the Chamber. In front of the Dome's main entrance, Jerome opened the rear limo door and Sherrie gracefully stepped in. A score of people crowded around the Dome side of the limo, several shouting, "Congratulations, Paul!" Those closest slapped him on the back. Another said, "Couldn't happen to a nicer guy!" Yet another chimed in, "About time, Paul. You should have won the award years ago."

As Jerome closed the car door behind the couple, he casually saluted and said, "Congratulations, boss."

"Thanks, Jerome. Hey," Paul held the face of his watch out at Jerome. "It's 9:42 . . . and, *we're* outta here! Told you the Chamber'd get this thing done by ten. Thank God it's over."

The limo pulled away from the Super Dome's circular VIP entrance. In the back, Sherrie leaned over and kissed him on the cheek. "Paul, your acceptance speech was incredible! And" whispering, "by the way, don't forget, I'd like you to be *incredible* again a little later!" The same seductive smile she'd shown before they left the house made a repeat appearance.

After a pause, she continued, "Where was John tonight? You'd think for an event this big – one honoring *his own brother* – he could show his non-social whiskered face and be there to support you. *Everyone* noticed his absence. The empty table setting with his place card on it really said a lot about brotherly love!"

"I don't know, hon," said Paul. "Even though it's been more than a couple of months, I think he's still feeling a little *off* after that face-off with the streetcar. He almost got killed, you know."

As if on cue, Paul's cell phone rang.

"Yeah," he answered as he loosened his bow tie with his free hand. Listening to the voice on the other end for several moments, he replied, "Okay. Okay. I can probably do that. You're really sure you want to do this, huh?" After a pause for a response, he smiled and said, "I'm on my way. Meet you at the office." He hung up.

"Sorry, Hon. I told you on the way over we'd received

a customer . . . but, since we're talking about John, that was him. He's at the office now and says he wants to – get this: 'Relive his youth!' He's asked me to . . . now, get this, '. . . *drop me off at a truck stop out on I-10 after we're done so I can*' . . . and I quote, "*. . . hit the road hitchhiking to Tin Cup*. Says he's, '*. . . always wanted to go back there,*' and, '*. . . the best time to get a long ride is to work the truck stops late at night.*'

"He should know, I guess. When we're finished with the customer, I'll drop him off at the TA out where I-10 and I-12 meet and then come right home. Maybe with luck, we won't see him for a while."

"After he didn't show tonight, I wouldn't care if it was never!" responded Sherrie.

"Jerome," Paul changed the subject saying to the chauffeur. "We need to turn around. Take me to the office please, and then take Mrs. Pope home. Make certain she gets inside before you leave. Hey, and then, please give our babysitter a ride home."

"Yes, sir," came the expected reply. Seconds later, the limo braked and made a three-point 180.

"You promise you'll be home soon?" whispered Sherrie. "Hurry, but don't take off that tux . . . I wanna do that."

"Alright," he smiled. "I promise. But don't wait up for me. If I'm not home by midnight, we can catch up in the morning. Hey, uh, can you take this and put it in the study?" He handed her his *Three Under Thirty* award plaque.

A large white three-story castle-looking building

bathed in bright light, the recently remodeled Beiderweil and Pope Funeral Home, appeared on the corner of Royal and Nichols just off Bourbon Street. A large lit sign over the angled front doors proclaimed the name as well. A slide of the same view had been part of the multimedia shown on the big screens earlier that night at the *Three Under Thirty* event. The limo pulled to the side of Nichols, slowly passing the main entrance, halting in front of a small semi-hidden doorway. Paul stepped out of the limo, leaned back in, and kissed Sherrie.

"Sorry about this, Hon. Be sure and set the security when you get home."

He closed the door and watched as the limo moved on, turning left at Rampart street. Paul continued to watch until it was out of sight. Extracting keys from his pocket, he unlocked the nondescript door. A small, barely visible sign over it read simply, "Office." Closing the door behind him and making certain the lock triggered, Paul headed down a dark hallway, walking *past* a door marked, "Paul Pope, President, Beiderweil and Pope."

When he reached a door on the opposite side of the hallway marked "Do Not Enter", he withdrew another key, unlocked it, entered, and climbed the stairs to a small lobby on the second floor. At yet one more door, he used a third key to unlock this door as well.

Just as he was about to turn the knob, he was surprised as the door opened almost in anticipation. Cynthia Beiderweil, dressed in black stilettos, long red luxurious – *almost orange* – hair . . . . and only freckles, pulled him into her apartment and immediately began to undress him.

Behind her, a television reporter was breathlessly reporting breaking news, a live report from Vatican City. The reporter stuttered a bit with big news, "We're seeing . . . uh, seeing some activity around the Sistine Chapel . . ."

"'Bout damn time," Cynthia said to Paul hungrily. "I've been waiting *and waiting* for you! So, you got an 'A-ward' tonight, huh? How 'bout a 'RE-ward,' right now?" She gave him a long deep kiss while he took inventory.

The two shuffled toward her bedroom dropping pieces of Paul's clothing behind them.

As they moved down the hallway, they passed a series of photographs lining the wall: Cynthia with her parents, Walter Beiderweil shaking Paul's hand in agreement to a partnership in front of the main entrance to the funeral home as Cynthia stood to the side smiling, Cynthia crossing The *New Orleans Classic Marathon* finish line wearing an all-black running outfit featuring the orange European symbol for "No" across her chest.

In it she looked as fresh as the moment the race had begun and her outfit looked as if it might have been sprayed on. The final wall-mounted optic featured a framed newspaper story about Walter and Emma Beiderweils' fatal airplane crash as they had made their way to a fishing camp in north Louisiana.

The door to her bedroom closed behind them.

VII

Paul re-entered the second-floor lobby exiting Cynthia's apartment. Turning back he said, "Go ahead. Have your run. Then get a shower. I'll be back in an hour or two. I've got something to do for a while. Keep it warm. Maybe I'll meet you in the shower later."

Behind them, an excited television reporter was saying, "Breaking news! White smoke is pouring from the chimney over the Sistine Chapel. It seems we may have a new Pope! Let's go to Brian Murray in St. Peter's Square in Vatican City . . ."

Paul closed the apartment door and smiled. It was a smile of immense satisfaction. For him this was a captured moment . . . a photograph if you will of his life: *He had it all.*

Skipping down the stairs and into the hallway, Paul unlocked the door to his office and flipped on a ceiling light, illuminating the incredibly luxurious office that reeked of leather and expensive cigars.

Barely audible through the ceiling speakers, Arturo Sandoval's Piano Trio had just begun *When Smoke Gets in Your Eyes*. Paul entered the office . . . *his office*. On the wall behind the massive desk, two large photographs captured his, as well as every visitor's, attention. The slightly smaller version on the left was of the shabby-looking *old* Beiderweil Funeral Home. The newer one on the right was a larger shot, in color, and a nighttime image of the building's beautifully restored façade. To bring it to its authentic former appearance, the old building had been whitewashed. Bathed in lights. As remodeled, it bore a strong resemblance to a small European castle.

Just as in the earlier smile, and the one in the live view earlier from his limousine, this night photo could just as easily be titled, "*Success*." A story from the *Times-Picayune* about the building's remake was posted below it, detailing how the historic old Beiderweil Funeral Home building was at that time being enclosed by the new version, to preserve a historic New Orleans landmark dating back to the early 1800s. It had served many functions over its life and was perhaps best recalled locally with some fame as the former home of an 1830s husband and wife whose last name was LaLurie. The story about the old home was legendary.

Next to it was a smaller framed architect's conception of what the newest Beiderweil and Pope *branch* funeral home would look like when completed and opened a few months later in Metairie. On one bookshelf perched a photograph of Paul standing . . . *almost posed* . . . and leaning back on his fire engine red Ferrari in front of the Cathedral on Jackson Square. On Paul's desk were photographs of Sherrie, Ace, and one of the entire family, each holding a good-sized fish aboard a large yacht named, *Bon Temp, Destin*.

Life *was* good for the Popes.

Paul picked up a remote from his desk and pointed it at the latest and flattest television hanging on the wall. It was only four inches deep. Up popped a reporter standing in front of St. Peter's in the Vatican. Rain was falling in the square and the man was dressed in a slicker with a CBS logo on it. He said, "Christy, we'll probably know the name of the new Pope within the hour. In the far background, you can see white smoke still coming out of the small chimney on the roof of the Sistine Chapel so, it won't be long, probably thirty minutes or so before we hear the words, *"Habemus Papum!"* – We have a Pope!... Brian Murray reporting from St. Peter's Square."

Paul grunted, "Hmmph!" and remoted the television back to darkness and arranged the few things on his desk to make it perfect.

Finally, he extracted a large corporate checkbook from a locked drawer and wrote a check out to *Three Under Thirty* for $100,000. Placing the check in a tray on his desk marked, *Roberta*, he picked up the phone, punched a button, waited a second, and said into the message system, "Roberta. I've left a check for you to mail. It's in the tray on my desk. It's for those crooks at *Three Under Thirty*. Send it to them first thing in the morning with a letter from me describing how honored I am at their selection and for the ceremony. Maybe they'll quit bugging us for it."

He hung up the phone and replaced the checkbook. For a moment Paul steepled his hands and rested his chin on his fingertips in contemplation. He then took a deep breath and pushed his chair back. Walking over to a seven-foot mahogany cabinet in the corner, he took out a clean, folded, white doctor's style work jacket. A label on its upper right side read, "Beiderweil and Pope Funeral Home," and in smaller letters below: "Paul Pope, President." He put it on, turned, walked back to his desk, and reached under it to retrieve a mostly empty wastebasket.

Walking around the huge desk, Paul carried the basket over to a rolling leather chair stationed next to the desk. Next to the chair, a small table lay on its side. Several pieces of broken glass were there as well. They had once formed a crystal flower vase. A dozen withered cut lilies lay on the floor. Paul carefully collected the glass pieces, placing them in the wastebasket. The lilies followed. On the floor next to the chair was a 4 X 6-foot piece of carpet displaying a large, clotted bloodstain plus watermarks from the broken vase. He rolled the carpet into a tube.

Paul checked the floor to make certain no blood had soaked into the hardwood. It hadn't. Placing the rug under an arm, he retrieved the wastebasket and opened the office door, checking down the hallway. As expected at this hour, it was empty. Turning, he doused the office light and pulled the office door closed behind him, rattling it to make certain it had locked.

Paul carried the two items down the long dim hallway to another door marked, *Beiderweil and Pope Preparation Room – Employees Only – Do Not Enter.* Punching in the access code, he unlocked it. At his entrance, fluorescent ceiling lights triggered *on* in a large, sterile, antiseptic-looking room. At first glance, one might easily have suspected this was an industrial sterile laboratory. A large clock on the wall showed the time as 12:45 a.m. An irritating buzz sounded from the ancient fluorescents.

Paul, of course, was in the older portion of Beiderweil

and Pope where he'd first been introduced to the business by old Walt Beiderweil. A large garage-style door, high and wide enough to allow access by an ambulance, was located at one end. Stainless steel autopsy-style tables stood starkly in the center of the room with floor drains centered under them. At the moment, the tables were empty.

Paul walked to the far wall where a three-by-three foot, four-inch-thick insulated steel door with a locking metal handle was mounted. The door was located a precise 42 inches up from the floor. He flipped a switch on a small panel next to it on the wall and a light began glowing behind the door which was barely visible through a small observation window. Paul looked in while absentmindedly rubbing his hands together. A small sign above the door read: "Crematory Oven, Authorized Personnel Only. Do Not Touch!"

Paul stared for a moment, seemingly in contemplation, and finally smiled. Inside, the walls of the oven appeared to be constructed of dark-colored brick. The eight-foot-long chamber was lined with refractory bricks that when new had been colored a light grey. Over time and under frequent use, they'd turned a toasty black. The roof of the chamber was dominated by a vent hood similar to what one might find over a kitchen stove but obviously, one that served a much more industrial purpose.

Grunting in satisfaction, he flipped another switch, this one marked *Pilot*. A subtle pop sounded as a small flame inside the oven ignited. He then turned and retrieved an empty gurney parked next to the oven and pushed it across the room to where several morgue-style locker doors, also precisely 42 inches above the floor, lined the wall.

Parking the gurney under the middle door, he opened it. A puff of humidified air escaped, dispersing noiselessly. Before pulling out a metal drawer, he lifted a white-colored plastic sheet to make certain the body under it was *not* wearing a toe tag. Satisfied, he dropped the sheet back over the feet.

The body was now fully covered . . . again.

Paul then slid the heavy cardboard tray containing the body out from the locker and onto the gurney. Closing the door, he absentmindedly began to whistle an old Walt Disney *Snow White* tune as he rolled the gurney across the room, positioning it just below the crematory door. He opened the oven, slid the cardboard tray a few feet into the oven, and then stopped in contemplation of what he was about to do.

It was time to face the deceased, the enemy, the victim, the brother . . . the twin.

Standing at the head end of the covered corpse, Paul finally peeled the sheet back far enough to expose its head and chest. His brother John looked back seemingly in disbelief at what was happening to him.

Paul smiled. Having expired more than ten hours ago now, John's skin had turned grey and thanks to the passage of life and the cooler itself, he was now almost ice cold to the touch. Paul's twin remained fully clothed, wearing coveralls and the flannel shirt that had almost become his trademark. It now showed a circular, almost black stain directly over the heart. His escaping blood had congealed and glistened in the harsh light of the Preparation Room. John's open eyes were fixed, glassy, and vacant. As Paul studied them more closely, he smiled at the frozen expression of shocked surprise.

Paul then imagined what John's eyes could see were there life still in them. He'd of course have an upside-down view of his own brother leering at him from above. Paul allowed another moment of silence. Finally, he smiled down at the form, gave John a dismissive two-fingered salute, and said, "So you wanted to go to the State Police with a story about the deaths of the Beiderweils, huh? Guess you'll have to tell your story to St. Peter." In the sterile mostly empty room, Paul's laugh echoed several times off the cold walls.

Recovering, Paul retrieved the tubed carpet and placed it over John's lower body but didn't bother covering the face. He then placed the wicker wastebasket containing broken vase parts on top of the rug. Knowing that the intense heat of the crematory would vaporize the carpet, the ceramics, and the wicker basket, not to mention the body. He was easily disposing of evidence. As a final touch, he placed the lilies on top of the carpet and smiled one last time.

On a panel mounted to the right of the oven door, he punched numbered buttons to digitally read "2,200 Degrees." He almost slid his brother's body on its cardboard tray the rest of the way into the oven but realized he wanted one more moment with John.

Nearly a minute of silence ticked by. The moment wasn't in memoriam for his slain brother though, Paul just wanted to recall when the idea had first occurred to him.

Or was it Cynthia's idea first? He recalled.

Then, in a sing-song voice, he stared into the vacant eyes of his brother and said, "Goodbye, John. Have a nice trip! Get used to the heat!" and pushed the cardboard mattress all the way into the chamber.

Again, the walls heard a laugh that seemed to echo forever.

Paul closed the oven door. Taking a deep breath, he pushed a button on the panel marked, "Ignition." A loud whoosh sounded as the oven's gas burners ignited. A bright orange glow showed through the observation window. Paul turned to a wall clock and noted the time as 2:33 a.m. Absent-mindedly, he again rubbed his hands together and pulled out a flask.

* * * *

Ninety minutes later, still dressed in his white medical professional's jacket, Paul carried a silver urn down the hallway and through a door near the ambulance entrance marked *Casket Display Room*. Inside, seven empty and open caskets failed to draw his interest. Walking quickly, he halted before a door that was almost hidden from view behind a curtain.

He opened the urn for one last glimpse, and whispered, "John! Is that you? Man, you look like shit!"

Silently, he unlocked the door which opened to a small

dark, mostly empty closet. Two upper shelves were filled with identical silver urns, all with labels on them. There were fifteen on the top shelf and seven on the lower. He placed the urn he'd just carried from the oven containing the cremains of his twin brother, next to the others on the lower shelf. To its newly applied blank label, using a black Sharpie, he wrote *Pope, John XXIII* and closed the door.

VIII

APRIL 19TH, 2005 (TWENTY MINUTES LATER) – NEW ORLEANS NORTH SIDE

A Beiderweil and Pope company car screamed to a stop on the concrete pad next to Paul's magnificent home which was shrouded in darkness. Storm clouds swirled overhead. His security system sang of urgencies as a nearly full moon slipped in and out of clouds like a faltering flashlight.

Paul first heard the alarm whooping as he passed through the entrance gate. He was irritated because it appeared that no one was home, or worse, no one was conscious. The outside alarm warning also flashed a beacon of white light creating a strobe effect. Just before he shut the car's engine down, he noted that the dash clock read 4:45 a.m. When he swung open the car door, the noise of the alarm became much louder, screeching at him like a monstrously large, irritated mama bird protecting its young.

Screech, screech, screech. Whoop, whoop, whoop . . .

Paul jumped from the car, pulled out his cell phone, and punched 9-1-1. When the operator answered, he said angrily, "Yeah. This is Paul Pope. Where *are* you? My security company called me five minutes ago tellin' me there'd been a break-in at my house. You should have gotten the same call . . . and you *should* have had your guys here by now, dammit! Hurry, will you? I'm goin' in."

The operator bit her tongue and chose not to remind her worried caller that she maintained no contact with the caller's security company but warned him anyway not to enter the dwelling until police arrived. But Paul was already running to the front door which he found secure. He looked through the living room windows but could see nothing out of line. Still, the window tinting in the darkness made night observation difficult.

He ran around the corner of the house to the glassed-in porch that overlooked the Bayou Oaks' fifth tee. Lake Pontchartrain reflected the moon's presence as it occasionally emerged from behind clouds. The swirling winds had juiced up the waves on the big lake.

Whoop, whoop, whoop . . .

Police sirens joined the chorus as they approached, still though from a far distance.

Paul saw that the glass door to the porch had been shattered. He grabbed a small lantern that normally sat on the floor near the doorway and switched it on. With it, he was able to see drops of blood sprinkling the walkway into the house. Or was it *walking out of the house*? He stepped onto the porch and over the glass as it crunched under his shoes. Quickly panning the lantern he concluded that the porch was empty. He tripped over his *Three Under Thirty* award lying on the floor and it confirmed for him that at some point his wife had been there. He called through the doorway, "Sherrie! Sherrie! Where are you?" No answer. In fact, the only sound he heard was . . .

Whoop, whoop, whoop . . .

Paul punched 9-1-1 again and waited only for a second. "They got my wife and probably my son too. And maybe even my dog. Hurry dammit!"

He punched the phone off before the operator could respond and walked back out the shattered glass door stepping on more shards of glass. Before placing the phone back in his pocket, he remembered to punch in the code to open the security gate for the approaching police. He cursed himself for not thinking about that detail earlier. Paul moved out onto the patio where more blood trails led him toward the lawn bordering the golf course. The sirens were nearer and louder now. Heavy rain began to fall.

Whoop, whoop, whoop . . .

Paul pointed his lantern to follow the trail of blood droplets across the tiled patio and then into and across the downward-sloping yard. The blood spots were becoming larger and easier to track. That, in itself, was worrying. Through the chaos of the warning speaker, the approaching sirens, and the gusting winds, he heard a dog barking out on the fairway. In the darkness, though, he could see nothing.

There was a brief growl of thunder and a short lightning

burst that illuminated two small public restrooms between the fourth green and the fifth tee. The burst of lightning had pulled his attention to them. Now blurred movement near there caught his attention. He shot the lantern in that direction and could make out several figures standing near the buildings. He heard barking, then a woman crying, and finally, a child's voice hollering, "Daddy!"

"I'm coming Ace!" he shouted through the myriad of sounds – storm, siren, animal, human – they all grabbed at his mind and propelled him forward. It was chaos.

As Paul closed in on the figures, he recognized his Golden Retriever Trip in the middle of the swirling maelstrom and soon saw that he was standing at alert, teeth bared, growling furiously at something just out of sight. Another slight roll of thunder was followed quickly by a flash of lightning

Whoop, whoop, whoop . . .

Paul withdrew a Glock 9 from the cummerbund of his tuxedo and charged toward them. Lightning illuminated one of the figures holding his wife from behind with a gun pointed at her head. The figure shuffled and he noted it was dressed in black and had an orange slash on its chest. He, of course, recognized it immediately. It was the universal European symbol for *No*, an orange reflective circle with a slash across it. The terrorist was Cynthia.

Paul picked up his pace and closed in on her, on Sherrie, on Ace, and on the dog Trip. His face mirrored the same expression he'd last seen on John's face just before he'd closed the crematory oven door.

As he closed in on the small congregation, the dog, Trip, tugged on his leash especially hard, yanking Cynthia's left foot. It was bleeding from its right rear flank and had apparently been injured in the defense of Paul's family. As he came to a halt, the dog whimpered and yielded to Paul, and then growled menacingly. The dog was planted only feet from Cynthia, prepared to attack her if the figure of his wife hadn't blocked the way. Cynthia though, continued to hold Sherrie at bay with a gun pointed at her head. Ace cried, "Daddy!" again, and in tandem, Trip growled.

Whoop, whoop, whoop . . .

The moon peeked out weakly from behind the scurrying clouds. A monstrously huge yellow flash followed, and a simultaneous boom sounded, echoing off the trees long after . . .

As the flash and the thunderous echo faded away, an eerie silence took over. The night clouds still scurried past in fast-forward, leading eventually though to a brightening dawn and a brilliant blue sky filled with puffy white clouds.

7

TICNUP

I

May 19, 2016 – Near Tin Cup Peak, Colorado

In Charles Pierre LeBlanc's fitful dream, he was flying an ultra-light aircraft powered by not much more than a lawnmower engine, catching updrafts over the sun-drenched snowcapped mountains of central Colorado. It was a beautiful morning! The sky was blue, and the temperature was in the mid-50s. Even in his dream, Pierre wanted to pinch himself to see if he'd perhaps died of exposure from his night on the mountain and was now in heaven with the Lady Jolie.

He circled his small craft down, descending below the rims of the wondrous Rockies all around, above, and below him. Even at this height, he could easily make out the heads of early spring flowers showing themselves through the last snowdrifts of the season. They joined millions of others popping their heads out all around, emerging from bright green mountain grasses. They seemed to be reaching up their red, blue, and purple heads to touch him.

Astoundingly, in the dream, he knew it was all *just a dream*! Had he frozen to death or was he in a pre-death euphoria?

Descending, he saw below him a small car angled into a melting snowdrift on a dirt road. Recognizing it

In Better Times

immediately as his 1980 International Scout rental, he brought the small craft lower and lower until landing in the melting snow just behind the vehicle.

Anxious to see what he would find in the car, Pierre climbed out of the craft and stooped to look through the vehicle's rear window. He could see completely through it, and even through its front windshield. A large sign emerged from the melting snow. It was mounted not ten feet in front of the automobile reading, "Welcome to Tin Cup, Colorado, Population 178." Further, behind the sign, perhaps two football fields further, were three or four white-framed homes and buildings located on both sides of the road. Behind them was a larger, white-framed structure as well, supporting a church steeple. It dominated the skyline of the tiny town.

A hand was rapping on the windshield.

"Wake up, mister! Mister? Mister! Are you okay?" It was the voice of a preteen boy. Pierre opened his eyes groggily. He was still in the front seat of the Scout shaking himself into full consciousness. The ultralight flight *was* in fact just a dream. He'd survived his night on the mountain after all. His last candle lay melted on the dashboard before him, its stub standing in a mess of congealed red, white, and blue wax.

Pierre waved the boy off, opened the car door, and immediately realized that the temperature had climbed to at least the fifties. *Incredible*, he thought. *A few hours ago, I nearly froze to death! Now, the snow at my feet is melting into rivers.* He looked over his surroundings and again saw, just as his dream predicted, a large sign only a few feet ahead of the Scout welcoming him to Tin Cup. It was mounted on a weathered piece of plywood just to the side of the road twenty feet in front of the car. Had he risked leaving the vehicle during the storm last night, he would certainly have found the sign and surely managed to walk the hundred yards or so to one of the five or six structures in the town. Someone then would have no doubt offered him shelter and a bed. The closest building was a small barn and even it would have served better as a shelter than the Scout.

He stretched and felt the kinks in his body react.

The boy, wearing bib overalls, was now shouting behind him to a full-bearded man in matching coveralls who approached from across a meadow – a meadow not covered with snow but with lush moist green spring grass. There were still small mounds of snow, of course, but they were quickly melting in the brilliant high-altitude sun. The combination of snow and warm sunshine was pushing the grass and flowers to grow and bloom almost before his eyes.

"Dad! Dad! There's a man in the car! Hurry!"

Pierre, still in a bit of a pre-wakening fog, continued to stretch and yawn as the man, probably around 40, approached from the direction of one of the small white-frame homes perhaps 100 yards away. Neither he nor the boy were wearing shirts despite the cool temperatures. Both had shoulder-length hair and the father's beard was well on its way to turning fully grey.

In Better Times

"You okay, mister?" asked the man, stepping across a small stream of melting snow and extending his hand to help Pierre out of the small car. "I'm Pastor Pope of the Tin Cup Community Church just up the road. Can I help you?"

Pope and his son stared at their visitor who, incredibly, was wearing a suit coat, over pajamas over ruined oxfords.

Fully awake now, and because he was a lawyer after all, Charles Pierre LeBlanc III assumed command. He shook the man's hand and said, "Pope? Pope, you said? John Pope?"

"That's right. What can I do for you?"

The boy came up to him and offered his hand as well. "I'm Deuce. Deuce Pope. Glad to meet you, sir."

"Hello . . . Deuce, is it? Huh? Good to meet you, son."

Pierre turned back to the Reverend John Pope. "As I said, my name's Charles Pierre LeBlanc III. I'm an attorney with LeBlanc LeBlanc LeBlanc and Blois of New Orleans. I've been looking for you, Mr. Pope . . . Pastor Pope, rather . . . for a long, long time – *ten years if it's a day!* Is there a chance I might talk to you over a cup of coffee?"

"I can do better than that," said Pope. "How about some bacon and eggs to go with the coffee."

"Delighted," said Pierre, realizing his last meal had been a can of Spam and a stale cupcake. "And . . . over grits and a second cup, I'll tell you why I'm here."

As they headed into the small house, Pierre asked, "How long have you been living in Colorado, Pastor Pope?"

"Seems like all my life. Colorado, I mean. When I was

younger, I lived a pretty wild life as a hippie in a number of communes here on the southern slopes, including *Libre* over in Gardner. Last one I was part of though, was here in Tin Cup before it disbanded maybe fifteen years ago. I think it was also one of the last ones still going . . . although a few, like *Drop City*, are still hangin' on.

A large kitchen window opened over a meadow in the frame home allowing fresh, pleasantly cool breezes to flow through. Over the best coffee he'd ever tasted, Pierre poured out his story. "Your brother was Paul Pope, right? I'm handling his estate. Actually, my firm is. We've been trying to track you down for years. I'm not certain our FedEx's have been getting here."

Pierre looked around him at the small kitchen, outfitted a bit sparingly. If the furnishings were representative of the entire home, this dwelling in New Orleans could have easily been classified as *impoverished*.

Curiously, John Pope's face wore a frown, even with the probability of good news from his visitor.

His brief pause to admire the furnishings ended and Pierre continued, "Well Pastor, it took forever to find you, but now that I have, I want to resolve this affair. I think you'll be quite pleased when I reveal the details . . . If LeBlanc LeBlanc LeBlanc and Blois is to wrap this up, one of the members of our practice was required to travel here to Tin Cup and finish it, once and for all, face-to-face. I am that person."

Pierre forced a business card into Pope's hand and waited for what he expected was going to be a happy but curious response.

He was wrong.

"If anybody survived that awful night," said Pope looking at the business card and suddenly fully aware of Pierre's purpose, "I'd give all the proceeds of Paul's estate to them. Frankly, I really don't want to have anything to do with whatever's left of it. Tainted money! That's what it is. I hadn't seen him in more than ten years when it happened and even the awful event that brings you here took place more than ten years ago. Thank you, but no thank you, Mr. LeBlanc."

Pope turned toward a kitchen cabinet and then spun around. "I'll be happy though to find you transportation back to Denver, or we can get a tow truck out from Gunnison or Crested Butte to get your car out. Which would you prefer?"

Nonplussed, Pierre replied, "I think I understand your feelings on the matter, Pastor, but this affair *really* needs to end. It's been going on far too long. I'd like you to fly back with me to New Orleans . . . today, if possible . . . and we'll take care of the whole thing once and for all. You'll be back here in Tin Cup in 48 hours. All expenses will be on LeBlanc LeBlanc LeBlanc and Roux, of course. You won't have to worry about a thing. Paul's funeral home and the Monroe and Pontchartrain properties were sold off long ago. In other words, everything in the estate is liquid. All we need to do is sign some papers and pay a visit to PGTBNB."

"PG . . . what?

"PGTB, Pierre Gustave Toutant-Beauregard – he was a Civil War General from New Orleans, and a bank is named for him – Pierre Gustave Toutant-Beauregard National Bank of New Orleans. The bank is the repository for all the cash and deeds in Paul Pope's estate.

"Then, let's just get rid of it, can't we? Or give it away?" asked Rev. Pope earnestly. "I don't want to go back to New Orleans for all the tea in China." John Pope raised his arms to indicate the land around them. "This is my home and *has been* my home now for more than 10 years. I am not gonna bring back bad memories if I don't have to. You can give all the proceeds to the Anderson Institute. That probably would make Paul happy too, I suspect, and maybe even our father."

Pierre replied, "But, sir, *you* must make that decision legally, and *you* are required to be the one to *come back* to New Orleans to do it. You're the last one standing in your entire family, Pastor Pope."

"Do we know that for certain after what happened that night? I flew back for the funerals for Paul's wife and my nephew, but that was a week-and-a-half later . . . and they hadn't then . . . and still haven't found Paul's and my nephew's body if I recall correctly."

"No sir. Still haven't, Pastor Pope. A big mystery, but the police believe that the lightning bolt was so intense, if you don't mind my choice of words, it vaporized your brother and your nephew. No DNA . . . and no burial. Seven years later Paul Pope was declared legally dead, and now I'm here to make you rich.

In Better Times

"Sorry for your trouble, Mr. LeBlanc, but I don't want any of the sixty million . . ."

Pierre and John Pope were interrupted as a door off the kitchen opened and an attractive woman stepped through it. She was a bit younger than John Pope and dressed in faded 70s-style hippie clothes.

"Seven . . . What's going on?" she asked.

"Cyndy! Come on in. I've someone I'd like you to meet," said Pope. "Mr. LeBlanc this is my sleepyhead wife, Cyndy."

"Very nice to meet you," said Cyndy Pope, her long carrot-colored hair blowing in a fresh breeze.

Her eyes squinted a bit when she smiled and the freckles on her face showed in the light. She did that again now. It was a smile big enough to kill a cat.

"Seven, darling. What was that about sixty million dollars and settling Paul's estate?"

At that moment a large black and orange butterfly stole the moment floating through the open kitchen window. It landed on Pope's left shoulder, wings beating slowly. Deuce pointed to the beautiful monarch open-mouthed.

Pastor Pope turned his head to peek at the creature and said, "Interesting. Two things just popped into my head. Both were sayings my father taught me a long time ago. One was 'Live. Die. Repeat.,' and the other had something to do with the *butterfly in the room*, or was it an elephant?"

The End

A Christmas Tail

A *Very* Short Story
By Ken Hinrichs

My story begins in late 1843 and, as with most tales, a female is at the center of it all.

Late on a cold December afternoon, I found myself walking London's narrow winding streets with no real purpose in mind, my solicitor work completed for the day.

Smoke from the nearby chimneys held low to the ground forcing from me an occasional struggling cough. With the passing of the winter solstice, *Old Sol* had been setting earlier and earlier each afternoon and so, above the narrow streets and the city-blocked horizon, very little direct sunlight was available to warm me.

As I moved down the shaded lane, I perused the contents in the many shop windows. A few were empty, but in one, there she lay.

Seemingly posing just for me on a carpet set on a raised fireplace hearth, the lady, a cocker, I believe lay reclined, curled in a fetal position in front of a roaring fire. Because of the bright orange flames from the fireplace behind her, she appeared mostly in silhouette.

My feet froze on the walkway for I became instantly entranced.

Barely discernable in the shadows above the fireplace was a crudely painted sign reading *Aesop's Tables*. A similar sign, albeit one more professionally crafted, hung above the shop's entrance. Like those above the doors of most of the other shops, this one illustrated the product for sale within. *Hand Crafted Wooden Table*s is what the sign would have said had it been made of words and letters instead of an illustration of the objects for sale within.

The fireplace mantle was littered with candles and other things one often finds in these small shops. This mantle also held the holsters for a man's woodworking tools. They reminded me of Christmas stockings. It was the season after all.

In a corner to the right, a small malnourished and unadorned Christmas tree sat atop a woodworker's chest near where an aproned, elderly, man, most likely the shop's owner, held a broom as sweetly as he might a Stradivarius. He swept dusty fluffs of sawdust toward the shop's doorway, and I imagined him humming a Christmas Carol or perhaps a concerto as he played his broom so sweetly.

Fading shafts of diffused light streamed through a side window silhouetting suspended particles of sawdust. To the man's right sat a newly fashioned wooden table, no doubt a product of his own hands, perhaps even completed earlier that same day. It showed to be highly polished even in the softly fading light of late afternoon.

When the old man paused from his sweeping and lifted his face, I viewed an almost perfectly round head. Bald on top, the man wore a heavy growth of hair in the back and on both sides not so neatly framing a large bushy mustache. The bright flames in opposition to the shop's dimness made it difficult to discern the color of the man's hair, but because of his obvious age, the hair and mustache were most probably grey, perhaps even beginning to turn white.

A smudged pair of wire-rimmed bifocals perched on the end of his round nose. The man, however, chose to look above, rather than through the glasses at the uncovered form reclining before him on the carpet. I could not of course hear it, but the old man appeared to sigh heavily, his chest rising and falling, his face crinkling as he did so, smiling with an obvious love for the figure sleeping by the fire.

I was able to observe all this from my position on the other side of the narrow lane where I stood in shadow, only a dozen or so steps across from the shop's door.

Before me, gazing through the same window, were the backs of a woman and a boy who I decided must be mother and son. Both were too shabbily clothed to long survive the cold. The boy leaned heavily on a crutch. I expected their stop to be momentary.

The curious scene inside the shop had stopped them and then entranced them as well as it had me, but from a closer vantage than I. Both rocked back and forth, quietly amused. The boy pointed to the sleeping figure on the rug. Both mother and son giggled loudly enough for me to hear. Her voice was soft and loving, the boy's full of curiosity and joy.

Snow had begun falling an hour before and by now the drifts were accumulating at the corners of the shop. A small mound of it was easily pushed aside as the shop door opened and the craftsman swept out his small bits of dusty detritus, startling a small blackbird that had taken refuge in the transom above the shop's door. In breaking the general silence, the bird took to flight squawking and fluttering its wings. The air was crisp and crystal clear, the falling snow quickly closing in over the noise of the bird's escape.

The vision before me was so still and hypnotizing that I had to remind myself to even draw a breath. I felt immersed in warm tones of sepia, the falling snow appearing to me almost in shadow. Time slowed and stopped for a moment in the fading sunlight. I became suspended in the scene before me.

Despite the chill, I remained comfortable; my body continued to fully relax. The fullness and sense of solitude holding me captive seemed beyond description. Indeed, as I stood in my shadow, I became convinced I'd become a part of a most beautiful painting.

It occurred to me then that this was such a unique moment, it might prove a wonderful memory to replay again and again in my mind's eye. And so, I committed to memorizing each individual puzzle piece in the scene to recall it all later.

As I impressed each detail into my mind, I discovered something significant I'd heretofore missed. Crouching behind a dark-colored vase on the mantle above the figure on the floor, and almost blending into the background, was a small fox. Its coat was auburn; its eyes alert to the shopkeeper.

Somehow it must have earlier gained entrance to the shop, probably seeking refuge from the abiding chill. Now, by the actions of the shopkeeper, it was aroused from its hiding place. Perhaps it now sensed a need and an opportunity for escape.

Riveted by the creature's discovery, I watched as the fox leaped from its position on the mantle, landing lightly on the floor, and quickly scurried out the open shop door, side-stepping the surprised shopkeeper as well as the mother and son. It disappeared through a narrow opening between two adjacent buildings.

It was then that the boy broke the silence and exclaimed, "Look, Mother! The quick brown fox jumped over the lazy dog's back."

His mother smiled and replied, "Timothy Cratchit, you have become a complete person. Your father will be so proud."

And together, hand in hand, they moved down the lane.
The End

Acknowledgments

Regarding *Seven Stories*, several small sections of New Orleans's geography have been changed to protect the innocent. They would have been corrected but I ran out of time. Please forgive. The LaLurie home does in fact exist precisely where I placed it and has seen its own set of real horrors.

Pete Stickney, critic, proofer, mountain driving expert, English teacher, arcane arts instructor, and self-styled humorist provided critical incidental help on this project . . . about every third word. He appears in it as a golf pro, which would not be an entirely inaccurate avocation for him. A cousin, Joel Hinrichs, also an author, deserves thanks for helping me realize after the fact, that this volume is actually a collection of short stories.

In 1916 Albert Einstein wrote his foundational treatise, *Relativity: The Special and the General Theory*. In it, he posits, "The separation between past, present, and future is only an illusion, although a convincing one." Perhaps the man had something there. Then again, *The Time Machine* by H.G. Wells, published in 1895, and the short story, *A Sound of Thunder* by Ray Bradbury, published in 1952, are the inspirations to pen *this* story as well as *every* time travel story written since by thousands of more successful and talented authors. Without their efforts, this work of fiction would not have been possible. Now that I can claim to be a neophyte member of that pack of hounds,

I admit it is a bit conceited, but also necessary, for me to gratefully acknowledge and thank those three brilliant men – Einstein, Wells, and Bradbury – for their genius.
   the author

Disclaimers

Please memorize this section before reading *Seven Stories*. Quantities are limited while supply lasts so buy several now. Thanks. Previous editions are obsolete. Any similarity between the characters described herein and the names of, and resemblance to, actual people who now live or who have ever lived is strictly coincidental. This book is not recommended for children. No animals were harmed in the writing of this book. This end up. Shake well before reading. Caution: This book may cause drowsiness, nausea, dizziness, or blurred vision. Readers of this book must wash their hands before returning to life. WARNING: This book may become hot after heating; please handle carefully. Some assembly required. Make certain your seatbacks and tray tables are in the locked and fully upright position. If this product comes into contact with your eyes, wash them with clean running water and consult a physician. Pay no attention to the man behind the curtain. Do not drive with sun-shield in place. Not responsible for typografical errors. Do not try the stunts depicted herein in your living room. Actual mileage may vary. If this product is heated, it can catch fire or melt; reheating is not recommended. Do not remove these disclaimers under penalty of law. Floss between meals. The Publisher is an equal-opportunity employer. In the event this book catches fire, keep calm. Eating rocks may lead to broken teeth. This book is provided as is without any warranties. No salt, MSG, artificial coloring, or flavoring has been added. Avoid alcoholic beverages while using this product. Do not read while sleeping or unconscious. This book is safe to read around pets and is gluten-free, however, once digested, it will not be glutton-free. Avoid contact with mucous membranes. This book has been sanitized for your protection. Batteries not included. This book is for indoor or outdoor use only. Please remain seated until the book has come to a complete stop. Bridge will freeze before the highway. Strike before closing cover. Remove wrapper before consuming. When reading this book while traveling in an automobile, buckle your seatbelt. Excessive page turning may lead to paper cuts. The truth is out there. Not responsible for sunburn if reading this book in the direct sun on the beach. Apply this book to the affected area. In the event of an emergency, an oxygen mask will drop down from the compartment above your head. In the event of reprint, add toner. All rights reserved; tax, title, and license extra. Approved for veterans. This book is ribbed for your pleasure. Substantial penalty for early withdrawal. Break glass in case of emergency. Caveat emptor. The performance represented here is historical and is not a reliable indicator of future results. Consult your physician before reading. Look both ways before crossing. The Surgeon General of the United States warns that the smoking of this book by pregnant women may result in fetal injury, premature birth, and low birth weight. This book is not to be used as a personal flotation device. Wear safety goggles while reading. If you do not understand or cannot read all directions, cautions, disclaimers, and warnings herein, do not read this book. All sales final. All major credit cards accepted. Void where prohibited. All books leaving this store, full or empty, must be paid for. The above terms subject to change without notice. Certain conditions apply. Avoid extreme temperatures. Store in a cool dry place. Sales tax not included. Because some jurisdictions do not allow the exclusion or limitation of liability for consequential or incidental damages, the above limitations may not apply. Results may vary. If you do not agree to the conditions stated in this warning, put this book down or log off immediately. This information is not intended as legal advice. Pavement ends without warning.

Any reproduction, or retransmission, without the expressed, written consent of the Publisher, the author, or Major League Baseball is expressly prohibited. Please call with questions. Your call is very important to us. This disclaimer should not be considered a true and legal disclaimer. Amen.